11-12-13

Best Wishes Bob!
precious Bob!
God Bless You,
Love always,
Connie

Happy Baha'u'llah's
Birthday

Enjoy the book!

Enjoy the story –
Regards
Tom D. Carb

The BROTHERHOOD of PURITY

THOMAS DICARLO
CONNIE D. ATKINSON

Published By
Hummingbird Press – New York – New Zealand

Library of Congress Control Number: 2013905658

ISBN: 978-0-9888553-0-4

 Printed in the United States of America on acid free paper
Springhill Cream contains 10% post-consumer fiber

First Edition
A B C D E

Requests for permission to make copies of any part of this work please write
or call:
Hummingbird Press
Box 58
Roslyn, N.Y. 11576
Hummingbirdpress@verizon.net
516.697.5001

Book Design and Symbol by: KarrieRoss.com
Editing by: Mary Wang

www.thebrotherhoodofpurity.com

To all those souls, touched by 9-11,

still wondering 'why,' and for our greatly loved

mother, who encouraged us, as

youngsters, to write. We finally took your advice,

heard your voice, and it resides

on every page.

"Let the charity of the brotherhood abide in you. And hospitality, do not forget: for by this some, being not aware of it, have entertained angels."

— Hebrews 13:1-2.

Table Of Contents

PROLOGUE

"God must be dead."

David Anderson spat out the words as a matter of habit now, almost mindlessly and without scorn; words born of weariness and a vague sense of revulsion that came upon him from time to time. It was sunset and David was standing on Iran's Dasht-i-Kavir desert. The linen pants and shirt he wore, hanging loosely on his tall slender frame, were moving back and forth with the rhythm of rising breezes on the afternoon thermals. In the immensity of the surrounding wasteland, he appeared as an insignificant grey and brown shape, silhouetted against an enormous orange semicircle sinking into the desert sand.

He knelt and scooped up a small clod of dry earth, meaning to throw it at the relentless sun that dared to shine so hard on this land and its people. Instead, it burst through the fingers of his clenched fist as his grip tightened along with his mood. He let what remained of the broken soil slip from his palm, back to the barren spot from where it had come.

"That's a wrap," said David to the camera crew, as he removed the microphone from his lapel and flicked the earpiece out of his ear.

The crew set about packing away their equipment in the rented van, while the somber journalist, leaning against the passenger door, looked out at the barren sands and red tinted dunes one last time. The desert, a vision busy in its own wild play, teased his senses, creating an imposing phantasm of light and form; a grand crescendo of descending twilight, fading away, leaving only vermillion-colored glints of light shimmering in his eyes. Torn and tired at the end of the final day, he hung between exhaustion and satisfaction about what had been a tumultuous time.

David Anderson was completing a new documentary; his first major assignment for Global News Network. He had spent the past year researching, and then recording, an investigative report on the children of the Middle East's radical madrasah schools. The unsettled sense of indignation gripping him after 9-11, swept over him again one month into the assignment, growing stronger as he dove more deeply into the subject.

The storm at the heart of his fury began in the prime of youth when David, in response to the initial catalyst of his mother's death, chose to forego the centuries-old family tradition of membership in the Lutheran Church. No longer certain he believed in an intelligent Greater Power as creator of the physical universe, and even more circumspect about any such Force's involvement in human affairs, David decided religion and its offspring were more of a plague upon mankind than a blessing. This belief, he knew, challenged his objectivity even as it fueled his resolve.

While initially pursuing his interest in exploring the madrasah school system, the world continued to experience an ever-rising number of terror-related events, and David, like most other Americans, tended to believe that anyone educated in a madrasah had to be a terrorist. Feeling every bit as angry and stunned as the rest of his countrymen, David decided to set off in search of answers to the pressing question of how in God's name a man, not much out of his childhood, could be convinced that blowing himself up with as many other human lives as could possibly be taken with him, was actually condoned and rewarded by God. Just another example of how organized religion has commandeered a people's faith for its own hideous ends, David reasoned, adding yet another justification for hammering one more nail into the coffin that used to be his faith.

Prologue

Newly hired and assigned to an affiliate of Global News in Anaheim, California, David posed this question to Steven Holt, a friend and mentor. One rainy afternoon the two men sat together in Steven's office, discussing David's thoughts and misgivings. With small rivulets of water streaming down the window behind Steven's desk, David poured out his ideas and anxieties to the soft melody of the falling rain. Steven was a man of few words. His advice was simple and straightforward but they held heavyweight impact.

"David, I have come to believe that the basis for such fierce hatred, in men who are not clinically insane, will make a vitally important story. As much as I empathize with your anger, believe me, the truth hidden behind the doors of those schools, whatever that may be, cannot be unsealed unless you hold back your own rage. If you can't do that, don't go."

Thus began David's research. The following morning he hit the electronic stacks in the nearly limitless Global News Library and, shortly thereafter, began a series of interviews with local Muslim clergy. Soon enough, David's interest and knowledge in this area, and affinity for the children affected by it, grabbed the notice of his superiors.

The news director, impressed by the synopsis of David's documentary proposal, the research details and the project timeline, was able to be especially generous with the budget. Thanks to a new climate of interest in the country created after the Towers fell, David was afforded the best producers on staff. They ensured his instructions were carried out to the letter, the preliminary research completed with plenty of time for review, his itinerary planned, and the travel arrangements for the staff and crew made well in advance of the trip.

It was not long before he was on his way. David traversed seven Middle Eastern countries and put in countless hours, interviewing anyone who would give him their time. David's natural ability to display a humble reverence and genuine curiosity for the peoples he visited sometimes afforded him the privilege of trust and, in turn, a glimpse into their mysterious world. For this he was sincerely grateful.

David's passion flared even higher when his journeys led him to discover the rich and varied history of the madrasah school system that continued to thrive throughout the Mideast. It appeared that these schools where not just training grounds for future terrorists. He discovered that any secular or parochial school was referred to in Arabic as a madrasah and David's guide in Iran, a well-respected, wise, and congenial old man named Haji Shaykh Mahmud Azzizi, was happy to edify David on the topic during their first outing.

"The word 'madrasah' literally means 'school'," said the Shaykh. "A political affiliation is not implied, just as the word 'Allah' literally means 'God' and in no way implies that Muslims worship a god other than the God of the Judeo-Christian tradition."

"Got it," replied David, "'Allah' means 'God' in Arabic."

"That's right, David Effendi," the Shaykh said, smiling. David understood the old man appreciated his response. "There are as many ways to say 'God' as there are languages."

The subsequent weeks held an ocean of new information for the neophyte journalist and his crew. Deeply interested in what the Shaykh had to share with him, they walked the city perimeter for hours, David's cameraman quietly filming as the Shaykh continued his missive.

"During the rule of the Fatimid and Mamluk Dynasties, and their successor states in the medieval Middle East, many of the ruling elite founded madrasahs through a religious endowment known as 'waq'f'. The madrasah became a potent symbol of power and a means of transmitting wealth and status to their descendants."

"Yes…but don't people of all backgrounds attend madrasah schools?" David asked. "That's been my observation up to now."

David's guide was now deep in thought, thumb and forefinger earnestly raking back his eyebrows as he walked along.

"That's right, David. Over time, the madrasahs have come to admit orphans and poor children in order to provide them with education, training and services not available from their local governments. Even female students are enrolled, although they always study separately from the boys. The madrasahs, at times, resemble Western colleges where people can take evening classes or reside in dormitories. Many students will move on to become Imams. The programs are often rigorous and a certificate, such as an 'alim', requires twelve years of study. It may interest you to know, David Effendi, the university system in Europe owes a great deal to the madrasah school model."

David nodded, in silent affirmation, as they walked.

On David's last day with Shaykh Mahmud, the old man asked for a promise. "Tell the world that not all madrasahs are radical training grounds for terrorists, and it is to their benefit to learn about, respect, and appreciate so great an educational system. Without it, people would be completely ignorant and sink into dire poverty."

David assured his mentor that any criticisms leveled at the madrasahs in his documentary would remain strictly confined to those radical elements of Islam responsible for the indoctrination of children in the principles of hatred and violence against, not only the non-Muslim peoples of the world, but even more moderate Muslims who dared to oppose their radical brethren.

As Shaykh Mahmud Azzizi prepared to leave, David looked into his eyes and smiled; a look anchored in the deep admiration and respect the journalist had come to feel for this man who spent countless hours instructing and guiding him on the initial and most important leg of his journey. The old man had given David a most priceless gift – his time and an open heart. David knew that the days he spent with the Shaykh, however short, far surpassed in depth and insight, any time he, or his staff, could spend in a library. The old Shaykh returned David's smile and, with the humor that comes so naturally to Iranians, he winked, "You better be careful, my dear David Effendi, or I will turn you into a devout Muslim."

His shoulders shaking with a good, deep laugh, the Shaykh put his hand firmly on David's shoulders and said, "That's all for today, David-joon. Khoda hafez, my friend."

He lightly tapped the tips of his fingers on David's cheek, a sign of great affection. This revered Shaykh was treating him as he would a young family member and this honor greatly moved David. He, an American journalist, an infidel, had not expected such openness from this Muslim shaman, and, to his surprise, he felt humbled. Sensing David's reaction, the old Shaykh smiled – the smallest and kindest of smiles that one can only see on the face of the wise who have suffered much. David tried to thank the man but he just waved it away, saying, "It is nothing."

Unexpectedly, from an inner pocket, the Shaykh produced a papyrus scroll; its fragile parchment was tied with hemp string and sealed with wax. Embedded in the wax was a collection of gold loops gleaming with ancient luster and mystery.

"What is this?" David asked.

"This was rescued from the holy fire…it is the beginning and end of your search…guard it well." Handing it to David, turning with a sigh and an almost imperceptible limp, the old man headed for the door, leaving the newsman's question unanswered.

Before returning to the hotel that afternoon, David found a sturdy box in which to store the mysterious scroll the Shaykh had entrusted to him. Fearful that breaking the wax seal might damage the parchment, David wrapped it with cloth, laid it into its temporary home, and secured the box with several layers of tape, packing it carefully into his luggage.

During his subsequent travels throughout the Mideast the newsman kept well Shaykh Mahmud's council, visiting many madrasah schools with a renewed sense of perspective. David found the Jami'at al-Qarawiyyin, located inside the Al-Qarawiyyin Mosque, to be one of the most intriguing.

The school, nestled majestically in Fez, an ancient city in northeastern Morocco, was once considered the spiritual and intellectual nerve center of the ancient world. David discovered it to be not only the oldest madrasah in the Muslim world but the oldest continuously operating institution of higher education on the globe. The university became a place for men to gather together in the early Islamic custom of that time, seeking enlightenment of both simple and abstruse metaphysical questions relating to the Holy Qur'an. Fierce arguments raged among them over the authenticity of the Hadiths, which were reported sayings of the Prophet Muhammad collected by his followers for the century and a half following his death.

David stood in the mosque's courtyard and pictured these men pondering religious and intellectual questions. Some would eventually emerge as informal teachers who later became known as shaykhs. As David pondered the stories of a nascent culture pouring out of the ancient walls, an old man, with a long staff fashioned from Madagascar Ebony and trimmed with intricate patterns of gold and silver, appeared and interrupted his imaginary trip into the past. David greeted the man as he crossed the tessellated mosaic of interwoven china blue and pale yellow tiles, but the man chose to walk by without acknowledging David, as though he were nothing more than a shadow. David knew most of the local community found his presence inside the mosques disturbing; their proclivity was to ignore foreigners. There wasn't any umbrage intended or taken, and so, with a respectful temperament, he simply pushed on.

David's work did not proceed entirely free of obstacles. Throughout his sojourn in the Mideast, David would, inevitably, encounter Islamic militants with an extremely conservative view of Islam, wielding considerable power, in whose schools radical indoctrination of students was occurring. The madrasahs started or dominated by these militants became ideological training grounds for hatred against the West. In Pakistan, Saudi Arabia, Iran, Egypt, Syria, Iraq, Lebanon, Northern Africa, and spreading rapidly across the region, the heavy emphasis on radical religious teachings in many of these madrasahs was to the exclusion of more academically diverse subject areas. To make matters more complicated, the radical madrasahs generally denied their ideological orientation and obtaining accurate and reliable interviews at these schools was difficult and often impossible, leaving David to rely heavily on the reports given him by their more moderate counterparts.

As David traveled throughout the region, he occasionally encountered an unusual symbol affixed to some of the mosques and madrasahs. The symbol was hard to miss; a collection of vibrant gold loops forming an infinite knot, gleaming like a beacon in the brilliant sun, silently calling, with the Muezzin, the devoted believers to prayer. Local residents in towns where the symbol was displayed, reluctantly whispered rumors about an early Sufi order founded in ancient Baghdad; a secret sect whose members renounced a life of material pleasures and, instead, were dedicated to a journey of self-knowledge.

Blasé at first, the newsman's interest peaked when he realized the gold symbol was identical to the one on the scroll. Once back in Iran, on the final leg of his journey, David finally had the time to investigate, but whenever he started asking questions about the sect, public officials would appear, cautioning him to drop the topic and any further inquiries. He considered putting aside investigation into the mysterious symbol when he discovered that his casual conversations with some local townspeople wound up in an official dossier.

Damping down his sense of caution, David decided to press on with his inquiries until one day when the religious police, known as the 'Blood of God', intervened.

It was the last full day of his working sojourn in Iran. David left his team to spend some time alone in a small forgotten village on the edge of the Dasht-i-Kavir, not far from Tehran's southeastern border. David was walking along a path, admiring the detailed carvings on the thick wooden shutters covering the windowless openings of the buildings. The air was hot, dry, dusty, and filled with a foreign and mildly unpleasant odor.

He stopped and raised a camera to photograph a man cleaning the sand from the road with a palm branch freshly cut from a nearby tree. The man struggled under the weight of the intense desert sunlight. He wore sandals whose color had long ago been bleached away by the sun along with a tattered, loose fitting faded grey robe as protection from the heat. He appeared monochromatic, except for a decoratively embroidered head cap of red, yellow and blue, and the iridescent green palm held loosely in his hand.

One hundred feet further down the road several dozen men, similarly dressed, sat in a row along the wayside with nothing to do but stare at the subtly swirling sand. David approached and was surprised to see they were actually sitting on the heels of their feet. They looked completely comfortable in this position, not moving and not speaking, staring intently out into the desert, mesmerized by the waving currents of heat rising up from the sand.

Again, David raised his camera but, before he could press the shutter, a military jeep pulled up, stopped abruptly, and two men jumped out. They were dressed in paramilitary service uniforms. One grabbed David and slammed him against the jeep's hood. Another, obviously the superior of the first, took hold of David's collar and stood him upright, twisting one arm behind his back. David grimaced. Determined not to betray his ever-growing sense of rage and disgust, he asked casually, "Is there a problem, officer?"

The man holding David released his grip and pushed him to the dusty ground. "You were warned not to ask about things which do not concern you. If you do this again you will go to jail. Our jail is not like your jail; you will not survive our jail! You would be wise to leave our country...very soon."

Although incensed by the intrusion into his business, David held his peace, presuming, quite rightly, that to fight or even protest, would get him thrown into the notorious Evin prison in Tehran. His boss would be royally pissed off at that one. He liked his job and intended to keep it. Instead, from down in the dust, he tried to make eye contact with the two men but the opaque black lenses of their sunglasses made this impossible.

Instead, David offered his most contrite smile, praying he would not be shot. The men loomed over him, kicking the choking sand at David with the tips of their boots and then jumped back in the jeep. They drove off as quickly as they arrived, speeding away in a noisy cloud of desert dust, their raucous laughter audible over the rumble of the jeep's engine.

Slowly, David straightened, stretched his aching back, and dusted himself and his dignity off. Flashing an embarrassed grin at the row of gentlemen, who had not moved a muscle during the entire incident, he bowed a short but elegant bow and, turning, headed for the car that would take him back to the hotel in Tehran. There he would have a nice long bath, and perhaps even a nap.

That evening, his arm still in pain from the encounter with the police, David, determined to put aside the incident, placed the finishing touches on his documentary. Although he was glad the project had been completed on time and he could finally go home, he knew he would miss the children depicted in the documentary and many of the people he met along the way. In an odd sense, this exotic and unfamiliar place, seemingly out of a Bible story, had become intimate and homey and it beckoned him to stay.

Surely, if needed, his diplomatic connections could afford him a reprieve, despite the warnings of the two thugs who had threatened him that afternoon. Yet he knew that it would be a grave injustice to delay this story. It was a primary journalistic principle by which David governed his life; something his father told him long ago: "If no one is telling your story, go pick up a pencil."

David wanted this work to prove a watershed moment for those brave enough to believe that we really do have much more in common with each other than not, and that the impact on our own children, by turning away from the suffering of the children in other cultures, although subtle, was still profound.

So, David completed the final voiceover and packed his belongings, thinking again about the strange gold symbol on the buildings and the Shaykh's scroll. He worried there might be some connection between it and all the threats and warnings and, deciding to make sure the scroll was kept safe, he gently placed it into a narrow white tube about twelve inches long and labeled it with a black marker to read simply: 'Hummingbird.' Later that night, the journalist slipped silently down the service stairs to the hotel's lobby and handed it to a refined looking Iranian man at the front desk, who nodded his affirmation that he knew exactly where, and to whom, it was to go.

David returned to his room and promptly fell into a deep sleep. His dreams were filled with images of Bedouins riding across the desert in black turbans, the wild green folds of their robes flying behind them like magic carpets. Images of the now familiar pails of spices, for sale in the curry souk, transformed his dream into an evanescent memory of intoxicating colors and a whirlwind of scents lifted on a sudden current of hot afternoon wind.

The next morning, while waiting for a car that would take him to the airport, David sat at the edge of a beautiful stone fountain just on the boundaries of the local madrasah school. Its inner bowl was lined with blue and gold ceramic tiles whose color and brilliance appeared to mirror the heavens in their depths. The fountain seemed to spray its blessings out into the world through the gleaming shower of water that shot up from its center spout.

A young student was sitting a few feet away on one of the steps leading up to the base of the fountain. The boy was slight of build but the barest shadow of a beard led David to guess he was about fifteen or sixteen years of age. He wore an immaculate robe of a raw and un-dyed material David guessed was probably hemp. The robe fell almost to his brown leather sandals and gave him the look of someone lost in ancient Biblical times. He had shining thick black hair that was cut close and neat, its wave just visible, and his skin was satin smooth with a milky chocolate color that looked almost too perfect to be real.

David sat down on the fountain's step near the boy, who glanced up briefly before returning to the book he held in his lap. David could see that his eyes were wells of deepest black that held a murky quality, reminding David of the ponds deep in the woods at home that would lose their clarity as mud from the bottom was swirled to the surface by a thunderstorm.

David noticed at once that he was not like the other children in the square. He was, instead, intent on the book he was reading rather than the active play in which the others were engaged. The sandy robe he wore blended almost seamlessly into the fountain's stone and he barely moved except for the faint rocking that could only be detected as David looked more closely. The boy recited, in low tones, the verses of the Qur'an he held, but he most surely did not need the open book. His dark eyes did not move across the beautiful calligraphy of its pages but held, instead, an intense stare, revealing he knew the holy book by heart.

"Hello. My name is David. Would you allow me to talk to you for a short while? I saw you sitting here, reciting so intently. It made me curious to know you."

The boy looked distractedly up from the book, acknowledged David with a brief nod, but would not give his name and immediately went back to reciting the verses. Oddly, he did not have the familiar look of curiosity and eagerness common for a boy of fifteen meeting a stranger from a distant land. He seemed older, not in general appearance, but his eyes held sadness in them that David sensed was profound and his voice was absent the animation David heard in the shouts and laughter flowing endlessly from the other youth in the square.

"Why do you not play with the others?" queried David.

Finally, the boy stopped rocking and looked up from the Qur'an.

"I have no time for their foolishness. They are going to hell for their foolishness," replied the boy impatiently, once again returning to the prayer book.

"Do you live close by?" asked David, unsure how to keep the conversation moving.

"I should not speak to you. You are an infidel. I will go to hell," he told David in a resolute, but almost casual way, conveying an innocence and directness one generally finds only in the pure heart of a child. David was momentarily stunned by his directness and finality, but resolved to press on.

"Then I promise I will not stay long. I mean you no harm. Is Tehran your home?" asked David hurriedly, again trying to keep up the momentum; hoping this young boy would not rise from his spot on the steps and rush away.

The boy at last seemed disarmed. His shoulders relaxed as his head fell to one side and he said wistfully, "I live at the school. I was sent by my parents to study here."

"You sound as though you miss your home. Are your parents far away?"

"My family moved to Shiraz. When they lived in Tehran, I could go home every day. Now they are all very far."

"I can tell you miss them very much," David replied in a gentle voice.

"I should not be telling you this. I should not speak to you. I will go to hell for speaking to an infidel." The boy's words should have silenced David, yet his tone had not changed and David felt that the boy wanted to talk despite his admonishment.

David used this last comment as a springboard to delve more deeply into this boy's world. "You have said you will go to hell a number of times. Who told you this is so?"

Finally, the boy, his eyes fierce and hot, looked directly at David. A faint glow blossomed on the boy's cheeks as he raised his head.

"The Holy Qur'an tells us the truth of what will be. You are dressed like an American."

David nodded and the boy, pointing his finger in accusation, his face twisted in an expression of condemnation, resumed his admonition.

"America has lost its soul because of its materialism. You have rejected the one, true God and His Prophet, His Holiness Muhammad, may my life be sacrificed for Him. You must pay for your sins. You are infidels and the neck veins of the infidels will be cut. You have seen the greatness of Allah in the acts of our martyrs and you will see more. Islam is the true road to democracy. This is a war Islam cannot afford to lose and we will not lose it. It is the Will of God and I am an instrument of Allah's Divine Will."

The boy grew silent, diverting his eyes once again. By the slight quivering of his hands David could tell he was quite agitated.

"How do you know God wants you to do this?"

"It is written in the Holy Qur'an."

"Maybe the Qur'an is wrong," David challenged tentatively.

The boy pulled back as if physically slapped by the words. "Never breathe such a thing in my presence. I will go to hell for listening to you and you will go to hell for saying it. The Qur'an is the Divine Will of Allah."

David could not hold back. "What proof is there that God exists at all?"

The boy, with utter scorn, the fear leaving his face, said, "Only the infidels of the West ask such foolish questions. We have no need of proof. Proof is in the Word itself. Open your eyes and see. It has the power to recreate the entire earth."

"The world is so imperfect," replied David. "How could a perfect God create this mess, let alone recreate it?"

"How is it that you, who are so imperfect, think you can imagine what perfection is? How do you know the world is not perfect just as it is? How do you know that the Will of God is not unfolding as it should? Little by little, step by step. It is an honor for me to be part of its unfoldment. I submit to His Will. I submit freely."

"If the world, as it is, reflects the Will of God, then your God is cruel and one whom I cannot believe in," said David in his most earnest tone.

The boy grew quiet for a while. David thought that the conversation had ended. He was preparing to rise when the boy spoke, "God's Will has nothing to do with the suffering in the world. God's Will is for us to be happy, but we disobey God's Laws and, as a consequence, we cause ourselves and others great hardship and suffering."

David was startled; not expecting such thoughts pouring from the lips of a youth only just on the brink of manhood. The boy seemed to read his very thoughts, partly piercing the heart of what troubled David since his mother's death. Yet still, something in his demeanor was not completely right. For all the wisdom quite beyond his years, this boy seemed to have his own demons to tame, his own doubts to reconcile. He was not at peace and David could sense it. This was obviously a very frightened child; his intensity a way of dealing with those fears and, despite insisting he submitted freely, David knew the boy was far from able to exercise free will. David felt pity for this boy, alone, a child still, and his heart opened up to him entirely at that moment.

David let his arms drop. "Has anyone ever told you they love you?"

This time the boy turned ashen as the blood drained from his face. He closed the Qur'an and rose. "These things are of no importance in comparison to the Will of Allah. We have no right to expect such things. There is enough time for love in the next world."

Before he had a chance to reply, the call to prayer sounded, and David knew the boy would leave.

"It was a great honor for me to have met you," David said before the boy could turn away for the final time, "If I lived here, I would hope that we could be friends. If you had been my son, I would have been very proud of you and kept you close to me. I would have told you I love you every day. If I believed in God, I would believe in a God who wants all the people of the world to live together in peace, no matter what they believe. I would believe in a God who had a good reason for sending so many different messengers to His people. My God would want you and me to free the angels within us."

The boy paused and again looked directly into David's eyes. With that same startling intensity, he said, "You are an infidel and I am bound to kill infidels. There are many things that you do not understand. I will pray that Allah will open your eyes. But I am surprised to find that you are a good man...that you respect me, and what I believe...though impossible, you wish to be my friend. There are many sacred trusts that I am sworn to carry out, but I swear by the Holy Qur'an that, in honor of the friendship and respect you have offered me, I will never in my life hurt you or anyone you love. Khoda Hafez, David Effendi."

Then the boy collected his belongings, turned and walked slowly away while David, his eyes shining, watched him go.

Because Good Men
Do Nothing

Eric Anderson was finding it practically impossible to set his mind on work. The sky's dazzling beauty was so clear; it's blue so deep, he wanted to dive in for a swim. Sighing softly, hands warming on a second cup of coffee, his face bathed in the welcome rays of golden sunshine streaming dependably through the kitchen's bay window, Eric gazed with envy at the early morning golfers playing on the Diablo Hills Golf Course. Its fairway, shining in luxuriant serenity, sat on the far side of his back yard lawn. He wiled away the early morning critiquing each player's swing path and mechanics, his thoughts lost amid the lure of lustrous sunlight, vivid green grass, and the silver arcs of the golf clubs. In the background, barely discernable, the siren's song of industry beckoned him to the world of commerce; demanding he make a simple choice: work or play.

Eric inevitably chose work. He was, in the end, a reliable and trustworthy leader, the envy of his colleagues and the paladin of his staff. And so, feeling a bit melancholy, yet satisfied with his decision, Eric arrived at the Omni America Building precisely on time to plan the agenda for the eight thirty flash meeting with his sales and capture team.

At eight o'clock that morning, Eric, engrossed in thoughts of the coming meeting, was startled by a thunderous noise that drove him to the window. In alarm and disbelief, he stared intently at the empty space that was once the center span of the newly completed San Francisco-Oakland Harbor Bridge. Mangled cars were floating upside down in the bay amid the wreckage and debris. Eric, sure there had been massive loss of life, felt a wave of revulsion sweep over him.

In the next moment, a head splitting explosion from somewhere below knocked Eric to the floor. A premonition whispered he and many others in the tower would soon suffer the same fate.

Shaking, holding tight to the window frame for support Eric lifted himself to his feet. He could just make out an emergency team down on the street pouring into the building even as its occupants on the lower floors, soot-covered and gasping, streamed out past them. He could tell they were all frantic. He knew there were firefighters in the building trying desperately to rescue suffocating workers trapped in their offices. And he knew something else: they would never be rescued and, once more, despite the efforts of the city's best security minds, those brave and determined souls ascending the staircases would soon die trying.

A second more violent blast from the basement of the building jolted Eric nearly off his feet and he began to tremble. Smoke, laden with toxic chemicals from the materials used in the construction of the building, began to fill the room. Eric, his nostrils burning, could taste the acrid compounds. The chemicals in his tortured lungs now made it impossible to breathe normally. He tried to block off the choking fumes by pressing his sleeve against his nose and taking short breaths through his mouth. A short breath, hold – then again. The heat scorched the weave of his suit jacket and his skin began to stick to the shirt underneath.

"Please God, let me see my son one more time!" he pleaded, somehow sensing his prayer futile. God had other plans. Sick at heart that he would never see his son again; never get to say goodbye, he prayed that David, who lost his mother as a teen, be given the strength to handle this loss as well.

As the searing heat drew closer, becoming unbearable, another brutal realization clamped his throat ever tighter: he must decide how to die – fire or freefall. Choosing descent through the torturous, smoking air, Eric knelt for one final moment to ask for guidance and forgiveness, and for courage with his last act on earth: to break the glass, force himself onto the ledge and, finally, to jump.

Tears battling the particles of soot invading his eyes, he moved around the desk, gathered his strength and lifted a chair over his head to smash the window. The world's conflicts, now very suddenly, were no longer far away. They leapt off the pages of the newspaper on his desk into his life.

Just as Eric was about to let the chair fly, the glass shattered inward and a blast of air pushed it from his grasp. He looked up, reflexively shielding his eyes from another fireball, expecting that this was his last earthly moment. All his senses were heightened; his emotions bubbling to the surface from his deepest places, except one – remarkably, he felt fear fall away as the chair flew from his hands.

A white light streamed passed the window frame causing prisms of color to spray upward from the shards of glass that had fallen to the floor. Instantly, while gazing up at the brilliant rays, Eric perceived a woman of astonishing radiance suspended in the space above his head. An ineffable sense of reverence forced him back down onto his knees. His hands wrapped around his sides, slipping under his armpits, and his head fell to his chest. When at last he summoned the courage to glance up into the ravishing face, Eric found in her crystal gaze a love so deep and pure that tears rushed down his cheeks and crashed in pools onto the floor. The woman stretched out her hand and he knew that she meant him to take it. Their fingers touched and in that single moment Eric witnessed the entire span and essence of his life reflected in the single shimmering droplet of a tear as it fell from his cheek. It was a good life and an overwhelming sense of peace enveloped his being as he, weightless, began to rise.

A few miles away, Ahmad Hasan was standing on the rooftop of an old apartment building where he rented the western topmost corner flat using the stolen identity of Walter Greenfield; a 73-year-old retired Methodist minister from Catoosa, Oklahoma. The parson's former congregation might have said the crime was poetic justice for all the poor box offerings the good Reverend had pinched over the years from these modest and devoted churchgoers. They kept their counsel though because, in every other respect, he was a gifted pastor; a perpetual mentor and guide at births, deaths, and the events in-between that marked the passage of their lives.

Today, however, the good people of Catoosa were of no concern to Ahmad who, dressed in casual clothes meant for traveling a far distance, stood openly on the roof in plain sight, recording the attack. Police helicopters flew directly above him but the pilots and passengers were too distracted by the fire and smoke to notice the lone man below holding a camera. They were, like all the witnesses this day, hypnotized by the destruction and death unfolding before them. Many wished to turn away, to will themselves to avert their eyes and push the horror out of mind, even for a moment, but most just could not. Had any cared to look, cared to turn away from the unfolding horror, they might have noticed Ahmad and the reflection of the ravaged city in the UV coated lens of the video camera held tightly against his face.

From his vantage point on the roof Ahmad scanned the morning's carnage. Flames were shooting from the smoking skyscraper, licking the air with incinerating fury. Desperate victims stood in open windows, waving clothing, manila folders, or anything they could get their hands on to signal distress and plead for rescue. Some leaned from their windows to escape the heat, others gradually recognizing the inevitable, allowed themselves to fall. Bodies began raining from the skyscraper like tears falling from a goliath that knows its time has ended. People on the street stood in such agonizing helplessness at what they were witnessing that only a gasp or a single tear was capable of escaping their tortured hearts.

Turning the camera away from the building and toward the destroyed bridge, Ahmad could see the steel pylons that supported and anchored the bridge's massive cables. They were designed to steadfastly hold the bridge in place despite the constant punishing procession of traffic that would run over its surface day and night for the next one hundred odd years. But a flash of light, followed by the delayed sound of a massive explosion, told him that the final detonation had occurred precisely on time and he listened and watched as the bridge came crashing down. He stopped to bow his head and pray for the souls of the martyrs who had driven the counterfeit emergency service vehicles to each location. They were in paradise now, having circumvented the wait for Allah's judgment with a martyr's remission of sins, and Ahmad hoped that, someday, he too could sacrifice his own life.

Ahmad was brought back to the present by another explosion. He jerked his head to the left in time to see the burning fragments of a passenger car flying through the air on the way into the bay. Cars and trucks, crushed by flying blocks of concrete and steel, were everywhere. Most of those who survived the initial blast were screaming, many broken and bloodied when their vehicles came into sudden contact with the cars belonging to their fellow commuters or with the twisted steel and pulverized concrete debris. Twisted metal, so ferociously hot it lay on fire on what remained of the center span, made the air on the bridge wave and curl. The walking wounded staggered down the remaining span, some roaming aimlessly in obvious shock, some crying in fear and disbelief.

Several victims in their cars survived the fall into the bay as the bridge fell. A few brave souls were diving from the shoreline into the swirling waters trying to save those not yet drowned or killed by the fall. Hordes of stunned and paralyzed spectators, assembling to witness the second leg of a national nightmare, stood mesmerized by the sight. The water of the bay appeared deceptively peaceful, quietly lapping against the concrete at the base of the steel pylons as if licking the wounds of the mortally injured bridge; just as a faithful dog would tend to a beloved master. Commuters, who shortly before had been enjoying a lovely morning drive across the bridge's span, were now floating face down in the water. Their souls, hovering above their own lifeless bodies bobbing on the troubled crests of the bay waters, were left wondering what had happened, even as they ascended into the next world.

A semi tractor-trailer was on fire at the gaping wound that used to be the center span, its nose sticking out into empty space over the bay. A loaded school bus had come to rest just beside the flaming truck; it too perched precariously near the jagged edge. A line of school children where hurriedly exiting the back emergency door of the bright yellow bus, some quietly crying; others trembling and frantic.

The driver, feeling dazed, but trained to care for his charges above all else, could hear the slow grinding of the bus axel against the cold steel of the bridge's jagged edge, declaring that he had minutes, perhaps seconds, to get the children off the bridge before the rest of the span collapsed. Shaking off the paralyzing pull of his shock, he began barking orders at the youngsters who, for once, did not hesitate or defy him.

Hundreds of rescue workers, emergency personnel, and volunteers began converging on the scene, followed by engineers, government officials, and the media in all its forms. Ghiradelli Square and the Pier had become a rescue staging area where medical personnel, the Red Cross, and local volunteers where assembling. A launch pad for medi-copters was improvised to take the wounded to area hospitals with available beds and the capacity to care for severely injured victims.

Ahmad looked out one last time at the harsh line of black smoke that left an ugly scar as it cut across the clear blue sky. Low thunder grumbled restlessly in the distance like an echo of the morning's rage, pressing him to get moving.

He tucked away the video camera in a nondescript canvas backpack at the same time removing a delicately engraved leather bound prayer book. It was time to move on, to blend into the confusion and to change identities once again. Before entering the stairway for a final descent to the street, Ahmad opened the prayer book, fell to his knees and, bowing his forehead to the ground, began to offer thanks. He rose from prayer and pushed through the grey, steel door that lead down from the roof, his thoughts drifting to home – the home he knew as a child and now dearly missed.

It had been a long, long time since Ahmad, as a child, remembered crossing the courtyard of his home, in anxious anticipation at the start of the school day. In this neighborhood of Tehran, high stone walls surround the typical Persian home. Ahmad's home was no exception. The wall offered safety for the children of the household. Rarely would a Persian child unlock the gate and wander away from his family. The custom also functioned to keep out intruders and unwelcome guests, but also to provide privacy for the women of the household so that no passersby could catch a glimpse of an uncovered head or an unveiled face, lest this sight destroy their purity and lead their neighbor to sin.

On one hot summer day a woman in the neighborhood, a close friend of Ahmad's mother, left the gate open and ran out of the house, unveiled, to pick up her fallen and crying child. A neighbor, passing by on the way to the local market, saw her bare face and reported the incident directly to the local Basij. The woman was arrested that very day and brought before the Islamic court. Convicted of breaking Shari'ah Law, a sin against Islam, she was sentenced to six months in the women's section of Evin prison, infamous for its harsh treatment of prisoners. Ahmad remembered his father commenting how she was lucky to have escaped the gallows. He told Ahmad that had it not been for her uncle, Mullah Mohammed, she would be swinging in the square by her own chador!

The boy had been frightened at the thought of this fearful chastisement and never forgot how severe the retribution was for those who break the Divine Law. He felt grateful that he was being raised to have a deep understanding and love for the Law and vowed that nothing like that would ever happen to him.

That was the day Ahmad realized the wall represented much more than physical protection from the dangers just on the other side. It also kept out the way of the world; his beliefs preserved and kept free and clean of any influence that might steer him away from his training, and lead to his destruction and an eternal punishment of both body and soul.

Sometimes, deep down, Ahmad wished he could be an ordinary boy, especially when Shahin, a neighborhood friend, called across the wall to come and play. On such occasions, he would remember the woman who had been dragged to prison and that was enough for him to suppress the desire. Ignoring his friend's plaintive cries, Ahmad returned to his studies.

The next morning, walking toward the madrasah, the student ran the day's lesson through his mind. He wanted very much to please his teacher, an Hojjat-ol-Esl'am, an authority on Islam, with a perfect recitation of the Quranic verses. This great teacher told Ahmad he was one of the chosen few; chosen to be a carrier of the pure and holy Qur'an. A living example! It was the greatest of honors.

Ahmad had truly come to believe the sole purpose for which he was created was to memorize and recite the Qur'an each day, fully internalizing and living the lessons enshrined therein. At the end of each lesson the teacher would shout, "Who are you?" and the boys in the class, led by Ahmad, would reply, "We are majahedeen! We are the resistance! We are the holy warriors!"

Ahmad rushed down the staircase from the narrow rooftop with a great sense of pride swelling over him. Having taken the first step in the fulfillment of his destiny, all the old boyhood anxieties melted away, replaced by a deep sense of love and gratitude for the old teachers and hard lessons in which he had been so relentlessly schooled. In a whisper he asked, "Who are you?" The voice of an impassioned boy replied with a familiar and reassuring answer, "I am a holy warrior."

The bright sunlight pouring in from the doorway snapped him out of his reverie bringing him back to the divine odyssey he had begun so long ago for the glory of Islam.

He wanted to share this joyful moment with the men who sent him, yet Ahmad knew any form of communication, for the time being, could mean discovery by the ever-vigilant international police agencies.

So now, once again, needing to disappear, to commingle with the crowd and become one of the victims, he slipped the prayer book into the outer pocket of the backpack and slung it over his right shoulder. Taking final aim at the shimmering rectangle of sunlight pouring through the open doorway, Ahmad sprinted down the last flight of stairs towards freedom and anonymity.

Merilee Brunswick was on her way to work, sometime after eight o'clock, on a perfectly delicious, sparkling San Francisco morning. Enjoying the warmth of the sun on her face and the brisk morning air rolling in from the bay, Merilee hummed a snappy tune. She worked for one of the largest real estate firms in the city and today she was hurrying to meet one of their most high-profile developers to show him a magnificent old apartment building in the Presidio Heights section of town. The property was worth twenty five million and if she pulled off this sale the commission would be the biggest hit ever, propelling the young agent to the top of the regional sales team. She had been working for this moment for two years and was daydreaming about winning 'Real Estate Sales Executive of the Year,' and standing up for her team at the Christmas Holiday awards ceremony - quite an accomplishment for a girl whose family never expected her to amount to much.

The apartments were a few miles from the Omni America Building and as she approached the facade the first fire engines flew by with their sirens screaming. The harsh blare awakened Merilee to the fact that the salt spray was not the only scent in the air. The faint smell of smoke, polluted by several acrid odors began to sting her nostrils, provoking tears. A feeling of alarm started to rise from her belly and creep up into her throat.

Merilee stood in the front entrance of the historic building watching the fire engines speeding by. It took a moment to see and register, from the corner of her eye, the man bounding through the doorway. There was no way to avoid a collision – the man was coming rapidly at her, head on.

"Oh, shit! Look out," she yelled.

His distant, resolute expression told her that he did not hear her cry.

She guessed by the sudden alarm on the man's face that he finally, too late, apprehended the situation. Bracing for the collision, Merilee suddenly knew how it might feel to be in a car, stalled on the railroad tracks, as a speeding train roared ahead, bearing down, ever closer, oblivious to the desperation and sense of helplessness its victim would feel.

As the inevitable impact occurred, the small valise she carried flew from her grasp, the bits and pieces of her day scattering on the pavement like water droplets dancing wildly on a hot pancake griddle. An illegally parked car saved her from being thrown directly into the busy thoroughfare and under the wheels of a large step van with flashing red and blue lights just turning the corner. It bore the markings: San Francisco Police – Emergency Response Unit.

"Hey, you jerk! Get back here and help me pick this shit up!"

But it was no use. The man merely flipped a cursory glance over his shoulder, muttering something low under his breath. He glanced at the police van for less than a second before hurrying down the street and out of sight.

"Yeah, well, screw you too!" she called after him with less anger than fatigue, kneeling down to gather her things along with a little of her dignity. Absent-mindedly tossing them into her valise, Merilee noticed a pocket-sized leather-bound book just to the right of the brick steps that swaddled the entrance. She threw it in with all the rest of the chaos swept up from the sidewalk, never noticing a single laminated card that fell from the book on the opposite side of the stairway.

"I can't believe this," she yelled to no one, "didn't even notice he dropped his book. I hope I find a phone number inside so I can call and rip him a new one! What's wrong with people today? No goddamn manners!"

She caught herself just as tears were beginning to pop into the corners of her eyes, "Ok, girl, get it together. This too shall pass."

She was about to mutter a racial epithet about the Middle Eastern-looking man who knocked her down without a kind word or second thought, but decided against it. The man was a jerk, full stop. It had been a long morning and all she wanted now was an exceptionally strong cup of black coffee and some friends who would listen.

Merilee sat down on the steps of the building and while waiting for the client to show, sorted through the sad pile of scattered belongings and returned each item to its proper place. She loved this new valise. It was red leather and she took pride when people would point out that they especially admired it because it was not standard-issue black. It was a bit of daring in her mostly convention-al life. Slipping the stranger's book into its front pocket and zipping it shut, she tried calling her client's cell phone and was told to leave a message by a mechanical voice.

"Hello, Mr. Abraham," she chirped, disguising her annoyance after hearing the voice commanding her to speak. "This is Merilee Brunswick from Dowling Realty. I realize that with all the chaos you must be having an impossible time trying to get here. I will be in touch soon so we can reschedule for another time at your earliest convenience."

She clicked off and flipped through her cell's address book until the number she needed appeared on her screen. She hit "send" and left a message for her boss, Christine, explaining that the meeting with Mr. Abraham never happened and she would not be back in the office until the horrendous traffic jam, from whatever accident was causing the tie-up, could be cleared.

"I'll try to make it in later," she told her boss with a touch of guilty-conscience, knowing that going back to work was the least likely of all the day's possible endings.

Putting aside thoughts of the office, Merilee swept down the street, away from the smoke. She made a left at the next corner to see if she could catch that cup of coffee at 'The Penalty Box' and maybe find out what was going on.

'The Penalty Box' was a little sports bar and grill on Cherry Street and the favorite lunchtime hangout for the local businesses. Merilee came down here as often as she could to get away from the office frenzy. The pub had taken to opening early in the morning, to catch any caffeine-deprived executive in the area who could steal away for a morning cup of joe, or a take-away meal for a working lunch.

Before getting back to the often-stressful business of high-end real estate, Merilee would meet her best friend and computer wiz extraordinaire, Justine Diamonte, who worked in the area, and they would share a meal and relax a bit when time permitted. As Merilee wandered in, she sensed something unsettling in the air. The usual lunchtime crowd was there, only it was way before lunchtime and Merilee thought they were somehow different in a way she could not immediately put her finger on.

Normally, the guys in 'The Penalty Box' were at the circular bar in the center of the room, cheerily discussing whatever ballgame happened to be on the night before, or energetically debating the night's recap as they bolted their hero sandwiches and chips and washed them down with a beer chaser or two. Today they might have been shouting their objections about an umpire, usually referred to, often and vociferously, as a euphemism for an illegitimate child, or yelling their hatred of the bum at the plate, who once might have been their hero, but who, the night before, had blown a last-inning chance of tying the score.

The ladies usually sat together at small tables with their soups and salads, chattering away, ignoring the screens above their heads, except occasionally, as the replay of some particularly memorable play was interrupted by the rising decibels of male voices. Merilee had been looking forward to melting into this normally chaotic but carefree mob to help her salve the unpleasantness she had just left behind.

That's it, she realized, the noise…it's gone!

It was quiet…too quiet…eerily quiet. The only sound was the constant din of the ubiquitous television sets. The jibes, the chatter, were all silenced and everyone present, the bartenders and women included, were raptly staring up at whatever television screen was closest. In the next instant, Merilee registered the fear and concern on the faces of her friends. Scanning the room, her eyes fell on Justine who was now staring at the screen with a tear softly running down one cheek. Crossing the space between them, she slipped into the empty chair Justine had been saving and put an arm around her friend's shoulder.

"What is it? What's happening here? Has someone died?" she whispered to Justine, noticing again the knot forming in her stomach.

"They took it down! They bombed the Harbor Bridge and the Omni America building!" Justine sobbed, now burying her face in her hands.

With the silence finally broken, her friends at the table began frenetically recounting bits and pieces of the morning Merilee missed.

"They did it again," shrieked Justine's coworker, Lianna, banging both fists against the table. "Those bastards! How could the fucking government allow them to do this again?"

"They told us we were safer!" another friend exclaimed as a look of terror settled across her face, her eyes becoming sunken and narrow.

"You believed that bullshit? They're all a bunch of liars. Nothing can protect us from insane men who are willing to die to kill us," said Bernadette Rosario, a criminal attorney who had put aside her idealism a long time ago as she watched the guilty go free time and again. She finally gave up practicing criminal law for the relative civility of a small corporate office.

"Fuck you, you bastards!" she screamed in frustration and grief, making an obscene gesture at the television monitor suspended overhead.

"I don't think I can stand this. Not again. I had friends in that building. Good friends." Justine began to cry hard now.

Merilee, at first, did not understand what her friends were telling her. Looking back later, making her way home in a daze, she would realize that it was just too big to let in all at once, her mind could not accept the enormity of an event like this, and so, she whittled it down to a manageable level, her defenses initially telling her everything would be fine.

For now, she sensed the desperation, shock and urgency in her friend's voices but was not registering exactly what had happened. Had someone died on the Harbor Bridge? Was there perhaps a suicide bomber on the bridge that blew up a few cars? Surely, everyone was expecting something of that nature to happen eventually. Had it? Her thoughts strayed for a few seconds to a Chronicle photo of a bus in Tel Aviv, recently exploded by a Hezbollah suicide bomber. Forty-two people died, women and children included. Could what happened in her city today possibly be as bad as that? Merilee desperately hoped not.

Finally, however, the gravity and deadly seriousness of her friends began to soak through and her mind allowed her to understand that something unspeakably horrible, something very much like September 11, had just happened. Now the urgency to know took over.

"Wait! Could you all stop talking all at once!" cried Merilee turning to Justine, "What the hell is going on out there? What do you mean, they took down the Harbor Bridge? The bridge? How? Start at the beginning and tell me exactly what happened!"

Justine recounted the morning's horrific events, the knot in Merilee's stomach again migrating up into her chest, then her throat; becoming so tight that she could no longer speak. Tears began to flow in rivers down her cheeks, easing the tension in her throat, and all she could think of was escape.

Jumping up, excusing herself with a raspy whimper, she picked up the red valise, and started to leave. Justine came after her but Merilee bolted out the door and ran down the street. Justine called out after her, "Merilee, get back here!"

"I'll be alright, Jus. I've got to be alone. I've just got to…" Merilee said looking back, calling to her friend as she hurried away.

"I'll call you later," promised Merilee, even as she knew she would not.

BROKEN SYMMETRY

There's an unbroken current of energy that runs through the streets of New York City. A virtual buzz, distinctive and unique, coming from some enigmatic dimension in non-Euclidean space and is, at the same time, tangible as the city's skyscrapers and elusive as a toddler's attention span. Residents of the city who discover this flux use it to propel themselves throughout the day.

Suzanne Biasotto, a New York City native, allowed the tiniest of sighs to escape her lips, her feet hitting the city streets as she descended the steps exiting the tenderly restored brownstone she called home. For the past eight years, each of her mornings began with, pretty much, the same routine and life was beginning to feel like a ray of light trapped between two mirrors carrying the same image back and forth into infinity. Only the "buzz" saved her and she climbed on top of that energy wave and rode it like the surfers on Hawaii's Pipeline. Suzanne's near constant animation impressed her colleagues as born of steely motivation and a relentless drive to get things done. Extreme multitasking was her recognized forte. Suzanne hid well, often even from herself, that an anxious dread of living her life in a pattern of static repetition was the true source of her enterprise.

Unlike most of her fellow New Yorkers, Suzanne actually enjoyed the morning commute. Although she occasionally wished that she did not have to compete with throngs of commuters simply to travel a mile uptown, at heart Suzanne was a 'people-watcher,' enjoying the daily ballet on the city streets, as ardent mothers corralled their young children to school, earnest businessmen tapped out terse coded messages to their colleagues on the latest smartphone, and teens, swaying with the rhythm of the subway trains, reclaimed lost sleep as pop or hip-hop music was piped through headsets into their dreams. Suzanne drew pride and comfort at how most everyone moved in such kind syncopation with seldom a ripple in a veritable symphony of rush.

It was a few minutes before eleven in the morning, Suzanne was late, and the streets were still congested with people hurrying in every conceivable direction. New York City was one of the few places remaining in the country with livable salaries and people traveled for many miles and sacrificed countless hours of their lives just to get there. Unless it was Christmas Day, there were twenty-four hour crowds in New York, either working or visiting, and today would be no different.

Lucky to have found an apartment only a block and a half from the subway line connecting directly to her destination, Suzanne descended the staircase leading into the damp and cavernous tunnel with a resolute determination. She moved toward the crowded sub-way platform and into the stochastic madness New Yorker's call rush hour, making her way through the crowd, adroitly avoiding obstacles and commuters in her path, finally arriving at the exact spot on the platform where she calculated the train doors would open. Suzanne paused just long enough to notice the dramatic climate change floating through the air on the station's platform, the numbing cold of the concrete walls and steel columns that made the station feel like a tomb all winter long melted into that uniquely mild and sweet sensation characteristic of a spring day in the City. Thoughts of the wet heat of the coming summer tried creeping in but she held them at bay with the sheer enjoyment of the present. Spring was her favorite time of year and today she would immerse herself in a reverie of its pleasures and promises.

Suzanne, daydreaming about taking the day off, scowled at the deafening screech of the steel wheels on the tracks; the sound bouncing off the ceramic tiles as the train rumbled into the station.

Stepping into the packed subway car she found, by some miracle of the lesser gods that rule over subways, a seat. Pulling out a morning newspaper she purchased at a kiosk that stood at the subway's entrance, she began flipping through its pages, scanning for stories or items that might shape world events.

The major headline was a story about a retired athlete announcing he would return to play for his former team, the front page filled with career highlights.

The next top story covered a fundraiser at the Beverly Wilshire Hotel in Los Angeles with pictures of smiling celebrities in elegant eveningwear, drinking champagne from crystal flutes. They had gathered to perform at the 'No One is Alone Concert' to auction their discarded tee shirts and gowns while asking, once again, ordinary Americans still employed, to dig deep into their already drained pockets and share what little they had with their out of work neighbors.

Two pages of local and regional news stories followed with details of crimes and accidents, plus a list of inane tips for coping with the worsening economic situation that government stimulus dollars had failed to quell. Tip number one read: Try not to lose your job!

"Ya think!" Suzanne blurted out loud, momentarily catching the attention of the passenger seated across the aisle from her. The woman shot a disapproving glance at Suzanne, and shook her head. Suzanne recognized 'the look' as typical of New Yorkers who were notoriously possessive of their 'alone time' during the morning commute and did not appreciate interruptions by cell phone users, loud conversers, or 'crazies' talking to themselves. Suzanne grinned sheepishly and shrugged her shoulders in apology, surmising it futile to try to explain her sudden outburst. They both went back to their own business: Suzanne to her paper, and the woman, to the fourth book in a thriller series.

Suzanne's subway stop was directly under a new building Constellation Media Group erected as their world headquarters. The influence and importance of Constellation Media was so great that the New York State and City governments, together with the Federal Transportation Department, built a subway station just to accommodate the company, christening it 'Constellation Plaza' during the building's opening ceremonies.

The beneficiary of this government largesse was Lance Rodgers, founder of Constellation Media. Born in London of wealthy parents, Lance immigrated to the United States after graduating from Oxford University with a degree in literature. His family name and background helped him to quickly land a position as senior managing director with Spencer Wilson, the oldest and most prestigious financial and investment-banking firm in the New York, London, Dubai and Tokyo financial centers. After several years on Wall Street, he published an article entitled 'Global Imbalances within International Monetary Systems.' The paper won international acclaim among economists and became the basis for a new theory of currency trading, inducing the heads of Europe and Asia's central banks, along with the governors of the Federal Reserve Bank in the United States, to offer Lance paid speaking engagements to address the banking elite in their respective countries. Lance properly deferred the generous speaking honorariums, sending them instead to various charities, raising Lance's esteem and influence in financial circles and eventually propelling him to celebrity status. Lance Rodgers became a fixture on news analysis and talk shows across the globe.

Armed with classic British polish and aplomb, Lance's popularity soared, as did the ratings of any program fortunate enough to have him as a guest. From the moment he addressed the US Senate's banking committee, lecturing on the looming fiscal crisis, Lance Rodgers became the world's foremost expert on financial and monetary matters. Scheduling kept him so occupied Lance was seldom in the office. In spite of extended absences, Lance was placed on a fast track at Spencer Wilson. The firm was enjoying the tangible benefits of Lance's notoriety and had no intention of forfeiting their golden boy or the free publicity Lance brought with him. Promoted to Chief Investment Officer with a seven-figure salary, Lance became the firm's spokesman and it soon became common knowledge, via a series of leaked news stories, that Lance Rodgers was in the succession line to become Spencer Wilson's next Chief Executive Officer.

Despite the generosity of Lance's employers, and the satisfaction derived from his position, Lance had a more global long-term plan which, at the most propitious time, he tenaciously pursued. Through a network of business and family contacts, and with the help of Spencer Wilson and anonymous private equity funds, he raised two hundred billion dollars and formed the Constellation Media Group.

With a seemingly endless war chest of cash, he embarked on a series of ruthless acquisitions. Constellation Media Group swallowed entertainment companies, publishing companies, newspapers and magazines plus telecom, satellite and cable interests, through friendly or hostile takeovers. To complete the conglomerate, Constellation Media acquired a collection of storied news organizations and combined them into the corporate crown jewel, Global News and Information Network. And that is where Suzanne Biasotto worked as the executive producer in charge of programming for the prime time block of evening news and analysis shows.

Suzanne hurried through the underground tunnels to the building's lobby and waited impatiently for an elevator. She stepped off on the thirty-eighth floor, which was the main entrance of Global News. Passing the receptionist she clipped her employee identification badge onto her jacket and placed her index finger against the biometric security sensor. The system immediately recognized her fingerprint, together with the radio-frequency identification microchip in her employee card, swinging open the heavy glass doors. Walking briskly through the newsroom, she nodded 'good morning' to the army of reporters, editors, and copywriters preparing the nation's news, when a production assistant, his arms filled with a voluminous bundle of research papers, intercepted the producer as she turned a corner. He looked disheveled and nearly out of breath.

"Suzanne, John's been looking for you. He's been down here twice since ten. You'd better call him."

"Yeah, thanks, soon as I get settled." Without breaking her forward momentum, she continued down the hallway.

When she entered the office, a yellow rectangle of sunlight was lying across the desktop, reminding her of Tasha, sleeping on the parquet floor in the front room of their apartment. The calico cat would wake every so often, to move and follow the shifting sunlight, as though nourished by its constitutive rays. Suzanne was grateful for an office with windows. It was her portal to the world outside the newsroom and provided some consolation over spending a beautiful spring day inside.

Suzanne plopped into her chair as if she were falling into a swimming pool, the sunlit cityscape behind her, and touched 'enter' on the keyboard. One of three computer screens came to life, prompting her for a password. The screen read, 'Global News and Information Network - Welcome back Suzanne'; the system setting her preferences at the same time. In a few seconds, the screens on her desk, and the monitors suspended from the ceiling, came alive with news feeds, information, and messages from around the world. The current project, she and David Anderson were editing, appeared on the center monitor exactly where they left off the previous night.

She began a carefully choreographed routine of multitasking; quickly running down the overnight news stories to see if there was anything the assignment editors might have missed. She was reviewing the unopened e-mail in her inbox, when John Stavos, Global News' Editor-in-Chief, walked in.

John Stavos was fifty-three years old and his fine hair and meticulously groomed beard were already pure white. Every day he wore the same uniform: a starched white shirt, sleeves rolled up, and a conservative tie loose around his neck. To Suzanne, he looked every bit an image of the newsman archetype played by Spencer Tracy during the black and white era of Hollywood films; the dangling cigarette, its tendrils of smoke a lazy witness to the words tapped in hurried ardor, as though his thoughts might soon escape him; the ace reporter hard at his craft, hunched over a chunky black typewriter, responding to the touch of its keys with that classic 'tap and zing' everyone still secretly missed. These were to her, the lost signatures from the most romantic era of journalism.

John had spent most of his adult life in and around the news business. Telling a story was his passion and John's enthusiasm for it affected everyone around. He started out in Montana, teaching sixth grade and writing about local events for the Butte Mountain News. After five years in Butte, John decided to pursue his dream and applied for a position as a reporter for the Wichita Herald. When offered the position, Stavos accepted without hesitation. Not two weeks after the school term ended in June of that year, John moved to Kansas, diving into his new job the very next Monday morning with great earnestness, leaving the brown cardboard boxes, containing what remained of his life in Montana, still unopened on the floor of his rented apartment.

At first, John was delighted with the opportunity to finally practice his craft full time but the heat of enthusiasm soon waned, replaced by daily arguments with the editor, who insisted John's stories be changed to fit a certain ideological worldview. This penumbra of truth, where facts were mixed with editorial, was increasingly uncomfortable for John. He saw himself as one of the 'old breed' of newsmen, who believed their job was simply to report.

Within a year, John decided to move on and he began looking for a new position. It wasn't long before he found one, reporting for a local network affiliate in Minneapolis where he settled in quickly and produced some of the best stories of his career. Industry insiders began to notice his work and, before long, John won several prestigious journalism awards.

Then, finally, the big break came. John Stavos was offered the prime time anchor spot at Chicago's most popular television station, becoming an icon on Chicago television for almost two decades and a fixture on the city's psyche. The high and low points of John's career came when a group of investors approached him and offered co-ownership of a chain of network affiliate stations across the Midwest. They promised that he would make all the decisions and focus on the hard news stories that were his passion. And there was a side benefit. "This venture will make us rich," they promised.

But that promise was soon broken. After several years of mismanagement, and with the sinking economy taking a toll on advertising revenues, the investors sold out to Lance Rodgers and John was an employee once again, his new title, 'Editor-in-Chief' of Global News.

Suzanne looked up and said in a cheerful voice, "Good morning, boss!"

"Morning, Suzanne," John said in a monotone, dropping an interoffice envelope marked 'confidential' into a stainless steel tray full of papers. "Here are the latest ratings numbers."

Suzanne leaned forward, reaching across her desk, thought better of it, and instead, letting the envelope lay untouched, settled back into her chair. "I'm guessing we still own all the major time slots."

"We even gained some ground," John declared with a touch of pride while scarcely managing a smile.

Thinking her boss's somber mood might be melting, Suzanne folded her hands neatly in her lap and asked, "John, have you given any thought to my reassignment request?"

"Still want to get out there and spread those wings, huh?"

"That was kind of my hope...yes."

"Well Suzanne, take it from an old warhorse. Reporting isn't all adventure and romance, you know. In any event, I need you here doing the superlative job that you do!"

John noticed Suzanne's look of disappointment and added, "Listen, when the time is right I will send you into the field. Okay? Now tell me, anything new?"

Suzanne rolled her eyes, that sick feeling of being caged in mounting yet again. Times were bad, though; people would die for her job. Forcing a smile, she said, "I just got in...Let's see, a state senator from Ohio was killed skiing...another Hollywood celeb checked herself into rehab...the usual fires, shootings, weather..."

Pausing the length of a breath, John's expression still dour, Suzanne offered, "We're continuing coverage on the civil unrest here and in Europe, the World Energy Conference demonstrators in San Francisco, the Mid-East War, and, of course, the global economic meltdown."

John knew Suzanne too well for any nuance to pass unnoticed, no matter how subtle; she understood the unspoken message attached to "anything new" and he looked unmoved at her attempt to assuage his concerns. "That's not what I was hoping to hear. We can't repurpose the same content…our viewers are getting news fatigue. For May sweeps we need to find something unique…a format change perhaps. By the way, where's David?"

"We stayed late last night editing his documentary for sweeps week, so we are both running behind. I was just about to review the close. He should be here any minute. Trying to fit the documentary in the allotted airtime is a challenge. It's a big subject…lots of historical content comparing the fall of ancient civilizations with current world events. Some great interviews though. I think you'll like it… a bit edgy but more on the positive side. It's timely and, hopefully, we'll get some buzz around the water coolers. Would you like a peek at the closing clip…might cheer you up."

"Sounds interesting," John said, curious, "Cue it up."

She clicked on the video file and the monitors above their heads came to life. In the background was a superimposed graphic representing fading republics from antiquity to modern times. In the foreground David Anderson was delivering a final thought.

"…for the human heart does not readily change. When cultures collapse and the ephemeral bond between the individual and society dissolves, democracy soon follows.

Is the loss of our core values, the distrust of institutions both secular and religious, the decline of a common morality, and the hollowing out of our treasury a harbinger of our future? Unlike the chroniclers of past civilizations these warnings will be recorded by electronic ink for future historians to debate, but mostly, it will serve as a warning for all of us participating in the noble experiment of freedom.

This is David Anderson for Global News…Goodnight and thank you for watching."

"Good stuff," John said sounding more positive. Look, since we're behind schedule, why don't we go ahead with the morning editorial meeting. You can fill David in afterward…say fifteen minutes?"

"Sure thing, John. I'll round everyone up."

The editorial conference room, located on the eighty-third floor, had floor-to-ceiling windows offering occupants a spectacular panorama of New York's skyline. The opposite wall was covered with rare and expensive artwork befitting a corporation with the stature of Constellation Media; the architects purposely designing the building's public spaces to impart a feeling of symbolic royalty to its visitors.

John sat at the head of a long table fashioned from a mammoth thirty-thousand year old Kauri tree discovered beneath a peat swamp in Northland, New Zealand; its exotic wood polished to a deep reflective luster. The table was sculpted as a single piece, the legs embellished with exquisite sacred symbols carved by a renowned Maori woodworker and flown halfway around the globe to New York. It was only one of several in the world; the others, national treasures in New Zealand. The table's symbols told a story only Lance Rodgers, and the table's carvers, would ever know. It was a testament to the prestige of Constellation Media Corp, something the Maori people called 'mana'.

Behind John was a wall of monitors controlled with a lighted remote rarely ever out of his hand. Suzanne usually sat at the opposite end of the table. The production directors, assignment, wire, copy, photographic and video editors, along with the research director, news administrator and segment producers were seated on each side. Although a seating hierarchy had never been established, everyone sat in the same chair each day. Creatures of habit, thought Suzanne with a crooked smile, amused by the monotony associated with human idiosyncrasies.

Suzanne's smile widened as she thought of Global's senior anchorman. David Anderson never sat in the same seat. She found him a completely fascinating and unique man and she adored him. The senior journalist signified a fearlessness Suzanne wished she possessed. Emulating David this morning, Suzanne selected a place three chairs down from the one she chose the morning before. It was a small gesture, but it was something, and it seemed to sooth her restlessness.

As Suzanne waited for everyone to enter and settle in, she was distracted by the endlessly transcendent view; a welcome relief from the predictable routine of the day. Suzanne was seized by the first inkling that she would someday want to work in a skyscraper when, as a youngster, her parents surprised her with a trip to the observation deck of the Empire State Building. She had never seen anything so remarkable and impressive as the city in the sky.

Suzanne couldn't understand why New Yorkers seemed so indifferent to the art above their heads. She admired the architects and builders who were compelled to spend so much creative energy and money adorning the tops of their structures with ornate decorations that would never be noticed by most people. These days, there were moments when she would be seized by an almost uncontrollable urge to grab her fellow pedestrians and say, "Look up! You're missing it!"

John, hurrying into the room, called the meeting to order. "Alright people, let's settle down…I'd like a rundown of what we're thinking for tonight's program. Suzanne, can you walk us through it?"

"Sure, John." Suzanne stood and looked momentarily at the staff. She had gleaned from John the fine art of non-verbal expression and her appearance conveyed a simple message of preparedness. She began with Drew Krohn, the newsroom administrator. "Drew, bring up the story listing for tonight's program, please."

Drew touched a few keys and the monitors behind John fused into a single display showing the proposed details. Each story idea was listed in order and included a title, story slug, correspondent, producer, research assistant, and editor plus the scheduled airtime and run length.

Suzanne nodded to Drew, signaling approval, and continued, "Our lead-in tonight is the president's White House meeting with the head of the International Monetary Fund. David will recap the events then go to our senior White House correspondent, Mike Lussardi, for the details."

Suzanne turned toward Robert Lutz, the political editor, "Anything to add, Bob?"

"Well, the meeting is scheduled for later this afternoon…we expect a brief news conference…mostly a photo-op, no major announcements…they don't agree on anything."

"Are you hearing this from a trusted source or is this your opinion?" John asked. The acerbic question was subtle and purposeful.

"Yes…sorry John…we got this 'off the record' yesterday from an EU minister."

Greg Nowak, Global News' foreign assignment editor, chimed in, "My understanding is that the IMF has been holding backchannel meetings, trying to win support for a new reserve currency prior to the World Banking Conference in Paris. They won't talk about it until they have the votes."

"Thanks Greg," Suzanne interjected, steering the meeting back on its usual positive track.

"For our second story, we're covering the World Energy Conference out on the West Coast. No major developments expected…the focus of our coverage tonight is on the demonstrations and the rioting going on out there. A group, calling themselves The Alliance for Global Advancement, is threatening to block bridges and occupy several buildings. It's a nice tie-in with our special coverage on the escalating economic deterioration around the world."

John raised his hands in a 'stop' sign. He wanted quiet in the room. He spun the chair around, placed his hands, fingers locked, behind his head, and began considering the stories listed on the screen. Everyone sat silently staring at John's back, anticipating his reaction, when the telephone rang. Suzanne picked up the receiver and listened intently for a moment then touched the conference button so all in the room could hear.

"Go ahead, I've got you on speaker."

"This is Dume in the Network control room, we have a…"

"Who are you?" John asked, sounding annoyed at the intrusion. He turned to stare menacingly at the phone.

"Dume Lumumda, assistant technical director for 'Live at Noon.' We have feeds coming in from our local affiliates and from the West Coast newsroom… something…there is something happening in San Francisco. It doesn't look good."

John reset the display screen. A shutter opened and through the convex lens of a camera's eye, wide angles of violence flooded the room. Minutes passed. No one made a sound, everyone in the room just staring at the video, hypnotized and repulsed at the same time. An inexorable force pulled them into a tight circle around John, the close contact offering a level of comfort and relief. Suzanne was the only one not to move, remaining seated, staring at the screen, waiting impatiently for a cue from her heart.

John, his signature inscrutability intact, quickly scanned the room. A pallor on the faces of those who gathered around the screen; a palpable stiffness to the way they held their heads on slumped shoulders; the frightened, questioning look in their eyes, told him to act quickly now, before he had to deal with a full-blown meltdown.

Standing to address the group, his legs suddenly felt weak, thin as wire, and barely able to hold him. He held fast to the conference room table for support. With instincts born of decades in the news industry, John took control. Like a military officer on horseback ordering a charge, he commanded, "Alright folks. We know what to do…get moving!"

The resolution was sufficient to break the spell holding John's loyal acolytes in a deer-like trance, initiating a complex series of actions. The staff, calculating the steps needed to engage the quick acting assets of Global News, raced in concert toward the elevators.

Standing together in the now empty conference room, their gaze fixed on one another, John nodded at Suzanne, like a parent assuring a child that the bad times in life will always be resolved for the good. "Are you okay?" he asked her.

"I can almost…hardly breathe," she replied, her voice breaking. John nodded a sign of commiseration and support. Suzanne broke away reluctantly and ran toward the elevators. Pushing her way into the packed car, turning around just as the doors were closing, she heard John call out, "Get David on the air and tell him it's going to be a long night!"

The doors slid shut. The elevator car began its descent. Suzanne realized the symmetry of routine and the reliable boundless current of energy she took for granted all these years, had been irreparably shattered.

After crashing into Merilee Brunswick, the second leg of Ahmad's journey began. Still bearing a long scratch on his forearm from the brass buckle fastening the woman's briefcase, he slid into the car purchased using Walter Greenfield's stolen identity. The car, an old Buick Skylark, its original cheery blue paint now replaced with a dismal dark green that gave it anonymity, was exactly what Ahmad needed. The salesman at the used car lot tried to convince Ahmad the car was 'a real little jewel' and well worth the twenty five hundred dollar sticker price. Ahmad, however, having been raised in a part of the world famous for its hagglers, drove away in the little 'jewel' only eighteen hundred dollars poorer and no worse for wear.

Ahmad's getaway car was parked close to the entrance ramp of the Golden Gate Bridge. Timing was crucial. He had to cross the bridge without raising suspicion and before the authorities had time to fully react to the attack. Ahmad let out the breath he was holding when he saw the police had opened both sides of the bridge to evacuate the city. In the ensuing chaos of the disaster there was little time to scrutinize passing vehicles and the patrolmen were only glancing at cars as they passed, looking for obvious signs of suspicion, hurriedly waving each car along.

Ahmad drove north past the police checkpoints and, with joy, recited a prayer, "La ilaha ill Allah," which meant, "I testify that there is no God but Allah." For Ahmad, it was both an affirmation of his faith and a prayer of gratitude.

Troubled by the notion he might be stopped and questioned by the police, Ahmad was determined to be a model driver. He made sure the speed limit was never exceeded, obeying every traffic light, signaling at every turn or lane change. His driver's license and the car's registration were issued in the name of the Reverend Greenfield and he did not want a traffic cop to notice that his resemblance to a Midwestern, white protestant was debatable.

Traffic on the interstate just north of Sacramento grew congested and came to a standstill several times, as police, haphazardly pulling cars off the road and onto the highway's right shoulder, hoped, by sheer luck, they might apprehend a suspect.

Passing Sacramento city center, Ahmad stopped once in Rocklin to fuel the car and stretch his legs.

The temperature dropped as Ahmad wound the old green sedan through the Sierra Nevada Mountains, soon discovering the sedan he bought, 'a proper car for someone from Catoosa,' didn't have reliable heat. The blower was making a ka-chunking sound, fraying his nerves. Ahmad hoped the fresh air from the open windows might help him stay alert, but the cold, noisy wind proved too much after a time and it wasn't long before he rolled up the window, buttoned his thin denim jacket, and, reluctantly, turned on the radio.

Ordinarily, Ahmad believed American music immoral but he did not want to drive off a mountain road or careen over a cliff. The dilemma was short-lived, since the 'no frills' car only had a terrestrial FM receiver and the stations were either out of range or broadcasting news of the day's events. Switching off the radio, he drove shivering and alone through the mountains as the sun moved across the sky.

Ahmad passed the time by reciting some of the Quranic verses memorized as a child. The recitations brought him comfort and strength, justifying, he believed, his very existence. He chanted, fervently in Arabic:

> "O you who believe! Fight those of the disbelievers who are close to you; and let them find harshness in you; and know that Allah is with those who are the pious."
>
> "Let not the Unbelievers think that they can get the better of the godly; they will never frustrate them. Against them make ready your strength to the utmost power, including steeds of war, to strike terror into the hearts of the enemies of Allah and your enemies and others besides, whom you may not know but whom Allah knows."
>
> "Allah has preferred in grades those who strive hard and fight with their wealth and with their lives, above those who sit. Unto each Allah has promised paradise, but Allah has preferred those who strive hard and fight above those who sit, by a huge reward."

The midday sun soon sank into late afternoon. On the outskirts of Reno, Ahmad drove into a gas station. His first order of business was to find the rest room, perform his ablutions and say his prayers.

His next stop was the gasoline pump, where he topped off the gas in the car's tank, and replaced the nozzle and gas cap before walking into the station's convenience store for something to eat. He selected several items before standing in line behind a man wearing a tee shirt that read *'The End is Near. Repent.'*

Sitting on a shelf, behind the shop clerk's head, was a small, old-style color television with a grainy picture, displaying the endless news coverage resulting from Ahmad's earlier activities. The clerk had long, dull, grey-white hair pulled into a ponytail. After spending thirty years in the fraternity of trackwalkers employed by the Southern Pacific Rail Road, the skin on his face was raw, bitten by the sun, and wrinkled like crumpled parchment. Day in and out, with only Sunday to rest, this counter clerk, who refused to quit working, had carefully examined every rail, joint and tie on the Tehachapi Loop: a tight helix constructed to decrease the angle of the track grade so trains could climb the mountain; it was one of the most dangerous tracks in the continental United States.

As Ahmad stepped to the counter, the old man looked him over with the same scrutiny he used when walking the tracks. He watched the clerk knit his brows over narrowed eyes as he registered every detail of Ahmad's appearance. Ahmed twisted his face away, pretending he was looking at some items on a shelf behind him.

"Just passing through?" the old man asked.

"Yes, I'm on my way to…err, Tahoe," Ahmed replied, turning back to face the man, his hand coming up in front of his face, slowly scratching his nose.

"You comin' from the west?" the old man persisted.

"Yes…Sacramento." Ahmad realized this was a mistake as the words passed his lips. "How much does this cost?" he added, hoping the clerk would let the error go unnoticed.

"Well, partner, you went a little out of your way. You should've…"

'How much does this cost?" Ahmad asked again, his hands flying down from his face in clenched fists.

"Nine sixty-one…mister," the clerk growled, his narrowed eyes turning into a glare.

The man began stuffing the items into a brown bag, his motions short and aggressive.

"Terrible thing that happened today…real scum, whoever did it…real scum…we'll get 'em…just wish they'd bring 'em in here… I'd like a crack at 'em."

Ahmad turned to go without a response, contemplating the insult of the foolish old man's words, his face flushing. He hated having to endure the daily encounters in America, with its ignoble and ignorant people, happy he would soon be gone from this country of infidels.

Turning the ignition key just as a Nevada State Highway Patrol Car pulled into the station and up to the adjacent gasoline pump, Ahmad noticed the clerk standing behind the weather-beaten aluminum frame door, watching him with steely eyes. He prayed the old man would not say something to the patrolman that would wind up getting him arrested. There is nothing I can do about it now, he thought. Without glancing at the patrolman, he waved at the old man and sped away.

About a quarter mile or so later Ahmed caught himself. He deliberately forced himself to slow down, continuing just under the speed limit on the dusty rest-stop road until he entered the I-80 on-ramp. He pointed the old Skylark toward the Black Rock Desert and, with the sun dropping behind him, Ahmad sped east, the gentle hills and dunes of the desert rolling by mile after mile, hour after hour.

Merilee felt a sense of relief wash over her as she climbed the stairs to her tiny second floor apartment in the North Beach section of the city, her sanctuary for the past five years. She was grateful for the retreat more than ever today.

At seventeen, Merilee escaped a sewer of abuse on the outskirts of St. Louis at the hands of her relentlessly hateful stepfather. Ray Johnstone was an ignorant and angry man who believed women and children were created essentially as a man's property and, as such, needed to be managed as one would manage a business. Ray's family 'business' had, as its overriding mission statement, the careful maintenance of his own comfort and convenience. Anything, or anyone, who got in the way of Ray's 'mission' was in a whole world of trouble.

Merilee's kindest memory of her stepfather was of him slouching in front of an ancient Frigidaire, it's massive dull grey door now scuffed and dented with dozens of fingerprints permanently imbedded in its once gleaming white surface, staring inside at the jumble of half-eaten jarred condiments and leftover remains, popping the top on a can of brew, silent, wearing a slightly crooked scowl on his gaunt, unshaven face.

Merilee learned never to ignore Ray's scowl. It meant Ray could suddenly erupt into an evil rage, usually fueled by a stop at the local bar on his way home from work. Whenever she saw the little curl of his lip, indicating someone he did not respect had disrupted his sense of comfort, inconvenienced him, or pissed him off, she ducked out of sight, quick and silent as a jackrabbit. Years later, memory flashes of that 'look' caused Merilee to squeeze her eyes shut, willing the image back down into the locked vault she kept inside. She still felt guilty about her ability to avoid the beatings as a child, usually by hiding in the back of her bedroom closet while her mother, Claire, and her brother, Tim, took the brunt of his rage.

Claire tried to soothe her husband, she tried hard, but Ray's rage was like a gathering storm and just as unstoppable. Claire put herself between her husband and her children and it fueled Ray's rage ever hotter. One particularly memorable episode, culminating in Ray grabbing Claire by the hair with a kitchen knife held to her throat, left Merilee with deep emotional wounds.

Ray exhibited his colossal penchant for cruelty with a particularly creative way of prolonging the suffering of his two terrified stepchildren. He would tell them to 'get ready' and tromp off to his bedroom to see what implement of torture he could fish out: perhaps a stick, perhaps a wooden slat that had fallen out of the louver door in the den. Other times, he would remove his belt and, if he wanted to be particularly sadistic, hit them with the brass buckle that dangled ferociously at its end.

As the two ill-fated children waited, anticipating the punishment to come, they would scamper upstairs like hunted rabbits and hold each other, trembling, "What do you think he will do? Do you think we'll die?"

"Maybe we should jump out the window. We might die. But it won't be as bad," Tim replied in anxious dread.

"We can't leave mom alone with him," said Merilee with finality.

"It'll be alright. It'll be over soon!" Merilee and Tim assured each other.

Ironically, the two children were soon to discover making it through the beating wasn't the worst part. The worst part was being forced to hold it in – all the grief and pain. Ray did not cotton to crying.

"Shut up or I'll give you something to cry about!" he growled between gritted teeth.

Merilee came to learn the term "choking back the tears" was no metaphor: it was the actual sensation of the lump she felt in her throat from the effort required to restrain her cries.

Holding back her tears was something Merilee would carry into her adulthood. Years later, her therapist, Joan, in response to the difficulty she had breaking through Merilee's steely calm, would remark, "Jesus, Merilee! For someone functioning in the world as well as you do, you sure have the best damn defense system I have ever seen."

As a child hiding from Ray's wrath, Merilee huddled in the back of her closet, anxious and wishing the wall would magically open up and swallow her into another world, rich and populated with the most fantastic creatures and places her young imagination could conjure. She often stayed well after the storm passed, not just because she felt safe there but because it was fun.

In this imagined world, the colors were bright as a sun-made prism created by the passing of a rain shower and the people were smiling and kind.

Merilee made detailed drawings of her imagined haven to bring to school and show Miss Carolyn, the art teacher at Hamilton Elementary. Miss Carolyn would beam down at the pictures and exclaim with sincere delight how well her young student was progressing. She would remind Merilee that her imagination was especially creative and she must remember to nurture this gift. Occasionally, Miss Carolyn would ask where Merilee received the inspiration for the drawings. Merilee would shrug and tell the teacher she copied them from a storybook. Miss Carolyn nodded and told her that, nonetheless, the pictures showed special talents.

Miss Carolyn was the only person who looked directly into Merilee's eyes and this instilled a sense of self she would not otherwise have acquired. Merilee's mother had once filled her need for recognition and nurturing but, finally, unable to find the courage needed to leave her abusive husband, she withdrew into her own tight world and left her two youngsters to fend for themselves.

The simple act of acceptance and respect consistently shown by Miss Carolyn was enough to inspire Merilee to believe that, indeed, she might possess inherent goodness and value. She clung to the teacher's kind words like a small child who clings to its mother's fingers while learning to walk. Ray could never take these memories from her. The warm feelings of affection that grew between Merilee and her teacher would serve her well in the times ahead when she would be forced to face Ray's frustration and rage at her growing confidence and independence, and later, when she would embark on a new life alone.

Merilee never told a living soul about her secret world for fear the door might be nailed shut forever by Ray's derision or the closed minds of even well-meaning adults. Merilee feared sharing her secret world would lead to a cascade of questions. There were things you did not talk about. There were things too horrible to reveal, even to your most trusted friends.

Once, empowered by something she heard at school, Merilee dared to try and step out of her frightening world of abuse. She threatened to call Child Protection Services.

"Go ahead, little girl," Ray said taunting, "Report me to the police. See if anyone is alive by the time they get here. No...why should I die or spend time in jail on account of you? Go ahead. Call them. They'll just take you away and you'll never see your mother or brother again. Here, let me get you the phone."

In the end, Merilee did not call and Tim did jump out the proverbial window. At their stepfather's insistence, Tim became a man by abusing alcohol with Ray and his buddies. The beatings stopped but the hurt was still there. Tim got good and drunk one night, hopped into Ray's four-by-four pickup, and took his last sweet ride into eternity. That's when Merilee left. She came to realize that her mother did not need or want protection.

The day Merilee ran away, she was certain Ray would not pursue her. He could not care about anyone but himself. He felt nothing but disdain and jealousy at the relationship between Merilee and her mother.

Good riddance, Merilee imagined he would say. Relief would be Ray's only response as he pressured her mother to call off the search for her missing daughter.

And so she went – as far as she could. But sometimes…sometimes…the memories came floating back and the tightness in her throat would return. It was then that she would climb into the back of her deepest, darkest closet, just as she had done as a child, to hide from her stepfather's wrath. She would stay there until the trembling subsided and she could face life in the real world once more.

Merilee took comfort knowing that in the unlikely event the bastard ever changed his mind and showed up in San Francisco, she could blow him away with a small handgun she purchased shortly after settling in. She took a few shooting lessons down at the local range, obtained a permit, and then kept it safely in the drawer of the bedside night stand for peace of mind.

As she let these thoughts drift away, Merilee slipped off her shoes and carefully laid them inside the door of her apartment. With the day's events lurking once again in her mind, she went down the hallway and rounded a bend to the left leading into a tiny efficiency kitchen. She opened the refrigerator to see what cold liquid she could use to rescue her throat from the clench of fear that, suddenly, felt like an icy hand emanating from the coldness coming from the open door.

Merilee shook off the sensation and stood there for a long while wondering what on earth her churning stomach could possibly keep down; hoping a sparkling mineral water and plain tea biscuits would suffice. She closed the refrigerator door, took a handful of biscuits from a vintage 'Little Red Riding Hood' ceramic cookie jar, and proceeded back down the hall, grabbing the red valise on the way. She turned into a small sitting room. Sinking down into her Victorian chair with the cabbage rose print, Merilee closed her eyes with a sigh.

Taking slow, thoughtless sips from the bottle of spring water, Merilee tried to blot out the day but, soon, anxiety won and her eyes snapped open. She pulled herself wearily out of the chair, crossed the room to where the remote lay on top of the television set, and clicked on the local news.

Every news organization had commandeered the airwaves to provide live coverage of the events happening in the city. Information gathered by the major news agencies pointed to the premise that a militant terrorist organization, intent on jihad, was responsible for the attacks. As Merilee watched the unfolding events, she pulled the valise into her lap and unzipped the front pocket. Televised scenes of reveling Middle Easterners reminded her of the book left behind by the distinctly foreign-looking man with whom she had collided, and she removed it from the valise. Merilee was quietly lamenting the level of hatred that had developed between east and west when she opened the embossed leather cover.

A few crumbs from the biscuit on which she was snacking fell onto the open page of the book sitting in her lap. She was not surprised to see the words were unreadable. The letters were beautifully drawn in a delicate calligraphy that she suspected must have been from somewhere in the Middle East. The outer edges of each page were illuminated by exquisite and intricate blue and gold leaf designs that gave her a little thrill of admiration for the skill and discipline of the artist. The paper was of the finest stock and texture. The entire book appeared painstakingly drawn and bound and was obviously of great value. She carefully wiped her mouth with a napkin to catch stray crumbs and gently blew away those fallen on the page, fearing that touching the pages with her fingertips would unalterably mar the beautiful writing.

The book was obviously well cared for and she wondered how the man could have been so careless with such a prized possession. She felt a deep sense of respect for the little book and guessed it must be an important text of some kind, perhaps a Qur'an. At the same time, an inexplicable sense of dread lingered as she recalled the face of the frightening stranger with the urgency in his eyes that knocked her down and ran away in such a frenzied rush.

Merilee carefully perused the book, thinking perhaps she might have the good fortune of finding the man's name or 'return if found' information. Thoughts of calling him up for a good scolding no longer preoccupied her. In its place she had the distinct feeling that, in view of the events of the day, the police might appreciate knowing about the odd man bounding down the stairs of a building not far from the attacks.

To her surprise, when she flipped through the book's front pages, Merilee found a set of five cards instead of the man's name and contact information. The cards were distinctly similar in workman-ship to the beautifully hand decorated prayer book. They were about the size of standard playing cards and each was coated in a clear plastic laminate. On one side, there was text printed in black ink with lettering similar to that in the book. On the opposite side appeared a golden mark, obviously created by an artisan of great skill. She sur-mised it might be an old fashioned writer's seal, the kind that would identify the author or place of origin of the owner. The symbol looked delicate and, at the same time, exquisitely intricate. The mark, a collection of loops forming an infinite knot, gleamed under the light of the lamp.

Merilee had no idea what this all meant but now every instinct told her to call the police. Years of abuse gave Merilee a finely honed sense of danger.

Merilee's chest started to pound and her breath quickened as she dialed the phone number of the local police department. She had not imagined that it would take her a full thirty minutes to get through to the sergeant at the front desk. Everyone in the city must be calling the police tonight.

"Sergeant Brooks speaking," was the cursory reply as she finally heard a voice. The man sounded exhausted and his responses strained, as though forced to go through the motion of talking to the public.

"Yes, my name is Merilee Brunswick. I collided with a man this morning running out of a building on Jackson Street, about a mile from the attack site. He was in an awful hurry and knocked me off my feet as he pushed past. I am worried that he may have had something to do with the attacks."

"What makes you think so?" The sergeant asked, irritated. "Did he have a gun or any other weapon?"

"No. Nothing like that, sergeant," answered Merilee, fidgeting in the chair and feeling as though she were being questioned as a suspect.

"Do you have any evidence that he was carrying a bomb? Did he threaten you or mention the attacks?" It sounded to Merilee like the sergeant was reading through a script for the thousandth time that day.

"No, sir, not exactly," Merilee said, trying to control her now wildly shaking left leg.

"No crime bein' in a hurry, miss. Maybe he was scared half to death like the rest of us. Why don't you just turn off the TV and try to relax. We have it all under control," the officer replied. This time he spoke with a definite air of impatience in his voice that was beginning to get Merilee just a tad annoyed.

"I am sure you are right, sir, but he dropped a book that I think may be significant. It seems to be a prayer book, of some sort, written in a Middle Eastern script, possibly Arabic."

"No crime in prayin', lady," came the sardonic reply.

The policeman was getting distinctly obnoxious and Merilee could have done without the condescending attitude. Her nervousness was slowly changing to indignation.

"Of course not," Merilee agreed. She refrained from adding, "You bloody, holier-than-thou, pisspot."

"Listen," she commanded. Her speech became high and rapid. "There's a set of cards inside with notes and symbols written on them. They could provide some clue to what is going on and I thought it my civic duty…"

"Do the cards mention a threat or list possible targets?" The sergeant interrupted, clearly reading from the script again.

"Sergeant, as I told you before, they are written in a language I do not understand," replied Merilee with deepening exasperation.

"Well, listen lady, you are welcome to bring them in. Don't bother coming in today though. All hell is breaking loose and we can't spare a detective. Wait a few days and then I'll see what I can do. Have a nice day, lady." Abruptly, the phone went dead. Merilee just stared in disbelief at the receiver as she listened to the dead silence.

Merilee hung up the phone and stopped to ponder her next move. Upon talking to the officer on the other end of the line, Merilee realized a detective who would see her might take days, if not weeks, to actually follow up on any leads given him. She thought the police must have hundreds of leads to look into, or soon would, probably some that will seem a lot more credible than this little leather-bound book.

Merilee, however, was convinced that what she had in her possession was significant, if not crucial, to the events of the day. The more she looked through the man's book, the more sinister the memory of him became. Years of living with Ray taught her to trust her instincts and she knew she had to think of a way to find and convince the right person to check out this book. But how? And who?

As she was turning possible alternatives over in her mind the doorbell rang. Oh, man. Who could that be? I'm really in no mood for socializing at the moment, she thought as she moved toward the door.

"Who is it?" she said as she pressed the intercom.

"It's me, you clown, your best friend," chided Justine. "The one you ditched this morning at the pub. I thought I'd come over and make sure that you haven't done anything desperate."

"Oh, must you be so melodramatic?" whined Merilee.

"Yes, I must," Justine insisted.

"Come in, mother hen, before I change my mind," said Merilee with a faint grin as she pressed the buzzer that opened the front entrance door. Justine was the one person Merilee was always pleased to see.

Justine settled into a small sofa and, without a second thought, tossed her purse on the floor.

"Merilee, what's up? You look like you've just seen a ghost," Justine observed.

The concern in Justine's voice gave Merilee a sense of security; she appreciated what a great choice she had made in this friend.

She knew Justine could be trusted with her story. Justine would listen, offer levelheaded advice, and, most importantly, keep the whole thing confidential.

Merilee decided, right then, she would tell Justine the entire story. She rose from her chair and began pacing the room. Intent on total recall, Merilee became absorbed by the pattern on the Persian rug as she paced back and forth. She started to talk as she paced, rubbing the sides of her temples, calling forth every detail. She did not look up until she came to 'The Tale of Sergeant Brooks.'

"He was the most patronizing little twerp, Jus. You should have heard him. I wanted to reach in over the line and slap that smart-ass mouth of his," Merilee said. Her voice was again rising.

Getting no reply from Justine, she looked over and saw her friend intent upon watching the television, seemingly not paying attention, one whit, to Merilee's account of the day's events.

"Excuse me, Jus? Am I interrupting your sojourn into TV la-la land? Have you heard anything I've said?" Merilee shouted, snapping her fingers. "This is important stuff babe, listen up!"

"Justine has heard every word that has come off your honeyed tongue, girlfriend, and now mama is gonna tell you exactly what to do." Justine's confidence always seemed to calm Merilee's anxiety, straight away.

"Oh, really," Merilee said. She was intrigued, as usual, by her friend's assurance, "And what, pray tell, would that be?"

"You are going to call him," instructed Jus, pointing to the television screen.

"Him? Him Who?" Merilee asked. She turned around to look at the man Jus was insisting she must call.

Merilee took one look at the journalist on the screen, looked back at Jus, threw her head back and laughed. "Oh sure. You want me to call David Anderson. Like he gives a rat's ass about my…"

"Merilee, just trust me. You know I am right!"

"And how, in heaven's name, am I supposed to get through to him? He works for the largest news organization on the planet. He's their biggest anchor. Do you really think they will put me through to him? I don't think so."

"Oh ye of little faith! Just call the local station and leave him a message that you have a tip about the attacks and he is the only one you intend to contact. If any of his coworkers are worth their salt they will at least relay the message. After all, he could be getting an exclusive lead in the hugest event to happen in this country since 9/11. He would be a fool not to at least have a producer call and check it out."

Merilee had to admit that Jus did have a good point. Still, she was skeptical, especially in light of the treatment she received at the hands of Sergeant Brooks. But it was her only viable option and she picked up the phone and dialed information.

Merilee called the number for the local Global News office. As she listened to the phone ring, she glanced up again at the image of David Anderson on the TV screen, standing in front of what appeared to be a mosque somewhere in the Middle East. He was presenting an exposé on the life of children attending local Islamic religious schools, where youth were apparently trained to become extremists and suicide bombers. Something above David's head kept capturing Merilee's attention. Suddenly, she recognized it and let out a yell that catapulted Jus off the couch and sent her almost to the ceiling.

"What the hell is wrong?" Jus demanded, her hands flying up in the air.

"This is un-freakin'-believable," cried Merilee as she dropped the phone and ran back to her chair.

She picked up the illustrated prayer book.

"Take a look at this, Jus, and then tell me what you see on the outside of that school." Merilee was trembling as she thrust the laminated cards into Jus' hands.

Justine's mouth fell open as she saw the symbols were the same!

"You have got to reach David Anderson as soon as humanly possible. He has to know about this and he has to know NOW! This means something and I have a feeling it ain't no small potatoes."

Justine's renewed enthusiasm inspired Merilee with the confidence she needed and Merilee was, suddenly, right there, in complete agreement with her friend. She crossed the room to the spot where she had dropped the phone, picked it up and, having forgotten the number, dialed information once more.

"What city and state?" Merilee heard the canned voice ask.

She was in no mood to play with the voice response system again. It never seemed to understand what she was saying. She groaned as she recalled the myriad times she heard, "I'm sorry, I didn't get that."

She decided to remain silent and wait for a live voice, hoping that the mechanism would not hang up on her. Within a few seconds, she heard the hoped-for live voice ask how she could be helped. She repeated her request for the Assignment Desk number at the San Francisco office of Global News and opted to have the number automatically dialed.

She barely waited for a 'hello' before asking how she might get in touch with David Anderson.

"I'm sorry," replied the pleasant-sounding assignment editor, "David Anderson does not work from this office."

"Listen. I really need to reach him. I believe I have some important information that might be quite relevant to the attacks today. He might be able to help me sort out what to do."

"Have you contacted the authorities, miss?" the assignment editor suggested. "They may be in the best position to guide you."

"Yes, I have already tried them and they are overwhelmed with people calling in leads. By the time they get to me…look…David Anderson aired a story recently on the madrasah schools in the Middle East. I really think he would want to take a look at what I have. Can't you at least relay a message to him for me?"

The assignment editor began to sense the urgency in Merilee's voice and thought this was something she, perhaps, should not dismiss.

"Well, I suppose I could pass your name and number to one of his production assistants," she told Merilee in a tentative voice.

Merilee was thrilled with this bit of compromise and gladly repeated the entire story.

She concluded the phone call by saying, "Don't forget to tell him that the information is directly related to the exposé that aired on Global this afternoon. Tell him I ran into someone who may be related to this morning's attacks and he left behind some important papers. It is very important you don't leave that out." The assignment editor did not miss the note of relief in Merilee's voice.

"Yes, miss. I understand. I will do my best. Goodbye, and thank you for calling Global News."

"Thank you. Goodbye," replied Merilee.

Feeling ever so relieved, Merilee turned back to Justine as she hung up the phone.

"You were right! I feel a lot better now. Let's keep our fingers crossed he gets the message."

"Let's hope it matters to him as well," Justine replied and then added, "Look, Merry, if you are okay, I guess I should be on my way to see how my own clan is faring through all this."

"Yes, of course. Thanks so much for being there for me today, Jus. You are just the best," Merilee said, walking her friend to the door.

"That's 'Jus, the best'," she smiled with the signature twinkle in her eyes, "You can always count on me, girlfriend. I'll call you tomorrow."

Merilee gave her chum a hug, and double locked the door as the sound of her friend's footsteps faded.

She returned to the sofa clutching the portable phone in both hands, watching the anchorman, anticipating his call.

THE SEEKER AND
THE SEARCH

"We've tried, over and over, David. We just can't reach your dad! David Anderson replayed the words in his mind until his head began to pound. The repetition stirred the memory of an antique record player once belonging to his great grandmother. It was called a Victor Victrola and it was grand. The old cabinet was made of a beautiful dark cherry wood, graced by two carved doors containing shelves filled with shiny black vinyl discs. The crank on its right side wound the hidden spring until sufficient tension was created to spin the record in a dizzying whirl. The needle, carefully placed on the revolving discs, would skip over scratches, repeating the same musical phrase, over and over, until it was gently lifted and placed on an adjacent track.

David wished life could be replayed like the skipping music of the old discs and, with a simple movement of his hand, he could return to New Town before his mother died and his dad went missing. Secretly, David was yearning for nothing more than a return to a time when the three of them were all safe within the historic centuries-old farmhouse his family called home.

Besides the comfort of a wistful memory, the old Victrola carried a greater significance for David. It turned out to be a harbinger of the man David was to become. The Victrola had, as its logo, a picture of a dog sitting next to a phonograph player, his head cocked, listening intently to the sound emanating from its large fluted horn. Beneath the picture was inscribed 'His Masters Voice'. David, fascinated by the logo, asked what the whimsical symbol meant, but no one knew. It became a mystery of irresistible intrigue to the young boy. David began hunting for information that would provide the key to unlock the door to this peculiar puzzle.

David's ardent search led him to discover the dog was 'Nipper', the famous fox terrier, who gazed with longing and expectant eyes at the Victrola's flute, bringing to him the last remnants of his beloved master, gone but never to be forgotten.

David found that an English artist, Francis Barraud, captured the peculiar interest the dog took in the recordings of his late brother's voice. He created the timeless painting that would make its way into history as the trademark of what would become, in all its manifestations, one of mankind's most enduring inventions.

When David told his parents the secret, they celebrated with milk and chocolate crème cupcakes and nicknamed him their 'clever sleuth.' What his parents did not know, what no one on earth could have known, was David had taken the first step towards his future. And that future would someday require their son to cross a wide and dangerous torrent of deliberately obscure and closely guarded secrets.

The sweet memories of long ago, mixed with apprehension, troubled David as he reclined in the grey leather chair of a Gulf Stream 450. Flying thirty five thousand feet above Kansas, heading toward San Francisco, David reapplied a cold damp towel to his forehead.

Noticing the news anchor's restless struggle to find a comfortable position, Suzanne inquired, "How's the headache?"

"Don't ask." David winced, closing his eyes again; attempting, without much success, to push aside the fiercely persistent thoughts of the day's events.

The last sixteen hours had become so blurred he could hardly remember the details. Within an hour of receiving Suzanne's telephone call, David was sitting behind the studio anchor desk.

Twelve hours of frenzied activity followed without a break, as he and the intrepid staff at Global News fought to make sense of the chaotic story threads relating to the unfolding tragedy in San Francisco. Collectively, they set aside their personal horror to sew together fragments of information and present a coherent series of events to their audience. The staff was charged with sorting through the mountain of conflicting data, which pointed to the escalating domestic tensions between political groups within the country and the ongoing threats from Islamic extremists abroad.

By mid-morning, the staff believed one thing for sure: the attack on San Francisco was a response from Islamic militants, intent upon, what they considered, 'jihad' for the United States-led attacks on their brethren in the war torn Middle East. Global's editors did not see what was happening to their countrymen as 'holy', and determined to call the attacks 'hirabah', which meant 'sinful warfare'- a great shame on any Muslim man. Regardless of what they were called, the persistent threats of massive, coordinated attacks on the West had finally been successfully initiated. It was clearly a call-to-arms, meant to intensify the struggle of forming a worldwide Islamic republic.

The buzz from Global's underground network all pointed to this conclusion. A short meeting with management affirmed David's instinct: they should go with the story. Within the next half hour, he was prepped and on the air.

From the moment David began anchoring the newscast, he became the nexus point for the massive information machine assembled by Lance Rodgers. The staff, and a shaken nation, looked to him for steadfast assurance that somehow things would right themselves. The hours passed as David presented a sweeping perspective of the day's developments, moving from story to story, finding a cadence, developing the temporal sequence, sorting facts from fabrication. With every pause or second of airtime he could steal away from the hard news of the tragic day, David offered his most heartfelt compassion to the survivors, none, of whom, had any idea that this newsman, broadcasting from the opposite coast, was also anxiously awaiting news of his own father.

Immediate reaction came from the Vice President, condemning the attack and assuring the public that the President, who had been evacuated by the Secret Service, would take full control of the situation upon returning to the White House.

The Pentagon held a news conference to assure Americans they were safe and the military was on full alert, guarding against all potential aggressors. Interviews poured in from stunned eyewitnesses and the sobbing relatives of the still unnamed victims. The governor of California and the mayor of San Francisco held a series of hastily arranged news conferences throughout the day, discussing the details of the rescue and recovery efforts. Governors and mayors from various states and cities around the country expressed their outrage and sympathy, offered assistance and, depending on their party affiliation, blamed the president and congress for not providing adequate funding to prevent this terror attack. Members of the House and Senate practically trampled over one another, vying for air time, each vowing to bring the perpetrators to justice while trying to strike a perfect balance of indignation and compassion.

The heads of most foreign governments, along with their citizens, expressed disbelief and shock, denounced the actions of the terrorists, and offered solidarity and aid to the United States. But the cameras also caught reaction from other countries whose governments insisted the attack was the fault of United States foreign policy. In some Middle Eastern countries, citizens, as in the past, celebrated openly in the streets, cheering the strike against the 'Great Satan'. Later in the day, the United Nations condemned the attacks and offered condolences to the victim's families but reiterated their assertion that counter terrorism efforts could not be the only tool for combating terrorism, asserting that steps to address human rights concerns were also crucial.

David ended the newscast by interviewing a gaggle of pundits, whose appearances had been hastily arranged by Global's producers. All, but a few, claimed to have some special insight as to what happened, why it happened, how 'they' managed to pull this off, and who 'they' were. Closing with grave expressions and considerable finger wagging, each offered some advice, or lesson learned, so 'this would never happen again'.

Throughout the twelve hour broadcast, near exhaustion and a premonition of tragedy caused intermittent cramping in the fibers of David's trapezius. He did his best to disguise the anxious discomfort but, once off camera, he would call over a production assistant, a producer, a writer, or anyone within earshot, and ask them to check if there was any word about his father.

The information they could gather remained inconclusive. The only thing the staff could offer was some vague promise that the FBI would investigate when they found time. David was fully aware, in the unfolding pandemonium, this might mean never. Undaunted, he remained behind the anchor desk. Although upset and swearing silently off camera, David managed to stay composed on air. He remained through the evening programming until, finally exhausted, he turned over the anchor duties and prepared to leave.

As David walked toward the newsroom exit, John Stavos, just leaving the assistant news director's office, spotted the anchor. John, stepping into his path, stood hands in pockets, exclaiming, "Excellent reporting tonight, David. Nice work!"

"John," said David, ignoring the complement "I need to fly to the West Coast…tonight, if possible…can you help me out"? The expression of worry and impatience on David's face, and the strain apparent in his voice, told John the rumors flying around the newsroom were true. Still, he presented a professional face, knowing his anchorman would reject any show of sympathy.

"Hmmm," John said, as though thinking out loud. "It might not be a bad idea for you to resume your coverage at the scene. In fact, I like the idea …anchoring from the field. Go for it."

Lowering his head, David whispered, "That's not actually what I had in mind."

"I know. It's ok, I'll make the arrangements." John placed a firm hand on David's shoulder. "Go home and pack. We'll call you with the travel details."

"Thanks, boss." David turned to go. John, grasping his arm, pleaded, "Do me a favor… take Suzanne with you."

David, out of countenance at the prospect, began to object, "Look John, I don't need…"

"David, as a favor to me...please! She's driving me crazy with this notion that she's missing out on life, or something. She needs to get it out of her system...and you need a friend. All right?"

David shrugged in tacit agreement and, without another word, headed for the exit.

The sepia shadows of the previous day, filled with tumult and commotion, flickered in David's mind like an old time newsreel, until the drone from the engines of the Gulf Stream, at last, lulled him into a fitful sleep. Before surrendering consciousness to exhaustion, David offered what, at an earlier time, would have been a prayer: to see his father alive once more.

Suzanne, sitting in the quiet of the row adjacent to her sleeping coworker, looked out the airplane's window into the empty space of the night as it flew by; the darkness speckled with the light of stars charged with caring for the wishes of generations past and present. She stretched and, kicking off her pumps, casually placed both feet against the opposite seat, revealing the delicate and feminine elegance of legs that were as well suited for eveningwear as a business suit.

Suzanne turned away from the twinkling constellations and glanced across the aisle. Seeing David so troubled made her heartsick. She wanted to reach across the aisle and take his hand. Better not...she told herself.

She recalled inviting the newly hired anchorman to join her for a 'get acquainted' dinner. They were discussing new programming ideas, when she reached across the table and placed her hand over his to emphasize a point. Expressionless, he stopped talking, and waited until she sat back in the chair, her arms folded. A hot flush flooded Suzanne's face. He always pulls back, she thought, wondering why David seemed so impersonal...even aloof at times. The question had been bothering her from the very beginning of their relationship.

Her thoughts were interrupted by the presence of a man standing beside her seat with intense, burning eyes, like those of a peregrine falcon, sharply focused for seeing distant objects. Flyers eyes, was Suzanne's first impression. She was grateful for the company.

"Hi there, I'm Mark Webb, your pilot," the man said in a half whisper while extending his hand. He was tall with bodybuilder's muscles complementing the tapered cut of a short-sleeved uniform shirt. He had salt and pepper hair, a ruddy complexion and deep lines on his face cut by years of experience. The pilot's slightly crooked smile underscored the joy he found in life and the joy he found in flight. It was the first time Suzanne ever really felt safe on an airplane.

I must seriously hang out with pilots more often, she thought, grinning inside.

She returned the greeting in the same half whisper, brought her feet down from the opposite seat and sat upright, slipping on her shoes. The pilot gestured for Suzanne to follow him to the tail section of the aircraft.

"I didn't want to disturb Mr. Anderson...you're Ms. Biasotto?"

"Yep...call me 'Suzanne'."

"Well, Suzanne," the pilot continued, leaning casually against the bulkhead. "I just wanted to apologize for the missing amenities. John Stavos' office requested the flight in a timeframe that precluded arrangements for food service or a full flight crew."

"Not to worry," Suzanne assured him. "I think David just wants to sleep and I grabbed a quick dinner before boarding."

"All right then," Webb said, squeezing past Suzanne in the narrow space of the aisle. "I guess I ought to get back to the cockpit and see how my copilot is doing." He paused for a split second to notice her perfume, took a few steps, stopped, turned and commented, "You know...Mr. Anderson looks awfully young to be a prominent national figure. It's quite an accomplishment."

"Correction, Captain, he's actually a global figure and it's quite a tale...if you're interested."

Mark Webb was intrigued, by the story of course, but also by the beautiful young woman telling it. Glancing at his wristwatch, calculating time, speed, and distance, figuring he had a few minutes to spare, he said, "Now you've piqued my curiosity."

Suzanne slid onto one of the galley benches and with a wave of her hand, and a sparkle in her eyes, invited the pilot to join her. They sat with the polished oak table between them, each leaning inward towards the other like old friends and confidants sharing a past secret.

She began calculating each word. "Most people don't know that David kinda got his job by a strange twist of, what you might call, fate. Even David doesn't know this story."

"Really? So tell me."

"About nine years ago...maybe ten...Constellation Media hired John Stavos...he's our boss...to take over and lead Global News. During the following months John hired me and the rest of the team. Those were wild times...working around the clock. But it was fun and, anyway, John made us feel like we were doing something important."

"What was so important it required nonstop work?" Webb asked.

"John decided to restructure and consolidate all the fragmented news organizations Constellation Media owned into one – a mammoth operation. It was my idea to select one person to become the face of Global News and Information Network. I thought our worldwide audience needed someone to identify with...a sort of media archangel or mega-anchor that would tie the brand together."

"I'm guessing John liked the idea," Webb said with an approving smile, acknowledging the accomplishment.

"You bet!" She answered, beaming. "The plan went all the way to the top; right up to Lance Rodger's office and John gave me the credit! Cool...right?"

"And David?" Webb prompted, looking at his watch.

Suzanne, not one to hurry through a story, sped up the pace so the pilot could return to the flight deck. "It all started at one of our stations on the West Coast where David was a local news reporter...fires, crimes, local political squabbles, stuff like that. With the brass in New York focused on the big picture, they didn't have time to notice a local reporter. But David wrote a documentary proposal called 'The Terrorist Incubator' and the local news director loved the idea, so he approved the budget and David was off to the Mideast. After he returned and the network aired his documentary, David went back there and for several years, covered conflicts and events in the area, sending back hours of investigative reports on government corruption, terror cells, child trafficking, genocide and slavery. More than once his life was threatened."

"Go on..." Webb said.

"Sure. One time, David was investigating child slavery in Sudan and the government threw him in jail and ordered his execution."

"How the hell did he get out of that fix?"

"No one really knows, exactly, but the rumor is, Lance's office called someone at State who threatened the Sudanese government. Before releasing him, they confiscated all the story materials. Only, David hid a copy of the digital video on a chip where no one would find it. When the story was broadcast, the people responsible were arrested in Europe."

"And so, David Anderson was discovered," Webb said, pushing up from the table.

"Not quite." Suzanne replied, her wry smile indicating the story was only half told. "That's just the back story. You have to be patient."

"Oh, sorry, go on," Webb said, sitting back in his seat.

Suzanne was pleased to tell the story, even if it was only an audience of one.

"Now, here's where things get interesting. John orders Human Resources to submit a list of candidates for the global anchor spot. We get ten names, five from other news organizations, the rest internal candidates...all anchors from our major news hubs. Real imaginative, huh? Anyway, we arranged for the nominees to come to New York and have live auditions and interviews. We worked round the clock for weeks doing mock newscasts, hiring image consultants, running audience trials and focus groups. And after all that, John still couldn't make a decision."

"Why not?"

"Because...they all basically looked the same, clones of each other. They read the teleprompter fine, acted concerned in all the right places and, of course, possessed the required air of authority. But John wanted something unique...an intangible kind of quality...someone who...connected...real...unpretentious...if you know what I mean."

"I think so," Webb said. "But why the change?"

"Because people simply don't trust the news media anymore." Suzanne said, paraphrasing her boss's philosophy. "John told us there were once news organizations considered gold standards of journalism. People had confidence in whatever they printed or broadcast.

But over time, they hollowed out their organizations, stopped doing real investigative reporting and stopped challenging the powers that be…essentially, stopped speaking truth. Then, when all the new media came on line, the audience fragmented, in search of more trustworthy information. After that, their business models collapsed."

"And that's where Lance Rodgers came in and bought everyone out for a song, right?"

"Sort of," Suzanne answered. "But it was more than that. John was hired to restore the gold standard of trust at Global; that was John's real mission."

"But when does David come in?" he asked having forgotten the time.

"Ah…right now. David's roaming the Mideast continuing his reportage in total obscurity. Meanwhile, late one night we're all hanging in John's office, well past two in the morning, trying to figure out what the hell to do next. I remember being totally exhausted and staring at the remnants of sandwiches, salads and cold pizza, trying to coax my mind into thinking up some creative suggestions. All I could do was look at this unopened bottle of Perrier-Jouet sitting in a silver bucket of melted ice. John ordered it to celebrate but it just sat there, lopsided in that bucket of water, looking hopeless like the rest of us."

"We decided to give up for the night when breaking news of a terrorist bombing in front of the Knesset in Jerusalem flashed across one of the monitors on John's wall. We stopped to watch for a second; everyone's in a panic, running for their lives, except this guy in khaki slacks and a white cotton shirt bolting toward the explosion and helping the injured. He had this floppy hair, bro look; preppy, but not lobster pants preppy…if you know what I mean, and by now he's spattered with blood. Next thing we know, he has a microphone in his hand…calmly describing the events and it turns out he's a Global reporter. When the cameraman zoomed out for a long shot, we saw people watching him…and it was amazing! David saw it all through their eyes…trust me, it was unbelievable. A month later, John announced David got the job, everyone in the industry freaked…and…well you know the rest."

Her voice trailed off while she quietly relived the experience. Captain Webb sat regarding Suzanne for a moment. Rising, he said, "Well I'd better get back to the flight deck. He's a lucky guy to have the support and admiration of a woman like you. Thanks again, Suzanne…great story."

Suzanne smiled at the pilot. "No, it is I who should thank you. I had kind of forgotten…."

Mark Webb shook Suzanne's hand, holding it just a second too long and walked silently toward the cockpit, hesitating a moment to look down at the sleeping anchorman whose rise to prominence seemed incredibly fortuitous. Not much a believer in luck, the pilot spent the next half hour pondering his own destiny.

Sometime later, David, waking from his nap with a luxurious yawn, opened his eyes, "How long have I been out?" he asked, stretching.

"About four hours," Suzanne responded. "How are you feeling?"

Sitting up, readjusting his seat back and glancing around the cabin, he replied. "Much better, thanks…good, in fact. Is anyone else here?"

"Only the pilots - they didn't have time to organize a crew."

David rose and began to pace up and down the aisle of the plane. It felt good, not only to stretch his legs but to alleviate the persistent anxiety about his father. Suzanne watched until he finally stopped adjacent to the same galley benches where she and Mark Webb were talking earlier. David glided onto the leather bench and gazed out the window, a look of wistful dreaming on his somber face.

Reluctant to break into David's reverie, Suzanne remained silent, rose and, moving to the tail of the aircraft, rummaged through the galley, returning with the only thing she could find: two royal blue bottles of sparkling water. She placed the bottles on the table without a sound, before finding a comfortable position leaning against the fuselage, legs stretched out across the leather cushion.

Taking small sips from the water bottle, Suzanne waited for what she thought was a respectable amount of time, then finally remarked, "You would think they'd stock a feast on these corporate planes."

David continued staring into the darkness. "You know, Lance Rodgers must have some serious influence in Washington – some really serious influence, right to the top!"

"How so?" Suzanne asked.

"The FAA grounded all private and commercial flights for forty eight hours after the attack…but here we are! Someone approved the flight plan, someone very high up."

"They probably made an exception for news organizations."

"Only Global News?" David asked. He turned to face Suzanne, hoping a challenge to her well-known analytical mind might spark a spirited discussion.

Suzanne, too tired and hungry to spar with David at the moment, didn't respond but, instead, resting her chin on open palms, said, "David, you over-analyze everything. Have some faith once in awhile! We'll land, go to the studio, get back on the air, and find your dad. They'll catch the monsters that attacked us and things will get back to normal…sort of."

"Suzanne," David replied. He could not help letting a hint of the overwhelming emotion he felt creep into his voice. "My father was in the building, no one has heard from him nor can they find him. There just isn't any logical basis to expect he is alive."

"I'm sorry for being insensitive," Suzanne said, worried that mentioning David's father was a dumb mistake.

David nodded but, before he could answer, the intercom crackled to life.

"Mr. Anderson, this is the Captain. We're beginning our descent into Oakland International. We should be on the ground in approximately thirty-five minutes. There's a phone call for you; pick up any black receiver in the cabin. I'll let you know when we're on final approach."

David reached over and lifted the receiver. "Hello…this is David." There was a moment of silence before the switching circuits of the satellites in orbit connected the caller and he heard John's voice.

"Hi David, how are you and Suzanne?"

"Fine John, do you ever sleep?"

"Now you know why I put a couch in my office. Listen, a couple of things. There will be a car at the airport for both of you. The local newsroom is set and the staff will be on hand for a noon meeting. We expect you back on the air by four o'clock, your time. That leaves a few hours to rest and clean up at the hotel, okay? Oh, and the limo is instructed to stay with you both for the entire trip."

David let several seconds pass while he considered the itinerary John just described.

"John, I think I'll skip the hotel and stay at my father's house, just in case he...by the way, what's the word on locating him?"

"I'm sorry," John said, embarrassed by forgetting to mention the older Anderson's disappearance. "I should have addressed that first! We have staffers combing the city, checking with the rescue teams, the hospitals and...well, morgues. The good and bad news is they haven't had any luck, so far, but Lance Rodgers personally called the Justice Department. The FBI is now actively looking for him and two special agents are assigned to the case...they'll make contact once you get settled."

Again David took a few moments, "I'm not sure about the broadcast today, I may need to take a few days to..."

John interrupted, "I know you're worried, but the city is in chaos. Even with your press credentials you'll have limited access...give the FBI and police a chance to do what they do and you do what you do...it's just a suggestion but...what do you think?"

"Tell you what, John, I'm willing to go and stay through the evening news program. Then I'm on my own time...agreed?"

"Fair enough...and ask Suzanne to call in when she gets to the newsroom and...you two, be careful. Let's talk later."

John hung up leaving David holding the receiver and appreciating the divergence between the concern he heard in John's voice and his brusque business repartee.

Suzanne, a pout beginning to form at either corner of her mouth, said, "From the sound of that call I am guessing someone's going to ditch me."

"I can't see staying at a hotel," David explained, "It doesn't make sense. My dad's house will be more comfortable and I'll feel better being there. Anyway, he has three empty bedrooms so, if you'd like, you're welcome to stay in one. Now consider yourself un-ditched."

"Thanks David," she said. The pilot interrupted her delight with a second announcement.

"Folks, this is Capitan Webb. We're on final approach and cleared to land on runway 9L. I'll be making a tight turn over San Francisco Bay and you can see the city from the right side of the aircraft. We should land in a few moments, so please return to your seats, fasten your seatbelts, and stow any loose items in the cabin."

Suzanne, jumping up, grabbed the water bottles on the table and disposed of them in the galley's trash drawer before sliding into the closest right side seat. Looking through the window she could only see lights in the distance. It was still too dark to see even a hint of the horrific images she had seen in the newsroom. David returned to his seat at the front of the plane, purposefully sitting on the opposite side, unable to look at the wounded city. As they hurtled through the darkness toward the lights on the runway, both wondered what trauma or challenge this new day would bring.

The Gulf Stream touched down making a perfect landing, not a bump or a thud - just a smooth roll spilling off the plane's kinetic energy. Webb taxied the jet over to the east end of Oakland Airport's north field, coming to a stop next to the Business Jet Center where Capitan Webb, David, and Suzanne disembarked from the plane on the stairs attached to the forward cabin door. The copilot tossed the luggage down to Webb who placed it gently on the ground.

"Where would you like these?" Webb asked.

"I'm not quite sure" David said, "John Stavos arranged some sort of ground transportation but I forgot to ask how to contact the driver. I pictured meeting in the terminal…didn't expect a runway."

"The lights are on. Why don't we look inside the building?" Suzanne suggested.

Webb looked back at the copilot standing in the jet's opening, "Say Jeff, can you taxi her over to hanger one and then meet me inside?"

"Sure thing," Jeff replied and disappeared back into the plane.

The Business Jet Center, an eclectic building, sparsely land-scaped, one bare light bulb over its entrance, was designed in an art deco motif. Surrounded by high contrast shadows, the trio began walking across the tarmac towards the building, kicking aside a thin pre-dawn mist.

Suzanne, swooning from the romantic aesthetic, said, "I feel like IIsa in Casablanca."

"Since I'm in uniform, I'll be Renault." Webb joined in Suzanne's play. By now, he was quite enamored with Global's executive producer.

David mustered a half smile, but he could not shake the sullen-ness he felt. Quickening his pace, he reached the building first, pausing to look around the field. The other buildings were dark. There weren't cars or trucks or aircraft or people. David shuddered. Life had changed…again, and the only hope was, like the attack in New York so many years ago, time would erase the pain, people would forget, and things would return to some semblance of the way they had been.

Suzanne and Captain Webb caught up and David held the door open for them.

"Everything okay?" Suzanne asked, noticing David's faraway expression.

David chose not to reply but followed them into the building.

"Hello" Suzanne shouted, "Anyone home?"

The building seemed deserted. Suzanne walked up to the count-er and again called out to the empty space. "Hellooo… anyone here?"

David and Captain Webb set off in opposite directions across the vacant waiting area to have a look in the surrounding offices. They found no one in the building and returned to the counter where Suzanne was waiting. David wore a look of growing concern and Webb was clearly puzzled.

"Now this is odd," Webb remarked, "an FBO is required by the FAA to man the station twenty four by seven."

"What's an FBO?" Suzanne asked.

"A fixed base operator," answered Webb. "They service general aviation…private aircraft. They're required to man these operations round the clock."

"Well then," David said, "Something's not right."

"I'm getting nervous," Suzanne announced.

Webb began thinking out loud. "Okay, we got clearance to land from the tower, they directed us here. There must be a ground controller on duty…let's call and ask what the hell is going on."

Before they could move toward the telephone sitting on the counter, the sound of a crash, reverberating through the huge space, startled the trio. Suzanne jumped as both the anchorman and the pilot spun around toward the glass entrance doors that had been thrown open hard enough to slam against the doorstops.

A man dressed in an ill-tailored, black, double-breasted suit entered the lobby. He stood well above six feet and was heavy set with dark eyes and black hair, slicked back and tied in a short ponytail. He had a bald spot on the top of his head and his hair gel created shiny patches on his scalp that reflected the overhead lights.

Walking up to the group and extending his hand to David, he said, "My name is Brian Saunders. I'm your driver. Sorry I'm late…got lost at terminal A."

Suzanne sighed in relief. David reached out and shook the man's hand. "I'm David Anderson."

"Yeah, sure," the man answered, as if he were completely disinterested. "I've seen ya on TV. The car's outside."

David hesitated a moment to regard the stranger and asked, "Who is it you work for?"

The driver produced a Constellation Media employee identification badge and an email from New York with his instructions. Handing one to Suzanne and one to David, he said, "I work for Mr. Rodgers but I rarely talk to him…only to Alma, his assistant."

"I see," David said, "No offense intended…been a long day."

"None taken. Like I said, the car's outside."

"Well then, let's get going. I'm tired," Suzanne said, handing the badge back to Saunders.

Outside, David pointed out their luggage. Saunders put the bags in the trunk of the black stretch limo. The car's license plate read 'Constell 9'. Despite the Constellation Media reference, David still felt uneasy about Saunders. Not quite the corporate type, he thought, but he shook off the feeling, blaming fatigue and the stress of the day's events. Turning to Captain Webb, David offered the pilots a ride.

Webb declined. "Thanks, Mr. Anderson. They leave a loner car for us in the hangar, so you go on. Besides, I want to find out why no one is on duty here. It was nice flying with you. Hope to see you and Ms Biasotto again soon."

Webb set off to find his copilot.

Saunders slammed the trunk closed, opened the rear door of the limo and stood beside the car to help Suzanne into the back seat. As she slid to the opposite side of the limousine, his coat fell open. David noticed the holster on his hip and turned to look around for Webb but the pilot was already out of sight.

David challenged Saunders in a manner akin to his natural investigative style. Unyielding, without being confrontational, he asked, "Tell me, Mr. Saunders, are all of Lance Rodger's drivers required to carry concealed weapons?"

The question had such a simpatico quality, as though the speaker felt sorry for anyone in Saunders' position, forced to carry a gun, that Saunders was disarmed.

The driver stood, his movements slow and deliberate as he straightened to his full height. With a nervous laugh, he said. "Ya don't miss a thing, huh? I guess everything they say about you is true."

"This isn't about me, Mr. Saunders. I was actually asking a question."

"I told those guys to let you know," Saunders mumbled as he walked around the front of the limo. Opening the front passenger-side door, Saunders opened the center console and retrieved a leather badge wallet. Saunders slid it over the roof of the car toward David. The wallet was worn and frayed at the edges but when David flipped it open, he discovered a gold shield and photo ID inside that read: San Francisco Police Department – Chief of Detectives.

"Sooo… you're a cop?" David wondered out loud.

"Retired cop. Truth is, I don't just drive Mr. Rodgers, I'm his bodyguard too…and yeah, it's legal for me to carry a weapon."

David stood still while he considered the situation. Handing the badge back to Saunders, he said, "Why don't we get moving?"

Driving along Hegenberger Road towards the airport exit, Saunders decided it might be a good idea to review the route he'd chosen. "Say, Mr. Anderson, the only way to your hotel is Interstate 880 south to the San Mateo Bridge. The Harbor Bridge is…well, you know…and part of Route 80 is sealed off. All right with you?"

David removed a folded piece of paper from the left inside pocket of his sports coat, slid over to the limo's partition and handed it to Saunders. "I'm sorry. With all the confusion, I should have mentioned it earlier. There's been a change of plans. We're not going into the city. Here's the new address."

Saunders held the paper up to his window to catch the ambient light from the airport. "Walnut Creek? Nice town. But I've got instructions to take you to the hotel, Mr. Anderson. I'll just call and get authorization."

"Who could you possibly call at this time in the morning?" David demanded. "I'm authorizing it! Let's leave it at that, shall we?"

Saunders, responding to David's imperative, agreed. "Okay, okay, Mr. Anderson. We'll head north then. I can get past the roadblock onto 24 east…no problem…we'll be there in a half hour or less."

"Thanks," David said, relaxing back into his seat. Looking out at the deserted road, his thoughts raced anxiously ahead of the car, anticipating what he might find, hoping for what he wanted to find.

Following David's written directions to the letter, Saunders turned the limousine onto Ygnacio Court, proceeding slowly along the darkened street until David spotted his father's house. They pulled into a circular driveway lit by copper ground lights that were shaped like leaves from sassafras trees and stopped under a carport. The shelter, its posts covered with vines, extended from the wainscot-paneled front doors, across the cobblestones, and to the flowerbeds aside the lawn.

Saunders hopped out of the limo and, with a low whistle, exclaimed, "Nice place you got here, Mr. Anderson! Was that a golf course I saw on the way in?"

David stood up, leaving the limo door open for Suzanne to follow and, moving toward the house, he remarked, "The yard sits along the Diablo Hills Golf Club. My Dad played…uh…plays here a few times a week. You're very observant, Mr. Saunders."

"Golf course, huh? Yes sir, really nice place!"

David walked up to the front door and, reaching into his pocket, produced a set of house keys attached to a remote control key fob. The dawn was just below the horizon and the motion sensor flared to life, illuminating the path. Suzanne exited the limousine and followed her colleague, climbing the two steps to the entrance doors. She stood beside David, waiting for the door to open. She tried to smile but was too exhausted to command the muscles of her face to form even the tiniest expression. Realizing the effort was useless, she entreated, "I think I need someone to show me to my room."

David turned the key in the lock and pushed open the door. They stepped inside the entrance foyer where David pressed a button on the key fob, deactivating the burglar alarm and switching on several lights throughout the house. "You'll be asleep in just a few minutes. Go sit in the living room for a sec while I get our bags...I'll get you a cup of tea, if you like."

"That's very sweet but all I need right now is a few hours sleep before we have to hit the studio again."

As David turned around, Saunders came up the front steps with the luggage.

"Here ya go, Mr. Anderson."

"Thanks."

"Why don't we take a quick look around outside?" Saunders suggested, producing a flashlight.

"I don't think that will be..."

"No sweat, just take a minute. Just checkin..."

"Look, I'm too tired to argue...you go alone...hold on while I turn on the outside lights."

"Be right back...just take a minute," Saunders repeated.

David closed the door and went down the steps into the sunken living room and sat opposite Suzanne on one of the matching sofas. A charming hand-made woolen blanket, David's mother crocheted when he was still a young boy, lay comfortably draped over an armrest with Suzanne lazing against it. David picked up a remote control, lying on a square oak coffee table, and touched a button to light the outdoor flood lamps. Walking around the table to Suzanne, who was, by now, reclining on the couch and nearly asleep, David took her by the wrist and led her down the hallway toward the bedrooms and opened the second door on the left.

A large four-poster bed dominated the room. The bed was so high off the floor a stool was placed beside it to help its occupant climb in and out. David placed Suzanne's travel bag on the bed, explaining, "The bathroom is through there. There are plenty of clean towels or whatever you need in the closet next to the Jacuzzi. You'll find soap, shampoo, and other supplies in the vanity."

"Thanks, David. I'll be calling you if I can't make it onto that bed."

David lifted his hand to gently caress Suzanne's face. "Suzanne, I'm the one who should be thanking you."

"What did I do?" Suzanne asked, surprised by David's touch.

"I know you're concerned about me…and that means much more than you know. Now get some sleep." David stepped out of the room, quietly closing the door behind him.

Brian Saunders waited, tapping lightly on the front door, until the news anchor noticed the faint sound and remembered he locked the driver outside.

"Mr. Saunders, sorry, didn't mean to lock you out," David lied. "Did you find anything out of the ordinary?"

"Nothing really, except the gate on the back fence was open onto the golf course."

"Well, my father probably, left it opened. That's how he gets onto the greens."

"Hmmm, mind if I just take a quick look inside, I'll get out of your hair in a minute."

Saunders stepped past the newsman without waiting for an invitation and began moving through the house in the efficient manner of a police detective. He stopped when David pointed toward the kitchen, signaling the ex cop to follow him.

Leaning against the center island, David said, "I would appreciate it if you would refrain from roaming, unescorted, through my father's home, Mr. Saunders. I have a guest and I ask you to respect our privacy."

"Ya know, Mr. Anderson," Saunders said, ignoring David and looking around the kitchen as if he might have uncovered something important. "Someone was here last night. There are fresh breakfast dishes in the sink and the black Mercedes sedan is missing."

"How do you know all this in five minutes?" David asked with frank incredulity, feigning admiration to disguise the fact he was growing ever suspicious of Saunders's actions.

"The sedan is in the background of several photos. It's a late model car so I'm guessing the photos are current and that it's your father's regular vehicle." He opened the fridge and continued. "There's a steak in here with a sell date several weeks old...it's still fresh...must have been thawing out for dinner. Basically, Mr. Anderson, it looks like a routine workday for a guy who was expecting to come home. It doesn't look like he intended to go anywhere else after work. Sorry for the bad news. I'm not usually so blunt with family members, least not at this stage...but you look like the type who can take it."

"Really? What type is that?"

"Well...back there at the airport, ya know, no one around, girl in the car, strange guy with a gun...you didn't flinch. I don't see that kinda cool in many people, especially after what's been happening. Say, why don't we go over to the local precinct...I have a few friends over there and we can look at the reports...the ones the public don't see? I'll bet there's some info on your father and we can wrap this up tonight."

The feeling of dread, haunting David throughout the morning, was back. Looking at Saunders, he couldn't help but think there was something else on the driver's mind. "Thanks for the offer but some other time. It's been a long night. I think I need to get a bit of shuteye...you do have a place to stay?"

"Sure, Mr. Anderson. Sure."

"Well, goodnight then...We'll be ready at noon...okay?"

"Roger that," Saunders said. He seemed oddly reluctant to leave, as though some unfinished business remained between them.

David escorted Saunders to the front door and watched as he drove down the driveway and the taillights of the limousine disappeared. He closed and doubled locked the doors and, on further thought, set the perimeter alarms before going to bed.

The morning sun, blazing with the fierceness of an Aztec god, rose in a clear blue California sky as David finally fell into bed. He was asleep almost instantly and slept, undisturbed by dreams or worry, until the bedside alarm roused him on a beautiful San Francisco morning. Too groggy to move, he lay in bed remembering how, as a child, his father took over the gardening when his mother became ill. He recalled how he had spent countless hours with his mother in her well tended, and much loved, garden. He pictured himself as a little boy with unkempt hair standing beside a beautiful woman kneeling over her flowerbeds. She was slender and youthful and had given the boy her pale blue eyes and her love for all God's creation. With patience, she cultivated the garden, one flower at a time, explaining to the boy the name and medicinal use of each plant.

He remembered, too, that once, as a very young child, unaware he was trampling the carefully cultivated garden, he had picked a liberal handful of flowers, gathered them into a bouquet and, stepping inside the pale yellow kitchen, presented them to his mother. David recalled how she could not help but place her hands over her heart, laugh in delight and then, lifting him, sang him a song while kissing his forehead, cheeks and nose. David could barely recall the song, something about please, no eating daisies, the memory as bitter as it was sweet.

Brian Saunders was waiting in the driveway, leaning on the front right fender of a black limousine reading the Chronicle, when David and Suzanne stepped outside the stately entrance of Eric Anderson's home. Pots of flowers lined the steps, their petals mixing in a riot of colors reminiscent of a painter's pallet.

The chauffer slid off the fender and opened the door. "Good afternoon, Mr. Anderson, Miss Biasotto." David stifled a grimace. Saunders's voice bothered him from their first meeting, provoking in David a subtle sense of dread.

The trip to the studio took longer than usual. The Harbor Bridge, a vital link between a wounded city living on a peninsula and the mainland of a country in silence and shock, had been severed.

Instead, they drove south to the San Mateo Bridge to connect with Route 101. Traveling north, David noted with some trepidation, the airport was closed. He expected it would remain that way, for some indefinite time, until Homeland Security could ensure airway safety had not been breached.

When they passed San Francisco General Hospital, Suzanne took out a small notebook and wrote down a reminder to check on the news crew covering the injured. The quiet draping the city hung in the air along with smoke from the still smoldering fires.

Saunders seemed quite familiar with the neighborhoods and roads along the route. Navigating around the quarantined area where the terror attacks occurred, he turned the car left, off Van Ness Avenue, onto Broadway. The Global News studio was located on the corner of Broadway and Battery Street several blocks north of the damaged buildings. The limousine pulled up to the curb when Suzanne was struck with a craving for her favorite coffee. "Hey guys, mind if we go up a few blocks to Green?"

David, amused as he stepped out of the limo, laughed and said, "You go ahead. One cup a day is enough for me...I'll meet you upstairs."

Saunders drove a few blocks to the Coffee Roastery. It was closed along with most of the businesses in the area.

"Would you like me to drive further on?" asked Saunders. "Perhaps someplace is open."

"Oh, forget it." Suzanne said. "We can grab something back at the office."

Saunders turned the car around. When they arrived at Global News, Suzanne instructed him to park in the underground garage.

Moments later the elevator opened onto the newsroom floor. Suzanne stepped up to the turnstile and presented her Global News badge to the automatic sensor, which instantly recognized her credentials, allowing her to pass through. Saunders followed close behind, causing the turnstile to emit a loud alarm. Two security guards stepped forward and took up flanking positions at the gate.

"Excuse me. May I see your identification, please?" One of the guards, the smaller of the two, stretched out his hand to accept the required authorization.

"Oh, is something wrong?" Suzanne asked. "Here, I'm Suzanne Biasotto," she said, handing over her badge.

"Oh, yes…Ms. Biasotto. Mister Anderson is waiting for you in the Collaboration Room. But ma'am, you need to go through the turnstile one at a time."

"I know that," Suzanne said, puzzled. She did not notice Saunders had stepped into the gate directly behind her.

"Sir, may I see ID?" the guard asked.

Saunders produced his Constellation Media badge. "Sure pal…here ya' go."

The guard waved the badge across the sensor; the turnstile made an ugly beeping sound.

"Sir, could you please come this way?" The guard's question was an order, not a request.

"What's the problem?" Saunders protested.

"Please come to the office while we call corporate security and verify this badge."

"Look, you telling me badges issued in New York don't work here?" Saunders irritation was clearly apparent. "I don't know what the hell is wrong with you people…screw this crap. I'll just wait in the car."

Suzanne interrupted, "What's wrong?"

"Sometimes the badges aren't keyed right…I'm sure that's all it is," the guard replied, looking worried about antagonizing a Global News executive producer.

"Ok, look. I'll sign him in as a guest while you do whatever," Suzanne offered.

"Fine, ma'am," the guard said, handing Saunders back his ID. "That was Brian Saunders, right"?

"Yeah, Detective Brian Saunders! That's Chief S-A-U-N-D-E-R-S, in case ya' can't spell."

"Look sir, I'm just…"

Suzanne asserted her authority, shouting down the escalating voices of the two men. "Hey guys, let's check the testosterone and keep it civil."

"Yes ma'am," the guards replied. Hiding their embarrassment, the two men hurried away, glaring back over their shoulders at their new 'guest'.

Suzanne walked Saunders into the newsroom. Pointing in different directions around the floor, she began a terse orientation. "Mr. Saunders, the coffee and snack area is over there at that end of the building...in there is a guest office where you can sit and surf the net, watch television, or do whatever...the cafeteria is on the fourth floor but you will need an escort if you leave this area. Is that clear? And please, stay out of trouble." Before Saunders could reply, Suzanne marched off to join David in the collaboration room.

The collaboration room was another Lance Rodgers innovation. Rodgers, an obsessively compulsive planner, hired well-known experts in ergonomics, work place dynamics, psychology, industrial sociology, cultural change, advanced communication methods and philosophy - all for this one project. He labeled this collection of PhD's the *Workplace Innovation Technology Team* or WIT Team for short. After three years, forty-three prototypes, and millions of dollars, they announced a scientific and sociological breakthrough: a workspace system and method that would enhance human productivity, creativity, and efficiency.

Lance Rodgers would often appear on business programs with one of the WIT Team members to promote their discovery; Rodgers claiming the CR would prove to be a new epoch in the ongoing business transformation underway in most western countries.

The CR was circular, its environment maintained by a system of computers. Programs continually set the optimum temperature and humidity for the exact number occupying the room. Listening sensors, connected to complex computer algorithms, responded to the shifting creativity of the collaborators by altering the images on the plasma screens and the colors of full spectrum down-lights lining the walls. In the center of the room was an enormous round table whose shape was meant to level the dynamics of management rank, compelling everyone sitting down to confer as equals. To ensure that the 'idea potential' of the diverse staff was maximized, all participants had equal say, so factors such as gender, race or assertiveness did not present a handicap. Lance was often heard to say, "Ideas know no rank, gender, or personal qualities. Ingenuity is all that matters here."

The table came equipped with in-built workstations. Each workstation had four flat panel displays embedded into the table's surface that would automatically tilt to provide the ideal viewing angle. The panels were arranged in an arc above a semi-circular keyboard. Facial recognition software automatically loaded the user's profile along with current projects from the desks at their office or home. In the center of the table a holographic projector was installed for producing three-dimensional images of the subject under consideration. A flip of a switch turned the hologram off so collaborators could interact during 'brainstorming' sessions.

Each chair had sensors that made automatic adjustments for a person's height and weight. Each was equipped with speakers in its headrest and neck strain was prevented by projecting mirror images of information displayed on one LED screen to every other lining the walls.

Collaboration rooms were installed in all Constellation Media offices and properties except at Global News in New York, where John Stavos was successful in lobbying to keep them out. When all the collaboration rooms were networked together, Lance Rodgers proclaimed at the annual shareholder's meeting, "Constellation Media is now, truly, a constellation of stars with each of our affiliates making up a point of light in our galaxy."

When Suzanne walked into the CR, she found David seated at the table, reviewing the coverage planned for the remainder of the day. The anchorman always asked everyone present to turn off their workstations during the meeting, preferring to look at a face rather than the top of someone's head. Upon seeing Suzanne, David motioned for her to take the seat next to his. They sat together, listening to the editors, producers, and writers as the assignments and stories for the day's program were outlined. The working title for the day was 'Tragedy and Courage – David Anderson Reporting Live from San Francisco.'

Suzanne began with a question. "Any opinions on whether David should start his coverage live from the field or anchor from the studio?"

Bill Fowler, the local assignment editor, was first to respond. "I think a remote link from the attack area is best. People want to see David on the scene, in the middle of things, as it were."

"It's going to take a little time to set this up," Mike Kauffman, the West Coast production manager, countered. "We need to get a crew together."

"Why is that?" Bill protested, "We have news crews on the scene."

"Yes, for the reporters. Roving news vans with a satellite uplink are different from setting up a remote anchor desk. We'll need to get the Outside Broadcast Van down there with a technical director, audio director, production staff...you name it...not to mention, an extra news van so David can roam as well."

"Mike," Suzanne asked, "How much time do you need?"

"Well...we have two locations to choose from that were approved by the city's emergency management office. My guys have already been working since early morning so...give me one more hour and I'll be ready to go live."

Hope Zanel, Program Manager for the San Francisco local station, interrupted.

"Folks, don't forget we will need some time...not long...but we have to arrange on-the-scene coverage and interviews for David...John Stavos expects David on air by four, our time. Promo's have been running nationwide since last night."

Suzanne looked up at the time zone display mounted on a wall of the CR. It was 12:40 local time.

"This is awfully tight," she said. "Is the copy for all the segments finished and fact checked?"

"All cued up," Hope assured her.

"And what time will the President address the nation?" David inquired.

"The White House press office told Mike Lussardi that it could be any time now," Hope answered.

Trying not to antagonize her West Coast colleagues, but feeling pressured by the deadline Stavos had imposed, Suzanne moved the meeting towards a quick conclusion, "All right, here's what I suggest. David will anchor the story segments from the studio and recap all events up to date. When the President is ready, David will switch to

Mike Lussardi at the White House for an intro, and then we'll cut to the White House pressroom feed for the speech. Afterward, David and Mike can do some analysis and we'll bring in some of our political commentators from around the nation. David closes with a follow-up reaction to the speech, that sort of thing…cutover to Studio B… continue with Vanessa Keyles and Matt Finan as co-anchors while David gets situated in the field. Is that okay with everyone?"

David stood up to leave, signaling he agreed with Suzanne's plan. Nodding at the group, he said, "I'm off to makeup…see you on set."

Except for Hope and Suzanne, the remaining news staff filed out of the CR behind David.

"David doesn't look like he needs any makeup to me," Hope said with an admiring wink.

"Amen to that," Suzanne agreed as both women burst into laughter. It was welcome relief from the previous day's events and the relentless tension that was now part of their lives.

Their ongoing review of opportunities for David's on-the-scene coverage was interrupted when a production assistant popped in with a sheaf of papers.

"Miss Zanel, here are the news tips you asked for from the assignment desk. Numerous people have called in with stories about the attack. There's a strange one in there that grabbed our attention. I marked it for you. Oh, and I have Mr. Anderson's messages."

"I'll take care of it, thanks," Hope said. "Just leave everything on the table."

"Any tips from the public?" Suzanne asked.

Hope began sifting through the papers, reading each under her breath.

Stopping at the tip the production assistant flagged with a large red check, Hope let out a low whistle. Handing the paper to Suzanne, she commented, "Well, here's one that's original…might make a good interview."

"She has to be kidding," Suzanne exclaimed, thinking out loud as she read the paper. "Merilee Brunswick…lets see…hmm… claims to be an eye witness…blah…blah…says she thinks she ran into one of the terrorists and he left something behind…doesn't know what it is…called the police but they blew her off…wants to meet with a reporter…oh…now this is good, she will only talk to David Anderson!"

"Well, I guess that's one way to meet a celebrity and get that fifteen minutes," Hope said, grinning.

"I'm not so sure," Suzanne answered, reconsidering. It was just an instinct but something in the message told her this might be more than just an attempt for fleeting on-air fame. "I may just call and check this out." Suzanne folded the paper and placed it in her notebook.

Hope and Suzanne finished their work and left the Collaboration Room. Hope, off preparing the on-scene interviews and stories for David, set in motion the unseen machinery behind the Global News cameras.

Suzanne tiptoed her way through the audio room, careful not to distract the engineers mixing the sound signals for the live broadcast. Quietly slipping through a soundproof door of the Studio Control Room, moving past racks of lighted equipment, she spotted a chair marked, 'Reserved for S. Biasotto'. She slipped on a set of headphones so she could listen in to both the newscast and the production crew.

On the other side of the glass, David was on camera talking by remote with Blair Fitzpatrick, one of the reporters covering the rescue and recovery efforts at the foot of the Oakland Harbor Bridge. Blair was interviewing several First Responders when David interrupted her mid-sentence, bringing his hand to his left ear.

"Hold on, Blair…what's that…okay, we are going live to our White House correspondent, Mike Lussardi, for an address by the President. Thank you, Blair. We'll come back later to your report."

Within the second it took to switch the circuits, David and Mike were on air discussing the president's possible reaction to the attacks.

"Mike, do we have any advance indication from the White House of what the President might say?"

"Everyone around the President is being pretty tight lipped." Mike reported. "We've only been told it will be a brief message. The press wasn't given an advanced copy of the speech. We were told there wasn't enough time or resources."

"And the reaction from the press?"

"Well...considering the Administration has been in office only a few months...and with the deteriorating economy taking up most of their time...there wasn't much we could say."

"Hold on, Mike, our director just signaled the President is ready...alright...ladies and gentlemen, the President."

Margaret Whitney, the first woman to be elected President of the United States, entered the Oval Office. She walked with a measured and deliberate pace in deference to the grave seriousness of the moment. She stood at attention for a moment, as though she was a boot camp recruit at final inspection, and then took her seat at the Resolute Desk. The sharp features of her face conveyed pride and confidence but her eyes reflected deep sadness and concern. Looking down at a hastily composed speech she began:

"My Fellow Americans...

I stand with you today in the most profound grief and sorrow. Today the blueprints and timetables of our lives are deeply disrupted as we come to terms with the loss of beloved family members, close friends, honorable colleagues, and cherished neighbors. And, although we are shocked and deeply grieved by these events, the courage, compassion, unity, and generosity of the American people, together with our friends the world over, will guide us out of this tragic moment and heal our minds and spirits.

I am taking personal responsibility for leading and directing every level of the federal government engaged in the rescue and recovery efforts in San Francisco. All federal assistance requested by the local authorities will be forth-coming without delay. We are granting to all agencies, responsible for dispersing essential aid and assistance, the authority required to ensure their ability to cut through the bureaucratic red tape that has, in the past, hindered assistance from reaching those in need.

Our military, Homeland Security, the FBI, and local law enforcement agencies are working around the clock to ensure our homes, public spaces, workplaces, transportation systems, and infrastructure are protected from any further attacks and that the criminals who perpetrated this tragedy will be brought to justice no matter where they hide.

My thoughts and prayers are with you. Indeed the sympathy and prayers of the nation and the world are with you. I have received messages from leaders around the globe offering their help and expressing their shock and horror at this reprehensible act.

Even as we grieve, let us resolve to work together as a single nation. Let not time erase our determination and passion no matter how long our struggle.

It has been said, the heroes we honor tell those around us, who we are, and what we value. Our choices are recorded in history, so future generations might know us.

Today we honor the beloved Americans whose lives were lost, the grieving families of the victims, and those who will take up the task of rebuilding. Thank you for your courage. You are in my heart and prayers today and every day.

God bless each of you…and God bless the United States of America."

COMPANIONS ON
A JOURNEY

There's a wearisome sameness to the desert; a boredom that takes its toll. Even time feels it and, like a major league baseball pitcher, alters its tempo in the hope of changing the unchangeable. On this particular afternoon, time, encountering a dark green sedan, decided to play a game.

Ahmad was finding nothing of interest to break the monotony of his long drive. The sameness of the desert vistas, a landscape without landmarks or waypoints, began to confuse him and he could not tell if he was actually making any progress. The speedometer read seventy miles per hour but the telephone poles along the roadside appeared to be standing still. He could see mountains in the distance moving closer, then further away. It was like looking at an object through a telescope, then turning it around, and looking again.

Ahmad, glancing at the dial of his wristwatch, became alarmed: the watch's second hand motion was stopped, as if unable to calibrate itself with this moment in time. He wished he had someone – anyone – to keep him company; he wished a car would pass; he wished shadows would fall across the road but there was no relief in sight. Instead, he was alone, trying, in vain, to ignore the faint screams of the ghosts inside his head.

At last, Ahmad spotted a patch of color a half mile in front of the car. An abandoned vehicle painted fire engine red lay in the sagebrush. It was turned on its side, its windows and lights broken, but to Ahmad it was a welcome sight. He felt like the captain of a square-rigged sailing ship who spots a lighthouse during a storm at night. Here was a beacon, something useful to measure progress. Approaching the object, time seemed to right itself again; once more, aligned with the stars and back in its natural rhythm. It lasted only a minute and Ahmad was sorry to watch the object shrink in his rearview mirror. The old car waved goodbye by reflecting a flare of orange, as the setting sunlight bounced off its chrome bumper. When he looked again through his windshield, clusters of objects grouped themselves into repeating patterns without beginning or end. Ahmad pressed on, fighting off his disorientation, certain that time, as it always does, would win the game.

It was dark when Ahmad pulled into a service station at the edge of Salt Lake City for fuel. It was a gamble to stop yet he was compelled to take the risk. The slight tremor in his hand was a signal that if he did not break his momentum, the journey might never be completed. He parked next to the first pump and began refueling the tank. At six and change per gallon, it took all his remaining cash to fill the compact car.

Ahmad locked himself inside the station's grimy men's room where a splash of cold water on his face and neck helped revive him. Using both arms to brace against the rust stained sink, he looked deeply at his own reflection, hoping for a vision of the Imam Ali, but the Expected One did not stare back. Downhearted, with no hope of the Divine guidance he so craved, Ahmad left the rest room without bothering to return the key. Driving on, he left the lights of the station behind.

The strain of the past several weeks pressed in on him. He could faintly discern the hills and rolling terrain on the horizon as he followed the pale yellow tunnel of the headlights cutting through the darkness. The pit of his stomach felt empty; not hungry but hollow. Ahmad's jubilation at the victory of the morning's attack was fading. In its place was a low, brooding melancholy. Somewhere between Laramie and Cheyenne, Ahmad turned off the car's headlights and stepped down on the accelerator, pressing it against the floorboard.

An ocean of stars came flooding in through the windshield as he begged Allah to spare him further suffering and take him to heaven. Suddenly, from the horizon, a single point of blinding white light began to advance toward the car. Ahmad had never seen an angel. He cried out in supplication to the apparition, "Mala'ikah'u'Allah, take me to paradise!"

The distraught man slowed the car in anticipation of divine deliverance. He soon discovered, to his bitter disappointment and embarrassment, the speeding light was nothing more than a west-bound Amtrak Zephyr. Ahmad began to laugh and the sound grew exponentially on itself until he was in tears. He was finding it difficult to drive and had to stop the car until his uncontrollable mirth subsided. The catharsis was just enough to sober him up and set him back on his journey. Switching on the headlights, he continued down the road and, in a short time, caught sight of a sign:

Interstate 25 South Denver
Exit 2 Miles

Ahmad pulled his car past the cloverleaf and onto the Interstate, at the same time noticing he'd been grinding his teeth and gripping the steering wheel with enough force to squeeze the resin out of the plastic. He cranked opened the window, stretched, and rotated one arm at a time. He inhaled the fresh Colorado air and held his breath for a moment before exhaling. I'll be there soon, he thought.

Arriving in the north Denver area, Ahmad reached into the outer pocket of his backpack for directions to the mosque where he was to meet the next contact. He pulled out a counterfeit wedding invitation with an address and a hand drawn map on the reverse. It took an extra half hour of backtracking, crossing and re-crossing the same roads until, familiar with the neighborhood, he finally found the destination.

Following the descending numbers, he arrived at a two story white brick building adorned with a dome constructed from a copper frame containing glass etched with geometric patterns common to Islam. Years of weathering and corrosion had changed the copper's natural salmon color to a verdigris patina. It was lighted from within and the green lights inside cast a gentle glow that spilled over the roof and onto the ground. Like the prophet Mohammad, green was Ahmad's favorite color and the dome, with its soft glow, reminded him of Islam's Holy Banner.

At each corner of the building, the tall graceful spires of the minarets were silhouetted against the brightening sky of early dawn. Afraid of endangering the mission, Ahmad had long avoided entering a mosque. The sight brought back memories of home, as joy mixed with anticipation welled up within him.

A wrought iron fence anchored to brick columns enclosed the mosque's compound. On the left side of the compound were arch-shaped gates. Sculpted into the metal bars was a gold-leafed crescent moon and star. Ahmad approached the gates, stopping adjacent to the keypad outside the driver's window. He picked up the wedding invitation and studied it again, but this time more closely. The first line read:

> Your benign presence is requested on the auspicious occasion of the marriage of Habib with Saeedeh.

Ahmad retrieved a pencil from the car's glove box and ripped a piece of scrap from the crumpled brown bag he had thrown into the back seat. In his head, he began to recite the formula to decipher the code. Using the mosque's address as the key, he outlined the steps in his memory as he had been taught:

> *The right most number is the equidistant letter spacing.*
> *Use it to find the correct letter in the sentence.*
> *Count backward from the end.*

Take and add the first number of the address to each letter's numerical place in the alphabet.
Multiply the entire number by the last number of the address.

From the brown scrap paper filled with letters and arithmetic, Ahmad entered the five most significant digits of the result into a keypad on the brick column and the gates swung open. Driving around to the back of the mosque, he parked the car in an area hidden by high bushes and pine trees. The grounds of the mosque weren't visible from the road. Its rear door had the same symbol on the lock as was imprinted on the key in Ahmad's pocket.

Ahmad entered the building and went straight to the basement where he found two plates of food: chicken with eggs and onions spiced with saffron, along with a plate of eggplant and tomato mixed with pomegranate and sour grape juice. There was flat bread wrapped in a red cloth napkin and a pitcher of water. He wondered who his unknown benefactor might be but it was a fleeting thought – the temptation to enjoy his native foods was irresistible.

Only three pieces of furniture were in the room. The table and chair where he sat to eat his meal and a narrow cot placed against the far wall. Ahmad walked over and sat on the cot for a moment, intending to say the fajr salat, the prayer before sunrise, but even before he could kneel, Ahmad collapsed and fell asleep. Before long, he heard a familiar voice calling out to him in his dream.

From the other side of the stone wall, Ahmad's boyhood friend, Shahin, called, "Ahmad, come out to play." Ahmad heard his friend's voice; at first it sounded far away, as it echoed over and over; it grew louder and closer each time. "Ahmad…Ahmad!"

"What!" Ahmad yelled. Startled, he jumped up, and found himself face-to-face with a stranger. It took a few seconds for his head to clear. He was not in Tehran. He was not a boy. This was not a dream. Preparing to defend himself, Ahmad took a step back. "Who are you?" he hissed.

"I am Sharif," the man answered softly. "May the most holy and merciful One bless you and bless your family…may Allah protect and reward you. With deepest respect, my brother, I have been sent to help you in our struggle."

Sharif handed Ahmad a card. Printed on one side was a prayer, hand written in a fine and delicate calligraphy. On the other side a symbol was printed. The symbol was gold-colored with several recursive loops nested around a center point; it was the same symbol on the key in Ahmad's pocket. Under the symbol were the same five numbers he had used to open the gate.

"Forgive me, brother," Ahmad said with tired eyes. "My journey has been long."

"It is I who should ask for your forgiveness. It was not my intention to startle you."

Ahmad moved to the table where the food had been set out. He had consumed most of the meal except for a piece of flat bread. "I am sorry, there is nothing to offer you," he said, gesturing toward the empty plates."

"I am not hungry, brother, except to do the will of Allah. I have train tickets to Newark, New Jersey, for us. No one knows when the planes will resume flying and the security at the airports is high, higher than the trains. From Newark, we will go to Patterson. There is a safe house where we will wait for our flight to Paris. In Paris, our brothers are preparing even now."

Sharif handed both tickets to Ahmad who began to study them as he considered the next phase of the grand plan he had been chosen to carry out. Before he could comment, the muezzin began calling the Morning Prayer. "Come, before we continue our journey, let us go and pray. It has been too long a time since I have been inside a mosque."

After performing the obligatory ablutions, the men walked upstairs and entered a large hall where small hand-woven rugs, each with its own individual pattern and color, were laid out on the floor. Just inside the doorway was a box containing kufi, the white knitted caps the men placed on their heads before entering.

It was early morning and the room was only partly full, so Ahmad and Sharif found a place directly in front of the Qiblah Wall, which contained a small ornate niche, or mihrah, pointing toward Mecca. This was the sacred direction, ordained by God, that all true believers were to face while praying. Ahmad knelt and began to recite the fajr salat.

As the prayers concluded, the mosque's Imam stepped up to the minbar, a richly decorated pulpit, shaped like a small tower, with gold inlays and exquisite carvings. Ahmad and Sharif were standing just a few feet away. The Imam climbed the stairs and stood at the top, looking out at the congregation. Then he began to speak.

"Salaam Alaykum," he greeted the assemblage of men. After another short pause, he continued, "Brothers, my heart is sad today. Some of our faithful do not understand the will of Allah or the words of the Prophet, peace be upon him. I fear there are some misguided amongst us responsible for the attacks in San Francisco. This will be another stain against all Muslims and cause reprisals against the innocent. More blood will be spilled. Jihad fi sabil illih…striving in the path of Allah…does not say we should kill non-believers. It tells us how we must struggle…and fight, within ourselves, to reach an enlightened and humble spirit. This spirit will bring us peace and we must bring peace to those around us. These few are not jihadists but hirabis…wagers of sinful war."

Ahmad listened to the Imam, his faced turning ashen, sure that the Imam must not understand the true meaning of the Quranic verses and the fundamental truths as taught in the holy writings. The fact that he was addressing this gathering, or any gathering of believers, troubled Ahmad. When the Imam concluded his remarks, Ahmad turned to Sharif and issued a terse command, "Let's get out of here!"

The men returned to the basement and, after gathering Ahmad's belongings, ascended the stairs toward the back door of the mosque. They would soon be heading to the railway station, only a short drive away. Ahmad reckoned that when the abandoned car was finally noticed, it would be days or weeks from now, and could only be traced back to a tired old Christian minister living in Oklahoma.

The men made their way to the landing at the top of the stairs then down a narrow hallway toward the backdoor where they saw the Imam standing there, blocking their egress. Ahmad stepped in front of Sharif.

"Good morning" he said, greeting the Imam. "Peace be with you."

"And peace be with you, my brother…the blessings of Allah upon you and your friend."

"Thank you, but I must confess we are in a hurry."

Ahmad tried to reach around the Imam to open the door but the man would not move.

Resolute, the Imam said, "You must be the one Shaykh Mohammad Al Abdulah told me of…the one for whom we prepared a meal. I have not seen you before but I hope you have felt welcome here."

"I do not know this shaykh so I do not know if I am the one you speak of. I only know that we have tickets on a train and must go now. I thank you for the meal."

"I see from your license plate that you came from California. The destruction is devastating. Have you been there? I pray to Allah that this was not done by one who claims to follow the Prophet Mohammad!"

Ahmad could not remain silent a moment longer. "And what do you know of the Prophet?" he asked. In a voice that started in a low growl and grew to a shout, he continued, "What befell the infidels in San Francisco is judgment as commanded in the holy Qur'an. You should pray for the martyrs. You have no right to rebuke them!"

"My brother," the Imam replied, "did not the Prophet say, 'There is a reward for kindness to every living animal or human'? Is it not written in the Qur'an, 'Allah does not forbid you from showing kindness and dealing justly with those who have not fought you about religion and have not driven you out of your homes'? The Qur'an tells us 'Allah loves just dealers'. Those people have done us no harm…they have done you no harm!"

"Do they believe as we believe, Imam? Do we not read, 'Fight and slay the Pagans wherever you find them, and seize them, beleaguer them, and lie in wait for them in every stratagem of war; but if they repent, and establish regular prayers and practice regular charity, then open the way for them: for Allah is Oft-forgiving, Most Merciful'? Do not speak to me of the Qur'an. I carry all its holy words in my heart."

The Imam looked at Ahmad with the sad expression in his eyes that one might have upon hearing of the death of a loved one. Lowering his head, he spoke in a raspy whisper.

"Brother, I can see you are a scholar and truly believe, but those people who were murdered…they suffered…horrible death…I pray for them…In the writings, it says: 'Any who believe in God and the Last Day and work righteousness shall have their reward with their Lord; on them shall be no fear, nor shall they grieve'. Surely, you cannot tell me all who died were evil and deserving of death."

Ahmad, feeling a sudden jolt of energy as though he were in battle, sneered at his opponent. Speaking slowly, he emphasized each word. "And so you feel pain for Christians and Jews?" Then he added, "And what about the others…those that worship only money and flesh…are they evil?"

"I am only a humble servant of Allah…it is not up to me to judge the human heart." The Imam continued with steady calmness. "Allah's words are plain to read that 'Not all of them are alike; of the People of the Book there are a portion that stand for the right, they rehearse the Signs of God all night long and they prostrate themselves in adoration. They believe in God and the Last Day; they enjoin what is right, and forbid what is wrong and they hasten in all good works. They are in the ranks of the righteous.'"

The fatigue from years of preparation finally hit him and Ahmad withdrew from patience. He just wanted to strike the Imam and end this argument. Sharif soon noticed the change in Ahmad's demeanor and immediately stepped between the men.

"It is time for us to go," he said without hesitation or deference. "We must leave now!"

With a stiff sweeping motion of his arm, Sharif moved the Imam away from the door and, taking hold of Ahmad's backpack, pulled him outside into the early morning sunlight. They began walking across the parking area to the dark green sedan.

"Thank you, brother," Ahmad said, apologizing to Sharif for having endangered their mission. "May Allah forgive me for my prideful sin."

Sharif turned toward Ahmad as they reached the car. "You have no reason to feel ashamed."

Ahmad noticed the Imam standing halfway between the car and the mosque. The Imam appeared both despondent, as though he had mislaid something precious, and interested, as though he were recording this incident in his mind. Not able to resist, Ahmad called to him as he was about to slide into the driver's seat.

"Remember, Imam, the holy writings say, 'Fight those who believe not in Allah nor the Last Day, nor hold unto that which hath been forbidden by Allah and His Apostle, nor acknowledge the religion of Truth, even if they are the People of the Book, until they pay the Jizya with willing submission, and feel themselves subdued.'"

The Imam took a step or two backwards, and raising his arm in a motion that looked like a blessing, replied. "Allah said to the prophet, 'Remember ye slew a man and fell into a dispute among yourselves as to the crime. But God was to bring forth what ye did hide.'" He turned and walked back into the mosque.

Ahmad sat motionless in the car, looking at Sharif who appeared confused and shocked.

Ahmad asked, "Do you think he knows who we are?"

"He certainly has a strong suspicion," Sharif answered.

"Do you think he would report us to the authorities?"

Sharif took a moment to answer. He was reluctant to express what he felt for fear of Ahmad's reaction. "After what he just said…yes," he admitted.

Retrieving the backpack from the rear seat, Ahmad pulled a compact Beretta Cheetah from one of the inside pockets. Without comment, he opened the door and walked inside the mosque.

Ahmad found the Imam in the hall where the Morning Prayer service had been conducted. He was praying, his forehead pressed against the carpet. Without a sound, Ahmad crept up behind the Imam. He did not hesitate for a single moment and fired one bullet into the head of the praying man, then knelt beside the Imam's lifeless body to recite the Salat Al Janazah, the prayer for the dead.

Without regret or a second thought, he returned to the car, put away his weapon, started the engine and left the mosque's compound. Ahmad and Sharif drove the twenty blocks to Union Railway Station in silence. They would never speak of their first meeting or the events of that day again.

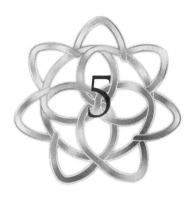

EPIPHANY

The Global Network remote news van sat parked on the corner of Washington and Montgomery opposite the wounded Omni America Pyramid. The van was given a premier spot beside the command post set up by the mayor and governor of the state just hours after the attack. The Omni, along with most other buildings in the area, was sealed off to all but police and fire departments, the FBI, and the National Guard. David Anderson, along with his news crew, was just wrapping up an interview with Governor Hanson Perez.

"Yes, the Federal response has surpassed our expectations… FEMA is on the scene along with Special Agents from the FBI," the governor told David, "They are marshalling resources to help with the recovery phase which will begin soon."

David, standing beside the governor and holding a microphone with the letters GN across it, asked. "By the sound of things,

Governor Perez, should we infer all the victims are accounted for at this time?"

"Well, according to my senior staff, the emergency responders have nearly accounted for all the victims," the Governor said. "Luckily, the building did not collapse and, we believe, all occupants have been evacuated. California has rigorous laws governing how buildings can be erected. Our earthquake precautions saved a lot of lives. Unfortunately, those who died or were injured, fell victim to the initial explosions and then the smoke and fires that followed."

"And how will you proceed from this point," queried David.

"At this point, I expect the commanders at the site will execute a final sweep of the building. We will then be switching from a rescue effort to recovery mode. I should have additional details later this afternoon."

The governor's answer did not satisfy David, whose personal interest in the outcome prompted him to ask the question again. "Governor, are all the known victims accounted for or not?"

"There still might be individuals who checked themselves into a hospital or went into hiding…just took off. We are trying to get employee rolls from the businesses in the building, along with admittance information from the local hospitals. There are also visitors from out of town who may have been there on business, and we are checking with the hotels in the area. People are still calling in missing persons reports. Then we have the victims of the bridge collapse to account for. Don't forget, there is some uncertainty with searching in water. Add all this together and you can see the picture is quite complicated. Oh…and, until all the debris is cleared, we don't have full access to the building's interior."

"When will the building access issue be resolved?" shouted another reporter who had taken his place in the group of journalists crowding around the governor.

"I'm not sure," replied Governor Perez. "My understanding is all the fires are contained or extinguished and the city engineers are checking to see which areas are safe to enter. Our environmental people are also checking for toxins and like substances."

"Governor," a third reporter asked "it is rumored these attacks were timed to occur during the World Energy Conference. Is there any link between the two?"

"I don't speculate about rumors" the governor replied. "I will say we knew of no prior threats to the delegates or the conference."

"Follow up question, governor...I hear that one of the organized groups, The Alliance for Global Advancement, called off their planned protests today. Any comments on whether they had advance warning?"

"Again, I won't speculate."

"One last question," said David. "Is there any definitive word on the whereabouts of Energy Secretary Kline?"

"We're still investigating...so, I'm sorry but I cannot comment." The governor hesitated before adding, "The Feds might have further details."

"Thank you, I appreciate your taking the time, governor, and good luck," said David.

"Right, thank you all," replied the governor.

As the governor departed with his retinue and a contingent of state police in tow, David concluded the field report.

"You have just heard from Governor Hanson Perez of California. He has expressed his resolve to find a solution for the many problems facing state and federal officials as they work through the process of rescuing those still trapped and the grim task of recovering the victims that died in the attack. This is David Anderson, reporting live from the Omni America building. Now back to Matt Finan at the anchor desk."

"Thank you, David. You can see David's next report, from the base of the Harbor Bridge. At the White House today..."

David removed his ear set, spinning his index finger in a circle to signal the cameraman to cut the segment. Sergio Leffert, his field producer, walked up and helped him remove the peanut mike from his lapel. "Nice work, David."

"Thanks, but I'm not so sure about that last answer...how did it sound to you?"

"The governor sounded sincere," Sergio replied.

"Serg...let's get a hold of Mike Lussardi and dig just a little deeper...I have a funny feeling that there is more to this energy conference than we are being told."

Barely containing his excitement at the prospect of doing a major story with David Anderson, Sergio said, "Well...you're the executive editor...do you want me to open an official investigative assignment?"

"Yes, and if anyone...even John Stavos, challenges you, refer them to me."

"Sure...err...to the bridge or Market Street next?" asked Sergio.

Before David could decide which story to follow first, a black limo pulled up behind the news van where the cameraman was packing the equipment. Suzanne stepped out and walked up to David who greeted her with a curious smile.

"Hey there, how are things back at the fort?"

"Good. John seems pleased," replied Suzanne, "I spoke with him this morning. I think he is still worried about you. You should give him a call."

"Absolutely," David answered. "I'll ring him up on the way. So, what is GN's executive producer doing out here in the field with the little people?"

Suzanne looked at David, one eyebrow held high, "Have you forgotten our lunch appointment with Miss Merilee Brunswick? Let's not be late."

David shot a glance at the black limousine. To his dismay Brian Saunders was sitting behind the wheel. "Did you have to bring that guy along?" There was no mistaking his consternation.

Dismissing David's concern, Suzanne said, "He's just our driver. Chill out!"

"Sure, just our driver..." David echoed, his voice trailing off.

"Excuse me, David," interrupted Sergio. "We should get rolling. Hi, Suzanne."

"Hi, Sergio, how are you?" Suzanne said with a sunny smile. "Sorry, I didn't mean to be rude. I am feeling rather harried. David and I have a lunch appointment, a possible story...we're not sure yet. How about we call you on your cell when we're done...we can meet you?"

"David?" Sergio asked, puzzled about the sudden change in plans.

David stood with his arms outstretched, the palms of his hands facing the sky. "You heard the boss," he quipped.

Suzanne rolled her eyes. "You heard the woman," she corrected. She walked away laughing and climbed into the limousine.

"I'll catch up with you later," David said, following his executive producer into the limo.

"Hello, Mr. Saunders, nice to see you." Whenever Brian Saunders was near, the newsman found it expedient to lie.

The car proceeded south and David moved to the rear bench seat, sliding in next to Suzanne. "Where are we meeting our contact?" he inquired.

"I'm not sure I would classify her as a contact, just yet, but we're heading to the Valencia Gardens section just north of Mission," Suzanne explained.

"Mexican food?" David said making a face.

"C'mon, stop! You like Mexican food," Suzanne protested, playfully slapping David on the arm.

"Okay, Mexican it is. So, bring me up to speed."

Suzanne opened her notebook. "The assignment desk got a tip from a Merilee Brunswick who called the day of the attack...rather, the evening of the attack. Anyway, she called and told the editor that she thought she ran into one of the terrorists."

David interrupted. "Could you define 'ran into'? Were they at a cocktail party or something?"

"That's very funny...you should try getting a job in television," Suzanne smirked. "When I called, she insisted this man she ran into was one of the terrorists, that the police didn't care, and that the guy left some papers, or something, behind. Oh...and...she will only meet with you because of a story you did."

"What story?"

"She didn't say."

"So what...you're thinking...if this information turns out to be...well, say radioactive, and the authorities ignored it, then we have quite a little story here," David responded, his eyes widening with approval.

"Exactly!" replied Suzanne, "Two stories, really...the missed follow-up and what might be in those papers."

"Smart gal…you know, Mexican food is beginning to sound like a good idea. What restaurant did you pick?"

"Don Ramon. Hope recommended it. She said the food's good, it's quiet, and not too many tourists. She mentioned the guacamole is to die for."

David smiled at the thought. The prospect of eating warm corn chips and guacamole made him remember his hunger. Leaning against the car door, he watched the city pass by and felt encouraged by the signs of activity along the streets. Slowly, but inexorably, people were returning to the routine of their daily lives. Businesses were reopening. Pedestrians were fighting with the traffic for supremacy of the roads. Tourists, some with families, were visiting the places they had circled on complimentary hotel maps. Shoppers were carrying packages and parents were pulling along determined youngsters who, to unlock the mysteries of childhood, insisted on blazing their own trails.

David looked back at Suzanne and let a chuckle escape. "I'm thinking everything may turn out all right, after all."

"Do you know, you're entirely too emotional for a hard boiled news reporter?"

"It'll just be our little secret," David whispered as the car pulled up to Don Ramon.

Although the sign read, 'No Stopping Anytime,' Brian Saunders ignored the parking regulations and pulled adjacent to the curb in front of the restaurant. It was coming on one o'clock as David and Suzanne opened the front door and walked up to the hostess.

"Welcome, two for lunch?" asked a pretty Latina woman with a broad Mexican accent. She grabbed two menus as Suzanne responded.

"Hi, I'm Suzanne Biasotto from Global News. Our office called to reserve a table for three…we're expecting another person."

A wide grin spread across the hostess's face as she recognized David Anderson as her guest. With the slightest hint of a tremor in her voice, she said, "Yes…yes there is someone here to meet you. Please, come this way!"

The two colleagues followed the hostess to the back of the restaurant where an attractive young woman sat at a table, her hands folded on top of a leather-bound book. Her posture was so erect it seemed unnatural. Shoulder length, curly brown hair matched the color of her anxious brown eyes. The woman wore a modest grey checked suit with a light blue blouse and looked up as David and Suzanne approached. She seemed hesitant to acknowledge them and it occurred to David that this woman was absolutely petrified.

In an attempt to lighten the mood, David stepped forward with a gregarious smile and offered his hand. "Hi, I'm David Anderson and this is Suzanne Biasotto. You must be Merilee Brunswick. It's very nice to meet you."

Immediately, the young woman's shoulders slipped into a normal pose and she returned David's smile, extending her hand. "Yes, I recognize you from TV. It's nice to meet you, too." With a nod of her head, she acknowledged Suzanne and gestured for them to sit.

David ordered beverages and appetizers for the group. For half an hour, David and Merilee chatted about their backgrounds and interests. Suzanne did not offer a word, thinking this resembled a date. She wanted to get right to the point of the meeting but David would not be rushed. He was interested in hearing all about this Merilee and, gradually, she was chattering away like they were long lost friends. David, satisfied with the rapport he felt with the pretty stranger across the table, called for the waiter.

After everyone ordered entrees, David sat back in his chair and asked, "Merilee, what made you call Global News and ask for me?"

"Well," the young woman began, "I…wanted to talk to someone I could recognize…someone I could trust…and I thought…well…"

"I understand and I'm glad you called."

A slight tension returned to Merilee's voice but she no longer seemed as anxious. David patted her hand and looked directly into her eyes, trying to reassure her but Merilee interrupted him, asking in a whisper, "Would you like me to tell you my story?"

"Sure thing, if you feel you can," David said.

"Do you promise not to use my name?" Merilee's eyes pleaded as she spoke.

"You have my word," David reassured her. "No one will ever know we met or where the story came from. Whatever you say here will be strictly confidential and off the record."

"Okay," Merilee began as she picked up the brown leather bound book and held it tightly against her chest.

"I went to work early the day of the attack. I had to meet a client at eight o'clock in front of an apartment building my company is trying to sell. I work in a real estate office in rentals and sales and I had a showing. I mean, someday I hope to be, you know, in management. Anyway, it's really nice, new floors and kitchens, bay windows, and...Well, never mind all that. I was walking towards the building and a man came running out of the door and down the steps."

"The building with the nice apartment?" David asked.

"Yes, I was about to walk up the front steps when he came running out."

"What happened next?" asked David, leaning toward his guest.

"The door," Merilee explained, "was already opened, like someone, you know, propped it open on purpose. It's supposed to be locked. Anyway, this man comes running through the door at full speed like he'd seen a ghost, or something...knocks me down and all my stuff goes flying all over the place. Then he does this weird thing. He sort of stops and looks at me, real strange, for a second, like he was going to say something...or do something, but when a police van turned onto the street...he ran away and kept looking back...as though he wanted to see if they were chasing him."

"Were they chasing him?" asked David.

"No, I don't think so," replied the girl.

"Then why do you think he ran away?"

"I'm not sure," Merilee said. "The thing is, he dropped this book." Merilee waved the book in the air and then began flipping through the pages. "He was in such a hurry to get away he didn't even realize he dropped it."

"And the book he dropped is the one you're holding?" David asked.

"Yes," she said, clutching the book tighter.

"What's inside the book? I'm guessing you looked inside."

"No, not right away." Merilee began to blush. "I was just hoping the guy might have left his name and phone number so I could call him and...well...tell him off."

David grinned and shot a quick glance over to Suzanne. So far, there was nothing newsworthy about her story but he was, by nature, a curious and thorough man.

"Does anyone else know about this?"

"Only my friend, Justine. She came over to my apartment that night after work because I was so upset. That's when we looked in the book...it's in a language neither of us understand...we guess it is Arabic, or something. Then we saw you on TV."

Suzanne's patience was wearing thin as the idea of the exclusive breaking news story seemed more and more remote. Shaking her head she murmured, "You saw David on TV and decided to call him...on a whim...just like that!"

"No, that's not how it happened," Merilee replied. The frightened woman reemerged and she began to speak rapidly in her own defense, looking at David with plaintive eyes.

"First, I watched the reports coming in that there was an Islamic terror organization claiming responsibility for the attacks. Then there was a report showing people in the Middle East celebrating. Later, the network aired a story about the profile of a terrorist. I thought the men in the story looked exactly like the guy who ran into me. I mean, I thought that, so I called the police."

"What did the police say?" David asked calmly, trying to keep Merilee composed.

"They said they were too busy and I should come to the station and file a report."

"Merilee," David asked. "So, you saw some middle eastern men who looked like the man who ran into you. Is that what frightened you?"

"Not entirely," replied Merilee, her voice growing almost too soft to hear. "It was the book..."

"Why did you call me then? What made you think of me?"

"I thought of you because of your story about the Muslim schools," Merilee answered, fighting to keep her lip from quivering.

"A story...I did a story?" David asked.

"David," Suzanne reminded him, "During a break, we cut to some file footage from your first documentary. Remember, the series on the madrasahs and how they indoctrinate their kids?"

Her voice rising, a warm apple glow spreading across her cheeks, Merilee said. "Yes! Yes, they are indoctrinated into terrorism in that school."

"Of course," David answered, becoming lost for a moment in memories from his early days at Global. "So why did that frighten you?"

Trembling, tears filling her eyes, Merilee looked at David. Her voice became strained and tight. "Because inside the book I found some cards and on one side of the cards there's a gold symbol…and the school you were standing in front of at the end of the news story had the same symbol over the entrance. The man who ran into me on the stairs…I'm afraid he's a terrorist. He's from there. I'm afraid he is the one responsible for the attacks yesterday and that he'll come back for this book and…do something. Please! I tried the police. They were no help. Please, help me."

Merilee handed the book to David. Her hands were shaking. Suzanne felt regret for scolding Merilee about contacting them. Then David gently took the book from Merilee's hands.

"Merilee, calm down…take a moment…breathe. Think about it for a second. This man doesn't know who you are…he could never find you…you have nothing to worry about."

David took hold of the strap holding the book closed and with a slow and deliberate motion pulled it up and opened the cover. He began flipping through the pages. Both women were glancing up and down, alternating between the book and David's face, waiting for his reaction. David looked up after a few minutes, and said, "Well, this is nothing but a Qur'an." Reassuring Merilee, he explained, "It's like a Muslim bible."

"You mean it's just a prayer book of sorts?" Merilee asked.

"Essentially," David responded.

"What about the cards?"

"I don't read Arabic but I've seen something similar when I was on assignment in the Middle East. I think they are some type of invitation…to a party or wedding. And the symbol is just a common emblem found all through the region."

"So that's it? There's nothing to worry about?" Merilee said, searching for more reassurance.

"There's no reason for concern," David said.

"Oh, man. I am so sorry to have troubled you," sighed Merilee, the telltale sign of her embarrassment clearly on her cheeks.

"Please don't have a second thought about it," insisted David, "It was very brave of you to call. It's good to know there are still folks out there who will step up to the plate when the occasion presents itself."

With a sigh of relief, Merilee began to thank David. Suzanne sat quietly watching the pass and re-pass of expressions on David's face as he looked over each card and through different pages of the book. Suzanne was sure the nearly undetectable changes on David's face escaped Merilee's notice but she knew David better than almost anyone, and she could tell there was something more than David was telling them.

Outside the restaurant, David offered Merilee a ride in the limo. Flattered at the offer, she accepted without hesitation. This vexed Suzanne, who was feeling pressured about the time away from the studio. She took her cue from David, though, and kept her conversation polite and friendly, managing to engage in some small talk with Merilee during the ride.

When they arrived at Merilee's apartment, David offered to walk her to the front entrance as Saunders stood holding the door for his passengers. When Merilee exited the car, she smiled at Saunders and with a polite nod of her head, said, "Thank you." She was not a user of limousines and wasn't sure whether to tip the driver, but sensed she should not.

David followed her through the limo's doorway, took her arm and began walking toward the brick steps ascending to the entrance when he stopped and abruptly turned. "Mr. Saunders," he called, "would you kindly hand me that leather book and those loose cards on the rear seat?"

Saunders brought the items to David, who escorted Merilee into the building's foyer. He said to her, "Merilee, remember…don't be afraid, no one knows you or how to find you. Here, these are yours."

"No, I don't want them. I left them in the car for you. Please, you keep them, okay?" Merilee pulled her hands back and away from the objects as though they were composed of toxic chemicals.

"Are you sure?"

"Yes, they have bad memories!"

David tucked the items into the inside pocket of his jacket, shook Merilee's hand, said goodbye, and departed.

During the rest of the day's activities that would end back at the studio, David remained pensive. On the way to meet Sergio, David just stared through the car's window at the passing scenery, lost in thought, seeming somber and distant. Suzanne remained quiet for a while, trying to gauge the appropriate time to inject a conversation into the gloomy silence hanging in the limo.

"David, are you going to tell me what the hell is going on?" she finally demanded.

"What makes you think...?"

Suzanne's eyelids narrowed, cutting David off mid-sentence. He could only see the jade green of her irises.

"That's a very alluring look," he said, grinning.

"Tell me, David...c'mon please! What's in that book?"

David closed the limo's privacy divider so Saunders couldn't see or hear them, and then removed the book and the cards from inside his jacket pocket. David held the book up in the space between them.

"This looks to be nothing more than a standard issue Qur'an," he said. It's in Arabic so I can't read it, but I recognize the format. Interesting thing, though, several of the passages have been highlighted and there's something handwritten on the blank note pages in the back. I can't read that either, but I think it's in Farsi."

"So are you saying this was a waste of time?" Suzanne asked.

"Patience, Suzanne. I'm not saying that at all. There is something else, something I was trying to remember." David shuffled the cards then held one up as an example. "I can't read these cards, I think they're in Farsi too, but I've seen this symbol before, scattered around the region."

"What do you mean by scattered...what region?"

"Well, during my travels throughout the Middle East, I encountered it on certain mosques, places strictly off limits to westerners. I also saw it on several madrasahs. I was granted access to one, I'll never forget it, in Tehran...the boys and young men were being trained to become suicide warriors and attack the enemies of Islam.

The mullah who was my guide inside the school, gave it a different spin. He told me they were to become the carriers of the holy message of the Qur'an, establishing Shari'ah Law throughout the world. I remember him telling me the West must learn to follow a strict code of Islamic law or the neck veins of America would be cut. He refused to elaborate but it was clearly a warning. It was chilling."

A sudden shiver shot through Suzanne as she listened to David. "Sounds more like a threat then a warning…hey, don't they speak Farsi in Iran?"

"Yes, and that has piqued my curiosity. That, and the fact my guide casually mentioned the symbol belonged to some secret sect. He was unwilling to discuss it! I was never able to find out more at the time…but for it to show up here…"

"David, do you think there's a back-story here that merits investigation?"

"It's possible…but to know for sure, we first need to get this translated. I know a professor at Notre Dame who teaches history and anthropology."

"Do you think he can help us?" Suzanne asked.

"He specializes in ancient cultures," David replied, "and is considered one of the foremost experts on the Middle East in the country. He is a consultant for State and Defense. We've collaborated in the past. I actually sent him a scroll to decipher that was given to me way back when I was in Iran. I guess we both forgot all about it…time to call in the results. Besides, he's also a close friend… I'm sure I can trust him."

Suzanne paused to consider the possibilities, momentarily occupied with hypothetical 'what ifs', story angles, and what an investigation might unearth.

"David, something is troubling me."

"What's that?" David asked.

"If you knew there was something unusual about the book at lunch, why did you try to return it to Merilee Brunswick?"

"I was simply checking her sincerity."

"Why on earth would you bother to do that?" asked Suzanne.

"I wanted to see if her reaction was authentic or if she was acting…contriving news to get attention or for some other personal reason. If her story was disingenuous, I don't think she could have maintained that level of dread for as long as she did. Her actions were completely consistent with someone who was truly frightened, terribly so, and just wanted to put this behind her."

"Very clever," Suzanne said. She admired David's natural talent for getting people to talk openly and his ability to discern truth from fiction. She was, in fact, a little envious.

Suzanne remained with David for the rest of the day, subbing as a field producer. After leaving Merilee Brunswick, they went to the foot of the Harbor Bridge, met Sergio, completed David's report and shuttled back to the field command post where the governor and mayor conducted a second press conference, distributing a list of the missing, injured and deceased victims. The list included a separate section detailing the names of the dignitaries and officials who were attending the World Energy Conference. Their last stop was Global, where David resumed his role at the anchor desk for the evening news, followed by an editorial meeting to discuss the following day's programming content.

It was nine o'clock that night when Brian Saunders pulled the limousine into Eric Anderson's circular driveway, ending a very long day. The couple was walking up the front steps of Eric's home toward the entrance doors when a navy blue sedan pulled up behind the limo. The white government license plate, contrasted against the dark color of the car, immediately caught David's attention. The car had arrived almost simultaneously with the limo. David wondered if they had been followed.

The driver, and his passenger, stepped from the car and walked up the path to the house where David and Suzanne stood waiting. As he approached, the driver pulled from his jacket pocket identification, which looked official enough to David.

"Mr. Anderson," he said, "we're from the FBI. I'm Special Agent DeMarco and this is Special Agent Martin. We're assigned to find your father. Is there someplace private where we can talk?"

David gestured for them to follow him. He unlocked the door and stepped inside the foyer.

When Suzanne, accompanied by the FBI agents, joined him, David called out to Saunders who was standing beside the car.

"Mr. Saunders, would you kindly wait a moment?" David asked, "We have a late dinner reservation, this shouldn't take long."

"Whatever you say, Mr. Anderson," Saunders said.

"Thanks," David responded as he closed the door, leaving Brian Saunders outside with the squirrels.

"Gentlemen, come in and make yourselves at home." David directed them to the living room.

The vicissitudes of the past few days left David feeling somewhat less than hospitable. He skipped the polite conversation and offer of drinks so they could get straight to the point. The sound of resignation was unmistakable in David's voice. Expecting the worst possible news, he asked, "Tell me gentlemen, have you learned anything new about my dad?"

"Nothing positive, I'm afraid," replied agent DeMarco.

"Go on" David said, prodding DeMarco to continue, his heart pounding.

"Well, sir...a security guard reported your father arrived at his office early. His access badge was swiped at the lobby turnstile and at his office floor. No one saw him leave after that time. What's left of his car is still in his reserved parking space underground. The search of the building and surrounding area is about complete and the victims' remains are in the process of being identified."

"Look," Suzanne interjected, "Will you please come to the point?"

"The point is..." answered Bill Martin, annoyed with Suzanne's impatience, "...most bodies...err...people...have not been identified yet. Some of them were burned beyond recognition and all we have to go on are dental records. Others will be more difficult as their remains are scattered but we have tentative identifications based on where we found them. Still others..."

Hoping to steer the conversation away from the morbid aspects of their investigation, and relieve David's anticipation without revealing too much in front of Suzanne, DeMarco stepped back in. "Mr. Anderson, I really don't want to be the one to tell you this but, as of now, your father is listed as presumed dead. We have a body we believe to be his. I'm very sorry."

David rose to his feet and, pacing the living room, finally stopped in front of an accent table placed behind a couch facing the stone fireplace. He stood, deep in thought, his eyes fixed on the framed photographs decorating the table. There were pictures of his childhood: his parents and their parents, a collection of faces, relatives, and friends of the family, some of whom he never knew, frozen on photographic paper, smiling at him from some time in the past. The collection was a cherished testimonial to lives of service and devotion to God, country, and family.

Suzanne walked over to the table, stood behind David and patted his back. Resting her head against his shoulder, she whispered in his ear, "David, I'm so sorry. I'm here for you."

They remained clinging to each other for a while until David turned, pressed her hands to his chest for a second, then moved back toward the sofa where the FBI agents were seated.

"Is that all?" David asked Agent DeMarco.

"We have other details," DeMarco offered. "Can we speak privately and off the record?"

"What does that mean?" Suzanne inquired.

"It means we have not released all the information to the public yet," replied Martin, the abrupt irritation in his voice meant to cut off Suzanne's line of questioning.

"I don't understand" Suzanne was puzzled. "Why can you tell David and not me?"

"Because he's immediate family," clarified DeMarco

"Not to mention, we have orders from Washington," Martin added.

David moved to her side, and taking hold of her hands again, he whispered, "Go inside, sit in my dad's study and watch TV for a few minutes, okay?"

Suzanne acquiesced. The newsman returned to the sofa, leaned forward and rested his elbows on his knees. He faced the two agents, allowing the pause in their conversation to grow into an uncomfortable silence. Finally, he said, "Now gentlemen, I should like to hear the details."

"It's like this," DeMarco volunteered. "There's kind of a mystery surrounding your father's ordeal."

"Could you explain?" David asked.

"Sure, yes ...err...whoever planned and executed these attacks were experts," replied the agent.

"Yeah...real professionals," Martin interrupted, nodding his head in agreement.

DeMarco threw a scintillated glance at Agent Martin before clearing his throat to continue. "It's like this. They drove two types of vans into the parking garage. First, they detonated a high velocity explosive encased in steel jackets. Next, they set off some sort of incendiary devices. The first blast targeted the elevator shafts. The sharp fragments pulverized the shaft's fire protective partitions but did little other damage...so they didn't kill their own guys. Then they set off the incendiaries, sending a fireball of expanding gases up thirteen of the eighteen elevators."

"Maximum damage, Mr. Anderson," Martin commented again, oblivious to his partner's escalating annoyance with the interruptions.

David was growing uneasy with the graphic details of the violence that took his father's life. He rose to his feet and glaring down at the agents, demanded, "What the hell does all this have to do with my father?"

"That fireball shot up as high as the thirty-seventh floor," DeMarco responded. "It blew out over three thousand windows. The contents and the people on every floor or office up to thirty-seven, who did not get out before the second explosion, were blown out the windows or incinerated. We are finding debris from the building six blocks away and victims' remains as far as two blocks away."

"Okay, I get it...so, are you saying my father was incinerated?"

"His office, is...well...different," DeMarco said, a sheepish look crossing his face. "We recovered a body. We presume it was your father, Mr. Anderson. We have taken the remains to the morgue. I have a picture, taken by the coroner. If you care to, we would like you to identify him now, but it is not mandatory. You can identify him, in person, at the morgue, if you prefer."

"Yes," said David without hesitation. "Please let me see the picture."

The agent reached into his valise and pulled out a photograph. He handed it to David. Immediately, David's head dropped to his chest and his hands went up to stop the tears."

"I'm sorry, I need a minute," David said.

"No problem, Mr. Anderson. Take all the time…"

David interrupted. "You said all the bodies recovered were burned, but my dad…"

"Exactly, Mr. Anderson, aside from some smudges of soot on his face and a few scorched patches on his suit, his body was in perfect condition…virtually, not a hair out of place. We can only guess he died from smoke inhalation. Nothing else in the office was burnt, either…not even paper…it's the damnedest thing I've ever seen. The office he occupied was in the same area as every other office that was completely destroyed. We just can't explain it!"

"Tell him about the windows," Martin reminded his partner.

"Right…the windows. Most of the windows in the building were blown *outward* except for your father's office. His windows were unbroken, apart from one window in front of his desk that was blown *inward*. We found shards of glass on the floor inside. None on the ledge…when we examined the shards more closely, the forensic guys noticed they were in a sort of starburst pattern…the same pattern was not seen in any other office! Bottom line, we don't really know what your father experienced during that time. It's a puzzle, Mr. Anderson, a puzzle," finished the agent, shaking his head.

"Our experts are completely baffled," added Martin.

Feeling powerless, like a man standing on a cliff as the ground begins to give way with nothing to grasp onto but hopelessness, David tilted back his head, fingers locked in his hair and stared at the ceiling. He tried hard to comprehend the description of the attack he just heard. He struggled to find a syllogism to explain DeMarco's recounting of the events but nothing fit. He felt sure of only two things: his father wasn't just missing anymore, he was dead, and that he hated the word 'dead'. He closed his eyes for a moment and leaned back in his chair.

For the second time in his life, he could not fix this and it left him feeling helpless and terribly alone. Through most of his life, David Anderson was self-sufficient and independent, nurtured by his parent's invisible support and unconditional love. But he was an orphan now. The very moment when he most needed their strength and guidance; when he needed his mother's loving gaze, or to see his father's approving smile, they weren't there.

In David's heritage it was commonplace, even natural, when confronting tragedy or facing great stress, to turn to God. But David hadn't spoken a word in God's direction since his mother's funeral. He came to disbelieve in God's existence with the simple reasoning that a benevolent creator would not take away a boy's mother; would never make her suffer; would never punish someone so beautiful and kind and good. David and Eric argued over this every year since her death. Now God's advocate was gone too.

Yet, in all this, a subtle sense of peace began to steal into David's grief until he found that his agitation was melting away. At least I can bury my dad, he thought, yet it did not fully explain this sudden feeling of serenity.

David opened his eyes and noticed the FBI agents were watching him, calculating his reaction to the information they had just conveyed. He had no doubt his reaction would be the subject of a report filed away somewhere in Washington, DC.

He composed himself and asked, "Is that all, gentlemen?"

"Just this," said Martin as he handed a card to David. "It's the number of the morgue. You will have to arrange..."

"Yes," David interrupted again, "I know...thank you."

"Oh, and Mr. Anderson," cautioned Agent Martin. "This information cannot be made public. The country has been in quite a state of disarray for some time now and this...well, this kind of thing, after the attacks and all...might cause widespread disruption if you know what I mean."

"I understand completely," replied David. "Thank you. If there is nothing else, I'd like to say good night."

The three men stood in the foyer shaking hands, when Vincent DeMarco said, "Mr. Anderson, there is one other small matter... perhaps it can wait until tomorrow."

"Not at all...please...what is it?" David asked.

"I'm not sure this is important but the security people at your studio mentioned they had a run-in with your driver. Do you know anything about it?"

"First I've heard...what happened?" David asked.

"It seems his credentials weren't working and Ms. Biasotto signed him in," DeMarco explained. "Apparently, there was a minor scuffle with the security guards."

"Don't tell me he slugged someone?" David asked, as that 'uneasy about Saunders' feeling began to well up again.

"No, nothing like that…but he gave his name to the guards and indicated he was somehow involved in law enforcement," replied the agent.

"That's true," David said. "He told us he was a retired police detective and showed me a shield when we first met."

"Did you check him out?" asked DeMarco.

"No. Why would I…that's Constellation's job."

DeMarco reached into his inside jacket pocket and, producing a small steno notepad, read out loud, "Corporate security at Constellation Media doesn't list any employee named Brian Saunders with that spelling…an FBI check with the San Francisco PD and the California State Police confirms they have no record of him either."

"In fact" added Martin, "we couldn't find a police department in the country that has a record of a Brian Saunders. We checked the Bureau and Interpol, Social Security, the IRS, he's not wanted but he doesn't appear to exist."

"Well, gentlemen," David suggested, "why don't we step outside and ask Mr. Saunders to clear this up?"

David opened the door and walked down the steps, followed by DeMarco and Martin. The limousine was no longer parked in the circular driveway. The group proceeded down the cobblestones and checked the street in the off chance Saunders parked the car at the curb.

"Well," said Martin, "the guy has sure split in a hurry. I'll call in a description of the car and see what we can find."

DeMarco and Martin set off for a walk around the house, looking for any physical sign that might have been left behind by the elusive driver.

"We're not going to find anything here," DeMarco said, at last. "Let's head on out."

The men approached David and assured him they would be in touch with any new information relevant to his father. David thanked them and went back into the house. For good measure, he double locked the doors and activated the perimeter alarms for a second night. He found Suzanne in the living room sitting on the couch, the nervous jiggle of her leg was a sure sign she was rabidly curious.

"Well, David. As usual, I have to ask what is going on."

"According to the FBI guys," said David, "There is some question as to what actually happened to my father. They don't know what to make of it. That's all I can share right now except that we can't mention this to anyone."

Suzanne's instinctive reaction was a feeling that they should expose any news from the authorities on-air, right away - play up the mystery angle and get the jump on the competition. But this involved David's father and she had to respect his feelings. David would tell her when the time was right. If someone else broke the story, for the sake of their relationship, she could live with that. Looking at David with a hint of irony, she said, "We're two for two today."

"How so?" David asked.

"First, Merilee Brunswick; now the FBI - two stories we can't tell the world."

"Actually, we're three for three," David added. "There's something else. Mr. Saunders, our driver, doesn't really exist."

"What are you talking about?" Suzanne asked, a look of bewilderment crossing her face.

"Corporate security checked his credentials after the confrontation yesterday...that you conveniently forgot to mention...and neither they nor HR have any record of a Brian Saunders. The FBI looked into his background...he's not a cop and has never been a cop. In fact, there isn't any data on the guy at all: no taxes, no driver's license, no phone or address...nothing. The guy's a ghost."

"Then who was he...do you think he's a spy or something?" asked Suzanne.

"I honestly don't know but I can't imagine why he would bother with us," David said, "Let him spy on John, or Lance, for that matter."

Suzanne shivered as she suddenly remembered that frightful feeling standing next to Saunders, alone in the elevator. She admonished herself for not heeding her instincts.

"What a jerk…I let the guy in the studio, past security…what was I thinking?" Her eyes darted toward David. "I wish I could read people like you…just saying, that's all."

"Don't get into a twist, we're covered," David offered, trying to calm Suzanne's frayed nerves. "I set the alarms and the FBI is sending out two policemen to guard the house. This guy, Saunders, is probably just some kook out for a cheap thrill."

David wasn't really sure he believed the part about Saunders being a kook but there was nothing he could do about it at the moment, so he kept quiet. They decided it was too late for dinner, their reservation was long passed, and agreed their best bet was to grab a quick bite from whatever they could find in the kitchen and get a good night's sleep.

After David bid goodnight to Suzanne, he began to walk toward the room where he always slept when visiting his father. As he was turning the knob, David glanced at his father's bedroom door, and instead, decided to sleep in the master bedroom. He washed, borrowed his dad's pajamas, set the alarm clock on the night table and slipping underneath the duvet, he sighed, feeling relaxed for the first time in days. A few minutes later, David Anderson was fast asleep.

It wasn't so much a sound; it was more like a feeling that woke David Anderson. He glanced at the clock on the table beside the bed. The liquid crystal display read 4:17 AM. David, startled, sat up and peered into the darkness. Two silhouette images stood in the room at the foot of his father's bed. They did not appear to come through his eyes so much as through his mind. At first, he thought he was dreaming.

David became alarmed. Had Saunders somehow gotten past the police and the alarm system? He strained to recognize the two figures and, ripping the comforter away, jumped to his feet.

In that instant, he saw a smile from his earliest memory; the smile in a man's eyes conveying unconditional love and approval; the smile of a man who broadened his life to become father, mother, friend and mentor. Behind the man, he saw a woman bathed in a soft white luminescence.

David fell back onto the bed. Voice cracking, he asked, "Dad, is that you?"

"Yes, David."

"You're alive?"

"More alive than I have ever been."

"God Almighty, dad, I thought I'd never see you again; they said you were missing and presumed...who is that with you?"

"This is the friend who helped me. Don't worry about me, son, it was a wonderful and beautiful moment."

"What do you mean...moment?"

"We live in two worlds, David. We are born into one of matter, time, facts. The other world - of spirit, timelessness, values, and faith - is where our souls live. That is where I am. After tonight, you won't see me...but I'll be with you and we'll see each other, one day, in the Lord's good time."

"No dad, I won't accept this. This is unacceptable!" David cried.

David glanced at the woman standing behind his father. She was beautiful, but in a way David had never seen before nor could he have ever imagined. Her hair could only be described as golden, although it was, actually, more the color of pure honey shining in the midday sun. It had such lustrous glints of light shining outward that, when she moved, it gave the impression that a halo surrounded her head. Her skin had that soft, olive glow of Mediterranean people that seemed to reflect her 'halo' and extend it to the very tips of her toes.

The woman's face was oval-shaped with a broad, prominent forehead and aquiline nose. She was not smiling, but a soft glow of warm affection shone through her eyes.

Those eyes, those shining, loving eyes...they were blue-green, deep and set wide, almond shaped with soft brown arched brows above them. David could sense it was the love radiating from those eyes which was the true source of her beauty.

The woman was dressed in what appeared to be a gown made of a diaphanous material that looked akin to pale pink chiffon. The gold thread running through it seemed, in itself, alive. It looked to form some kind of ancient script that kept changing as the folds of the gown waved in a gentle unseen zephyr. As the script snaked its way over the fabric, the soft whisper of voices that had entered the room when David was awakened, and which he could now just barely detect, also changed. It sounded as though they were singing the songs imbedded in the threads of the woman's flowing dress. David strained to hear the haunting voices but, the more he strained, the fainter they became. He thought the songs must be utterances of Divine Revelation, imparted through all eternity from the mouth of God, Himself. He was entranced by this vision and falling deeply into its ineffable sense of beauty, when David's reverie was suddenly interrupted by his father's voice.

"This is my guide and my guardian, David. She is here to help me."

"How can that possibly be?" cried David, "I'm so happy you're here, dad...but I can't believe these things are real...this is all just a dream."

David's voice began to crack and tears began forming at the corners of his eyes.

Allowing a moment to pass between him and his son, the man, who was once Eric Anderson, said, "David, I am here in answer to a prayer. It is a very special gift, son. Let's accept it and not question how or why. Now listen, carefully. When you were a boy I told you a story about Three Kings. Do you recall?"

"Yes, I remember."

"They embarked on a long journey to find the truth. Now it's your turn, son. Look east, toward the star, and always remember how much I love you."

In the next instant, Eric Anderson and the woman vanished, leaving David alone in the dark, awestruck, sobbing, and confused. David spent the rest of the night trying to make sense of the last words his father would, in this life, ever speak to him.

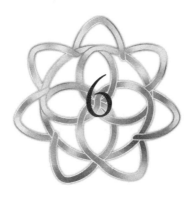

THE GOOD ROAD

Professor Ron Eyota stood in a small amphitheater behind the lectern, addressing a handful of graduate students. Other than finals, the semester was all but over and soon this small cadre of budding historians would be ejected into the world – a world of diminishing opportunities, of economic hardship, bitter ideological conflicts and escalating wars; a world that paid little attention to history or to history's caretakers. Dr. E., as his students often called him with affection, sadly reflected on this and on the year-over-year diminishing enrollment of the history department. Soon, he thought, there won't be anyone left to remember.

As the lesson concluded, a pretty young woman, intelligent and earnest in her studies, raised her hand. She had dark eyes, the color of mocha coffee, and the resolute demeanor of a young crusader out to change the world. Dr. E. felt despondent over the fact he would not be able to protect her much longer.

"Yes, Victoria, what is it?"

"Dr. E, seeing as school ends in a couple of weeks, I thought this might be a good time for you to tell us about your new book. I bet everyone would like to hear about it…right guys?"

The class enthusiastically agreed with deafening applause and, rising to their feet, they began chanting as one voice, "Book…book…book!" Dr. Eyota had the sense that this little display was preplanned.

Trying to regain control of the class, Ron Eyota reproved his students; "Okay…Okay, settle down." He reached inside the lectern, producing a thick, hard-covered volume that he held up for all to see. "Here, I have an advance copy from my publisher. You are welcome to come up and take a look."

"What's it about?" shouted a young man seated in the last row.

"What's the title?" called another young man who had selected college as a career and was just completing his second degree.

"The book is titled 'Ancestors Tell Our Story,'" explained Ron Eyota. "It's a historical perspective of cultures from around the world as told through the tales, legends and past accounts of individuals who pass down the history of their families from generation to generation. Essentially, it shows how a person's culture shapes their perspectives and experiences and how, in turn, they then shape and drive cultural change."

"Dr. E.," Victoria shouted, as she moved toward the lectern, "may I read a page or two out loud for the class?"

Again, there was an immediate and unanimous reaction from the students, followed by the same chant of book, book, book. Ron held up his hand like a traffic cop stopping cars at an intersection. Once the class quieted, he reluctantly surrendered his book to the student.

She opened the cover, holding the volume with a reverence normally reserved for documents of immense importance, like an original copy of the Bible, the Dead Sea Scrolls or the United States Constitution. She turned to the table of contents. Each chapter was named after a culture once vibrant and dominant; its people having made a special contribution to the ascent of humankind.

One chapter, in particular, caught her eye. It was titled 'Navajo Remembrance'. She placed her finger beneath it and looked toward

Dr. E. His gentle smile told her she had indeed found *his* story and Victoria began to read:

"I was born with three names: a European name, a Navajo name and a warrior name. I am called Ron Eyota. I was never told what the name Ron meant, or why my mother and father chose that name, but my Navajo name, Eyota, means 'great' and that is how I remember my family, my people, and my youth.

Names are as important to the Navajo as they tend to be in most cultures. Navajo names establish our standing in the community. They provide telltale characteristics of a family or the region from where the family originated. Names can tell the story of generations without a single word being spoken. This is the way of our indigenous people.

It was once the tradition of the Navajo, a practice similar among many Native Americans, to give an individual a name describing some special characteristic they possess. Most people are familiar with this concept through the media, especially old western movies, where the chief is named 'White Wolf' or the quickest of the braves is called 'Running Bear'. Sadly, as our culture became dominated and, in some cases, supplanted by cultural norms brought to the Americas by Europeans, this and other traditions slowly disappeared. This is why I was named Ron.

My father and grandfather, along with other tribal elders, heroically tried to preserve many of our Navajo traditions, even as the young members of our tribe left our ancestral lands seeking education and opportunity. So, in keeping with Navajo tradition, my father also gave me a warrior name when I was born. It was a secret not even my mother was to know. We never spoke my warrior name in the presence of another human being but when we found ourselves alone in the forest, among the animals, trees and other elements of nature, my father called me by that name. He said he did this so that the earth would know the great power I possessed.

My grandfather also used other names to preserve our traditions. He called me 'Da-he-tih-hi' which means 'hummingbird' in Navajo. He called me by this name because as a small boy

I darted from place to place, never sitting still for more than a minute or two.

So, to the world, I was known as Ron Eyota, to my grandfather, family and friends 'Da-he-tih-hi', and to my father, a name that must remain a secret until I die.

There were occasions when my grandfather and I would travel deep into the wilderness, following the trails along the mesa floor. Although the sun was hidden behind the cliffs, and the trails were overgrown, my grandfather never carried a compass, for he could never be lost.

When we came to a clearing we would stop and rest. My grandfather would gather small stones and place them in a circle. Once inside the shelter of the circle, we would lie back in serene repose, unconcerned with time, while grandfather recounted the tales and legends of our Navajo ancestors.

This is a story he told me. It's about the time my great-great grandfather lived:

The soldiers of the white man came and took our people from the land. They told them that they had to move to new land to keep peace. The people talked to the land and said the soldiers told them they had to leave...our people were sad and the land wept. On the journey many children were stolen but the soldiers did nothing to stop this. Many got sick and many others died...the soldiers did nothing to stop this either. The chief's war counsel decided to fight, but after a time they made peace with the white man's star chief. Our people waited at a soldier's fort for the star chief to let them go home.

Finally, the people went home. But the soldiers forced the people, their horses, and livestock to travel on the soldier roads. When the people came home the white man built schools and places for trading. They said this was civilized. They built roads and told the people they must follow the roads. They said this was civilized too.

Before the roads came our people always knew the way. And their horses and cattle also knew the way. We were uncivilized like the sun that without roads knows its path through the sky. Our people forgot the way and we traveled on the white man's roads. Many of the people died in shame because they were civilized. Their horses and cattle died in shame too.

When my grandfather finished a story he would always stand within the circle and sing a song in our native language. I remember to this day his favorite song. He sang it so I could always find the courage of the mythic Navajo warrior. He sang it that I might remember the songs of my people. He sang it so I would not forget their struggles or their greatness."

Hozo-go nay-yeltay to...A-na-oh bi-keh de-dlihn... Ni-hi-keh di-dlini ta-etin

Translated to English, my grandfather's song would go something like this: 'May we live in peace, hereafter; we have conquered all our foes. There is no force in the world we cannot conquer.'

Late at night, when I am alone and the house is quiet, I sing my grandfather's song, and I hear the voices of my family, and the voices of my people sing with me..."

Victoria's voice trailed off. Tears clouded the sparkle in her eyes and, without comment, she walked over to Ron Eyota, handed back his book, gave him a hug, and left the amphitheater. One by one, the other students followed her in silence. Most approached Dr. E., stopping to pat his shoulder, shake his hand or simply smile in acknowledgement and understanding.

Ron Eyota remained alone in the amphitheater, contemplating the recognition and the relevance of the past few minutes, then gathered his belongings and, as he walked across the campus towards his office, he felt a spark of hope. Perhaps I was wrong, he thought, perhaps there are some who will remember.

Professor Eyota stepped inside the anteroom of his office and glanced at the row of young people waiting to speak with him. It was the usual collection of students looking for guidance on completing

coursework or seeking teaching assistant positions. That is, all but one, who did not look quite like a typical Notre Dame student.

She was wearing an expensive black business suit with a cream colored camisole underneath the jacket. Ron Eyota couldn't help but notice that the formality of her suit was in contention with her short, tight skirt and her long legs. Strands of light brown and golden blond hair were pulled tightly behind her head, revealing the delicate features and soft lines of her face. She sat with a burgundy-red, Burberry leather briefcase in her lap, upon which she was impatiently drumming her slender fingers. Ron Eyota went over to greet her. When she looked up, Ron was surprised to find her deep green eyes had the same color and luminescence of sea glass.

"Good afternoon, miss, I'm Dr. Eyota. Is there something I can do for you?"

The woman popped to her feet. She reached inside the breast pocket of her jacket with two fingers and, producing a business card, handed it to him.

"My name is Suzanne Biasotto. I'm from Global News. Is there somewhere we can go and speak in private?"

"Certainly, my office is through there. Go inside and make yourself comfortable. I'll be with you in a moment."

Dr. E. spent a few minutes with his students answering questions, giving advice or making referrals. He reminded the group that anyone requiring a protracted conversation needed an appointment. Then he rattled off a few available dates, told them to select one and write in their names on the calendar hanging on the outer door to his office, finally, retreating to his office and closing the door behind him.

Ron Eyota sat behind his desk, placed his hands palms down, flat on the desktop and asked. "At the risk of repeating myself, what is it I can do for you?"

"I hope this doesn't sound too strange," responded Suzanne. "I'm a colleague of David Anderson. He's spoken of you so many times, I almost feel like I know you."

"Yes, David and I have been close friends for many years. We haven't spoken since he called on my birthday…we're both busy, I guess…but I do follow him on the news. Say, where's he been for the past few nights, some secret investigation?"

Suzanne was hesitant to continue the conversation. She sat in silence peering across the desk, trying to decide whether she could trust this man who, after all, was a stranger to her.

"Doctor Eyota, David talks about you with such great respect and affection. He mentioned that you work at Notre Dame so I looked you up and jumped on a plane. Now that David no longer has his father around, I have a sense you're the person I need to see. What I'm about to tell you must be kept in the strictest confidence. Do you understand? It's about David."

"Yes, of course. Is David all right?"

"I'm not sure. You see, several days ago, David and I spent the day in the field, reporting from San Francisco. We were staying at David's father's house and when we returned home the FBI showed up. They told David some fantastic story about the attack and that it's all hush-hush. David promised to tell no one any of the details. The next thing we know our limo driver vanishes into thin air and the FBI can't find him either. David and I went to bed…to sleep I mean…the next morning I woke up and David was gone too. He left this note in the kitchen."

Suzanne opened her briefcase and removed a sheet of paper. Leaning over, she placed the stationary on Ron's desk, facing him.

The top read: From the Desk of Eric Anderson. Underneath there was a note in David's handwriting:

Hi Suzanne,

Last nite something strange happened. I can't explain it. I'm not even sure if I was awake or having some weird sort of dream. But, you know, it doesn't really matter. There is something I have to find out. Something I think I am supposed to discover but I don't know what it is or where to look. I'm leaving for a while. Sorry to be skipping out like this. Believe me, I wish things were different. Tell John I'll be in touch when I sort all this out.

David

Ron looked up at Suzanne with a puzzled expression. "This is not the David I know. Maybe something the FBI said?"

"I heard most of what was said," Suzanne countered. "They told him his father was dead and, of course, that was a shock, but he looked okay after they left. I don't think it could be that...I mean I don't really know. I just know I'm worried."

"Do you have any clue as to where David is now?"

"Yes, he's in his apartment. He sequestered himself and won't see or talk to anyone. John Stavos, our boss, spoke to him through the door. John said he was asked to leave and that David sounded angry. He won't speak to anyone else, including me. Not friends, not relatives. Basically, you're my last chance."

"Me? Why me?"

"David said you were his best friend. So will you help me...help David, that is?"

"Sure, I'll do whatever I can. Shall I call him?"

"No! He wouldn't answer the phone anyway. What I need you to do is come with me to New York City. I have a small jet standing by at South Bend Regional Airport. We could be in town in a few hours."

Ron Eyota sat a while considering the situation. His friend might be in trouble and need help; a mysterious and beautiful woman just invited him to fly to New York on a private plane; he had no idea what the circumstances were or what to expect. The whole thing sounded like the product of some mystery writer's imagination. Ron finally gave Suzanne his answer.

"Miss...David is my closest friend in the world. I need a little time to make arrangements here and throw some things into a suitcase. I can meet you at David's apartment the day after tomorrow, alright?"

"Are you sure you don't need a ride?"

"I have work I must attend to first..."

"That would be quite satisfactory. Thank you."

Suzanne retrieved David's note from the desk, turned, and exited the office without another word, not even a goodbye. She vanished in the same strange way she had appeared.

In generations past, immigrants living in the inner cities often gathered on the brick or concrete steps leading up to the front door of their brownstones. The 'stoop' was a central place for adults to socialize or it might be the centerpiece for a child's game. Ahmad and Sharif were standing on the stoop in front of a neglected three-story brownstone located in Patterson, New Jersey. The weather was gloomy and overcast. A slight drizzle was beginning to fall. Ahmad fumbled anxiously in his pocket for the key to the front entrance. He and Sharif hoped to get inside before the threatening downpour arrived.

The door was at least a century old. Its heavy, carved oak contained a framed window with thick beveled glass, allowing light to spill onto the broken black and white tiled floor of the foyer. The door's craftsmanship had been lost under layers of chipped paint carelessly applied for decades. Assorted names and graffiti were carved into the paint. Just below the name, 'Jazzi 22,' and above the door's lockset, a small symbol was engraved. It was the same symbol stamped on the key Ahmad used to enter the mosque in Denver.

Ahmad and Sharif climbed the once splendid staircase to the topmost apartment. It was sparsely furnished and configured in the old railroad car design of walk-through adjacent rooms. The front-most room had floor-to-ceiling, double hung, wood windows looking out at the crumbling brownstones across the street. Grey light leaned in from the windows. The light seemed as tired as the buildings, barely able to muster the energy to enter the room.

Ahmad dragged a rusted folding chair across the floor and sat in front of the windows looking down at the late afternoon activity on the street below. Sharif brought over an old folding table and a crate to sit on, placed a napkin on the table, and set out food the men brought with them from the corner delicatessen.

"What time will the tickets and passports arrive?" asked Ahmad, removing the wrist watch he was wearing, tapping it on the window sill - it had not kept proper time since his desert crossing.

"It should be soon," conjectured Sharif. "The flight leaves at ten. They know how much time we need."

"We should finish eating...then pray," suggested Ahmad. When we finish the 'Maghrib Salat,' I will repack so we are carrying only one small valise. I think it is best if we leave behind our backpacks."

"And the gun...we don't want to be caught with it at the airport," cautioned Sharif.

"Of course not, brother," Ahmad assured him, "I will give it to the messenger...he can find a good place to throw it somewhere it will never be found."

The men finished their meal and Ahmad disappeared into the middle room. By now, Sharif's admiration had become near reverence and he found Ahmad bowed to his knees, expressing his acceptance and respect for Allah's eternal power. Sharif, having performed his ablutions, did the same, as Ahmad prostrated himself and began to recite the rakah.

The room was dark when the men opened their eyes. The grey light of the late afternoon had acquiesced to the evening twilight's deepening gloom. Ahmad stood and went to find the light switch on the wall. It was a relic from the early days of the Edison Company, originally coexisting with the gas lamps of its time. He pressed each of the two buttons protruding out from the switch plate but nothing happened. He glanced up at the brass fixture nestled in the plaster medallion on the ceiling. Its light bulbs were blackened and covered with dust. Ahmad could see that their filaments had burnt out long ago. He looked in each of the rooms and found the same condition – a combination of neglect and despair.

The room in the rear of the building had a floor lamp standing in its corner. It wasn't so much standing as it was hiding. It was made of bronze with a claw foot base and a fluted stand that flared into a rose petal shape at the top. The matching floral print of the tattered lampshade was still faintly visible.

Ahmad picked up the lamp cord. The insulation was made of interwoven threads of silk, frayed in spots, but when Ahmad plugged it in the lamp lit up the room with a soft glow. He was staring at the floor lamp when Sharif came in carrying the backpacks.

"Is there something troubling you, my brother?" Sharif inquired.

"No, I was just thinking this lamp must have once been some-one's treasure, yet here it is now, discarded."

"Because it is old," intoned Sharif. "Americans have no use for anything old."

Sharif emptied the contents of the backpacks on the bed. The bed was narrow; just wide enough for a small adult, and the springs of its mattress had worn through the quilted padding. There were irregular brown stains soaked into its surface.

Ahmad unlocked the suitcase and set it open on the bed. He removed the magazine from the Beretta, retracted the slide and made sure the gun was unloaded. Releasing the disassembly latch, he pulled the gun apart, folding its parts and ammunition inside an old shirt, using its sleeves to secure the bundle. When Ahmad was satisfied the package was secure enough for the messenger to carry, he carefully folded the few articles of clothing the two men owned and neatly placed them in separate piles inside the suitcase.

Ahmad began transferring the contents of his backpack into the small suitcase, including the video camera he used on the rooftop in San Francisco. Finally, he would put his Qur'an and coded cards under the clothes in the luggage.

"Sharif, have you seen my Qur'an? I put it in this pocket."

"No...when did you see it last?"

"Here, I put it here!" Ahmad insisted, pointing repeatedly at the empty pocket on the front of his backpack. "You must help me find it."

Ahmad and Sharif scoured the apartment, then the staircase, to see if it had fallen out of the backpack. When they failed to find Ahmad's Qur'an, they searched outside around the building and along the street with no success. Finally, they returned to the apartment, damp from the light rain.

Sharif, trying to reconstruct the steps of their journey, questioned Ahmad. "Could it be you left it behind in the car, or on the train?"

"No!"

"Did you pray with it at the mosque in Denver?"

"No, no!"

"When did you see it last?"

"I last saw it when I put it in..."

A memory flashed across Ahmad's mind like a film projected inside his forehead. He saw the shimmering sunlight in a doorway and the silhouette of a woman beyond. He remembered confusion, a collision, a police van, a woman screaming at him. Looking down at the scab healing on his arm, he knew exactly where he lost the book.

Sharif could see panic on Ahmad's face and wondered what was wrong. He did not know the prayer book held cards with instructions Ahmad needed and was unaware certain passages marked in Ahmad's Qur'an were the decryption keys to decode the cards.

"Brother, I would be most honored if you would take my Qur'an."

Ahmad placed a hand on his companion's shoulder; he was beginning to see Sharif as a younger brother.

"You are most generous but my Qur'an has a…personal meaning for me. I must get a replacement."

Ahmad went into the crumbling kitchen, found a pencil and a piece of yellowing paper, and wrote a note in Arabic which read:

My dearest uncle,
I am so sorry but I have misplaced your kind invitation. I left it behind while visiting the city. Would you, please, ask my cousin to deliver a copy to me when I arrive home?
Your devoted nephew

As he was returning to the front room a knock on the door startled him. "Who is it?" Ahmad shouted through the entranceway.

"It is 'Abdu'l-Azim."

Sharif nodded at Ahmad and said. "It's the messenger."

Ahmad opened the door for the messenger who was tall and wiry and badly in need of a bath. He handed Ahmad tickets, passports and other identification documents. Ahmad inspected each one and, finding them impeccable, handed a set to Sharif. Without speaking, the trio went downstairs where a white Toyota with rusted fenders and doors was waiting at the curb.

"I've been instructed to drive you to the airport," 'Abdu'l-Azim said.

Sharif climbed into the rear seat behind the driver and Ahmad slid in beside him. As they drove away, Ahmad opened one of the backpacks and removed the bundled shirt, placing it on the front passenger seat. He placed the empty packs alongside the bundle.

He leaned over the seat and said, "Listen carefully, brother. Inside this shirt is a gun. Get rid of it for me. It can never be found. The same for the backpacks…they must never be seen again. Do you understand this?"

"Yes, Sidi," the driver assured him.

"Good. Now the most important thing…I am placing a paper in your top pocket. The message on it must be delivered tonight. Do you understand this?"

"Yes, Sidi."

Ahmad retrieved the note he wrote to his 'uncle' and put it in the breast pocket of the man's threadbare jacket. As he did so, he explained the details of the missing items to 'Abdu'l-Azim. Then he sat back and, watching the cars go by on the highway, felt genuinely glad to be leaving America.

They arrived at the airport with time to spare. A surprising calm enveloped Ahmad as he stood in line at Newark International Airport waiting to board the flight to Paris. Ahmad's arms were crossed, his dark eyes alert, as he gazed over the crowd. Approaching the security checkpoint, he began to rock back and forth, slowly chewing on a fingernail – gestures only a seasoned behavioral profiler might notice.

After a thorough search of his meager baggage, a check of g overnment watch lists, and a second interrogation with more search-ing questions, Ahmad was sent on his way. He silently repeated "God is Great" in perfect Arabic, grateful to pass through a rigorous securi-ty check with nothing more than looks of disgust on the faces of the officers who could not, legally, find any reason to hold the Iranian national. Through it all, Ahmad remained calm and disinterested.

His calm was surprising, not only because of who he was and what he was planning to do once he reached Paris, but also, as a rule, he was terrified of flying. Ahmad had formed the, not uncommon, notion that an airplane was as delicate and capricious as a soap bubble flying from the tip of a child's wand on a warm summer's day seconds away from its fatal pop.

Passing the smiling stewardess, Ahmad and Sharif boarded the plane for Paris. As the plane ascended, Ahmad settled his gaze out the window. The moon had risen and he could not tell the snaking highways below from the earth's rivers and streams. Aware as he was of their differences - one manmade, chiseled and ground out with sweat and fumes; the other, nature's grinding artistry – Ahmad perceived that it all seemed as one.

Then, at once, the vision was gone as the plane climbed into the thick cover of the clouds, only to emerge into the dazzling star-filled night with the thick blanket of fluff below. It seemed such a serene and heavenly place and he wished he could leave the plane and walk around out there in the clouds.

The vision brought to mind a happier time in his boyhood, before he was sent to school in Tehran. He had befriended an old spiritual master whom Ahmad was counseled to avoid. The man was considered unclean and, because he was not Muslim, suffered imprisonment and torture in his youth. Yet, he bore the scars on his body with joy. Ahmad could not understand why he should avoid such a gentle and engaging neighbor and stole tiny moments with the wise old man.

One hot and sunny afternoon, Ahmad and the old man stopped to rest by the side of the lane. Ahmad mentioned the mullah in the mosque that morning who had painted a vivid portrait for the men present, of the glory in heaven awaiting true believers, with the happy faithful enjoying the lavish luxury of their eternal reward.

"Heaven is not a place that can be imagined, my child," whispered the old sage with a chuckle. "It is sanctified above time and place. The spiritual worlds, my young friend, cannot be described in human words any more than an infant in his mother's womb can describe, or even imagine, the world into which it will be born."

Then the old man grabbed Ahmad's knee, slowly pushing himself off the ground, ruffled the boy's hair, and bade him a blessed day. The memory faded with the old man strolling away, the hem of his abba flapping gently in the soft breeze.

As the plane headed across the Atlantic, Ahmad wanted to sleep, but his seat stubbornly refused to tilt back more than a few degrees. In spite of his discomfort, Ahmad closed his eyes and started thinking about Clichy-sous-Bois, a suburb northeast of the city center where he had been living for nearly two years. He knew Paris well and, with his memories still thick, pictured himself and his beloved Sholeh, strolling along the Rue Mouffetard just after sunrise, shopping for food at the open-air market. Holding tightly to this memory, he finally nodded off.

The blackness surrounding Brian Saunders penetrated his head like spikes being driven into his skull. He was sure he would smother, inhaling and exhaling the same air over and over, feeling the oxygen deplete with each breath, his hair wet and matted, droplets of sweat hanging from his nose and chin, he knew he must will himself to slow his anxious breathing and conserve what little oxygen remained. Handcuffs bound his wrists together so tightly his hands felt numb and heavy, like bloated sacks of wet sand. So what, he thought, I'll be dead soon enough.

He tried to plan how he might escape but could not think past the pain. Regret was useless, offering little distraction. He figured death would be a portal to something better. On the other hand, maybe he would be facing something much worse, and this prospect made his numb hands tremble.

A blinding instant later, there was light and air and the captive started panting. Saunders craned his neck to catch sight of the men who had just removed the black velour hood covering his head. His captors stood in darkened corners he could not see. The only illumination came from a small naked spotlight placed directly above his head.

He squinted, trying to see past the slim cone of light emanating from the overhead lamp. Saunders could faintly discern three figures sitting behind a long table about twenty feet in front of him. Their identities were cloaked by the semi-darkness in the room. They were discussing something urgent, and he knew when they turned their attention to him, it wouldn't be a good thing. Great, the fun is about to begin, he thought, with a mixture of dread and disdain.

At last, a deep baritone voice with an accent Saunders couldn't quite place, addressed him. "Well, Mr. Saunders, you haven't quite distinguished yourself on this assignment, have you?"

"I wasn't done!" Saunders pleaded. "The FBI showed up. It was a temporary setback. I would've gotten...it would've gotten done with one more day...I swear it!"

"We've spent a good deal of resources to execute this plan, Mr. Saunders," scolded the booming voice. "You were ordered to discover the whereabouts of our property and assassinate David Anderson the night he arrived in San Francisco."

"Look, I had the team at the San Mateo Bridge," Saunders implored, shaking now. "It was supposed to look like another terror attack...that's what you said...make it look like an attack. The fucking guy decided to bag the hotel and stay in Walnut-fuckin'-Creek."

"Why then, didn't you reposition your team?"

"I tried...so help me...I tried! The son of a bitch wouldn't let me use my phone. He hands me a paper and says go north, no phone calls."

"You were armed, weren't you?"

"Yeah, sure...but this guy...there's something with this guy...anyway, he's with this stuck-up bitch who follows him around like a fuckin' puppy. What was I suppose to do, kill 'em both? No one told me about her! That's an extra charge."

"What was that?" The three men looked at one another in disbelief.

Saunders ignored the question. "I walked outside his house hoping the bastard would follow but he stayed inside...I even offered to take him over to the local police station to look at secret reports and he wouldn't budge. You give me one more chance and I'll go shoot that motherfucker right now...tonight."

"We have made alternative plans, Mr. Saunders. You are no longer any use to us."

At that moment, someone entered and stood behind the men seated at the table. He interrupted the interrogation, explaining there were further details concerning the matter of 'their property'. Brian Saunders strained to listen.

"Well, what have you learned?" asked one of the men. His voice was deep; the tone low and menacing.

"Our nephew lost his Qur'an in the Presidio Heights district of the city," replied the man. "He ran into a woman and, apparently, dropped it in the confusion of the ongoing police activity. The location and building is known and the woman is described as average with wavy brown hair. We assume she may have retrieved it, since it wasn't to be found by the man we sent to recover it."

"And his instructions?"

"All six cards were in the book, they are missing as well. Our nephew requires a replacement."

The group huddled together, proceeding with their confidential deliberations but Saunders was able to hear snippets of the conversation and could tell they were more than a little agitated.

"Well, there's nothing to be concerned with," concluded one of the men. "As long as the items are replaced...they are, after all, unreadable."

"Yes, I concur...let's carry on and forget it," agreed another. "Why waste further resources."

"Because the lock is with the key!" vituperated the man that had been questioning Saunders. "We cannot accept the risk of these being discovered together. We must send someone to recover the items!"

The debate raged on as Saunders began speculating who would prevail. He took notice of each argument and rejoinder, and bet with himself on the outcome. It was a welcome diversion from what was about to happen.

Suddenly, in a transient flash of thought, Brian Saunders had the idea of a lifetime; what some might refer to as a moment of clarity. It started to germinate until it had become the biggest scheme he had ever concocted. Like magic, a puzzle was solved. Facts fell neatly into place and a straight and logical line of reasoning was born. Brian Saunders liked this feeling very much!

"Yo...hey...hey, can I get some attention here," Saunders shouted at the men, interrupting the debate. "I've got yer answer, pal."

"Mr. Saunders, I am surprised you want to call attention to yourself and your pathetic record of underachievement," said his inquisitor.

"Well…just maybe I've got a solution to your little dilemma."

"You, Mr. Saunders?" replied the baritone with more than a hint of incredulity and ridicule.

"Go ahead…laugh pal…laugh all you want…but you lost a little brown bookie with a strap that holds it closed, right? And some plastic cards with a yellow squiggly thing on one side…right? Just maybe I know where all this stuff is."

"Go on," uttered the baritone.

He had their attention now and Saunders took his best and final shot.

"Look, Anderson and that bitch-on-wheels woman he works with, met up with this chick at a Mexican place a cuppla days ago. When they come out, this chick gets in the limo and Anderson says to drive her home. I got a real good look at her…real good…nice lookin'…she had curly brown hair, just like the man said. Anderson gets out of the car and walks her to the door of her crib. Next thing I know, Anderson is orderin' me to bring him the junk she forgot in the car from off the back seat. I grab her stuff and bring it over…that's when I get a good look at everything; sounds exactly like what you're describing,' cards and all. Look! If I had killed the bastard on time, you guys wouldn't have a clue where the stuff ya lookin' for went."

A moment passed between Saunders and the man he was addressing. It was, probably, the most anxiety he had ever experienced. A sweat broke out on his forehead and began to run down his face.

"Are you offering to recover our lost items, Mr. Saunders?"

"Damn right! I'm thinkin' this chick found your stuff and called Anderson…probably wanted to get herself on TV…everyone wants to get on the fuckin' tube…right? I'm also thinkin' Anderson turned her down and dropped her off to be nice. I saw the dumb bastard give her all your crap back. I know where she lives…it ain't where ya think. You give me a chance and I'll go getchya stuff and I won't leave any witnesses, neither. And I'll take care of that fuckin' guy, Anderson, too. Well…is it a deal?"

For a third time the men fell into a hushed deliberation. The man with the baritone voice finally spoke.

"All right, Mr. Saunders. We accept your offer on the condition that you work with the team we assign and follow instructions this time. If you complete this assignment, we will pay you the original fee…plus a bonus. On the other hand, if you fail…well…you know the consequences. Are these terms satisfactory?"

"You bet…I'm in!"

"For your sake, Mr. Saunders, let's hope so. Release him."

The grey silhouettes without faces or identities, the men with the power of life or death over Brian Saunders, stood and quietly exited the room.

An instant later, everything went black and again the air was stale. Inside the velour hood time and feeling were frozen. The only thing Saunders could perceive was the vague sensation of motion and then relief as the cuffs were removed and the blood returned to his hands.

Standing alone at daybreak, in the crisp morning air, at the intersection of Lexington and 20th Street, Saunders pulled off the hood and watched as his captor's car drove away, turned the corner and vanished. He started to walk along the deserted road and, thinking he heard voices, spun around but there was no one in sight. Later on, something touched his shoulder but when he turned again, there was no one on the street.

Feeling haunted and watched Saunders moved along the road towards home. It was a road whose street sign read 'last chance'.

Inside his studio apartment, rented from a landlord of questionable reputation who specialized in snapping up foreclosures, Saunders pushed aside the clothes in the room's only closet. Behind a false wall, the assassin had stashed a large sum of cash together with an assortment of passports and drivers licenses bearing new identities. With them were hidden a cache of weapons and a theatrical makeup kit, so his movements could not be tracked by facial recognition cameras at airports and secure sites. He threw the items into an open valise lying on the floor, covered them with the garments hanging in his closet, and set off to find David Anderson.

MASQUERADE

The yellow taxi negotiated its way through the twenty-four hour congestion at New York City's Midtown Tunnel; its insolent driver forcing the cab into the packed line of crawling cars, practically daring the other drivers to ram him. He moved from one lane to another, cursing and gesticulating obscenities at the surrounding traffic, head swiveling side to side, trying to win an extra inch of pavement or, perhaps, an extra minute of precious time to spend elsewhere hustling for other fares. The driver's frenetic attempt was useless; traffic was delayed at all crossings into Manhattan since the random vehicle searches resumed in the immediate aftermath of the West Coast attack.

Ron Eyota sat comfortably in the back of the cab, window open, allowing the warm spring air to wash over his face, reading the billboard advertisements that lined the Long Island Expressway. He was genuinely enjoying a sunny day in the shadow of New York City's skyline. Maintaining his naturally quiet serenity, a Navajo trait developed over centuries and born of the struggle for survival, Ron gracefully accepted the events unfolding around him.

In the perfect display of irony, the cars in front and behind his taxicab were pulled over for a random inspection. The professor's eyes widened in surprise when both drivers jumped out of their autos and began fulminating at the police officers, squandering even more precious time by delaying the inevitable.

The tedious trip from the airport, long and boring, in typical barely-moving Long Island traffic, was amplified by the anticipation of seeing his closest friend. When the taxi finally stopped up-town, on Fifth Avenue, pulling alongside a building with a hunter green awning that extended out to the curb, Ron Eyota took hold of a single piece of luggage, paid the driver and went inside, pausing at the doorman's desk.

"Good morning, sir. Whom do you wish to visit?"

"I am looking for David Anderson."

"And whom shall I say is calling?"

"Tell him, no wait...tell him Da-he-tih-hi is here...he'll know!"

Somewhat ill at ease with the pronunciation of Ron's sobriquet, the doorman reluctantly called, replaced the phone in its cradle and announced, "Mr. Anderson is pleased to welcome you sir...any elevator...top floor."

David, casually dressed, shirttails out, greeted his friend in the hallway and, after bonding for a second as close friends who have been out of touch will do, he invited Ron inside.

Ron walked through the vestibule and into a spacious and well-appointed living room. Its most prominent feature was the line of Roman arched windows that offered a panorama of Central Park. In the center of the room were two sofas and a coffee table made with a wrought iron base and round polished glass top. On it sat a crystal bowl half filled with the smoothly polished turquoise stones Ron gave to the newsman as a gift when he landed the anchor spot.

"What's your pleasure?" David asked.

"That coffee smells good...how about a cup? Black, one sugar."

"I know," David said.

David returned with two ceramic mugs filled with a pungent coffee; a variety he had purchased while on assignment in Kona, a region on the Big Island of Hawaii. Exotic coffees were one of the few luxuries David reveled in and he had an impressive collection of roasts from a diverse range of faraway locations. He handed a cup to Ron and reclined against an overstuffed pillow on one of the leather sofas that circled the table. "So what brings you into town? By the name you gave reception, I'm guessing this is about something special."

Ron had not looked forward to this moment, yet he knew it would come and imagined any attempt to spare David's feelings might be construed as lying, or even worse, whinging, so he spoke plainly.

"This is a bit awkward, David, but I came at Suzanne Biasotto's request! She is worried that you have been too distraught to work." With emotion rising in his voice, he continued, "You know how very sorry I am over the loss of your father, David. Eric was...well, he was my role model, mentor, and friend...you know how much I'll miss him."

David appreciated his friend's forthrightness and compassion. Thanking Ron, he abruptly asked in disbelief, "How did she get a hold of you?"

"She came to South Bend...to the university, and told me about what happened...at least what she knew. Have you noticed she cares about you, David...very much! I read the note you left behind," Ron added, "I understand why it disturbed her."

"Ron," David said, his face becoming mildly flushed with embarrassment, "I'm sorry you came all this way. I just needed some time alone, that's all."

"When is the funeral?"

"Soon, I'll organize it soon."

"Is that all?" Ron asked with a note of apprehension.

Ron traveled halfway across the country, motivated by an enduring friendship, and David knew he was owed an explanation.

"Basically," David began, "the FBI came to my father's house with this rather quixotic tale about the attack. I guess their story upset me and I had a...strange dream...sort of a vision, which really threw me. I rushed back here trying to sort things out…to deal with the hurt. There was no goddamn way I could sit at that anchor desk anymore and act like I am not devastated by this. I'm getting better, now…I think."

Ron looked at his lifelong friend with concern. He had rarely seen David looking so grave. Finally, he spoke, "You seem pretty edgy and you're usually a rock."

David took a long breath in and then let it out with a deep sigh. He was stalling and Ron knew it. He couldn't keep his thoughts to himself much longer. Ron would hound them out of him. Actually, the newsman was relieved that there was, finally, someone close he could confide in about this; it made life infinitely more bearable.

"Ron, either I had a nervous breakdown or I'm stark, raving bonkers…maybe from the stress of the last few days." David gave his friend a weak smile.

"I had this crazy dream…like I said, maybe a vision…I don't know. Tell me I'm not nuts," David pleaded. "Maybe I was hallucinating, maybe I've finally lost it. You know about these things, Ron, I need your help."

"Whoa! Slow down and tell me what happened."

There it was, the strong friend who David had come to know as a brother, this man who, now that his father was gone, was his most trusted confidant. David began to tell Ron what happened – the dream, his father's cryptic message, how vivid it was, and how different it had been from any dream or experience he ever had before. When finished, he looked at Ron plaintively, waiting for him to interpret that night so he could put to rights the event and feel okay again.

"I don't think you are crazy at all. You were simply given a great gift few ever receive. There is wisdom in these experiences that are, somehow, different from our dreams. I have to say, I think it's apparent that Eric was foreshadowing some future event."

Shaking his head, David sighed, "I wish I could believe you."

"Just honor your father," counseled Ron, "by following his message. Begin your life with a new vision and hope, and get busy finding this 'eastern star.'"

David finally grinned. It was a wide grin that Ron could tell was genuine relief. "Thanks for the talk, but what now?"

"Follow your destiny, you have no other choice."

"I don't believe in predetermined events. We always have a choice."

"Then explain how you chose to go from obscure reporter to the anchor spot in a global newscast."

"Coincidence, I guess."

"There's no such thing. A coincidence is only a coincidence until all the facts are known!"

"How would you explain it then?" David asked, feeling a bit better now, debating his old friend. The verbal sparring took his mind off his grief and brought a sense of normalcy back into his life.

"Downward causation...what some of us call 'Divine Providence'. I was hoping your marvelous Aristotelian logic, free of emotion, would have told you that your father's message might, in fact, be your destiny."

"Don't you believe it," exclaimed David. "It was only a bad dream which likely started with that ludicrous FBI report...and that ridiculous assertion about some oddball illogical paradox. I'm thinking, they probably botched the investigation, hence the weird account."

"The real paradox of our lives," Ron said, "is that the things we most want are the things we most fear."

Before David could answer, the intercom chimed. He pressed the call button on the remote control sitting on the table.

"Mr. Anderson," the doorman announced, "there's a Ms. Biasotto here to see you."

"Right...send her up...please."

"Suzanne's here," David said, noticing Ron's anticipation as he unconsciously shifted back and forth several times.

"Mind if I ask a personal question?"

"Not at all"

"I'm not prying but...anything...you know...between you two?"

"Maybe, on some subtle level," David answered. "But you know the drill...colleagues, professional ethics, decorum...hold on, let me get the door."

Suzanne entered the room with her usual effervescence. She was wearing a cream colored suit and her grooming was refined and painstaking. Ron observed that it was the same classic fitted jacket and skirt style she'd worn before and that it very much suited her personality and slender form. She walked up to Ron and, extending her hand, said, "Thank you for coming, professor."

"You're welcome…just call me 'Ron'."

David splashed onto the sofa. "What's up?" he asked.

"You seem a lot better," Suzanne said. "Has Ron performed his magic? Can I tell John you'll be on air tonight?"

Crossing his eyes, the newsman joked, "You mean, is David still crazy?"

"That's not what I meant, at all," exclaimed Suzanne with a petulant expression. "I've been genuinely worried about you!"

"I know…I know," David said, shooting Ron a glance from under arched eyebrows. "Call John and tell him I'll be in."

"Cool! John will be relieved. Are you sure you're ready? You know that banking conference in Paris is coming up…we thought you might miss it."

"Nope, I'm going."

"Sweet!" Turning towards Ron, Suzanne said, "I can't thank you enough! I guess David explained the note, the FBI agents, and Merilee Brunswick."

"Who is Merilee Brunswick?" Ron asked.

"Didn't David tell you about Merilee and the book?"

"No…I didn't get a chance," David said.

"May I?" Suzanne asked David.

"Why not," David replied with a shrug.

Suzanne told Ron the entire story, beginning from Merilee's telephone call to the assignment desk, through to their meeting and departure. Ron asked her to repeat parts of the story, several times, posing questions to clarify the details. As Suzanne was wrapping up their encounter, David walked over to the bookcase, retrieved a book bound in exotic leather containing five small laminated cards, and handed them to Ron. He examined each item with great care and interest.

"David thought you would be able to interpret these," Suzanne explained.

"I can interpret them," Ron assured her, "but the question is whether I can decode them."

"I'm not sure what you mean."

"Why don't we start with the contents?" David suggested. "Then we can move on from there."

"Very well," Ron agreed. "This is a Qur'an...it's in the Arabic language, which is consistent with Islamic law and traditions. There isn't anything unduly alarming about it except...several passages throughout the text are marked. Normally, when a person marks a book in this way they are highlighting a favorite prayer or a passage with some special meaning. The phrases marked here are quite common."

"Then why mark them?" Suzanne asked.

"That's the million dollar question, isn't it?" replied Ron.

"And the cards?" David inquired.

"They appear to be commonplace. They are printed in Farsi. Here, if you look closely you can see the difference. Each lists one article of faith or tenet of Islam." Ron shuffled through the cards reading them, one by one. "One God, angels of God, scriptures of God, prophets of God, supremacy of God's will...that's odd, judgment day is missing."

"Maybe it was lost," Suzanne said.

"You think so?" Ron asked.

"I'm just saying...in all the confusion, anything could happen...couldn't it?"

"I suppose. Hey, David, do you recall this gold mark?"

"Yep. By the way, what did you find out about it?"

"Nothing. I never found time to pursue it. When I got back, Stateside, I sent out pictures of it to universities, libraries and intelligence agencies requesting information. I received one response to my inquiries but by that time I was heading for my post at Notre Dame. Sorry I dropped the ball. Hmmm, do you remember an old news story...years ago...something about messages hidden in Qur'ans... Afghanistan I think...wasn't it?"

"I remember. What about it?"

"Well, there are six highlighted passages in this Qur'an. Look here, for example. In Surih 112 there is the Tafsir of Surat Al-Ikhlas. In this passage, it says, 'He is Allah, One. He begets not, nor was He begotten. And there is none compatible to Him.' It ties back to the article of faith printed on this card. I'm thinking this isn't a random coincidence. There must be another card. I wonder what was on it...if there is a missing card."

David knew his friend well enough to suppose that Ron suspected the book and cards were parts of a code, so he asked," Do you know what the message says?"

"No, I'm not an expert in cryptography. In any case, the only clue we have to the messages' origin is the gold symbol on the front of the cards. That's the place to begin looking."

Suzanne appeared confused, and holding her hands perpendicular to form the letter 'T' shouted, "Time out! What's going on here...what are you guys talking about?"

"David," Ron suggested, "maybe we should back-brief her."

"There," Suzanne pleaded, "that's what I mean...back-brief; cryptography! Who talks that way?"

"Suzanne, sit down and relax," David began. "It's simple, really...during my travels, when I was just starting out...I occasionally provided certain information to help our government."

"You were a spy?"

"Nothing so glamorous, I simply conveyed local events to an analyst for review and...and after that, I don't really know."

"And I'm the analyst," Ron admitted.

"So you're both spies!"

"NO!" they shouted in unison.

Suzanne wasn't buying it. She still looked anxious so David decided to share some details, recounting how he and Ron met at the university and their travels overseas. He even explained what happened the night Eric appeared.

"So you understand why I was upset and left," David concluded. "Promise me, you will never repeat this to anyone."

Suzanne hesitated, staring blankly into space. She murmured, "Is there anything else about you I should know?"

"I went skinny dipping once," David joked, "at the senior frolic." Then he asked again, "Do you promise?"

"Yes!" she insisted.

"Listen guys," said Ron. "I don't want to interrupt...whatever...but I think we have some things of interest to discuss...like this golden knot...or whatever it is."

"You're right," David agreed. "Suzanne?"

"Sure," she replied. The far-off look was still in her eyes.

"Ron," David said. "You're right, my friend. It's about time we solve this, it's been hanging out there a long time."

"Yes, since your sojourn in the Middle East when you sent me a picture of the symbol. As soon as I received it, I sent out several queries. I found one lone expert in this sort of thing willing to help. His name is Cardinal Alberto Esposito. He is the only person who acknowledged my queries. He asked for additional information so I also sent the papyrus scroll you sent me from Tehran...remember?"

"Yes, the one from the Shaykh. What was on it, anyway?"

"I don't know. It looked so fragile, I was concerned I might damage it...never opened it up. I had it sealed in a Lucite tube filled with argon gas."

Ron noticed the puzzled look on his friend's face.

"It's an inert gas we use to preserve old manuscripts. Once I landed at the university, I was so busy, I forgot about the whole thing. But, at least, it's a place to start."

"A cardinal?" Suzanne asked surprised.

"Yes, the archivist and librarian cardinal of the Archivum Secretum Apostolicum Vaticanum. It's the Vatican's secret archives. You'd be quite astounded at the remarkable collection of documents and research that's stored there. I met him at Sapienza, the University of Rome, while studying. He was a good friend and mentor to me."

"Is he still in Rome?"

"Last I heard. David, may I use your PC to send an e-mail? Perhaps we can get in touch with the Cardinal today."

While Ron went off to David's library to contact the good Cardinal Esposito, Suzanne called John Stavos and happily reported that David would be back at the anchor desk that night. She and John agreed to rearrange the schedule, postponing the editorial meeting till after lunch. Paging through the contact list on her cell phone, she called key members of the news staff, checking on the content and progress of the various news stories slated for that evening's broadcast. Meanwhile, David went off to the bedroom to dress for work.

About a half hour later, Ron found David and Suzanne sitting at a wrought iron table out on the balcony, enjoying some fresh air and the sounds of the city rising from the street below. The area had been pressed into service as a provisional conference room and there were papers scattered all about. Suzanne had just finished updating David on Global's news coverage for the past few days and their discussion had turned to an earnest review of facts from the attack. They stopped mid-sentence when they noticed Ron standing there, holding a sheet of paper.

"Oh, don't let me interrupt," Ron offered.

"Actually, Ron, what we were talking about might tie in to all that's going on. Take a seat and I'll explain. Any luck with the Cardinal?"

Ron let the paper in his hand float to the table. It landed in front of David. The e-mail response came from a priest who identified himself as the Cardinal's assistant. It read:

> Dear Professor, It is with deep sadness I must inform you, Cardinal Esposito passed away last month. His replacement, Cardinal Oriastro, is not available at this time. We ask your kind indulgence but his Eminence is en route to Rome from Haifa, Israel. If you cable the Carmelite Monastery, you might catch him there.
> Sincerely Yours in Christ,
> RR. Anchel Estalla

"Well, there goes that lead," Suzanne shrugged. "Sorry about your friend."

"Thanks," Ron said. "Maybe we can still get an answer, though, if we reach out to the new Cardinal. I read an article about a Carmelite Friar who recently unearthed an Essene scroll during renovation on the Cave of Elijah, or something. Oriastro must have gone to retrieve it. Oriastro...hmmm, by the way, anyone speak Italian?"

"Quite well, in fact," Suzanne said with a touch of pride. "It's a family thing."

"The name, Oriastro, what does it mean...translated to English?"

"Oriastro is Oriastro," Suzanne replied plainly. "It's just a name."

"I see," Ron said. Ron looked down at his feet, tapping his knee with a spoon he picked up from the table.

Ron's brooding, downcast stare provoked Suzanne to think a little deeper, prompting her to add, "I suppose you might consider that a name can be made from fragments of common words. I don't know…err…oriente and astro. How's that? Put them together and, presto…Oriastro."

"And what would each word mean?" Ron asked, encouraged.

"'Oriente' means 'east' and 'astro' means 'star', so 'eastern star'… I would think."

Paraphrasing David's father, Ron intoned, "'Your journey is just beginning, look east and find the star.' Well David, it seems you have an answer."

"David, you look dubious," Suzanne said.

"I think there is a logical answer to all of this." David was adamant. He was not ready to concede to Ron's mystical interpretation. "Maybe, I saw his name on a news wire, or something, and it somehow ended up in my dream."

"Are you certain?" Ron asked.

"Funny, you should say that. When I was a kid my mother used to challenge me to solve riddles. It was a game we played. The very last one…when she was sick…just a few days before she died, went something like: 'The only thing for certain is nothing is certain; if this is true it must also be false.'"

The newsman let the solemnity of the moment hang in the air for a minute, then motioning to his friends said, "Let's get to the newsroom…I need to be certain about something."

Ahmad could feel only relief as he and Sharif stepped off the plane at Charles DeGaulle Airport in Paris. The flight across the Atlantic was uncomfortable but everything was proceeding with the smoothness of a perfectly tuned grand piano. With Canadian passports from French Québec, they moved through immigration and customs unchallenged. It was just past eleven o'clock in the morning, they had no checked luggage, just one carry-on, and were happy to avoid the long wait at the baggage claim carousel. Instead, they proceeded directly through Immigration and Customs.

On the way out of the airport terminal, Ahmad stopped into a shop in the mall that sold a variety of travel gear. He picked out the cheapest backpack he could find, paid the cashier, and stopped at a small café and sat down with his companion. While they sipped coffees, Ahmad opened the small piece of luggage and transferred everything belonging to him, including the items the messenger brought him, into the new backpack. He handed the half-empty suitcase to Sharif, finished his coffee and the two men left to find the nearest taxi station; each man reserving a separate cab.

Ahmad was glad to be out in the open again. The cool air felt good on his face. The excitement that is always Paris lingered in the crisp morning air, mingling with the omnipresent tinge of jet fuel.

Hopping into the taxi, whose door was held open for him by the concierge, he bid the driver, 'bonjour,' and handed him a crumpled piece of paper upon which was printed an address. It directed the driver to one of the poor, high-rise, housing projects known as the city's HLM, an acronym for 'Habitation à Loyer Modéré'. It was Paris' rent-controlled section, located in the Clichy-sous-Bois banlieue, east-northeast of the city center. Sholeh's parents resided high in a building, deep inside the complex. Ahmad would visit them as his first order of business in France. The visit was intended as, not only, a sign of deep respect but to make a much-needed request.

The suburb, mainly inhabited by North African and Arabic Muslims, was the epicenter of riots that began in autumn a few years earlier. Within a few days, the riots had escalated and hundreds of cars on the streets, along with several public buildings, had been incinerated in the nightly raids. The riots soon spread to all fifteen of the large *aires urbaines* in France.

The unrest was triggered by the death of two Muslim youths, electrocuted in a power substation when they tried to hide from police, whom, they believed, were intent on interrogating them for a neighborhood burglary.

Their deaths set off a series of violent protests and nightly riots as preexisting tensions ignited. The French Government's official stance was that the source of the conflict lay between the business community and the resident Muslim youth, tired of being treated as outcasts in their own country, tired of high unemployment rates, and tired of constant isolation.

Leaning forward, Ahmad asked the cabdriver, "Do you know where this is?"

"Oh, but of course, monsieur," replied the proud driver. "How could I claim to be a true professional if I do not know Paris? Oui? I know every street in the city and beyond. I must say, I get few calls for this section of the city; not since the President declared it a 'no-go zone' after the riots. Taxis stopped going there. Me? I couldn't care less. I go where my customers need to go."

Ahmad fell into silence and did not reply, tacitly letting the cab driver know he was not interested, even in the slightest bit, in small talk. The cabbie respected his passenger's wishes having learned, from years of experience, that there are different kinds of riders, all of whom could be put into their own distinct class.

There are those passengers who get into the cab chattering away, a free-association diatribe of their journeys and their business that continues, virtually non-stop, even as they are handing him their money and getting out of the cab. Only as he pulls away, do they hurriedly slam the door shut, still waving and yelling, "Au revoir."

There are also the riders who are rather shy but are ardently waiting for him to initiate a conversation, not wanting to be rude or appear unfriendly. He knows them because, even though they do not speak, when he glances in the rearview mirror, they are staring at the back of his head, anxiously awaiting the driver's first sentence. Once a conversation starts, and it doesn't always, depending on his mood and whether he likes their looks, the passengers are often quite engaging and delightful people with whom to converse. These are the foreigners that come from all over the world to see or do business in his city. They are curious to know everything he has to share, and once he begins, they have endless questions, mostly about where to find the best food, a foolish question in Paris. "Everywhere is good," he tells them. These passengers sometimes give him real enjoyment, as they are genuinely interested in his life, and he in turn, theirs; so that at the end of the ride, he has a distinctly good feeling that he made a friend.

Then there are passengers he calls 'the self-important'; people who have only business on their minds. They talk on cell phones or tap out messages to their colleagues. They do not greet him; just give him an address, immediately resuming their business. They could be from anywhere and their business is not to be interrupted.

This is why Jacques loved his job. It wasn't the money, of which he made quite a good living; it was more because these intermittent and fleeting relationships sometimes would truly enliven and enrich his life. He considered the little yellow cab to be a rolling university. At supper he would share, with his wife and children, endless stories about his passengers.

But there were, of course, people like Ahmad. Jacques thought that, unless you were clueless, you had to know they wanted to be left alone, to cogitate in the thick soup of their own dark thoughts. These riders were polite but distant. Jacques did not disturb such men or women. He knew they were somewhere else - tired, sad, irritated, or just plain preoccupied. Ahmad said not another word for the rest of the journey and Jacques, respecting the silence, turned on the radio and proceeded on his way.

As the taxi drove along, Ahmad watched the city rolling by and thought about the place and the memories to which he was returning. Predominant among these memories were thoughts of his beloved Sholeh. She was the reason he was originally sent to Paris. Ahmad had meant to stay in Tehran and continue his studies. He intended to obtain a doctorate in Islamic law and join the Imams in administration of their Faith. But his parents were worried that he, being of age, had shown no interest in beginning a family.

One evening after dinner, while visiting the family home in Shiraz, his father told him that he was set to leave for France. Ahmad sat astounded as his father explained that he would be leaving Iran in one month and flying to Europe. There, he would meet a young woman whom his parents hoped would become his wife.

"Surely, you are joking, father!" exclaimed the distraught student. "I cannot leave Iran. I am scheduled to begin my law studies next week."

"The law will be there when you return with your new bride, my son," cajoled Ahmad's father.

"But, I have enrolled in the course." Ahmad replied in distress.

"You can reapply next year, Ahmad," interrupted his mother.

"I will not go. I cannot go," insisted Ahmad.

"You can go, and you will, my son," his father assured him, maintaining a calm that infuriated Ahmad. "Your mother and I have discussed this at length. You are ready to assume the responsibilities of marriage."

"I am ready for nothing," Ahmad said, his voice rising again. "I will not go."

"I am afraid that you will," his father said. "It is your sacred duty as my son. You will not shame us with this disgraceful refusal. You will honor the family and you will go to Paris and receive your bride, or you will forfeit your place in this family."

"But..." Ahmad tried to say.

"No, Ahmad, it is enough! We have given our word. This girl is from a well-known and respected family. She is your perfect match and her family is honored to have you as a husband to their daughter. We have already agreed upon giving you a very large dowry for her, Ahmad. Yes, you will go! That is my last word," said his father, turning his back to the argument and leaving the room.

Ahmad, horrified, looked plaintively at his mother. Tears were streaming down her face. Then, without a word, she stood up, kissed Ahmad on the forehead, and went to her husband.

Ahmad smiled at the memory, a small sigh escaping his lips, too small for the driver to notice. Ahmad remembered the many sleepless nights, before boarding the plane, that would take him from his homeland and fix his destiny forever. Before the day arrived when he was to leave for Paris, he lay awake night after night, distraught, planning, and discarding, countless ways to escape his fate. He finally decided his best option was to run. He would go back to Tehran and ask his instructors to shield him within the walls of the madrasah. Ahmad prepared everything he would need to flee but, in the end, could not defy the ingrained taboos of his upbringing. He could not shame his parents. He could not live with that sin.

And so, Ahmad went to Paris, as his parents commanded him, with a large sum of money to support him during the period of his courtship and to pay his wife on condition of their marriage, should the need arise.

The moment he stepped off the plane, he felt his fears begin to fade. For the first time in his life, this sheltered student was independent and it felt fresh and good and right. Ahmad was surprised to find that he suddenly felt an anxious anticipation. He did not know why but, for the first time since his parents told him the news, Ahmad felt hopeful and energized. The moment he looked into Sholeh's astonishingly beautiful dark eyes, Ahmad knew why. He knew that he would love this girl forever; that they would traverse all the worlds of God together.

Both sets of parents were delighted to find that their match was a good one. They were thrilled to be merging their families; fathers congratulating each other and mothers planning the lavish wedding that would take place in Ahmad's hometown of Shiraz as all the family members and friends gathered for the joyous occasion.

Sholeh felt a tingling in the pit of her stomach whenever Ahmad was near; her knees weak, palms sweaty, like any other young woman in love. The couple shared their days together, happily planning their lives, sharing secrets of their childhoods and their dreams and aspirations. They would marry, yes, but first, Sholeh would spend the next several months finishing her teaching degree. Ahmad refused to go back to Iran and would wait by her side in Paris.

In the days that followed, Ahmad and Sholeh spent as much time together as they could beg, borrow, or steal. Ahmad found her radiant exuberance a pure delight, like that first fresh whiff of spring that rises up from the thawing earth after a long and cold winter. Sholeh was a naturally happy girl and he found, through her, a new feeling, and a way to see the world in a different light.

Ahmad especially cherished how Sholeh loved to play, especially outdoors. She would pester Ahmad until he agreed to go bicycle riding with her on the wooded path that was not far from the commune where they lived. They laughed and chattered on while they rode.

One particularly fresh and lazy day, as they rode along, Sholeh told him about her schoolmate, Genevieve, who always tried to coax her into, what she referred to as, a 'normal' relationship with the boys in school. Sholeh continued her story, describing how, whenever she became cranky, Genevieve would say, in the superior perfect French she used only when she was teasing, "Oh, Sholeh, I know what you need...a really good man!"

Sholeh would just laugh out loud, amused by her friend's teasing, certain that, although she refused to judge her friend for the choices she made, she would not break the strict moral code she held inside, knowing the joy of pleasing God and her parents. Sholeh would remain chaste until she met the man she would marry, and that was that. But Genevieve was her very best friend, and she was not offended by her playful banter.

"Now I have him!" declared Sholeh.

"Who, may I ask, is that?" asked Ahmad, feigning ignorance, wanting to hear her inevitable reply.

"My really good man..." she sparkled.

"I want to meet this friend, this Genevieve," Ahmad told Sholeh as they got off their bikes to sit a while, hand-in-hand.

"Yes, of course you will meet her, my dear Ahmad," said Sholeh. "She will love you as I love you, but you must promise me that you won't fall in love with her. She is a very beautiful Parisian woman, you know."

Ahmad laughed with delight, "Foolish woman, I could never love anyone besides you. You are my whole life. You are my heart; you know you are."

Sholeh's eyes shone with pure pleasure as she gazed into the eyes of her new beau; her fiancé. She would love him forever as well, of that she was sure. She lifted his hand to her mouth and kissed the palm. It was an indiscretion of which she knew her parents would not approve, but she did it anyway, a mischievous grin peeking out from her pretty face. Ahmad did not object. The little kiss was her pledge to him that she belonged to him, alone, forever.

Sholeh was the best, the only, truly intimate friend that Ahmad ever had. He was not only grateful but amazed he had been given such a great gift. Although she had been raised in Paris, she was a committed Muslim, obedient to Shari'ah Law, wearing the chador incumbent upon all pure Iranian women. She had Ahmad's utmost esteem and respect.

Sholeh had experienced the prejudice of the French people toward her kind, and although she was sympathetic toward the radical views Ahmad had acquired during his years in the madrasah, she never felt completely comfortable with Ahmad's assertion that jihad was the only way to maintain the purity of Islam. Ahmad, on the other hand, was certain that, as their love grew, Sholeh would come to see the soundness of his position and back him with any decision he would deem necessary for the good of Islam.

Then the riots began in Clichy-sous-Bois. Ahmad was as angry as his neighbors at the deaths of the two teens, after witnessing Muslim youth ostracized from real participation in French society, marginalized by the government, and isolated from economic progress. Ahmad, still yet to find a job, and scrimping the money he had come with to France, began to join the groups of young men who took to the streets each night in protest, burning public property and every car in sight not owned by their neighbors.

Sholeh was not happy with this turn of events and pleaded with Ahmad to stop. She finally convinced him to help her and her schoolmates build an organization that would bring pressure on the French Government to create laws and programs that would ensure the liberation of the Muslim communities isolated from the rest of the French population. Ahmad agreed but insisted they could never allow integration of their neighborhoods with 'infidels'. Sholeh was content. They had come to believe they were an excellent match and together would be an unstoppable force.

The night Sholeh was killed during the riots in Clichy-sous-Bois was the final blow to Ahmad's fragile and emerging sense of well-being. The devastation it left on his psyche, and the rage that followed in its wake, ensured that the fire lit by this tragedy, along with his years in the madrasah, would consume him. It was shortly after Sholeh's death that Ahmad committed himself and pledged his undying fealty to jihad.

Tonight Ahmad was returning to Sholeh's home to pay his respects to her parents, whom he considered as his own. They were the only people in France that he knew he could trust and he intended to ask them to hold onto some personal effects. He did not want to be carrying these in the event anything happened to him, and he knew he would shortly need to leave France in haste.

"Pardon, monsieur," said the cabby, startling Ahmad. "We have arrived."

Ahmad, his mind still hazy, did not reply.

"Are you all right, monsieur," Jacques asked. "Is there anything else I can do?"

"No...no," replied Ahmad, finally. "I have not been here for a while, and..."

"It is hard for you, I see," replied Jacques, "This is a sad place. Do not be sad, monsieur. I think that you will soon meet a woman who will help to heal your sadness. Oui?"

Ahmad looked up at the cabby, startled that he would make so impudent and presumptuous a statement. Then he relaxed as he saw, not the licentious grin he was expecting, but a look of genuine concern on the driver's face.

"How much do I owe you, monsieur," asked Ahmad, not knowing what else to say.

The driver handed him a ticket with the fare printed on it. Ahmad rummaged in his pockets, settled the fare, and stepped out of the car. He stood a few seconds on the curb holding open the door to the cab. At last, leaning in again, he said, "Merci, monsieur. Adieu." Then, closing the door, he disappeared into the commune. Jacques smiled and drove away.

Ahmad walked up and down the sidewalk in the high-rise apartment complex for several minutes before he recognized the building where Sholeh's parents lived with their youngest son. He stood in the foyer with his hand on the buzzer, waiting for the voice of a family member who would let him in the building. He was about to give up when he heard a young man's voice at the other end of the intercom.

"Hello," said, Sholeh's youngest brother. "Who is calling?"

"It is me, Farzam...Ahmad," he said, delighted to hear the voice of the boy who had become like a brother to him. "It is wonderful to hear your voice again!"

"Ahmad? Ahmad joon?" said the voice. "Momma-jan! Momma-jan! Come quickly. Ahmad is home!"

"Let him in! Let him in! Hurry, Farzam! Come up, Ahmad-joon. I cannot believe this. It is a miracle! Shokreh Khoda! Shokreh Khoda!!" said Sholeh's mother, thanking God, her voice cracking as Ahmad took his finger off the intercom buzzer and quickly pulled open the door as he heard the click of the lock.

Minutes later, Ahmad had ascended to the ninth floor and was waiting for the door to open on the place where he had first laid eyes on his beloved Sholeh. Ahmad stood breathlessly, wiping the sweat of his palms on his black denim trousers, as he heard the door latches click open, one by one.

The door finally flew open, Sholeh's mother and younger brother standing there to greet him, utter joy adorning both their faces.

"Khodayeh man! Khodayeh man!" shrieked Momma-jan. "Salam, Ahmad-joon. Papa, come look. He is here. Ahmad is here!"

Ahmad's joy at seeing his 'adopted' family was in precise counterpoint to the immense sadness he felt as soon as the door opened onto his ruined future, and he could not bring himself to move past the doorway.

Suddenly, Sholeh's father, Habib, rushed out from the room in which he had been working. He saw Ahmad, pushed past his wife and son, and grabbed Ahmad in a tight embrace.

"Ahmad, my son, come, come in," said Habib. "Mama, why do you let our boy stand out in the hallway like a stranger? He is our honored guest. Sit. Sit. Tell us how you are. Where have you been? We have missed you, Ahmad. Mama, get Ahmad tea. Have you eaten, my son? Please, come to the table. We have plenty of food. Mama, make Ahmad a plate."

Ahmad let Habib lead him to the dining room table. He felt overwhelmed with intense gratitude at their warm greeting. These people still treated him with the same kindness and respect they would shower upon their own son. Ahmad loved them, in return, as if they were his family, making the pain of losing Sholeh all the more acute.

For the first time, Ahmad looked around the apartment. It was smaller than he remembered. He shook his head as he thought of how this was a family who had thrived in Iran; they were practically royalty. Surely, they deserved better than this tiny hovel.

Habib and his wife, Maryam, came to France to escape the severe Shari'ah Law imposed upon them by the imams and mullahs after the deposition of Reza Pahlavi Shah. Habib and Maryam were not particularly religious and liked the freedoms they enjoyed while the Shah was in power. Habib was part owner in a successful clothe-making business, exporting his exquisite silks all over the world.

Maryam especially appreciated going about her life unveiled during the Shah's reign. She was one of those lovely, fashion-conscious, professional Persian women, and wore all the latest cosmetic trends she could find or order out of catalogues from the fine salons of Europe. She had been a physician in Iran, well known for the special attention she paid to the poorest patients. Although she was born into one of Tehran's premier families, and enjoyed the finest clothes and furnishings money could buy, her greatest joy was in giving abundantly to the poor, ever trying to lend a helping hand and relieve the sufferings of those less fortunate than she. At the age of twenty-nine, she set up a free medical clinic in her town to treat the elderly and the indigent. All in all, the couple had started life comfortable and prosperous. They were admired and respected. Their future looked brilliant.

When the Shah was gone, all this ended. Restrictions on businesses, strict dress codes for women, and many more restrictions, impacting nearly every area of their lives, forced them to consider leaving their beloved Iran. They decided, after many family consultations, to set out for France in search of a better life, a freer life for them and their children.

They came to Clichy-sous-Bois on the advice of a friend who told them that they would feel most comfortable in this area in which resided a predominantly Moslem community of people. The couple started a new business here, intending to move to more affluent surroundings more suitable for a growing family but, before long, it was apparent that the business would fail and they would be raising their children in this cramped apartment.

Ahmad blamed the bigotry he saw in Europe against the Muslim people for the failure of Habib's business but Sholeh's parents held no resentments, they were free and happy. They loved their friends and neighbors and, until Sholeh died, the family considered their lives to be greatly blessed and near perfection.

Ahmad removed the backpack he was carrying and leaned it against the clean, white wall behind his chair. He took off his sable-brown tweed jacket, hung it on the back of an old dining room chair and sat down at a table covered with a fine olive green jacquard silk cloth and a feast fit for a Persian king.

Ahmad saw that his favorite food was all there, almost as though they were expecting him. "Khodayeh man! You have prepared Chelo kebab, my favorite meal, Mama-jan? Did you know I was coming?"

"Yes, of course!" Maryam said. "I can read your mind." They all roared with laughter.

"And, tell me, where is the rice?" asked Ahmed. His mouth was watering. He could hardly wait to begin shoveling the food into his mouth.

Maryam took the lid off a silver plate.

"Bah! Bah! Bah! Loobia Polow! It has been a long time, mamma-jan." Ahmed's wide smile conveyed the gratitude he felt for this special occasion. The reunited family sat there for a time, in silence, looking at Ahmad, tears gathering in their eyes.

Finally, Ahmad grinned, grasping Mama-jan's hand and kissing her on the cheek, letting his nostrils fill with the delicious aroma of the Persian rice and green beans. It was colored a delicate shade of golden yellow from the imported saffron and dried lime Maryam used as a seasoning. "I hope you saved me tahdig!"

Waving him aside, she continued fixing a huge plate of food for Ahmad to eat. "Sit. Sit. Let me finish. I will spill the rice everywhere," she said, tears beginning to flow down her cheeks. "Of course... tahdig...your favorite! Have the rest. Here is some fresh yogurt with cucumber and dill. I made the yogurt just yesterday. It is good, yes? Tell me if you like it."

Ahmad began to eat, not so much hungry for food as he was hungry for homemade Persian food, and the love that had gone into making every single bite.

"I like it, Mama-jan," said Ahmad, "I like it very much."

As Ahmad sat, eating the Persian meal he missed so much and chatting with the family he missed much more, they laughed and cried as they talked about what had been happening in their lives since they had last seen each other. Of course, Ahmad declined to mention his most recent enterprise. They acted as if they were still all one, as though Sholeh was not gone, only out shopping with friends and would be back shortly.

After a while their conversation slowed. They sat quietly, at last, finishing off the meal with homemade baklava and jasmine tea. Then Sholeh's father grew serious.

"Ahmad, we have worried about you," said Habib, the furrow of his brow growing deep. "We hear reports about the Renseignements Generaux and Interpol planting spies here in Clichy. They are looking for jihadists. They know our young men are being recruited and trained. Security is very tight in France since the incident in San Francisco. They are afraid there are men who might be planning an attack at the banking conference in Paris. They are searching in Clichy for these men. Surely, you have heard."

"Yes, I have heard, Habib Effendi," said Ahmad, looking away.

Unable to force himself to meet Habib's eyes, Ahmad stared, instead, at the elegant brass samovar the family had purchased on a visit to Turkey. It sat in the middle of the table, a constant brew of the fragrant jasmine tea at the ready; all day, every day. Ahmad allowed his eyes to follow the intricate pattern embossed on its surface as though it were a map of the world that would tell him where to go and lead him into the future.

"We have been worried about you," said Habib. "We worry that you were so angry when Sholeh died. We know how you feel. But we love you and do not want you to do anything…rash."

"You must trust me, Baba-jan. I will do nothing to bring harm or shame to this family. Do not worry about me. The future will take care of itself. I work only for the glory of Islam, and Allah protects His loved ones."

"This talk, Ahmad, it scares me," said Habib. "You will do nothing to harm anyone, or yourself?" Habib looked plaintively at Ahmad, hoping for some sign that Ahmad did not mean what he suspected.

"My dear husband is asking you to be wise," interrupted Maryam, finally unable to hold her silence. "We know how you feel,

Ahmad-joon. We know that you are angry and sad, but exacting revenge will not bring back our daughter."

"As much as I dream of it, I know Sholeh is not coming back," replied Ahmad in a barely audible voice, "but there is something I can do."

Maryam's mouth set, and pushing back from the table, she rose from her chair. She left the dining room and headed down the hall to the back of the apartment. The trio of men sat there knowing that there remained, heavy in the air, something unspoken - the secrets of their broken hearts, profound but unutterable.

Only minutes passed when Maryam returned and sat back down.

"Would you like more tea, Ahmad-joon?" she asked.

"No, please, Mama-jan," replied the man who was to have been her son-in-law.

"Please, have some more, you are still thirsty."

"Is this tarouf, Mama?" asked Ahmad, smiling. "If so, there is no need to ask a third time; I really do not want more, I promise."

Maryam looked at Ahmad with a delicate and tender smile. Reaching into the hip pocket of her dress, she said, "I want you to see something."

"Yes, Mama-jan, of course," replied Ahmad.

"It is from Sholeh," said Maryam, "She wrote it the night she was killed."

"What?" said Ahmad, his face ashen, his voice trembling with alarm.

"It is not much," said Maryam, "As you can see, it merely says she needs to see you right away and will return home soon. We never saw her again."

"She was coming to see me? I don't understand. She told me she needed to stay home to study for an exam. What could have possibly been so important? She promised me she would stay inside at night until the riots subsided. Why would she do something so foolish?"

"Sholeh came home from school that afternoon, crying and heartbroken," Maryam explained.

"Why? What was it? What happened? She was fine when we talked that morning. She was looking forward to seeing her friends at the university."

"She told me that she saw a reporter talking to one of the youths involved in the riots," Maryam continued. "The youth was laughing, holding up a cell phone, and showing the reporter something. Sholeh was standing nearby and saw that it was a recording of someone, whose face was hidden, in the act of beheading a man."

"No, no! This cannot be," cried Ahmad. "My poor dear…my poor darling…" Ahmad began to rock back and forth in his chair.

"I am afraid there is more," Maryam said. "There is something she wanted you to know. She left the house because she wanted you to know that you must stop."

"Stop, what?" cried Ahmad. "What are you talking about?"

"Sholeh wanted you to stop the rioting and the talk about cleansing the world for Islam," Maryam said, tears now forming on her eyelids. "Ahmad, Sholeh listened to your ideas about how all the peoples of the world must come under the banner of Islam or die. She listened to you because she loved you. She wore the chador for you and wanted to be in the same place as you are, but when she saw the man in the suit and tie being beheaded by a man shouting 'Allah'u'Akbar,' she finally understood that it wasn't what God would wish. She left the house that night because she felt compelled to tell you to stop before it was too late. My daughter was ready to beg of you to stop. She wanted you to do this for her. Please, honor our daughter's last wish. Please, stay with us. Work with Habib. You will be a comfort to him and a help in his new business. You are like our son, Ahmad. You are our son. Please stay."

Ahmad wrapped his arms around the woman who was supposed to have been his mother-in-law. He lowered her head to his shoulder and kissed her forehead. They held each other and, for the first time since Sholeh's death, cried together for the beautiful girl they had lost. Habib and his son, sobbed with them.

Finally, his tears all but dried, Ahmad released Maryam from his embrace. The family sat together for a time, until Ahmad broke their silence.

"I thank Allah for giving me this family," Ahmad exclaimed. "You are my true family; the family I have longed for my entire life. I can never tell you how much I love you all."

"Stay here with us," Habib pleaded. "We love you too, my son. Work with me."

"Please forgive me," replied Ahmad. "May Allah bless you in every world of His worlds. I only wish it were in my power to stay here with you and live my life in peace, but I have work that I must do, work that I have sworn to complete. I ask you to trust and respect this. I promise you that I will honor Sholeh's memory."

"No, Ahmad-joon," cried Maryam, "No!"

"Please, Mama-jan, I must go. I ask that you do not ask me where or why. I have something, though, that I must beg of you. I must ask you to tell no one that you have seen me."

Ahmad pushed back his chair and put on his jacket. He leaned over and picked up the backpack that had been leaning against the wall all evening and laid it on the table.

"What is this?" asked Habib.

"I must ask you one more favor," said Ahmad.

"Of, course, Ahmad," replied Habib. "You are like my own son and will always be so."

"Please hold on to this for me," said Ahmad, handing the pack over the table to Habib. "This is my Qur'an, hide it somewhere safe. Please tell no one that it is here. I have business in the city but will be back to pick it up soon. It is vital this is still here when I come for it."

"We will do as you ask, of course, but are we doing something illegal, Ahmad-joon?" asked Maryam. "Please, I must ask that you do not jeopardize this family."

"No, Mama-jan," said Ahmad. "Do as I ask and no harm will come to any of you, I swear it."

"We will honor your wishes then, Ahmad," said Habib. "I ask you to honor our daughter's memory."

Ahmad did not reply. Before he departed, he embraced each family member and bid them all Allah's most great blessings.

Though the broadcast ended an hour earlier, Ron waited patiently, sitting alone, observing the bar patrons and marveling at the complex dynamics of human interactions. Just as Suzanne instructed, he retained firm possession of the only private booth the Green Room Lounge had to offer. The bar had an unpretentious mood that was lively and light and it was Suzanne's favorite place. She loved the ersatz animal skin print sofas that formed small gathering places for conversation and drinks with acquaintances or strangers. She would frequently stop there after work, listen to the restorative sounds of the crowd's cheerful gaiety and, for a moment, forget her problems and ignore the rampage of constantly changing world crises that stole most of her time.

Ron was talking on a cell phone as David and Suzanne entered and approached the table. "...I understand and thank his Eminence for the gracious invitation...arrivederci."

"Was that Rome?" David asked as he slid in across from Ron.

"Yes," answered Ron. "Cardinal Oriastro received my message in Israel just as he was departing and has agreed to meet us at the Vatican. The invitation should be in my inbox by now. Looks like we're set. How'd it go on your end?"

"All good news...John approved the trip, including your travel expenses. The arrangements should be complete within the hour."

"Great! Nice to have a friend with influence."

"It wasn't me...it's all Suzanne's doing."

"I'm a very influential gal!" Suzanne said, laughing and snapping her fingers. "But there is a slight wrinkle."

"Wrinkle?" Ron asked.

"Well...to convince John to allow me to go, I agreed to be field producer for the banking conference, so we will not be coming back to New York when we have finished our business in Rome. Instead, we'll be going straight to Paris to meet up with Mike Lussardi, our White House correspondent, who's traveling on Air Force One with President Whitney. The thing is...you don't have a plane ride home unless you fly commercial...of course, you're welcome to join us in Paris...its only two days."

"Tell you what, let's play this by ear. After we see the Cardinal, we'll reevaluate and decide then...you can always cancel a hotel room, right?" Ron offered.

"Fine with me," David said.

After a round of drinks, Suzanne signed a chit that billed their refreshments to a Global News expense account. Then they left the bar looking for a taxi. There weren't any to be found on the side streets. They waited a few minutes but wound up walking around the block to the broadcast center where a line of black town cars waited along the curb, ready to take Global News employees home.

David and Ron jumped into one of the cars and headed for David's apartment. Suzanne, who lived in the opposite direction, rode alone. When she was sure the broadcast center was out of sight, she opened her purse and rummaged around for a few seconds until she found an interoffice memo. It was, purportedly, from David requesting that she accompany him to the World Banking Conference. She wrote it, hoping that, if John balked at her request to travel with David on the Paris assignment, the note might tip the scales in her favor. To her surprise, John didn't hesitate for a second and now, Suzanne felt foolish and guilty for even thinking of trying to deceive her boss. With a generous measure of self-reproach, Suzanne tore the paper into tiny pieces, opened the car's window and tossed the remnants of her intrigue into the wind, hoping the vastness of a nameless New York night might offer some forgiveness. The pieces floated like the crushed petals of a dried flower; first on the slipstream of the car, then in the gentle spring breeze before falling to earth.

It was near midnight when Merilee Brunswick opened her eyes, once again finding herself asleep in the living room, curled up in her cherished wing backed chair. Overcome by emotional and physical exhaustion since the attack on the city, she stretched and pushed herself up, so weary, the walk to the bedroom, its door only ten feet away, felt like a climb to the top of Everest. Her malaise persisted day and night, and even meeting David Anderson did little to shake off her lethargy.

Every night Merilee would sit at the edge of the bed, looking at the only picture she owned of her mom, saying a little prayer for them both. Her real dad snapped the photograph during a family reunion when Merilee was five years old. She deeply regretted someone else was not asked to snap the picture so dad could have been beside her mother. A year later he was gone; a drunk driver, speeding into oncoming traffic, had killed him, instantly.

As she entered the bedroom and began changing into her night clothes, Merilee looked at the needlepoint hanging on the wall above the bed's headboard. Her mother's meticulous handiwork was a gift to celebrate her sixth birthday. It was a delightful piece of whimsy, perfect for a child - a rendering in yarn, of gossamer pink and white clouds set against a baby blue sky, over an open sea. Rising and falling with the crests of the waves, her mom embroidered a rendition of the last line of lyrics from one of Merilee's favorite childhood songs about rowing your boat.

The needlepoint elicited Merilee's most wonderfully warm and cozy feelings and she hoped to someday hand it down to a little girl of her own. But that was several days ago, before the strike, before the man with the prayer book and before life was interrupted with such unrest and uncertainty.

Merilee sat at the foot of the bed reflecting on the years gone by. The day she left home, she packed a frayed suitcase with a few clothes, the picture of her mother and the delicate needlepoint. Wrapping them in a roll, she placed them with reverence on top of a white cotton jumper. Christening it with a stray tear that fell into her suitcase just the moment before she closed the lid, Merilee zipped up her old life for the last time.

The week's incidents convinced her that it was time to contact her mother. Perhaps she had divorced Ray, by now. Maybe her mother was searching for her all along; maybe she could go home again.

Merilee lifted the portable handset summoning the courage to dial the number. A rising sense of alarm abruptly stopped her. If her mother was still married to Ray, it might set off one of his rages. Clair might suffer a severe beating as a consequence. After considering several options, she elected to call a childhood friend, Candace, who lived next door to her as a child. Merilee would give Candy a call and ask her to relay the message.

Merilee trusted Candace. They grew into the very best kind of friends when Candace's family barreled into town and moved next door. Their mutual creativity bonded them from the very first moment. Ten year olds playing dolls, hopscotch, roller-skating. Innumerable games, unnamed and conceived on the spot through the gift of childhood imagination, made the pair inseparable. They ended that first day by talking together through the upstairs windows; their houses separated only by a narrow alley on either side of a white picket fence dividing the homes.

Some months later, on a warm and dry summer night in late July, Merilee was lying on her bed under the window, looking up at a canopy of stars. Something hitting the screen got her attention. At first, she thought it must be moths attracted by the soft nightlight she read by until feeling drowsy enough to fall asleep. After a while though, the soft ping was accompanied by a low "psst" and Merilee finally got up and peeked out. Candy had her screen open and was throwing little objects towards the window: erasers, paper clips and the like, to attract her attention. Merilee opened the window screen and they giggled away about all sorts of things, knowing that, if caught, both would be in the worst sort of trouble.

Before long, Candy bet her aim was good enough to get all sorts of stuff through Merilee's window. Deciding to make a game of it, the girls devised a scoring system and, giggling with abandon, spent the next hour throwing every small object within reach out the windows in an attempt to make them fly across the alley and through the opposite window. All manner of items ended up in the alley, of course, among them small dolls, stray buttons, marbles, tennis balls, and the usual assortment of pens and pencils. Even small note pads and storybooks went sailing through the air. For the most part, they dropped to the ground; both girls laughing too hard to be much use at actually hitting their targets. Finally, worn out and out of projectiles, they said good night, closed the screens, and went to sleep.

The next day, when looking down into an alley strewn with all the items that missed their marks, they burst out into a series of more, long giggles. The girls made a plan to meet in the yard before both their mothers discovered the treasure and grounded them for life.

Candace was soon waiting for Merilee in the yard and the girls, giggling away, began hurriedly throwing things into a bucket. Thinking how very clever they were, Candy said, "We can hide the bucket behind the shed and then sort through it later." They parted, but not before promising lifelong devotion, sealing the vow with a secret handshake.

Merilee was sure calling her old mate, first, was the right thing to do. Candice was a trusted friend who would certainly convey the message to her mom. Merilee grabbed the phone and ran into the kitchen to search the junk draw beside the sink for her telephone-address book. She found Candy's phone number and found something else in the process - a renewed vitality to reunite her family and redeem the past.

"OK...let me think...what time is it there? Damn, it's past midnight back home...better call tomorrow."

Placing Candy's phone number and the portable handset together on the counter, Merilee returned to bed with a spark of anticipation to fuel her dreams. She picked up the picture of her mother, kissed it gently and began to pray when the doorbell startled her.

Mrs. Taylor, she thought, with a touch of antipathy. Why can't the woman record her own television shows?

Merilee slid off the bed, went into the foyer and up to the front door mumbling something about lonely old people with insomnia.

"Yes, Mrs. Taylor...what seems to be the problem tonight?" she called through the door, expecting to hear the aged voice of her neighbor.

"Ms. Brunswick...Ms. Merilee Brunswick?" replied a deep voice. "Sorry to disturb you at this hour, miss...David Anderson sent me over...he said to tell you...it's urgent."

"Who are you, again?"

"You're the lady we met with, right...at the Mexican restaurant...the one I drove home...remember, David and Suzanne from Global News?"

"Yes...I'm her...err...she...whatever."

"Good, good...I have an important message from David Anderson."

"Why didn't he call or come himself?"

"Um...he's on a flight...to New York, big story, breaking news about the attack. David asked me to say he's sorry he couldn't be here."

"Could you please come back tomorrow? It's really late."

"I'd be glad to, miss...only I've got to catch a plane in an hour. It'll only take a minute and I could lose my job... help a fella out...whadda ya say?"

"What's the message?"

"Look, I'm gonna wake up the whole building standing out here yelling...how 'bout opening the door just a crack?"

"Wait a sec," Merilee said, placing her face against the door and spying through the fisheye lens of the peephole.

She immediately recognized the man as the driver who helped her exit David Anderson's limo. She recalled the man was nice, even friendly, offering her a hand when they exchanged greetings. Merilee reached up and unlocked the deadbolt, pulling the door open as far as the security chain would allow, and peeked out.

"Hi miss, remember me...Brian Saunders...Mr. Anderson's assistant? Here's my Global News ID." Saunders handed Merilee the credentials through the small opening and stood shifting from one foot to another, eyes down, looking a little like a small boy reprimanded for bringing home some type of live amphibian in his pocket. "I'm really sorry to disturb you...really, really sorry," mumbled Saunders.

"It's okay," Merilee answered as she tried to unsuccessfully squeeze the ID back through the narrow space. Feeling sorry for the poor guy standing out in the hall with the hangdog expression, she decided to invite him in.

"It must be awkward standing out there," Merilee said. "I'll let you in but only for a minute...then you have to go...okay?"

"Yes miss...I appreciate this very much...it will only be a minute. I promise."

"One minute," Merilee repeated as she slipped the chain out of its bracket and opened the door.

Brian Saunders stepped inside and past Merilee. She closed the door and, leaning against it, grabbed her robe at the lapels and pulled it tightly closed.

"Sooo...what's the message?" she asked.

"Ms. Brunswick," Saunders replied, looking into her eyes with great intensity. "Mr. Anderson would like to know if he can borrow the items he gave you from the car...they're part of a big investigation...and he promises to return them by tomorrow afternoon."

"What items?" Merrilee asked, puzzled.

"You know…that little leather book and those cards I brought from the back seat." Saunders, noticing Merilee's bewildered expression, rattled on, "David asked me to get the stuff from the car for you…bring it over to you…remember?"

"Oh yes…and David sent you? Are you sure?"

"Yes ma'am, I work directly for David. He told me exactly what was needed. You don't have to worry, your stuff will be safe and returned right on time…and no one else will touch it but him."

Merilee was confused. Her confusion grew into fear, threatening to rise into panic. She desperately wanted to believe this was nothing more than a mistake, and Brian Saunders would never deliberately try to deceive her, but no matter how she tried to rationalize this, so-called, David Anderson message, there was no denying that Saunders was, in fact, just plain lying. A voice in her mind started screaming, you're in danger…get out now. She remembered the voice from her troubled past; it had always been unwavering and true. Trust your instincts, Merilee told herself.

Merilee was trapped between the door and the man's shear bulk. She was positive, in a struggle, he could easily snap her bones like dry twigs. The impulse to grab the phone, lock herself in the bathroom and call the police, came first, except the phone was left behind on the kitchen counter and the bathroom was accessible only through the bedroom.

She calculated her escape in a matter of seconds. She would pretend the book was in the kitchen, get the phone and hide it in the pocket of her robe, then excuse herself to search in the bedroom and lock herself in. Her gut, in that unwavering voice, screamed back, that flimsy bedroom door will never keep him out until the police arrived, but what was the alternative?

The past few years, living alone in the city, had changed Merilee. She believed violence would never again touch her life. But now the memories of Ray's abuse flooded over her and the buried fears began to well up inside, multiplying the terror she now faced. It took so much courage to escape from the horror of her childhood and now it was back. Except this time, things were different.

This time Merilee could protect herself.

This time she wasn't helpless.

This time there was a 38 caliber Lady Smith in the nightstand next to the bed.

So a new plan evolved in her mind. I'll get the gun and force him to leave...then call the police. I'll shoot him if I have to. She was ready to face Saunders.

"Oh yes," Merilee said, glancing in the direction of the bedroom, trying to maintain a casual demeanor to hide the tremor rolling across her body.

"Yes, yes, now I remember. Under the circumstances, I have been trying my best to forget it. I must have left it in the bedroom, probably in my night table draw. I'd be glad to lend them to Mr. Anderson. In fact, he can keep them...just wait here." She squeezed past Saunders and hurried toward the bedroom.

As Merilee reached into the night table's draw and grabbed the pistol she heard a noise behind her. Indeed, Saunders had followed and was standing in the doorway. She spun around and, pointing the gun at Saunders chest, yelled, "Get out! I know you're lying!"

Saunders began to laugh, deep and booming, the sound enraged Merilee and she warned him again.

"I mean it," she growled through clenched teeth. "Get out now or, I swear, I'll shoot you right where you stand!"

"Now, now...you seem upset...let me help you relax, baby," Saunders replied, chuckling, taking a step toward her.

Merilee aimed and squeezed the trigger just as the instructor at the range taught her. Saunders fell to the floor and didn't move. She lowered the weapon and walked over to see how badly he was wounded. She stopped beside him and Saunders' arm shot out, sweeping her legs out from beneath her and she fell hard to the floor. The gun flew out of her hand, crashing against the wall.

Saunders recovered the pistol, slipped it into his pocket and stood up. Merilee looked at him, dumbfounded, her head reeling.

"How...How..."

"Kevlar vest, ya stupid broad...who'd ya think you're fucking with," Saunders hissed, scorn shaping his mouth. "Besides, if you got me then *he* woulda got you."

Saunders opened the shade and pointed toward the window. Merilee could see a man crouching on the fire escape, his face framed by the wooden sash. She was sure he was the man who dropped the prayer book. She began screaming, the pitch moving up through the octaves toward High C, until Saunders bent over and grabbed her robe. Easily lifting her into the air, Saunders tossed her onto the bed then reached over and unlocked and opened the window.

"C'mon in, Jamal. Join our little party. Why don't we take a few liberties with our girl friend over there."

"Those are not our instructions," Jamal said, jumping down from the sill onto the parquet floor. "Besides, a gun just went off and a woman screamed. The police will be here any minute. Get the book and the cards and we go."

"Damn towel-head, party-pooper," Saunders muttered under his breath. "Okay, bitch, I'm gonna make this real simple…where's the stuff Anderson gave you?"

Merilee didn't answer; couldn't answer. Saunders went over to the bed and took hold of her robe, lifting her up again and slamming her hard against the wall. Tearing open the front of her nightclothes, he pulled them down to expose her shoulders. Stunned, she looked right through Saunders; she could see only evil – raw, merciless, malevolent. Images of Ray raced across her vision. Saunders, emboldened with the scent of her horror, closed his huge right hand around her throat, nearly encircling her neck.

"I'm asking one more time…where's the brown leather book and the five cards I brought you from the car?"

"I don't know…I swear, I don't know," Merilee gasped. "Please, you're choking me." She struggled, pushing against his arm, but his grip only tightened. She began to whimper and cough.

"I'll do a lot more than choke you," Saunders threatened, slapping her across the face.

Merilee's head snapped back and forth, her brown curls falling over her eyes. Saunders tightened his grip a bit more, lifting her head, and snarled, "Baby, I'm gonna do things to you that you never dreamed of…then I'm gonna kill ya, if you don't tell me, and my friend here, what we want t' know."

"I don't know where they are…I don't." Merilee sobbed. "I gave them back to David Anderson…he has them…he…has…them."

"Sure, you gave them back. When?"

"The day you…dropped me off…at my apartment!"

It finally dawned on Saunders just how Merilee knew he lied. Releasing his grip, the thug took several steps back, looking at her with a malicious smile that spread across his face like the contents of a cracked and rotten egg. This turn of events was quite unexpected. He knew the pathetic sobbing girl, standing frozen against the wall, was telling the truth, and felt annoyed for missing the moment when she returned the items to Anderson. But his thoughts abruptly turned to *those men*; the ones that sent him here, unarmed, with Jamal as a chaperone. What excuse could he give them?

Terror rose up Brian Saunders' spine like a flame exploding from a gas leak. He was afraid; afraid of that darkened room, of the grey silhouettes, of the man with the baritone voice. Outsmarted by David Anderson, again, it was time for a new course of action.

"Mr. Saunders," Jamal said with a reproachful tone. "Our items aren't here. You've led us on another useless chase. And now there's a witness…too bad."

Jamal pulled a 9mm Glock from a holster under his jacket with one hand and a silencer from his pocket with the other, and began to assemble them, as Brian Saunders moved away, backward toward the bedroom door.

"Now…hold on, partner," Saunders pleaded raising his hands.

"Get to your knees, hands in your pockets and don't move," snapped Jamal.

The hired killer fell to his knees and slid his hands into the pockets of his sport coat, just as Jamal commanded. In that instant, his hand came to rest on Merilee's 38 caliber Lady Smith. From this lowered position, Saunders aimed the pistol and fired two shots through the fabric of the coat's lining, hitting Jamal in the neck and head. Jumping back to his feet, Saunders walked over to the fallen man, lifted the Glock from Jamal's slack fingers, and tucked it into the waistband of his trousers. Sirens screamed in the distance. Someone, a man, was pounding on the entrance door, calling Merilee's name.

Saunders looked over his shoulder and saw Merilee standing alongside the bed, staring in stunned shock at Jamal who no longer had a recognizable human face. With the casual ease of someone boarding a yacht, Saunders drew the Glock and fired a single shot that struck Merilee in the abdomen. She fell onto the bed, moaning.

He wiped his fingerprints from both guns, and placing the 9mm in Jamal's dead hand, and the pistol just out of Merilee's grasp, climbed through the window onto the fire escape. He closed the sash, kicked the glass into the room and, hearing the sound of sirens coming ever closer, Brian Saunders disappeared into the night.

The last thing Merilee saw as the blood ran from her veins, soaking into the bedspread, was her mother's needlepoint; its' pink and white clouds floating lazily in a baby blue sky. Her final thought was of a melody and a lovely sunny summer day, lying with her mother on fresh cut grass, the bottoms of their feet pressed together, pumping the air with an imaginary bicycle between them. As her eyes slowly closed Merilee heard her mother's tender voice singing the familiar words of the lullaby, lovingly embroidered over the gently rolling waves so long ago, a gift for a six-year-old girl on her birthday:
Merilee,
    Merilee,
        Merilee,
            Merilee,
                ...Life Is But
                  A Dream...

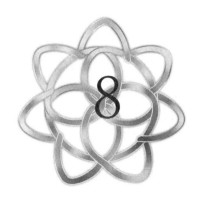

An Uncertain
Destination

When he stepped through the grand entry-way of the Boeing Dream Liner, Ron Eyota looked around and, astonished, let out a whistle. He thought it incredible that anything like this could be made to fly. The interior was lavishly appointed with blonde wood paneling, accoutrements of brushed stainless steel, and furnishings that would have been at home in any five star hotel. Adjacent to the flight deck there was a fully functional conference room with seating for twenty, plus a suite of small, semiprivate offices. The center of the aircraft had a completely equipped studio with state of the art production facilities, connected, via satellite, to all of Global's news feeds. Behind the news studio, there was a lounge that included a standup bar, two staterooms, each with its own faux marble bath, and a fully-equipped gourmet kitchen that would be the envy of even the most discerning chef.

Ron marveled that he wasn't just looking at a corporate jet but at a symbol of the new global aristocracy. Monarchs, emperors, shahs, despots, potentates and rajahs may have disappeared into time past, but human nature would not let the sovereigns completely die out. Evolving like earth's crust, throne rooms became boardrooms or legislative chambers; the ubiquitous corporate brands and political logos replacing coats of arms as badges of royalty. Conquering armies were becoming obsolete as the political and corporate elite assumed power by controlling more and more of the world's most precious and dwindling resources.

The irony caused Ron to chuckle under his breath, perhaps it was more of a scoff than a laugh, when an unctuous young man, sporting a practiced smile of gleaming white teeth, intruded on his ruminations.

"Professor Eyota, may I presume. My name is Bobby and I'm the purser and crew chief on our airship, 'Constellation Voyager'. Do allow me to take your luggage, Professor. Come this way."

Waving his arm in a grand arc of pride and ceremony, the purser ushered Ron to the lounge and introduced the bartender. Before disappearing into the labyrinth of rooms inside the fuselage, he said, "Please, do let me know if there is anything I can do to make your flight extraordinary."

Ron couldn't help notice both the purser, and the crew, were wearing uniforms that blended the look of an old-time movie usher with a paramilitary youth movement and wondered if that was by design.

David and Suzanne entered the lounge soon after and sat next to Ron. Marveling at the airplane's opulence, David remarked to no one, in particular, "Have you ever seen anything like this?"

"It's a sybarite's dream," Ron commented.

"Let's go see the rest," Suzanne suggested, excited to tour the plane. Taking hold of David's arm, she pulled him along.

When they reached the first stateroom, Suzanne sat on the edge of the bed, lightly caressing the satin bedcover with her slender fingers. The spread had a sensuous quality, smooth and cool to the touch, and she became momentarily absorbed in its tactile pleasure.

Stifling a yawn, she said, "I could sure use a nap. I didn't get much sleep last night."

'Why not?" asked David.

"I stayed up to do a final run-through of the new format."

What she told David was only part of the truth. She explained how she reviewed every detail of the day's programming, from audio to graphics. She didn't tell him that her insomnia was intensified by the thrill of joining David on this assignment.

She looked up at David with a demure smile. "I can't wait till we're in Rome. I hope we have time to see the city together, it's so beautiful." There was a breathy quality to her voice and, for the first time since he'd known her, David noticed a coquettish side to Suzanne that he found alluring.

She raised her head, brushed back several loose strands of hair and looked into his eyes. The softly diffused highlights from the cabin lamps, reflecting in her green eyes, created in them a luminescent glow. Warm pleasure raced up David's shoulders, past the back of his neck, and towards his temples. He held her glance for a brief moment but the spell was soon broken by an announcement blaring from the overhead speakers, declaring takeoff was imminent and asking the passengers to return to their seats.

They hurried back and sat down, snapping closed the seatbelts. As the plane climbed through the clouds into rarified air, both reflected on the moment that had passed between them. David was surprised and mildly embarrassed; Suzanne was quiet, nursing her disappointment.

At forty two thousand feet, the seatbelt indicator was turned off and David signaled to the others to join him around the conference room table. Bobby, their imperious purser, showed up moments later with two flight crew members in tow. He instructed them to take the group's food order as he stood by, looking down his nose. When the ordering was complete, he collected the menus and all three marched off to bring the food and beverages.

David and Ron exchanged glances at the charade. Over the years, both had developed a refined nonverbal communication skill that was so accurate people often mistook it for telepathy.

"What the hell was that?" David asked.

"Never send one guy when three can do the job," Ron said, laughing.

Suzanne, otherwise distracted, switched on a monitor and tuned into Global's network feed. She watched the screen, engrossed in analysis, as Matt Finan anchored the noontime news segment, comparing the program to the notes in her smartphone, making sure the new network format was followed to the letter.

"No rest for the tired and weary?" Ron asked her.

"I promised John a more dynamic product," she replied, explaining her diligence. "I hope he likes the changes. I hope the audience likes them too…even though we're in the lead, a ratings uptick would be nice."

"You get John a one-point bump in the ratings and he'll be your best friend," David said, joking.

Just then the food and drinks arrived. To everyone's surprise, it was very formal with fine china, silverware, crystal goblets, vintage wine, and white glove service; all executed under the withering glare of Bobby who stood, arms folded, several feet away from the table.

When the crew stepped back, the purser approached. "Will there be anything else?" he asked without the deference he extended to the uppermost classes of men it was his usual job to serve.

"That will be all, thank you," David said, mimicking the purser's supercilious demeanor as he dismissed Bobby with a flick of his wrist and a mischievous grin directed toward Ron.

Once they were alone, Ron, who couldn't hold back his reaction, said in amazement, "This is some spread. Your boss has expensive taste!" They ate while watching Global News, the provider of the feast.

Midway through the meal, Suzanne was called away from the table to answer the telephone. When she returned, she was staring off into space.

"Something wrong?" David inquired.

"No…why?"

"You seem a bit…far away."

Suzanne seemed hesitant to continue. "David, there's something…I don't know, exactly, how to say."

"Tell me. What?"

"It's bad."

"Just say it quick…don't think!"

"That was Hope Zandel who telephoned. Last night a report came into the newsroom…they…the police…found Merilee Brunswick murdered in her apartment."

"Murdered?" David repeated, stunned. "How? Who?"

"The details aren't all in, yet," Suzanne answered. "They found her on the bed with a gun nearby, shot once. The police also found a Jamal-something-or-other, lying on the floor, holding a gun. The window of her bedroom was smashed and the cops think it might be an attempted burglary. Maybe, Merilee caught the guy climbing in through the window and a gunfight broke out."

David could not hide the revulsion on his face. "I promised she would be okay…I gave my word."

"David," Suzanne insisted, "It's not your fault. This has nothing to do with us…it was a robbery."

"I'm finding that hard to believe," David shot back. "It's too close to our meeting. Isn't it possible this Jamal was trying to retrieve the Qur'an and cards she gave to us? I think we owe it to her to find out."

"But Merilee gave you the book when you were standing by her front door," Suzanne said, correcting the newsman.

David, thinking for a second, asked. "Suzanne, who knew we were meeting Merilee Brunswick?"

"Well," Suzanne began, searching her memory, "Hope Zandel, for one, and the assignment editor who got the call, several production assistants, Hope's admin…I think that's it."

"What about our friend, Brian Saunders?" David asked. The question sounded as though he were positing a theory.

"You think?" Suzanne said, her voice growing tense.

David continued, "He knew where we met and where she lived. He retrieved the book from the car but he didn't see her return it to me and, as far as I know, he's the only one to disappear into thin air without a trace."

"This man…Saunders…who is he, and why would he kill your friend?" Ron inquired.

"He's our limo driver on the West Coast. I'm betting he wanted the book and cards back."

"David," Suzanne interrupted, struggling to understand the anchor's line of reasoning "Why would Saunders want it…what's so valuable about it? I mean…to kill for something you can easily find…I don't get it."

"Actually, Suzanne, you can't find 'this book' just anywhere," Ron observed. "The Qur'an, and five cards inside, likely contains a hidden message. The most reasonable supposition is that your driver tried to retrieve it for whoever dropped it…and…whoever that man is, he might be connected to the events in San Francisco."

"I never trusted Brian Saunders…not even for a moment," David added. "There was something about him, something…strange. When the FBI told us he disappeared, I thought…well, he's probably just a guy with a checkered past who needed a job, so he faked an identity to get one and got caught. It's not that uncommon these days. Now I wonder whether he was intentionally sent to be my driver to spy on me and, accidentally, stumbled onto Merilee's secret. He's the only one, besides us, who saw the book. Maybe, he wound up killing Merilee to get what he thought he was looking for. It's the only thing that fits."

"Why, in heaven's name, would he want to spy on you in the first place? This sounds made up," Suzanne insisted. "I may have to rock-paper-scissor you guys on this one."

"It's clear to me," David said. "Look at the facts, if…"

"I'm too tired to argue the facts, now," intoned Suzanne. "I need to recharge."

David said, "Why don't you go lie down and take a nap?"

"And sit up for the rest of the night in my hotel room with jet lag? No thanks!"

"A few hours won't matter and I promise the newsroom will still be here."

She glanced over at Ron who twice nodded his approval. "A nap might help clear your head. Go on…if anything happens, we'll call you."

Suzanne rose, hesitated for a second, then acquiesced and tromped off to her suite without wishing them good night.

"I guess this is all a bit much," David told Ron.

"It is abstract," Ron agreed, "especially, this thing with Eric."

"My father is gone and I had a bad dream. What's so inexplicable about that?"

"You don't believe in life after death…a soul…a higher spiritual plane…an eternal entity?"

"No, as a matter of fact, I don't!"

"I understand your feelings, David. Certain things challenge your faith. It happens to everyone sometimes."

"There's no challenge if you deal in deductive logic and reason." David hesitated a moment. Then, he added, "Leave my dad, faith, God, and the Navajo Great Spirit out of the discussion… okay… please!"

"Fine with me. All I am saying is that deductive reasoning doesn't come first and logic is only a tool to prove a premise. The premise is the first cause, and it comes from inductive reasoning… like… insight, inspiration, a wild flash of an idea…even a hunch or a guess. You must first have faith in your premise, then you set out to logically prove it. You do believe in cause and effect, within the context of existence and a non-empty universe?"

"Sure. I cede the existence of causality. Can we move on?"

But Ron would not move on. For some time now, he was concerned that his friend was so vociferous in his refusal to discuss his lost faith. He was done being rebuffed whenever he broached the subject. "As a philosophy minor this might interest you."

"What's that?" David said, pouring a drink, holding the bottle up as an invitation for Ron to join him. Ron lifted his glass and, swirling the ice with his index finger, answered.

"Aristotle first put forth a first cause, or an uncaused cause, pointing to the origin of existence. Aristotle's proof never addressed the uniqueness of the first cause…indeed, there could be more than one, and he never made any claim about the nature of God, or whether the first cause was purposeful and conscious. Of course, Aquinas, Maimonides, and Avicenna expanded on his proof for just that purpose."

"To prove God exists," David said, matter-of-factly. "Ron, I know what you're trying to do and I appreciate it…I really do! I may not be a scientist but I have heard of the Big Bang. I just think it happened at random. Can we leave this alone for a while?"

"Which brings us back to the beginning of this argument," Ron observed. "When you look at the universe, don't you see cause, pattern and purpose? And for now, I will say no more."

The conversation switched to more prosaic topics and after an hour, or so, both men decided to heed the advice they gave Suzanne and relax for the remainder of the flight.

Ron returned to the row where he had been seated when he first came on board the jumbo jet, opened the overhead compartment, and retrieved some handwritten notes and a laptop from his luggage. He remained in deep concentration, working on his eleventh book comparing the ascent of disparate cultures to the development of a set of language skills common to all.

David sat in the row farthest away from the conference area. The sun was behind them now and, with night falling in Europe, the aircraft, along with David and his companions, raced into the oncoming darkness. He dimmed the window, reclined his chair and, closing his eyes, tried to fall asleep, but the uncertainty surrounding the trip made sleeping impossible. So he sat in the stillness of the cabin trying to rest, when the conversation with Ron kindled an old memory. He pictured a young man, barely out of boyhood, eyes black as onyx and as intense as a summer thunderstorm. He remembered the boy sitting at the edge of a beautiful stone fountain, its inner bowl lined with blue and gold ceramic tiles. Suddenly, he heard the boy's words as though he was sitting there in the adjacent seat, "America has lost its soul…you must pay for your sins…open your eyes and see."

It was 12:34 AM Central Europe Summer Time when 'Constellation Voyager' landed in Rome. The airport was named after an historical figure who had envisioned flight half a millennium earlier. His iconic drawing of 'The Vitruvian Man' adorned the terminal's concourse. It spoke of the classical orders, of architectural proportion, and of the relationship between humankind and the clockworks of the universe. To the more discerning eye, it depicted the symbolic link between the material and spiritual existence of humankind.

Their arrival had been prearranged so it didn't matter that immigration and customs were closed for the night. Passengers on private aircraft were accustomed to special treatment and a lone immigration official, a man David guessed was in his late seventies if he were a day, handed back their passports without a hint of scrutiny. Then, off they went to the exit, piling into the Maserati Quattroporte waiting at the curb just outside the terminal. At that hour, the roads were largely deserted and the ground trip took less than forty minutes.

The bellman was standing at attention, a brass luggage cart at the ready, as their car pulled in front of the Hotel Cicerone. Suzanne, refreshed by several hours of sleep on the plane, hopped out first to organize the check-in process. To her surprise, the night manager quickly appeared, welcomed his new guests in musically accented English and handed each a room key. The man was tall and suave, with groomed, jet-black hair. That he was clearly charmed by the beautiful American woman, who spoke with him in his native tongue, was obvious. They followed the bellman to the floor where three adjacent suites had been reserved. David occupied the center suite and Ron and Suzanne met him there once they settled in.

"Everyone comfortable?" Suzanne asked.

"I'm good!" Ron said with a Cheshire cat grin that, just like in Lewis Carroll's story, remained in the air long after he stopped smiling.

David nodded. "That goes double for me." He opened the mini bar and asked, "Anyone up for a nightcap…might help you sleep!"

Both indicated they would join him, so David returned with three glasses of Nocello, a delicate liqueur made from blending husks of walnuts and hazelnuts.

He set the three glasses on the table next to Merilee Brunswick's brown leather book. "Ron, what time are we expected?"

"The Cardinal said noon."

David looked at his wristwatch. "It's getting late…why don't we catch some shuteye and meet downstairs for breakfast…say around ten. Then we'll walk over to the Vatican, all right?"

"Fine, fine…" Ron said as he finished his drink.

"Suzanne?"

"Why not," she replied. "Six hours of sleep is more than anyone deserves." She placed her glass half finished on the table and headed for the door with Ron in tow.

"See you guys in the morning," Ron said, walking toward his room.

Suzanne lingered just past the doorway, waiting in the corridor. She could not put into words, exactly, what it was she was waiting for, but reasoned that, if it wasn't named, it wasn't tangible, and if it wasn't tangible, it couldn't hurt her.

David followed her, leaned casually against the door jam and said. "Don't forget to double lock your door or you may find your friend downstairs with the master key standing at your bedside…dressed in a grin and nothing else."

"Jealous, David?"

"Let's say…cautious."

"I think you're being silly!" Suzanne said, smiling at David's awkward attempt at flirting.

Suzanne felt a bit cautious, herself, having been in this situation with him before. She moved toward her room, walking backward, watching David and swinging the room key on her outstretched finger. David made no move toward her, so she unlocked the door, threw back her head and brushed the hair away from her face. "Good night, David," she said, and slipping past the room's portal, she disappeared.

"Good night, Suzanne," he said quietly to the empty corridor. He slowly closed the door, thinking the emptiness might make a good metaphor for his life.

Leaning against the closed door, shoulders slumped, David thought, go knock on her door, right now…what are you waiting for? He turned to go, grabbed the door handle, but stopped, letting his hand drop.

Instead, the newsman crossed the room, picked up Merilee's leather book from the table, and walked out onto the balcony. The city was quiet at this hour and everywhere he looked there was something from antiquity that caused him to marvel. Sitting on the terrace's only bench, looking out at the Justice Building, David began reminiscing about a night just like this, warm with a gentle breeze;

one of many nights his family spent visiting his grandparents in Connecticut.

It was late summer and David had just turned eleven. The family was sitting outside on the wooden veranda of an expanded Cape Cod-style house his grandparents kept north of Mystic. The view, peaceful as one could ever want, looked out over the setting sun that gracefully danced and spun gold over the Sound, casting a pink glow on the anchored sailboats, quietly rocking to the soft, warm breeze that came up off the Long Island Sound. The leaves of the maple trees lining the shore were just turning that brilliant yellow-orange that was one of the hallmarks of his mother's love of nature.

At his wife's insistence, David's grandfather added a wrap-a-round veranda to the little house years ago, and it was here that the family, starting from early spring and well on into autumn, most liked to gather to eat and chat and laugh. The veranda was made of a now creaky, but well-kept, old pine with a classic white railing and a green and white striped awning that protected the family from the sun and rain. Green Adirondack chairs sat helter-skelter among white wicker tables piled high with assorted books, magazines, empty cookie plates, coffee cups, tall iced tea glasses, and his grandmother's hand-crocheted linen napkins.

David's father and grandfather were watching the ball game on a tiny portable television set. It was plugged into an electrical outlet connected to one of the wrought iron porch lights hanging next to the entrance of the house.

The New York Yankees were playing the Boston Red Sox and they were, once again, neck and neck for the American League Pennant. The competition was white hot, hotter than a summer day, and the men in the family were heatedly debating who had the best chance of winning the Series. David noticed his mother quietly staring at her husband with a small, but unmistakable, smile turning up each corner of her mouth ever so slightly. She had a look in her eyes that David recognized, even at his age, as bordering on adoration.

David leaned over to his mother and asked her what she was thinking. His mother grinned and sighed. "Ahh, yes, I should know I can't hide anything from my clever boy. I was thinking how a relationship is just, exactly, like a baseball game. The similarities are remarkable. In baseball, one side pitches but you cannot play unless the other side steps up to the plate. That's why I married your father, David. Even though he truly can drive me crazy, every time it's my turn to pitch, your father's at the plate. It can't have been easy…I have a pretty wicked fastball, I must admit. Sometimes I throw curves, and, once or twice, I have thrown a slider that must have been truly painful. Some things I threw at your father could, quite frankly, be called wild. But your dad stepped up to the plate every time, like a real pro, and hung in there with me. I tried my best to do the same for him, although I'm not sure I was quite as good at bat as I was on the mound. When I think about those times, and I see him sitting there, watching ball with my dad, and I think about how we are still here; it just takes my breath away. In our years together, I guess we have seen just about every kind of play there is in the game…strikes, walks, hits…lots of home runs, one or two grand slams even, but no matter what, we both keep playing. And you know what? Now we have a championship team. I was very lucky, David. I found someone who was willing to play ball with me, no matter what I pitched at him."

David's daydream faded to the memory of cheering baseball fans on a late summer's night. He could hear his mother say, play ball, David, play ball. And he did, for no matter how hard it was to cover a story, David always stepped up to the plate. But the real game, the important game about which his mother was talking, had nothing to do with the news business and everything to do with finding someone special. Yes, there were brief liaisons to keep a rising star occupied or distracted, perhaps even happy for a short while. But he knew the truth and it was simply this: for a long time now he was alone in a dark and empty stadium and the one light that was always on, his father, no longer shone.

Absently, David flipped the pages of Merilee's book, again and again, listening to the sound of the fluttering sheets stirring the air. Had he really come to Rome to find the answers to some contrived mystery or had he agreed to this trip to be with Suzanne? Wasn't he positive that all these isolated events were nothing more than a coincidence despite Ron's insistence that they were not? Did he really think some musty cardinal whose name meant 'eastern star' might have the insights he'd been searching for since his mother's death? Now there was a dead girl to add to the mix. Surely, wasn't it his obligation to get answers to why Merilee met such a sad end?

David realized he was too exhausted to answer his own questions. Retiring for the night, he left the doors to the balcony open so the curtains, dancing hypnotically in the gentle breeze, combined with the soft urbane sounds from the eternal city below, would lull him to sleep.

Clichy-sous-Bois, a small municipality about ten miles northeast of the Paris city center, is one of the capital's poorest suburbs. Its minority population, mostly Muslim, is isolated from mainstream French society and largely unemployed. Except for a single bus, the commune has no public transportation. Visitors are a rare sight.

Should a tourist stumble into the area, the stark contrast between it and the picturesque streets of Paris would be overwhelming. Instead of quaint bistros, tree lined boulevards, and an astonishing fugue of art and architecture, graffiti is scrawled on the walls of unadorned, urbanized, plain rectangular apartment buildings. Utilitarian is about the only complement you could pay to it.

Ahmad and Sharif spent the day waiting inside one of these nondescript white buildings. Their apartment was sparsely furnished, containing only two mattresses, a worn sofa, several wobbly chairs and a folding table. These would have to do. Luxury was not something they, or the men coming with them, craved or cared for; there was time enough for these trivialities in paradise. The hardships of this life were embraced with gratitude. It made them stronger than the enemy.

Immediately after the sun set, Ahmad and Sharif knelt for the maghrib, the evening prayer, and asked Allah to deliver their souls from the temptation to do evil. Then they rose and ate a light supper, their appetites hampered by a combination of the late hour, impatience, and anxiety.

Ahmad waited, staring out the window into the nightfall, thinking back to the days when he was younger, more earnest, more carefree, and in love with a beautiful woman from Iran. He could not forget the plans that were dashed when she was killed in the riot –

one of the many riots that were erupting at the time in this part of France.

The community leaders in the area claimed she was an innocent bystander targeted by a prejudiced police department. The French authorities claimed it was a tragic accident but blamed those same leaders who had instigated the rage within the community to grow out of control.

As always, the truth was lost in a fog of conflicting information. The only thing left to survive was her memory and the bitterness Ahmad carried in his heart. But soon, he would strike again at the very heart of the oppressor and Ahmad's bitterness, a ghost that haunted him night and day, might finally be mollified.

These memories, events from the past, dead to others but very much alive to him, were interrupted by a soft knock. He jumped out of his chair, startled.

Ahmad pulled opened the apartment door without looking through the peephole. Four men were standing in the hallway. Their skin was the color of almonds. Two had black hair and short cropped beards; another, the tallest of the group, was mostly bald and clean-shaven.

The forth man was much older. His face was gaunt with deep cut lines. A grey beard, lining his jaw-line, was accented with patches of black. His intense brown eyes communicated a message of firm resolve, even foreboding, and spoke silently about the years of struggle and pain he had endured.

Ahmad stood aside like a sentinel at attention, which was a small gesture indicating they should enter. The men came into the room, none speaking a word, each handing Ahmad a small card. On one side, there was an embossed gold symbol with seven loops on the outside and four on the inside, in a knot that seemed to have no end or beginning. On the other side, there were three short incantations in Arabic with blank spaces where some words were missing. The incantations were all different and the men inserted the missing words, separately, to complete each sentence.

Ahmad gathered the cards and, without a word, went into the bedroom. He retrieved Sharif's Qur'an and the nine-millimeter semi-automatic given him by the contact who met them outside the airport terminal. On the back page, there was a hastily scribbled list of cipher keys transcribed from the prayer book left behind with Sholeh's parents. He applied a different key to each card, producing a set of numbers. The numbers pointed to pages in the Qur'an and to a specific passage where the exact words, entered on each card, could also be found.

Satisfied, he returned to the group, this time with a softer, almost benevolent, expression and greeted the men properly.

"Salaam, brothers. May the blessings of the Prophet be upon you."

"And may Allah's blessings be upon you," one of them replied, the others nodding in agreement.

"Come in," Ahmad said, "Please, sit down. We have our future to discuss."

They gathered around the table. Sharif placed a matchbook under one leg of the table as a remedy for its wobble, and the men sat down. Once everyone was comfortable, Ahmad introduced himself and Sharif did the same. Each of the men followed, anxious to impress their new leader.

"My name is Ali bin Hussein al Mubi," said one of the younger men, "and this is Josif bin Abdullah Al Farran. "We work as apprentice chefs for the conference at the Hôtel de Ville. We prepare the food...the food for the reception!"

Speaking in Arabic, Ali al Mubi outlined the exact jobs for which he and Josif had been hired. He reviewed every detail surrounding the food preparation and related security, often repeating a description or speaking slowly, as though Ahmad would not understand what was being said. This annoyed Ahmad. He had to force himself to maintain the impression of someone interested in the proper technique for cutting vegetables. The over-eager Ali al Mubi continued describing his work in excruciating detail, using his hands as a visual aid, and was halfway through recounting proper knife skills when the tall bald man spoke out.

"Thank you, Ali," the tall one said in English, "I do not believe our imam requires the intimate particulars of cooking for your station. My name is Roshed bin Hamid Ismail. I am the assistant banquet manager. My job is to oversee..."

"I know your job," Ahmad said, losing patience.

"Yes, yes of course. I only wanted to assure you that we were able to get both of you the proper passes for entering the hall."

"How are you sure this isn't a trap?" Ahmad asked.

"I…we, have been working there for almost ten years," Roshed answered. "The French, they are lazy and we do most of the work in the building. We are paid very little but never complain. We do as we are told, work hard and long. We are always smiling and grateful for our jobs. They hold us down, but we never show displeasure or too much ambition. There is a very old proverb, my brother, 'If you cannot cut your enemies hand…then kiss it'. This is how we live. I promise you, we are trusted and no suspicion falls on us."

"I see," Ahmad said, looking toward Sharif, a small nod signaling his agreement.

"And the security arrangements?" Sharif inquired.

"They are complete." Roshed responded without hesitation. "The night security chief is a lazy man named Philippe Noiret. He has a job solely due to his brother's high position in the Interior Ministry. The man has a girlfriend and a wife. Once, or twice, a week he spends the evening with this girlfriend. Because I am there for many years, one day he asks that I put his code into the computer, every hour, until he returns. For this, he gives me his password. Soon after that, he asks every week. I stay late with no pay, until he comes back. Sometimes he brings me the leftover food she cooks. A dog could cook a better meal! Once he gave me twenty Euros. He thinks I'm a fool. Two days ago, when he went out, I uploaded the programs as I was instructed. Show him, Abdul!"

Abdul bin Khalid Al Jahni, born in Egypt, was a foot soldier in the Islamic revolution that overthrew Hosni Mubarak. His family claimed some tenuous lineage with the eighteenth dynasty of Pharaoh Amenhotep. He looked as old and weathered as the Pyramids and moved in a slow and deliberate manner.

From a pouch hidden under his shirt, Abdul produced a flash drive, two security badges, one for Ahmad and one for Sharif, plus a small bronze-colored glass vial. The vial had been smuggled out of Russia by people with the same values and vision as Abdul. Born inside a nuclear reactor, the substance within the vial contained traces of an isotope found in uranium. Less than a hundred, or so, grams of this substance were manufactured each year and Abdul's vial contained about one tenth of a gram. Abdul sat, silent, leaving the objects on the table, staring at Ahmad with that same foreboding look, waiting for a reaction.

"This looks like salt," Ahmad said, lifting the vial level with his eyes.

"It was disguised to look that way," Roshed replied. "The salt contains the poison. The alpha radiation it emits is almost undetectable. It is safe as long as it does not enter the body…but once in the body, there is no cure and death comes in a week. A millionth of a gram is enough to kill."

"Will they feel sick?" Sharif asked.

"Yes," said Roshed. "They will suffer food poisoning symptoms. The authorities will investigate, looking for bad meat or shellfish or something. When they discover what has happened, it will be too late to save anyone and we will be gone."

"You don't talk much, do you, Abdul?" Ahmad commented. "What is your job?"

Lowering his eyes, Abdul replied, "I am a janitor, nothing more."

"May I, Imam?" Roshed asked.

"Yes."

"Abdul brought the necessary materials to us, from far away, at great risks to himself. Also, we are searched when we enter work for an event such as this, so we cannot bring this vial in. I stole one of the kitchen saltshakers. It will replace the vial, and it will be hidden in the handle of Abdul's mop. During the meal service, we will create a diversion by spilling a tray of drinks on the floor. When Abdul comes in to clean this up, he will give the saltshaker to Ali. Abdul is a quiet, humble man…but he is most important."

"And Ali will season the conference delegates' food with this new salt…yes?" Sharif asked, with an unmistakable air of approval.

"And they will die," Abdul said, displaying no emotion. His face, at best, could only be described as sullen.

Ahmad and Sharif exchanged nods, first to each other, and then to the group at large. The men looked relieved as Ahmad complimented their initiative.

"You have done well, brothers. Your deeds will bring blessings on you all. But I am curious about the security arrangements and the contents of this flash drive."

"These are your entry badges." Roshed explained. "With these, you can go to the assignment area where you will get a badge to work in one part of the building. You must not go anywhere else or you will be detained and questioned so, be careful. The programs I uploaded are on the memory stick. They are like a computer virus. First, your facial features have been added to the security database so the camera scan will recognize you. Also your badge identification with your fingerprints is there and it will match the scan. After the reception dinner, late that night, the virus will completely wipe out all the security data and all the disks, including the backups on the network. It will destroy the security program and any other programs it finds, anywhere. It will cripple the city and erase our identities. Even the traffic signals will freeze. In this confusion, we will escape."

"And in case the plan fails?" Ahmad asked.

"A year ago, they replaced the kitchen wall ovens. An RDX compound was built into these ovens. It is a very powerful explosive, given to us by a friend in the Pakistan military. It was hard to disguise so, to be safe, we left out the remote detonator. We were afraid security might find it when they scanned the shipment. However, by setting the oven to auto clean, the timer to 714, and the temperature to 471, the bomb will be triggered."

"Excellent," Ahmad remarked. He returned the vial to Abdul and kept the flash drive and badges, placing them in the front pocket of his trousers.

Roshed folded his arms across his chest and slid his chair back from the table. He appeared embarrassed by Ahmad's praise. "We cannot take credit, we only carried out what was told to us, what we must do!"

According to the plan, as presented, Ahmad and Sharif did not need to enter the hall or attend the banquet. It was a dangerous and risky thing to do. But both wanted to witness, and be a part of, this holy act of justice.

To Sharif, this was more than just an assignment, or a mission. This was the moment of his initiation, the moment that would prove he was worthy and truly dedicated. Ahmad, on the other hand, had proven himself long ago, time and time again. In his mind, this was a reckoning, a chance to even the score, a chance to make a statement beyond the press reports and public opinion. It didn't matter if only he knew. It would suffice to drive out the demons of Sholeh's death; the relentless tormentors of his thoughts and dreams.

So the plan was set. Six men with menial jobs, unimportant and characterless, working at the reception for the World Banking Conference, would poison the attendees, decapitating several levels of leadership from the attending countries, along with the executives of their central banks and financial institutions. In the ensuing vacuum and panic, they prayed a magnificent new Caliphate would arise.

Inviting the men to join them in Isha, the night prayer, Ahmad moved to the center of the empty room and adjusted the placement of several small threadbare rugs. Each man washed as best he could in the decrepit sink that barely clung to the wall of the tiny bathroom, praying that God would purify them of their sins.

They knelt together, reflecting on the majesty of Allah, each reciting, in muted voices, the four elements of manifestation – all except Ahmad, whose thoughts were occupied with a manifestation of a different kind.

The Unveiling

David Anderson began the morning with a continental breakfast of juice, coffee, pastries and a lively discussion with Ron, centering on speculation about the meaning of the book and its five laminated cards. Suzanne listened, distracted, her head filled with anticipation at seeing the Vatican Library and meeting Cardinal Oriastro. She was still practicing the greetings she would use when David asked, "Everyone ready? Shall we go?"

The weather was nearly perfect: warm, with an unclouded sky and a hint of humidity. There was plenty of time for a bit of sightseeing. Dressed in business attire, the trio wanted to arrive for their audience with the Cardinal still looking crisp and fresh, so they walked along, unhurried, taking in the city. All three found it surprising and somewhat disappointing, that so many shops and cafés were shuttered along their route – the closed businesses were a testimony to the story of Europe's continuing economic problems.

The restaurants still open for business were busily preparing for the afternoon meal. Suzanne stopped at several of these to consider the menu, take in the ambiance, and make notes for possible dinner locations. Forty minutes later, they found themselves, along with a group of tourists, inside the great ellipse of white Doric columns surrounding Saint Peter's Square.

"Which way?" David asked Ron.

"It's this way…to the right of the Basilica…at the end of the colonnade. There, see…next to the Scala Regina."

The Swiss Guards, dressed in uniforms inspired by Renaissance design, looked over Ron's academic credentials and the Cardinal's invitation. Carefully, they checked each passport before providing directions to the Libraria Vaticana. After a circuitous walk through interconnecting passageways, the three finally found a long corridor with stone slabs set into its walls. Ron smiled; it was a sign of relief. "Okay, I know where we are now."

"Sharing would be nice." Suzanne prompted. She shrugged and added, as an answer to Ron's glare, "Just saying…I like to know these things."

"All right," Ron began, loving any opportunity to teach. "This is the Lapidarian Gallery. The slabs on the right walls are inscribed with pagan epitaphs that envision a dire destiny for mankind, filled with fear and hopelessness. The slabs on the left, contain Christian inscriptions expressing a hopeful future and a wish for peace and common understanding."

"It's dark and gloomy in here," said Suzanne, distracted from the lesson.

"That all depends on the destiny you choose," Ron quipped, noticing David smiling broadly and nodding in agreement.

At the end of the long passageway, they passed through two ponderous iron doors. Beyond the doors, Ron told Suzanne, "This is the Libraria Vaticana, or Hall of Sixtus, as it is officially known."

They entered a cavernous space of magnificent splendor. High above them was an enormous vaulted ceiling, supported by rectangular ornamental pillars that flared out, becoming part of the overhead arches. The hall was illuminated by medieval shades of gold, white, blue, and red and its walls, ceiling arches, and pillars were lavishly decorated with frescoes of exceptional beauty and grace. The architects and designers of this building, most assuredly, believed beauty essential to praising God and elevating the spirit.

"So...where are the books hiding?" Suzanne asked. The question had a timid quality about it, as if it was too greedy to ask.

"Follow me." Ron replied.

They continued through the galleries where Ron stopped for a second and pointed to a group of gilded cabinets with ivory carvings.

"The books are locked in there."

When the group came upon the reading room for periodicals, with its stacks and card cabinets, Suzanne relaxed in the more familiar surroundings.

"Now, this looks like a library," she said, walking toward shelves stacked with yellow binders.

"Suzanne!" Ron reminded her, "Don't touch anything! You haven't been invited to do research here."

David tapped his wristwatch. "Time folks...time."

At the end of the reading room they found an elevator that went directly to the administrative offices. The doors opened into a small anteroom, sparsely furnished with a formal hunter green sofa and a utilitarian wooden desk. Behind the desk, a young man, wearing a black Roman cassock, sat sorting a stack of pages with great care and attention. On the wall behind him was a crucifix, and on the corner of the desk, a statue of Saint George. He stopped, mid-task, looked up, and asked, with practiced politeness, "Buon pomeriggio, come posso aiutarla?"

Suzanne stepped forward and replied, "Ciao, il mio nome è Suzanne Biasotto. Questo è David Anderson. Noi siamo da Global News. E mi permette di introdurre il professore Eyota. Abbiamo un appuntamento con il Cardinale. Parli inglese?"

"Yes, yes," he replied, with a Slavic accent. "Welcome to the Library of the Vatican. I'm Father Jovan." Then he added with haste, "The Cardinal is expecting you."

They followed Father Jovan through a labyrinth of offices, full of other attentive young men dressed in black cassocks and white collars, dutifully completing their daily assignments.

"I detect a Balkan influence in your name and accent," Ron said, filling the silence.

"Yes, yes…you are a well-traveled man, no doubt. I am from a small suburb outside of Belgrade…it was destroyed during the war by NATO…my family was killed and I was placed in an orphanage until I joined the seminary…but that was long ago. Now I am very fortunate that I can serve God, and the world, here at the Library."

Father Jovan was anxious to tell Ron his life story and began recounting his personal history. The priest stopped, mid-sentence, when they reached a closed door with opaque glass and gold colored letters painted across it that read:

Cardinal Archivist and Librarian of the Holy Roman Church
His Most Reverend Eminence Card. Raffaele Oriastro, DSc, DTheol.
animadverto Deus quod ago

The good father knocked softly on the door. "Eminence," he called, "your noon appointment is here."

The door opened with exaggerated slowness, as though it was moving through liquid rather than air. The Cardinal was also dressed in a black cassock, but with red buttons, indicating his elevated status. He stood with a serene expression that suggested a wisdom born of the service required of his calling. There was the slightest hint of a smile in his deep-set eyes, conveying a sense of infinite patience and an enlightened understanding of the world and the affairs of its diverse peoples.

Ron was first to extend his hand in greeting. "Good afternoon, Your Eminence. I am Professor Eyota." Following a longstanding tradition, he kissed the Cardinal's ring, and stepped aside for Suzanne.

"I am Suzanne Biasotto, Your Eminence," she said, affecting a slight bow, also kissing the ring on the Cardinal's outstretched hand.

David stepped forward, shook the Cardinal's hand, and said. "Cardinal Oriastro, thank you for making time to see us. I'm David Anderson."

"It is my great pleasure to grant an audience to such a distinguished group and to meet, in person, such a noted historian. Professor Eyota, we have much in common and I have, how do you say, enjoyed reading your books."

"Thank you, Your Eminence," replied Ron, "you are most gracious to say so."

Raffaele Oriastro ushered them into a conference room where they took seats around a long rectangular table decorated with Byzantine carvings in its sides and legs.

"May I offer you a refreshment…some tea, perhaps?"

"Yes, thank you," said Ron.

Father Jovan returned minutes later with a silver tray upon which sat a white porcelain teapot, four white china cups, a plate with lemon wedges and a small bowl containing unrefined sugar. Each piece of china had a delicate rose design around its edge.

As the tea was being served, Ron asked the Cardinal, "How was your visit to Haifa?"

"Quite rewarding. Some interesting archeological artifacts were uncovered by a construction crew working at the Cave of Elijah near the Carmelite monastery."

"I can imagine it must have been very exciting. May I ask what was found there?"

"We discovered, what appear to be, two thousand-year-old fragments of a lost biblical manuscript. We're hoping it illuminates a blind spot in our understanding of that time."

"Any idea of their origin?"

"It's too early to tell…though I'm speculating they're from Qumran, possibly Essene. In fact, they bear a remarkable resemblance to the Dead Sea Scrolls. However, I have no idea how they ended up in Haifa at Mount Carmel."

"His Eminence is busy translating them now." Father Jovan said. "Most are in Aramaic."

"I would gladly volunteer to assist in any way…that is, if I can be useful." Ron offered.

The Cardinal smiled, a small but perceptible smile, at the history professor's interest. It was an acknowledgement of their common pursuit to understand the events and peoples of the past. He removed a few papers from a nearby shelf and returned to the table.

"The Church takes no position as to the origin or authenticity of these writings, and they will soon be available to various independent scholars for assessment. There is some indication they may have been created in the Middle Ages. We have a radiometric analysis scheduled, hoping to establish an approximate date. Regardless, the scrolls are ancient and it is quite fortuitous that they have come into our hands. The fragment is practically intact, which is quite remarkable. If you are interested, I will be happy to share a passage we translated today."

"Please do," Ron said.

David and Suzanne's expressions indicated that they, too, were in unanimous agreement at such a rare honor.

The Cardinal took great care as he ran his fingers through the pages, until he found just the right passage. He sat back in his chair and read:

"And He raised his hand and smiled upon a crowd of men, saying, 'Peace be with you.'

But they were in deep anguish and ashamed to return His greeting, for each, in his own way, had sinned. And the angels of the Heavenly Father, who are charged with guarding the earth, were distraught and, some wept. Then one man, his face twisted in torment, looked up and spoke: 'Rabbi, we are in painful need of your gentle guidance.'

So Jesus spoke to them:
'To lift your eyes towards your Heavenly Father
when all eyes are lowered toward the ground,
is not easy.
To worship God
when those around you worship only themselves and
their wealth,
this, too, is not easy.
But, I say to you, the most difficult thing of all

is to have the thoughts and the words of angels.

Act as angels do, and live without shame in the sight of God."'

"That's beautiful!" Suzanne said. The cardinal smiled.

"From the correspondence with your office," Ron interjected, "I gather the trip was brief."

"It was…I would have liked to spend some time visiting with old acquaintances."

"I know what you mean about quick business trips!" Suzanne said, anxious to join the discussion. "There's never any time for yourself."

Oriastro, charmed by Suzanne's concern, assured her. "As the former Auxiliary Bishop of Jerusalem, I am quite familiar with the area. Although short, my trip was, nevertheless, enriching. I've had many interesting experiences in that part of the world. Would you like to hear about a remarkable incident that happened while I was there?"

Ever the inveterate journalist, Suzanne urged the priest to begin. "Yes, of course!"

"Very well." Oriastro agreed, impelled by the young producer's interest. "Before returning to Rome, one year, I went to visit friends in a town named Shlomi. It is in Northern Israel, not far from the Lebanese border. Over the course of ten years, or so, it seemed, whenever I traveled there, the town was under attack from rockets launched from somewhere inside Lebanon. I was told the rockets had been falling intermittently for the past month. The townspeople were so accustomed to this constant barrage; they simply went about their day as though it was just another part of life, resigned to entrusting their lives to the army troops charged with protecting the settlement.

"Now…there are green rolling hills that run across both sides of the border and on these hills there are shepherds - Jews, Palestinians, and Christians - all tending flocks. They have no quarrel and, in fact, some are close friends whose families share the land and have done so for a thousand years. The day I left, we set off onto the highway and were driving along the 899 Motorway, north of town. We passed a garrison of Israeli tanks that had been sent to quell the rockets. The soldiers fired their cannons just as we passed. The percussion was so loud it shook the car. My driver slammed on the breaks and covered his ears. I was forced to do the same. When the attack ended, I looked around and, to my surprise, the sheep were lying on the ground. All, but a few, were dead; so frightened were they by the explosion. As we drove away, heartbroken for the families who had lost their livelihood, I kept asking myself, was it merely the sound that killed the sheep and ruined the lives of those who tended them?"

Suzanne and Ron, their full attention on the Cardinal, remained silent, reflecting on the cardinal's poignant story. David, head down, sat fidgeting with his smartphone, one foot tapping out a nervous rhythm.

Oriastro, sensitive to his guest's impatience, asked, "Tell me then, what is the nature of your visit?"

"Perhaps our resident academician should explain," David said. He was anxious to get to the business at hand.

Ron presented the events surrounding David's sojourn in the Middle East, when he received the scroll and had it delivered to Ron. He included as much background information and color as he could remember, hopeful the Cardinal, with his extensive experience in the region, would be able to help them interpret the strange series of events.

Mindful of the Cardinal's time, he tried to finish the story as quickly as he could, without sacrificing any of the salient details. He ended by relating David's vision of his father.

"In light of David's...eh...experience," Ron concluded, "and once I made the connection between the meaning of your name and David's recollection of his father's message, well, I naturally began to wonder if, perhaps, there might be something...say...precognitive, or...preternatural about this. On the other hand, we have been wondering whether it all might just be a coincidence."

"Of course, it's a coincidence!" David said. His voice, although barely above a whisper, was unmistakably quarrelsome. "At least, that's my working theory!"

Cardinal Oriastro looked at David, and then, turning to Ron, asked, "When you say, preternatural, is providential what you really mean?"

"One might look at it that way," Ron replied.

"Professor, do you recognize the phrase *Pluralitas non est ponenda sine necessitate?*"

"It is Latin for 'Entities should not be multiplied unnecessarily,' isn't it?"

"Indeed."

"Are you saying, according to the law of parsimony, I actually saw my father and he guided me to you? I don't mean to be rude, but I find this theory untenable. It has to be coincidence!"

The Cardinal continued in the same even, dulcet tone of voice with which he first greeted them. "I agree the simplicity rule may not be sufficient to explain the events as described, but to quote Shakespeare: *'There are more things in heaven and earth, Horatio, than are dreamt of in your philosophy'*. Accordingly, my young friend... I don't think coincidence, alone, is sufficient to explain the facts as described."

"Look, Cardinal..."

Ron, waving down David's willful persistence, interrupted, "Regardless of how we've come to be here, why don't we get down to the business of reviewing the items we came here to analyze?"

Orienting the five laminated cards and the prayer book, so they properly faced the Prelate, Ron added, "These are the articles we need you to review."

"I see," replied Oriastro, as he raised an opened hand.

Father Jovan placed a Lucite tube in the Cardinal's outstretched fingers, and laid a clear pane of quarter inch thick glass on the table. Affixed to the tube was a label with the familiar ND logo of Notre Dame University. It was addressed to Cardinal Alberto Esposito and the handwriting on the label, unmistakably, belonged to Ron.

"I discovered this in my predecessor's safe," noted Oriastro. "It is the reason that I extended the invitation for you to visit the library. I thought we should open it together."

David let a long sigh escape his lips. "I thought I would never see that again. I figured it was lost, forever, when Ron told me the Cardinal died. Now, I'm sorry I forgot about it."

Oriastro nodded and began to open the sealed tube in which lay the ancient scroll. As Librarian of the Holy Roman Church, Oriastro had extensive training in proper handling of ancient documents. With deliberate and painstaking concentration, he unsealed one side of the tube. It made a faint whooshing sound as the protective gas escaped. He then opened a drawer to his left, taking out a pair of white cotton gloves, and pulled them over his sturdy, timeworn hands. He extracted the scroll, placed it on the table, and removed the length of hemp that bound it. Ever so slowly, he unrolled the document; his movements measured, exact, and watchful. He listened for any sound to indicate the scroll was under duress. They held their breath until the papyrus lay flat on the glass plate. The five laminated cards and the scroll from the safe were imprinted with the same shiny gold symbol.

The Cardinal stopped his examination and looked up. "Now this is quite interesting. David, you look puzzled...tell me why?"

"I...um...got this from a Shaykh in Iran more than a decade ago," said David, clearly surprised. "That symbol on top was attached to quite a few buildings...in several countries. No one would talk about it and, when I pressed the issue, some unpleasant things occurred. I never found out what it meant, and I forgot about it until we received the cards from Merilee."

"Can you tell us?" Suzanne inquired of the Cardinal.

"It is possible...yes. But it will require patience and a few hours of your time."

"Agreed!" Ron said, without hesitation. "David?"

"Yes...we came all this way."

The Cardinal nodded. "Very well, let's see what this document tells us about the past."

Oriastro scribbled a list of references and handed it to Father Jovan, who then hurried away. The Cardinal began to peruse the scroll, character by character, taking notes, crossing them out, and then rewriting his notations over again. Not more than thirty minutes later, Father Jovan returned with several thick bound volumes from the library and placed them on the table. For several hours, David and Suzanne, mesmerized, watched Oriastro work, referring to the volumes, writing notes, rescanning the scroll. All the while, Ron stood behind the Cardinal, reading over his shoulder, nodding in agreement, throwing in an observation of his own, here and there.

The late afternoon light was pressing against the stained glass of the office windows, causing a cascade of medieval colors to flood the room, when Oriastro finally put his fountain pen down and addressed the visitors.

"This document is part of a charter describing the formation of a group and the symbol that will represent their purpose."

"Yes, of course!" Ron said, "It's all very clear now!"

"Could someone explain it to us?" David asked.

"First, a bit of history may help," Oriastro said. "Ancient peoples didn't have sophisticated numbering systems, so they relied on geometry to represent the natural order of the objects they were able to observe. Thousands of years before Christ, the Egyptians, followed by the Babylonians, and then the Greeks, discovered complex geometric formulas to explain their perception of the myriad shapes found throughout nature. One of their first accomplishments was to define the basic construct upon which our visual experience is based, that is, gravity is vertical and the perfect horizontal is at right angles to it. This discovery forms the basis of the builders set square and, from the time of the Pyramids to the present, we rely upon this relationship.

"Now, about five hundred years before Christ, the Greek philosopher and mathematician, Pythagoras, discovered a basic relationship between mathematics and music. He stretched a vibrating string to form a base note then demonstrated how dividing the string in halves, quarters, thirds, produced a pleasing harmonic tone. In essence, he discovered that the division of the string, by whole numbers, corresponded to harmonic notes that sound pleasing to the ear thus proving that numbers govern sound and these numbers relate to the geometry of the string.

"Over the next few centuries, traders and conquerors spread and, in some cases, formalized these ideas. Islam was one of those driving forces, along with the new numbering system devised by Arab scholars. But, because any representation of the human body was forbidden to Muslims, geometric designs and patterns, based on the discoveries of people like Pythagoras and Euclid, became the accepted form of expression.

"In time, the intrinsic relationships among math, geometry, harmony and music became accepted as universal truth. It was believed the smallest to the largest objects, within the natural world, resonated with harmonies. These vibrations have sometimes been referred to as the music of the spheres.

"It was thought all creation was based on geometric patterns and that understanding them would lead to understanding the origins of existence and, in this, the sacred truth of creation. As this concept was extended to the sciences and arts, the belief was born that the underlying geometric proportions, and their related harmonies, were sacred. Are there any questions so far?"

No one posed a question and Oriastro continued.

"Pythagoras' theories were developed in the Arabic world by, among others, a group known as Al Ikhwan As Safa...basically, translated as 'The Brotherhood of Purity'. According to our records, the group was started in Baghdad as an early Sufi order, sometime around nine hundred and fifty one years after Christ. Some of their early writings indicate they loosely followed a universalistic philosophy based on the music of the spheres or the intrinsic natural harmony. Members of the order were required to renounce all material things and live an austere life. They were encouraged to pursue a journey of self-realization and knowledge. Their leaders intended to discover the origins of intelligence, as they believed all intelligence was inherited from a higher power.

"As part of their sacred geometry, the Brotherhood placed special emphasis on the ratio one to four to seven, and the numbers one, four and seven. These numbers were thought to possess special powers. One moment...ah yes, here, in the text, are instructions for constructing the symbol. 'It is to be a single infinite object, the number one, in the form of a knot, with no beginning or end. Four interlocking loops, forming the center, flow into seven outer loops equidistantly spaced around the outside.' Apparently, the gold is meant to symbolize the rare and precious nature of the group and its philosophy. The concept of infinity was to show the Brotherhood was destined from creation and would endure forever."

"But what does any of this have to do with the cards?" David asked.

"It is the evolution of the group that may be of interest to you," the Cardinal declared. "Centuries before Thomas Aquinas and the Schoolmen addressed subjects like prime matter, substantial form, and the process of change, the Brotherhood began to reconcile reason, faith and knowledge. In nine hundred sixty one, they founded their first school. They taught that free will, justice, and perfect logic formed the foundation of God's creative actions and that, through reason, the meaning of existence could be discovered and our ultimate destiny, a product of conscious will, could be achieved by advanced states of reasoning. Later the group added Neoplatonism and Gnosticism as part of their general beliefs."

"Neoplatonism?" Suzanne asked.

"It's a doctrine of first causes." Ron explained. "The basic principle says that the first cause and source of all reality precedes existence, and is, therefore, unknowable. Until the sixth century, it was popular in pagan Europe. It also influenced early Christians, right up through the Renaissance. Elements of this philosophy are found in Islamic writings as well. It's interesting that indigenous belief systems, including the Navajo Way, which were not influenced by Renaissance thought, also teach that knowledge and reason light a path in the darkness."

"Universal truths are not the province of any one culture or religion," Oriastro observed.

Referring to another of the volumes on the table, the librarian continued. "The Brotherhood was arcane, to say the least, and the exact identities of group's members remain unclear, even to this day...although a number of scholars have investigated the group. They authored over forty codices...epistles that addressed diverse topics...math, natural sciences, astronomy, music and theology. There is one epistle, entitled 'The Light of Revelation,' which generated much attention at the time. It has never been found."

"I recall," said Ron, "reading about a missing codex with that title...it circulated in Europe around the time of the Renaissance. I thought it was considered a myth or legend."

"It, likely, is," Oriastro assured him, "but a very detailed myth. Purportedly, this epistle describes the duality of human nature, composed of both horror and bliss, explaining the ultimate battle between good and evil that rages within us all. I understand, it claims we are the fallen angels and describes paradise as a place of elegant logic and hell as a place without reason."

"That's quite a complete description for something that's never been seen," remarked David.

"References, describing the epistle, appear throughout historical documents," Oriastro explained. "However, according to legend, it was held close by the Brotherhood. Only the senior members of the order had access to it. Although many groups sought to possess it, some at the expense of their lives, the 'Light of Revelation' remains nothing more than a nice story."

"So...what happened to these guys?" Suzanne asked.

"They vanished from mainstream society around the time the Moors were driven from Spain and the Abbasid Caliphate collapsed under the Mongol siege. However, the Brotherhood continued to meet in secret and, sometime during the Crusades, came in contact with the Templar Knights, who became enamored with their accrued knowledge, and particularly, with the 'Light of Revelation'. Eventually, all the epistles were placed in their care."

"Why the Templars?" Suzanne inquired.

"It's always the Templars," David said, adding editorial color at the risk of drawing a rebuke from his friend.

"Is that all Eminence?" Ron asked, ignoring the newsman's attempt at irony.

"There's a bit more," replied the Cardinal. "The Templars operated many successful business ventures and attracted many wealthy merchant families. Through their extensive network, the word spread about the 'Light of Revelation'. Soon European nobles, Sheiks across Arabia, and merchant and banking families, formed a new Brotherhood. Christian, Muslim, Jew...the Brotherhood accepted the elite of society and grew throughout Europe, the Middle East, Northern India and Western Asia. Hoping to find the original members, several knights were dispatched to Baghdad. One of these knights was named Andre Saint-Omer and, soon after he left France, the unscrupulous King, Philip the Forth, in great debt to the Templars, contrived to dissolve the order. When Andre Saint-Omer returned from Baghdad, he realized that he, and his fellow knights, were going to face arrest and persecution. He fled to Prussia from France, changed his name to Abelard von Kinderlicht and joined the Teutonic Knights, becoming a faithful and devoted servant of that order. Trying to protect the Brotherhood and its members, he took with him the registry of names, the epistles, and the 'Light of Revelation'. Over time, he rose in stature and, eventually, became the Grand Master of the Teutonic Knights. It was he who expanded Marienberg Castle, adding hidden rooms where the Brotherhood would later gather."

"But why haven't I ever heard about them?" Suzanne inquired. "Until now, that is."

"I'll hazard a guess," David volunteered. "I'll bet, even a thousand years ago, it was politically incorrect for a European noble and an Arab sheik to be in the same club. And, whatever they were doing, they probably wanted to keep it a secret."

"You may be correct," Oriastro said to David. "Through the centuries, anecdotal evidence suggests that local townspeople knew The Brotherhood as a secret, but charitable, organization that built schools and hospitals and helped the poor. Of course, there were always rumors concerning their other activities, which elicited a combination of gratitude and fear from all who came into contact with them."

Suzanne, biting her pen, was trying hard to put the facts together to fit a storyline, when she asked. "So…what other activities? How does this…you know…relate to the present?"

"I'm afraid that's up to you to figure out," Oriastro replied. "Well, I am sorry to say that our time has run out. Professor, would you like us to return your scroll?"

"No…no, you keep it. It will be safe here."

"Then, my children," the Cardinal said, standing and gesturing that the session was over, "Do allow me to walk you out of the library."

They followed Cardinal Oriastro through a labyrinth of passageways to a private exit that opened onto a garden. The grounds were carved into irregular flowerbeds with narrow walking paths of crushed stone threading through and around them. The eight-foot walls, largely hidden by a curtain of Lombardy poplars, were made of tufa, a grey porous volcanic rock common to Rome and its environs. Hand carved travertine fountains were embedded into the wall; each had two stonework fish spewing water into an alabaster bowl.

Ron approached Oriastro. "Your Eminence, thank you, again, for your time. I know it is valuable and I hope we were not too much of a burden."

"You were not burdensome, at all," Oriastro insisted. "It was a rather nice distraction from our usual workday."

Turning to David, the Cardinal said, "It has been a distinct pleasure to meet you, Mr. Anderson. I pray that, with God's help, you will solve your dilemma...both of them."

"Both?" David looked at the Cardinal, puzzled.

"The problem of the scroll," the Cardinal explained, "and the problem in your heart."

"My heart?" David's eyes grew wide.

"I don't know what is troubling you," Oriastro said, "but I know it is something you must resolve. I will pray that God will help you."

"With all due respect, Your Eminence, praying is a waste of time."

The two men stood there, looking into each other's eyes. Finally, David added, "Religion has become obsolete, father...unless you need a good excuse to start a war, of course."

Ron cringed. Suzanne, embarrassed by David's candor, said, "David, that's quite enough. The Cardinal has been more than generous with his time."

Cardinal Oriastro raised his hand, signaling to Suzanne that there was no need to be alarmed.

"Perhaps, I can entice you to look at this in a different way. Every culture and civilization past and present, advanced or primitive has worship at its very core. Is it wise to destroy an instinct that has contributed so much to history and culture and gives, so many, comfort, strength, and a sense of purpose?"

"Perhaps not," replied David, "but, in the past, mankind needed answers to puzzles that, today, science and technology have solved."

"I agree with you, David," said Oriastro, "We no longer need supernatural explanations for natural phenomena. However, all the science and technology in the world will never tell you and me when life began, or more importantly, the question of why we are here at all."

"I'm sorry if I said anything to offend," said David, "but it is difficult to respect the institution of religion when it has been the cause of such prejudice, manipulation, hatred, and wars."

"Is it truly the cause, or is something in the human heart to blame? Ask yourself what, and who, really killed the sheep?"

David stood there. He had no words.

Making the sign of the cross in the air, the cardinal said, "May God bless each of you and guide you on your journey." With that, Oriastro hurried away, returning to the library by the same circuitous route, leaving them in the care of Father Jovan. As their visit began, so it ended.

Father Jovan led them along a path that stopped at a heavy rough-hewn wooden door with a thick black iron bolt. Opening the door, he pointed the way back to Saint Peter's Square. As they exited, the priest handed David a small envelop. "His Eminence wishes you to have this."

David looked puzzled for a moment, then tucked the note into the pocket of his jacket, extended his hand and said, "Father Jovan, thank you for everything." He thought a few seconds, and added, "That castle in Marienberg; do you think the Brotherhood is still headquartered there?"

"The town and castle were renamed after World War II," replied the priest. "It's now called Malbork. As for the castle, it suffered extensive damage in the war, though I think repairs have been made. It's a UNESCO site now, so I doubt the Brotherhood is meeting there."

"Well, someone is meeting somewhere and they're using the Brotherhood's symbol." David paused for a moment, considering the possibilities. "I'm wondering: if I were the Brotherhood, where would I go? And you know what? I might not put down roots in any one place. Too risky! No, I'd move around...a lot."

"Well, that may keep you hidden but it makes command and control quite a challenge." Ron observed.

"This is just freaking great! Oh, sorry Father." Suzanne was beginning to look cross. "What are we supposed to do, search the whole planet for these guys?"

"Who said they were guys?"

"David! For goodness sake, you're not helping!"

Father Jovan, with quiet calm, asked, "May I offer a different perspective?"

"Yes, please do!" Suzanne replied, glaring at David.

"Do you see the gardeners?" The priest pointed to where the workmen were just finishing their workday, pulling ivy away from the walls and trees. "For centuries, they have been removing that ivy. Yet it grows back because each vine sends out tendrils that form many roots. Because there isn't any single root, the plant lives no matter what the gardeners do. Instead of your 'not putting down roots theory' perhaps you should consider the ivy. Maybe you will find the Brotherhood in countless places, if you look. Just maybe, they have tendrils too."

Father Jovan bid them farewell and, as he closed the heavy wooden door, David, Ron and Suzanne waved goodbye for the final time. They made their way back to Saint Peter's Square in silence, each trying to find context and meaning for all they were told. After walking for about half a mile, David hailed a taxi to take them back to the hotel. The cab was small and they squeezed into the back bench because the driver's personal effects were strewn across the front passenger seat.

"Well, this was some day, huh?" David said, turning to his friends.

"Why do I always get stuck in the middle?" Suzanne groused.

"So," David continued, ignoring her complaint, "What shall we do for dinner? Any recommendations, Suzanne? I saw you taking notes."

"I'll give them to you before I go to my room."

"You're not coming to dinner?"

"No, I'm getting a headache and I'm tired. I just want to slip into a hot bath, sip a glass of Pinot Grigio, and sleep for ten hours."

"Sounds inviting," Ron said, hoping to inject some humor. "But I thought you would stay up all night tracking down 'The Brotherhood of Purity'."

"Tracking down whom? A group that's everywhere and nowhere at the same time...with roots, like a plant? Get serious! The trail's gone cold, boys...tomorrow, it's back to the real world!"

"Don't be discouraged," Ron responded. "We'll do a bit more research and something will turn up...you'll see."

"I wouldn't bet on it! I can't believe I flew four thousand miles for a history lesson!"

Ron raised his eyebrows, turned both palms up, shrugged and looked at David, who jumped to Ron's defense. "Suzanne, I know you're upset, but that comment's way off base. Anyway, there's still a chance something will develop, so take it easy, okay?"

"I'm sorry, Ron," Suzanne said, looking awkward and contrite. "When I'm over-tired, I sometimes blurt. I was just hoping, you know...to have something exciting...something...well...so, you're coming to Paris with us, right?"

"No, actually, since there is nothing else to do, I might as well head home. Like you said...time to get back to the real world."

"I guess this adventure is over then," Susanne said, punctuating the futility she felt with a wave of her hand.

Gloom hung over the group like one of those dark clouds in a cartoon that follows the characters around. They drove along, each thinking their own deep thoughts, staring out at the streets of the city. Even the sights of Rome could not dispel the sullen silence. There just wasn't anything left to say. What can you say when it's over, except that it's over. No one wanted to repeat, out loud, that the investigation might have hit a dead end.

When they arrived at the hotel, Suzanne tore a page from her notebook with a list of restaurants, handed it to David, and marched off to her room. David and Ron ventured out for a few blocks and ducked into the first decent restaurant they saw. Ron's Latin helped them understand the bill of fare, printed in Italian, and when the waiter arrived with the food, it almost matched what they thought they ordered. Both agreed to table any further discussion around the 'Brotherhood of Purity' and, instead, spent the evening reminiscing about old 'war stories' and people from their past. The dinner, the camaraderie, and a good long laugh at past lives, were restorative for both men, and they felt substantially renewed by the time they returned to the hotel.

When they entered the lobby, David began glancing around for the night manager, to assure himself Suzanne was alone in her room and not with him. He felt a bit foolish when he realized what he was doing.

"Something wrong?" Ron asked, noticing the peculiar expression on his friend's face.

"No, no...just thinking." David replied. "By the way, I'm sorry about Suzanne's outburst, she's just disappointed. She was looking forward to some romance and adventure."

"Aren't we all looking for romance and adventure?" Ron quipped

"I guess so. Hey, you up for a nightcap?"

"I'd like to turn in a little early tonight," Ron answered. "Could I have a rain check?"

"Anytime. Oh, and by the way, why don't you hold on to the Qur'an? I'd like you to take a crack at decoding it, if possible. Besides, I'll tell Suzanne you're doing some tests, or something, with it. Maybe, if she thinks you'll discover something new, it will calm her down."

"Are you positive about this?"

"I think so," David said. "There's nothing I can do with it and, like I said, it's just a bunch of random events."

"Okay," Ron agreed. "See you for breakfast?"

"You bet."

David, back in his room, sat at the edge of the bed drumming his fingers on the night table, realizing he, too, was disappointed with the day's outcome. Beyond romance, adventure, and a hell of a great story, David hoped this visit would heal the wound of his mother's premature death or unlock the mystery of his father's disappearance. Then he remembered the letter Father Jovan handed him as he was leaving, and retrieved it from his jacket, hanging in the armoire. Inside there was a handwritten note on Vatican stationary.

Dear Mr. Anderson,

I urge you not to let a troubled heart keep you from your destiny. Life may ask you to discover a landscape of unknowns; a strange land unlike anything you have ever seen. I believe, when you find this place, you shall discover its inhabitants have always expected your arrival. Perhaps you will find insight from the following excerpt of a Papal encyclical.

'People with hope, live their lives differently than people in despair. People, who believe, see things others cannot see. These are the stewards of God's love, the custodians of God's compassion, and the messengers of God's hope, who will have a depth of knowledge that those around them will never understand.'

It is my fondest hope that you find the answer that has, so long, eluded you and I will pray for your success.

Raffaele Oriastro

David read the Cardinal's note several times, until, finally exhausted, he let the note fall from his hand and onto the nightstand beside the bed. Still dressed in street clothes, he fell asleep. In one dream, thunder rumbled in the distance, growing louder and louder, until it woke him and, still semi-conscious, he realized the sound was coming from someone banging on the room's door.

It took a moment to clear his head. As he walked stiffly across the room, David called out, "I'm coming...hold your horses!" When he opened the door, Ron was standing there, practically panting, with a laptop and Merilee's book tucked under his arm. David turned to look at the clock on the nightstand; it read 4:17 AM.

"You have an odd way of turning in early," David commented.

"You have got to see this," Ron said, pushing his way into the room and placing the laptop on the table.

David followed him and asked, "What's so important, it couldn't wait till morning?"

Ron flipped open the laptop and grabbed Merilee's book and the five cards. "Allow me to demonstrate."

"By all means." David said, yawning.

"When I got back to my room, I was lying on the bed, staring at the symbol on one of the cards and ruminating about what the Cardinal said today. I kept thinking about the ancient Greeks, proportions, and all that. It occurred to me that phi has a relationship to the recursion of the Fibonacci sequence and I ran it starting with 1 then 4 then 7. Then, I took the real number where each sequence converged. On a whim, I typed into my computer the content of the cards and the marked passages in the book, then applied some old cipher decoding software I use when working with ancient texts. I ran the text through all kinds of algorithms, substitution ciphers, transition ciphers, transposition ciphers, using the real numbers and..."

"Hold on, Ron, you're losing me. Could you just explain, in simple English, what you are so excited about? You know, 'decoding ancient texts for dummies'."

"Okay, wait," Ron took a deep breath, holding it for a second, and then explained. "The book and cards contain a hidden message, right there, in the plaintext! By rotating..."

"Ron!" David said; his abruptness designed to stop his friend's diatribe. "Look, its late or early...or something...I don't know. What's the message?"

Ron turned the screen toward David so he could easily read it. "David, remember I said the cards were in order?"

"Yep."

"Well, on this first card there is a warehouse address in Nogales, Mexico that was used as a staging area. It includes a list of names, one of which is on the FBI's terrorist watch list. It has a crossing date several days before President Whitney reinforced the border. The second card has the targets that were attacked in San Francisco along with instructions."

"Tell me you're joking, right?"

"No! This is serious stuff! Cards three and four...a meeting place outside Paris in a suburb called Clichy-sous-Bois. I checked the names on this list and they are all immigrants to France with respectable backgrounds. Want to bet they're aliases? And a Paris address...eh...29 Rue de Rivoli and something about food.

"Hold on a second; that sounds familiar." David reached for his smart phone and opened the calendar. "I thought so…that's the Hotel de Ville, where the banking conference reception is going to be held."

"Don't you think we ought to call someone about this?" Ron asked, alarmed.

"I'm not sure what we would tell them. Why don't I bring everything to Paris and show the authorities what you found. Say, what's on that last card?"

"I don't know. The cards and Qur'an passages relate to each other. Without the last card the algorithm doesn't work." Leveling a stare of mock cynicism at his friend, Ron asked, "Still think this is just another random event?"

"Not any longer, no," David admitted, and with a self-effacing tone he echoed his friend's theory, "A coincidence is only a coincidence until all the facts are known. Ron, can I borrow your laptop?"

"No!"

"Why not?"

"Because, I'm coming with you!"

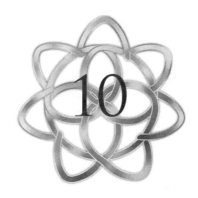

THE UNEXPECTED
ADVERSARY

◆

J t was unseasonably warm in Paris. David was relaxing on a bench at the southern end of the Hotel de Ville's courtyard. Looking across the Pont d'Arcole, he waited, anxious for Suzanne to return from a visit to the Cathedral. The newsman was sure she would regale him with tales of gargoyles and Victor Hugo's Quasimodo. Suzanne, absolutely rejuvenated after hearing about Ron's discovery, had resumed her quest for romance and adventure. It didn't matter if it lasted for a month or a lifetime, whether hazardous or benign; she firmly resolved to enjoy the experience.

Security for the conference was extremely tight and the French authorities closed the roads for ten blocks around Paris City Hall. This included all boat traffic on the Seine River and both the Île de la Cité and Île Saint-Louis, along with any metro stops in the quarantined area.

Five months earlier, anarchists infiltrated Belgium's state-owned news organization and managed to set off an explosive device at the European Union finance minister's headquarters in Brussels. The French response was to limit journalists working for accredited news organizations to the pressroom in the Hotel de Ville's basement where they could view a pool feed from France Télévisions. But after a telephone call between Lance Rodgers and the French President, Global News was granted permission to attend the reception. Except for a few bloggers, no one bothered to comment on Rodger's seemingly boundless influence.

Ron was off briefing representatives from the Minister of the Interior about what they had found. David didn't try to predict the outcome of the meeting and knew they would never cancel the reception, but hoped that, at the very least, they would add a level of increased scrutiny to the proceedings and attempt to track down some of the men who were mentioned in the cards.

At that moment, he caught sight of Suzanne. She was walking across the bridge toward him, wearing an expression of wonderment, her smart phone camera clicking away. As she approached, David could see the sheer bliss in her eyes and he found it a delight.

"So, how's the sightseeing coming along?"

"I'm in Paris," Suzanne said through a lyrical sigh. Taking a firm hold of David's arm, they began to stroll through the square. Suzanne opened her guidebook to a dog-eared page and began to read.

"This is the Hotel de Ville which serves as the City Hall of Paris. The building was originally…"

David strained to focus his complete concentration on the pretty girl next to him as Suzanne explained the history and architecture of the building, her discourse peppered with principles of the flying buttress and other well-known facts about Notre Dame. After fifteen minutes of effort, the anchorman held up his hand and said, "I don't mean to interrupt but where is our news van?"

"All work and no play…just saying." She pointed north to the intersection of Rue de Rivoli and Rue du Renard. "Right there."

A large silver step van, with the Global News logo painted across its side, sat gleaming in the sunshine, its array of microwave antennae in constant contact with satellites in geosynchronous orbit high overhead. In answer to Suzanne's knock on the door, a man appeared.

"Hello, Miss Biasotto, we've been expecting you. This must be Mister Anderson, no? But of course, it is! I am Richard Fournier, the directeur technique. Welcome, welcome…come in." He shook their hands, feeling quite excited about finally meeting a famous on-air personality and an international one at that.

Mike Lussardi, teasing his colleagues, called from the back of the vehicle, "Hey, you guys, it's about time you showed up! Where have you been?"

"Oh, we had to get some sightseeing in," David said, pointing to Suzanne's guidebook.

"See Paris and die," Suzanne quipped. "So gentlemen, shall we review today's coverage?"

They gathered in back of the van. The workspace was cramped but usable. Suzanne, reading the evening's conference schedule, was interrupted by a banging on the door. Fournier answered then turning to David, said, "Mr. Anderson, I think you are needed here."

Ron was standing between two uniformed policemen. A third man in a tailored grey suit appeared in charge and was leaning against the van, fanning himself with some papers held loosely in his hand.

As the news anchor stepped out of the vehicle, waiting for some sort of explanation from Ron, the man wearing the suit approached, stopping inches before David's face.

"I am Andre Noiret," the man barked, raising his chin and placing his hands behind him. "The Commissaire of Police for this commune."

David slid to his right, adjusting the proxemics so that he was no longer sandwiched between the news van and the commissioner.

"It's a pleasure," David said, offering his hand.

Andre Noiret had no patience for introductions and turned his back to David, waving the papers at Ron in an incriminating manner. "This man…this man claims to be with the Global News and he has just told us the most fantastic story!"

"Professor Eyota is a renowned historian and valuable consultant for our organization. I am sure…"

"I do not care what you call him, monsieur!" Noiret said, close to a shout. "He has made libelous remarks about French residents. It is against the law to say such things."

"Perhaps, if you explain what it is that upset you," David said, already knowing the answer.

"This allegation about terrorism is utterly ridiculous. Do you think only Americans can fight terrorists? Perhaps, you believe the French Interior Ministry is stupid? All such activities on our soil are scrupulously monitored, monsieur, I assure you. We appreciate your concern but the security for this event is well under our control."

The commissioner continued his fulminations, loud enough to attract the attention of other reporters from competing news outlets. The attention was more than unwelcome and David supposed that cameras were, likely, recording every second of the policeman's histrionics.

Noiret was working himself up into quite a tirade. As his voice grew louder, he began waving the sheaf of papers Ron had given him wildly in the air.

"I have checked the backgrounds of the names on your list. They are peaceful residents who have lived here for years. You and your friend, monsieur, are bigots. You seem to bear hatred toward our Muslim citizens. It is simple as that. Most Americans are bigots! Your fellow countrymen readily admit as much!"

David was more than a bit familiar with this tactic of using accusations, aimed at humiliation and belittlement, as a crude substitute for cogent argument and, just plain, telling the truth. He was used to experiencing it, over and over, in his journalistic investigations over the years. But this was the police, for God's sake. It was deplorable and he wasn't going to stand for it. There was always a story behind this kind of behavior and David aimed to uncover it.

"Commissaire Noiret," David shouted above the din, so everyone in the vicinity could clearly hear.

"We have provided well-researched information to the police. You have apparently chosen not to investigate this matter and have chosen, instead, to come here and insult my colleagues and I. Your behavior is completely unacceptable for a law enforcement professional, especially one of your stature. I caution you, Global News *will* investigate this matter and we will broadcast our findings, together with this little tirade of yours."

Both men were now standing toe to toe as Noiret shouted, "I will have you arrested!"

Unbowed, David replied, "Then arrest us or leave us alone! We have work to do!"

The police commissioner had the look of a bully confronted with someone taller and stronger. Noiret was not, so much, afraid of David as he was of the truth; a universal disinfectant that could quickly cut through the most artful deception. Realizing the newsman had won, for now, Noiret began to back away. He turned on his heels, motioning to the uniformed policemen to follow.

"Commissaire," David called after him. "The professor will have his items returned."

The policemen, carrying Ron's laptop and Merilee's book tucked under his arm, didn't wait for permission from Noiret. With a contrite bow, he returned the items to Ron and turned to David. He made a small gesture of apology, as if to say, please don't blame us, we're not all like this. As the group of gendarmes marched away, David kept the men in sight until they disappeared into a cafe across the street. Then he turned around and asked Suzanne to put a call into Lance Rodgers.

"Whatever for?" demanded Suzanne.

"If the French police will not investigate, we have to find someone who will. There are lives at stake. Lance Rodgers will know who to call and how to get them to move on this."

"I'm on it," said Suzanne.

It was mid afternoon when they returned to their hotel. Its location, only a few blocks from the Hotel de Ville, was situated safe inside the security zone. Global reserved the entire building for its news personnel to isolate the staff from the violent demonstrations and union strikes occurring throughout the city.

Sitting at the bar with his counterpart for the European Union news broadcast, and several journalists from Global's Paris bureau, David was discussing the continuing unrest and economic problems in Europe when Suzanne entered with Ron and Mike. She greeted everyone with a polite wave but followed the hostess to an isolated table in the far corner of the room, motioning for David to join them.

"Pardonnez-moi," David said, cutting short the conversation. "I see our executive producer and our crew. We need to discuss our programming for tonight's broadcast."

When he joined the group, Suzanne handed him a digital video file that was recorded on a small memory card. "Here's a souvenir from your dustup with the police this afternoon, complete with an Oscar winning performance from Captain Cantankerous... oh, umm...you were good, too. It's a little present from our French competition, by the way."

"How'd you manage...?"

"Charm goes a long, long way. It's a skill."

David laughed, shaking his head. "I'm not going to ask...I don't want to know."

Ron gave David a crisp salute. "Thanks for getting me out of that fix, sir."

David returned a puzzled look. "So what the hell did you say to that guy?"

"I'm not sure," Ron answered. "I waited for over an hour before they let me in, then I gave him the names and started explaining what I found. Noiret seemed interested at first...shouting orders to his subordinates to check into this or that. He rattled away in French so fast I didn't catch all of what he said. While we were waiting, I thought I might color in some of the background data from the Cardinal. Next thing I know, the guy jumps up and runs out of the office. When he returns...total hostility."

"Well, something set him off," Suzanne said, leaning in towards David. "I'll admit I was a little frightened. I was envisioning a night in the slammer for you boys and a news broadcast sans anchor."

"The names, maybe?" Ron proposed. "He seemed focused on the names."

David shifted in his seat and pressed his friend to reveal more. "Think Ron, what triggered his reaction?"

"Well, let's see. I was explaining the one, four, seven numbers, showed him how the symbol was constructed...wait, that's it! That's when he ran out of the office."

"When you showed him the symbol?" David repeated.

"Yes," Ron replied. "I'm sure of it."

"Did you mention the Brotherhood of Purity?" David asked.

"No!" Ron insisted.

"Wait a damn second here!" Mike Lussardi interrupted. He was scratching his head. "What symbol...and who the hell is the Brotherhood of whatever?"

David apologized, "I'm sorry, Mike. I didn't mean to ignore you."

Ron and David spent the next fifteen minutes bringing Mike up to speed on Merilee, the Cardinal and the coded cards. They gave him the condensed version; it was getting late in the day and they were all beat.

"You guys are kidding, right?"

"We're not kidding," David answered. Mike could tell David was as serious as the flu. "Show him, Ron."

Mike Lussardi looked perplexed when he saw the symbol on the cards, a whistle escaping his lips. "That's the damnedest thing."

"What is, Mike?" David asked.

"Well, remember when you asked me to investigate the rumors that the attack was aimed at the World Energy Conference and orchestrated by some group?"

"Sure, but I thought you came up empty on that one."

"I did...the FBI said no, Homeland Security said no; even the police said no...just another random terror attack with no link to any known organized group. The rumors were supposed to be some paranoid conspiracy theory from all the nuts that think aliens are sitting around Roswell playing Mahjong."

"So?"

"So this! You know the Alliance for Global Advancement?" Mike asked.

"They're an umbrella organization for social justice groups." David answered.

"That's right. They were primarily responsible for organizing the groups that showed up at the World Energy Conference demonstrations."

"There's nothing odd with that, Mike...these things have been sponsored for as long as I can remember."

"Okay, but...the night before, there was a lot of rioting and property damage until the police dispersed the crowd. Then the leaders called for a massive rally on Market Street the next day."

"I remember, we covered the story," Suzanne added.

"Then you probably recall the next day, before the attack, no one showed up for the rally. One of my producers pointed it out. I thought it was strange, at the time, but I lost track with all that was going on. One thing though, I remember glancing at their web site that morning and guess what...that loopy gold symbol was in the lower right corner."

"And you're sure about that Mike?" David asked.

"Positive!"

"Well, I'll be damned," said David.

"By the way, did you ever speak to Lance?" Suzanne interrupted.

"Yes, he promised me he would contact the international police agencies. He said he would give them my contact details so I can run all this by them. I don't understand why no one has contacted me, yet. It's getting late and I am worried something is going to go down at the reception."

David could tell the gears were turning inside Suzanne's head. There wasn't any telltale smoke yet, but he was sure that would come soon. Before he could reign in his executive producer's unbridled fervor, she said, "I think we should air this...put the whole thing out there, including the Noiret tirade, and see what develops. Maybe we can flush out the conspirators."

"Suzanne, we don't have a cogent story," David explained. "We have a set of facts that seem related...but any conclusion is far from certain and would be purely speculative on our part. Besides, we don't want to warn the bad guys, we want them to be apprehended. Let's give the authorities a bit more time."

Suzanne remained skeptical. "And what if someone else breaks this?"

"Who?" David replied, trying to assuage her unease. "Even if someone else out there knows about this, we're the only ones with all the pieces. If there's a story, we'll get it first, I promise."

"Legit?"

"Absolutely! By the way, Mike, I'd like to see that web site."

"You can't," Mike said. "It's down."

"When?"

"The other day when you guys were hanging in Rome."

"What should we do now?" asked Suzanne, puzzled.

"First rule of investigative reporting," David responded. "Follow the money! Someone's funding this group. Let's find out who it is."

"I'll start by checking the archives," Suzanne declared.

"Hold on," David said. "First, we need to cover the reception. There'll be time for this later on. We'd better get going…it's late."

As they were riding the elevator, heading for their rooms to change into their formal attire, Suzanne muttered something under her breath.

"What's that?" David asked.

She looked at him for a moment, insight dawning in her intense green eyes. Echoing Father Jovan's counsel, she said, "You may find the Brotherhood in countless places…maybe *they* have tendrils, too."

The boulevard in Clichy-sous-Bois, selected by the French Interior Ministry as a staging area for the conference reception, was, like many of the neglected roads in the Commune, in complete disrepair. The curbs of stark white cement were chipped and broken, their fragments strewn randomly about the roadbed. The boulevard's pavement was so severely eroded that the weeds springing up from its cracks, seeming to proclaim in defiance, we are taking back this land!

Packed in a tight line, hugging the broken curbs, were five municipal buses with a crisscross of metal bars covering the windows. A phalanx of police dressed in riot uniforms and helmets, armed with automatic weapons, surrounded the area. Wooden barricades formed a narrow queue where workers stood, waiting their turn for a security check, before boarding.

Ahmad was standing next to Sharif, rocking from foot to foot; stealing nervous glances at the proceedings around him. They should have expected this level of security, Ahmed thought. There would be no escape if he and Sharif failed the security check. To mitigate the risk, Ahmad insisted they keep a good distance from the four other men waiting to go through the checkpoint. Despite Roshed's frequent assurances that the credentials database had been compromised and they would be perfectly safe, Ahmed worried.

At the front of the line, a policeman examined Ahmad's badge, matching the photo to his face, and then scanning the badge into a handheld apparatus. Ahmed's anxiety threatened to overwhelm him, and he struggled to appear relaxed. At times, the discipline required to remain calm became almost unbearable. He fixed his eyes on the policeman's wristwatch, hoping the guard would not see his fear. The sweep hand ticked off a second, then another second, and then another still and, with each tick, Ahmad could feel a twisting sensation deep inside. Finally, the results came back and the screener looked up at him through narrowed eyes.

"What is your job?" he demanded.

"General Wait Staff," replied Ahmad.

"And your security number?"

"T51C52," Ahmad said, without hesitation.

"You're cleared. Go with that man!"

A gendarme, staring at Ahmad with a look that reminded him of a snarling wolf, escorted him to a trailer where a line of workers, also with escorts, entered through the front of the truck and exited by a door in the rear. Ahmad noticed that most of the workers leaving the trailer looked humiliated; their heads hanging, their shoulders slumped, eyes down and narrow.

When his turn came, the official escort pushed him up the two metal steps into the trailer, where he followed a darkened passage to a black circular door. When the door swung open, a voice from a hidden speaker commanded, "Enter the chamber now." Ahmad stood in the semi-darkened compartment, the voice directing him to raise his arms. He remained in the chamber for less than a minute, listening to a low buzzing sound, when the door on the opposite side opened and the voice said, "Exit, now."

Ahmad passed several policemen sitting behind a bank of monitors, unaware that he had just been subjected to a full body scan. He was motioned toward the exit, but stopped and turned, instead. Looking at the monitors as he passed, he was shocked by the images on the screens. The largest screen contained a high definition negative image of a naked man. A smaller screen beside it, labeled 'inverted,' displayed the color image of Ahmad's nude body and, on the row of monitors above, there were similar pictures of both men and women. Ahmed had been told that all the people on the bus were assigned to work at the Hotel de Ville and all were Muslim. Ahmad's red face, disguised by his dark skin, hid the deep shame and embarrassment he felt. The debasement of being subjected to such things was an outrageous affront to his modesty and privacy. Rage rose up within him and one of the guards noticed his resentment.

"What are you looking at?" snapped the policeman. "Move along!"

His escort met him at the steps of the exit and placed Ahmad on bus number three. Ahmad could not bear to raise his head to look at the workers around him. The dishonor of being unable to stop this most unholy intrusion was almost more then he could stand.

The convoy of buses arrived at the rear of the Hotel de Ville, passing through one of the ornately decorated wrought iron entryways. The motorcade parked in a secure U pattern inside the rear courtyard of the building. There was a heavy police presence and the workers were told to stand in two lines in front of the bus that transported them.

Andre Noiret, flanked by policemen, two on each side, stepped forward to address them.

"Bon soir, messieurs et madames, I have been informed of discontent with our security arrangements. You must try to understand that the leaders of the world are coming to France and we...all of us...are responsible for their safety and comfort. I should think that you would be grateful for your jobs and the tolerant hospitality of the French citizens. No matter...we all will work together to make this a memorable experience for our guests tonight."

As Noiret finished speaking, a portly gentleman with thick eyebrows, and even thicker lips, approached. He gazed at the commissioner with a lethargic stare.

"Hello, Philippe," Noiret said, greeting his oversized brother. "The arrangements are in place, yes?" Then, pointing to the tall balding man behind him, asked, "Who is this?"

"Hello, Andre." his brother replied in a nasal voice that sounded like he was talking through a heavy mask. "This is Roshed bin Hamid Ismail, the assistant banquet manager. He has the job assignments and building passes."

"Can you trust him?" asked Noiret.

With a nervous smile painted across his face, his brother hesitated for a barely perceptible moment. "Sure, sure, I know him for years."

"Then let's get on with it!"

Roshed and Philippe Noiret moved through the lines of workers, giving each a specific assignment and a pass for the area of the building where they needed to go.

Ahmad and Sharif were assigned as bar tenders in the main reception hall and stationed just outside the kitchen. Roshed treated Ahmad and Sharif exactly like the other workers. He was mindful that he could not act too familiar or too reticent. As the workers filed into the building, Ahmad suppressed a smile. The plan was working.

Like the cumulonimbus clouds of an approaching storm they gathered, slowly at first, in small groups of three or four, then seven, then ten, inexorably building volume until a critical mass was reached. By late that afternoon, the Parc du Champs de Mars became a colorful sea of protesters united in the solidarity of discontent.

The government announced, in response to the financial crisis, it was again reducing the generous benefits enjoyed by millions during decades passed, when politicians made deals with labor organizers in exchange for votes, without a care that, someday, the bill would come due. The elusive 'someday' had arrived, the economy was in decline with reduced tax revenues, and the money to pay the enormous interest on government loans had finally dried up. Without new loans, the bills could not be paid, and the masses were enraged.

French workers viewed these benefits as their birthright, so the public and private union organizers called for strikes and demonstrations in response. It was the perfect time; the eyes of the world were on Paris as host of the World Banking Conference.

Many of the rank and file raised flags colored green or blue or red, upon which messages and symbols were lettered in black ink. Others carried signs with slogans calling for social justice, global solidarity and the confiscation of private wealth. Several swarms of men, dressed in red tee shirts with matching bandanas, ignited road flares to signal the distress of the world's working class. The smoke cast a blue-grey haze over the sky and engulfed the crowds. The flags were scarcely visible. It was an image reminiscent of the French Revolution.

The entire legion, dubbed 'born-again social populists' by the media for the fervor of their ideology, moved as one body, coming east through the streets until they merged with like-minded students from the University of Paris.

Despite the quarantine, the protesters succeeded in finding routes, conveniently left unguarded by Andre Noiret's police. They marched through the Left Bank of the city to the edge of the Seine River where military, under the direct command of the Inspector General, succeeded in stopping their progress at the bridge entrances.

Now, only the cacophony of howls, shrieks, and jeers from the protesters could penetrate past the military and police personnel. Carefully scrutinizing credentials, they fashioned a tight formation through which the arriving dignitaries could pass. This curious security breach was inexplicable and most news organizations later blamed it on the apathy of the French Police, who were engaged in contract and pension negotiations of their own.

Less than a mile from the unrest, David Anderson was dressing in front of a mirror at his hotel, in a room that had been reserved for the makeup artists. As he fastened the last shirt stud, he tried to damp down his swirling thoughts, but his mind was like a burst steam pipe that couldn't be quelled.

Fragments of worry exploded in his head: Eric's disappearance, the FBI report, Merilee Brunswick, Saunders, Cardinal Oriastro, that book, those cards and that damn golden symbol following him since his documentary on the madrasah schools. They were becoming like waves in the sea; separate, yet, all parts of the same ocean. He tried to accept Ron's theory that all these things were connected, that there are no coincidences, but deep down he still questioned it. Still, he couldn't explain the seeming connections, either. Not with logic, not even with whimsy. And now, with the information Mike uncovered, the picture grew ever more complicated.

"Mister Anderson, are you all right?" asked Robbie, one of Global's makeup artists flown in from New York.

"Yes, why?"

"Oh...you just seemed so far away. So...what do you think I should say?"

"Say? I'm sorry, Robbie, I was concentrating on something else. What was that again?"

As Robbie started to reprise the details of his latest romance, David's thoughts, once again, began to drift. Soon he was thinking out loud, talking over the unwitting makeup artist.

"You know what, Robbie? I've been wondering about convergence...you know...how disparate events are really all coming from the same place. What's your opinion?"

Robbie shrugged. "Beats me, Mr. A."

David continued the verbal debate with himself when Robbie, utterly nonplused, interrupted. "Mister Anderson, you look absolutely stunning!"

David cleared his head and, stepping away from the mirror, saw the reflection of a tall and elegant figure gazing back at him. Robbie tucked a fine white linen handkerchief into the breast pocket of David's dinner jacket.

"Thanks Robbie. How's my tie?"

"Perfect!"

"Makeup?"

"Fabulous!"

"All right then, I'll see you later. Thanks."

It was still too early for cocktails, so with Perrier in hand, David, still lost in thought, sat alone at the hotel bar waiting for Suzanne and Mike. He didn't notice they had arrived until Mike called to him. He spun around and froze, his eyes locked on Suzanne. Seeing her dressed in something other than the usual business attire felt both odd and good. Slowly, he approached.

She was wearing an elegant, black evening gown that flowed to the floor, accenting the graceful outline of her figure. Except for the diamond tennis bracelet on her left wrist, the delicate and feminine lines of Suzanne's exposed arms and shoulders were the gown's only adornment.

The soft shadow of her smile illumined her face, and she extended her hand in the formal gesture of an introduction. "Good evening, Mister Anderson."

She spoke in the quiet, but confident, tones of a woman who knows beauty and knows she is beautiful. David took her hand and kissed it.

"It is a pleasure to make your acquaintance, mademoiselle." The words were spoken as though he was meeting her for the first time and, in a sense, he was. Offering Suzanne his arm, he said, "Shall we go?"

The three Global News journalists slid into the limo waiting for them at the entrance of the Hotel de Ville. The car sped away, escorting them to the site where they met the camera crew from France Televisions. Lance Rodgers negotiated an arrangement for the state-owned television company to provide all onsite production support and feed the video to the Global News van parked on the street. Camera crews were not allowed inside the Hall of Mirrors where the reception was to be held. Instead, they set up in the Salon Cheret, a small furnished room adjacent to the Hall.

As Suzanne was reviewing the production assignments with the French Televisions' staff, David turned to Mike and suggested he meet the President's party at the entrance. David assumed the leaders of other countries, arriving at the Conference, might not be amenable to a protracted interview as they stepped from their vehicles. He decided, instead, to greet them at the top of the Grand Staircase to capture reaction to questions about the globe's financial woes and their plans to address these during the Conference.

Suzanne was half listening to David and Mike planning their strategy. Realizing she would be alone for an hour, or so, she smiled at David. "What do you suggest I do while I'm waiting?"

"Mingle," he replied. "Go to the reception and socialize…try to pick up a comment, a remark or an 'off the record' statement. Let Mike or I know and we'll take it from there."

"Okay, that might be fun. Would one of you handsome gentlemen kindly escort me into the reception room?"

David and Suzanne entered the Hall of Mirrors and looked around. It was unusual for David to be rendered speechless, but all he could say was, "Wow." He wasn't fond of these events and didn't expect much to come from their coverage of the evening. Still, he had to admit, the splendor, the opulence and the sumptuous combination of Louis XIV décor with French Classicism architecture were astonishingly impressive in both detail and workmanship.

The guests were arriving and the shifting colors of their evening gowns, mixing with the flowers on the tables, created an intoxicating visual fugue. The diamonds, worn by most of the ladies, captured sparks of fire from the chandeliers and glimmered under the lights. The room's archways, walls, and even its furniture, were gilded and the rainbow flares of light showering down from the Baccarat crystal chandeliers, gave rise to the sensation of a fireworks display. The glittering lights made the figures on the exquisitely painted ceiling move with the rhythm of the evening.

On one side of the hall, a pianist and string quartet from the National Academy of Music were playing Claude Debussy's Clair de Lune. On the opposite side, a podium was setup for the evening's speech making. The wait staff, dressed in their proper crisp white uniforms, circulated among the guests, carrying silver trays of hors d'oeuvres. In spite of the dire economic conditions around the world, the affair had an atmosphere of brilliant excess and gaiety.

"Soooo…this is how the elite live!" Suzanne remarked.

"Will you be okay?" David asked her.

"Oui, but of course, monsieur!" she shot back, displaying her best French aplomb. David acknowledged her self-assurance with a smile and a quick bow before departing to carry on with his assignment.

After enduring ninety minutes of inane gasbaggery from the conference delegates, the news anchor returned to the reception. The reactions and comments he captured from world leaders were, as he expected, a disappointing array of banal, arcane and contradictory statements connecting, not to facts, but to wishes living in a fairytale. He hoped Suzanne or Mike would be more successful and began to scan the room for his producer. He spotted her under an archway, talking to a tall, fit-looking gent with black hair, pasted into a contemporary style by an excessive amount of grooming gel. He was wearing an expensive tuxedo and a lusty smirk. When a waiter passed by with a tray, the man turned to reach for a canapé and David recognized him as the President of the European Central Bank. Since Suzanne seemed to be more than holding her own, he decided not to disturb them.

A moment later, Mike Lussardi entered behind President Whitney and her retinue. He watched as a flurry of officials greeted the President and ushered her and the staff to their tables. Mike signaled that there was nothing newsworthy so far. David responded with a signal, indicating he would meet Mike in five minutes at the bar, where earlier he spotted a bottle of twenty-one year old Glenfiddich on the shelf behind the counter.

David walked up and asked the bartender to pour a glass of the whiskey over ice. A spark of something, maybe recognition, seemed to flash in the man's eyes. For a very uncomfortable moment, he just stood, silently, staring at the newsman.

"H-e-l-l-o...may I have a glass of..." David began, protracting the words. He was stalling for a chance to appraise the situation but the man walked away and whispered something to the second bartender.

"Yes sir," the second server said, after exchanging places, "a glass of the Glenfiddich on the rocks."

From the sound of his accent, David surmised that the man was foreign born, perhaps Middle Eastern.

"Did I say something to insult your friend?"

The bartender didn't answer, hurrying away to serve someone else.

David left the bar and took refuge in one of the archways. It was a good position for observing the bartenders. The exact reason he was interested in the men, he didn't quite know. There was something, just on the edge of his mind, an odd feeling of deja vu. He was watching the first bartender fill a tray of crystal glasses with Sauvignon Blanc, when Suzanne stepped in front of him.

"David, you won't believe what the President of the EU bank just let slip!"

"Suzanne, would you move a bit to your right. I'm trying to see if…"

"He just told me," she continued, oblivious of David's request, still standing in David's line of sight, "the EU is going to support the IMF's new reserve currency proposal. Well, no reaction?"

David stretched his neck, trying to see around Suzanne, just as Lussardi came up behind her. "Damnedest thing," Mike said to them both.

"What is, Mike?" David replied, distracted, as he tried to position Mike and Suzanne on his left side to create an unobstructed view of the bar.

"Several delegates just left the reception complaining about feeling sick."

David looked annoyed at Mike's interruption. "So, maybe there's a bug going around."

During that split second, as David diverted his eyes, a loud crashing sound of glass and metal split the dignified calm. All twelve wine glasses, along with the silver tray, were now on the floor in front of the bar. A janitor instantly appeared with a mop and bucket to clean it up. It was the timing between the two events - spill and janitor - that sent David's mind into hyper drive. He made a timeout sign and said to his colleagues, "Wait a moment, something is going on here."

He watched while the man with the mop cleaned up the spill. The janitor kept glancing at the churlish bartender; the two appeared to be passing signals. After the wine had been cleaned up and the broken glass swept away, the janitor retreated to the kitchen. The bartender, rather than make up a tray of new wine glasses, began serving other patrons. David's instincts told him something was not right. "Say Mike, do you know Jim Gilroy?"

"You mean the head of the President's security detail?"

"That's the one." David affirmed. "Could you ask him to come over here for a second?"

"What's going on?"

"I'll tell you when you get back here. Hurry!"

Suzanne looked puzzled as David grabbed her by the wrist and began walking toward the bar. He raised his index finger to his lips, indicating she should remain silent while they waited for the bartender to finish serving the party ahead of them. David was sure he had seen those intense, piercing dark grey eyes, once before. They belonged to a boy sitting at a fountain in Tehran many years ago; a boy who told him, I am bound to kill infidels.

When David stepped to the bar, he folded his arms and leaned casually on the counter top, hoping to catch the bartender off guard. "We've met before...remember?"

The man looked down, took a step backward, and said in a cold, dull voice, "You are mistaken. I have never seen you before."

"Surely, you remember the fountain in Tehran?" David pressed.

The man stared at David with a severe and menacing expression. David was now positive this was the boy he met on his last day in Iran.

"There are many fountains in Tehran, just as there are many traffic signs in Paris," the bartender insisted. "Order something, sir, or please, leave me alone."

David began to retreat, pulling Suzanne along, and stopped in front of the two swinging doors leading to the kitchen.

"What the hell was that all about?" Suzanne demanded. She was as curious as ever by David's strange behavior.

"I'll explain in a second."

Mike and Jim were joking and laughing as they walked over to meet David. "Okay, we're here," Mike announced. "So tell us, Kimosabe, what's the problem?"

"The bartender...over there...with the black, curly hair and murky grey eyes. See him?"

"Yeah...so?" Lussardi asked.

"A moment ago, he deliberately dropped a tray of wine glasses and, in something that looked like a well-orchestrated maneuver, this janitor shows up, cleans the mess, and then disappears into the kitchen. On top of that, I'm sure I met him before, when he was a kid. He told me he was sworn to kill infidels. I think we ought to go question the guy."

"I don't know, Dave," Jim Gilroy said. "That's not much to go on. And besides, we're on foreign soil. I don't have authority to question anyone, especially employees of the hotel who have already gone through a rigorous security check."

"Well, maybe you could ask one of the French security people to check it out!" Suzanne said, coming to the defense of Global's anchorman. "Oh, and people…call him, 'David'!"

"Look," Gilroy continued. He was becoming somewhat agitated. "Let's say, I go and stir everyone up and it's nothing…delegates leave the conference. Maybe there is a panic, who knows. What I do know is that I won't be the head of the President's security detail for much longer, after that. If you come up with something a little more solid, then maybe we can talk…"

David was only half listening to Jim Gilroy. He had steered the group over to the kitchen door and was looking through the small diamond-shaped window. The kitchen was abuzz with the activity of preparing the delegates' dinner. He spotted the janitor talking to one of the chefs. Suddenly, David saw the janitor pull the mop handle apart, remove a small clear glass container and pass it to the cook.

David turned and grabbed Gilroy by the lapels of his suit jacket, pulling him forward toward the window.

"Look in there…see the janitor and the chef?"

By the time Gilroy could find the men in all the kitchen's activity, the only thing to see was the chef holding a saltshaker that was just like all the other saltshakers in the kitchen.

"Let me guess, you're against excess sodium."

By this time, the bartender, looking quite upset, approached the group. "Is everything alright, monsieur? Is there something I can help with?" He ignored David and addressed Gilroy.

"Everything certainly seems fine, to me," said Gilroy. "Get this guy a drink." Gilroy pointed his thumb at David and walked away.

Jim Gilroy departed, mumbling a short diatribe under his breath about news people seeing conspiracies everywhere.

The bartender glared at David and returned to the bar.

David looked through the kitchen window one last time. The first course was warming on a long steam table and the chef was sprinkling salt onto each plate. David turned to look at the hall. The delegates were mostly seated now, talking, laughing, and waiting for their appetizers to be served. He turned back to the kitchen where the waiters were placing the plates on trays.

A sense of looming danger swept up his spine. Glancing at the bar, David noticed that, now, both bartenders were standing still, watching him. They looked ready to pounce. He looked to his left. On the side of the kitchen door, twelve inches from his hand, was a red box labeled FEU in white letters. He reached out and pulled the lever.

Immediately, the fire alarms in the hall began to flash and scream. Sirens blared. David grabbed Mike and Suzanne by the arm and dragged them to the center of the room. He began shouting, "FIRE...FIRE IN THE KITCHEN...FIRE!!!!"

Mike and Suzanne were embarrassed beyond description but the newsman spoke to them with the resolute authority that was David's hallmark. "I need your help to get these people out of here!" Without questioning, they began to usher people toward the main exit.

By now, the various security details and French authorities sprang into action, rushing world leaders out of the building to safety. President Whitney was one of the first to be evacuated. Behind her, a sea of impeccably dressed leaders rushed down the Grand Staircase and clamored for the exit doors. Several tables of people remained seated, watching and laughing as the crowd fought to fit through the door. They were waiting for the telltale smell of smoke before they would get up. David took up a position at the building's front entrance, helping people into the courtyard, while Suzanne and Mike ran to the Global News van to get a cameraman.

The realization of what was to be done fell on Ahmad like a piano dropped from a second story window. He sprinted toward the kitchen but was quickly restrained when Sharif grabbed his coat so violently that several of the brass buttons popped off.

"Why do you stop me, brother? We know what we must do."

"Please, my brother, imam, let the honor of this sacrifice be mine. You have been chosen; you must complete our mission and take us to glorious victory. I will see it from my place in paradise."

Ahmad, reluctant to concede, finally nodded, submitting to the inevitable. He placed his hand on the younger man's shoulder, held it there for a second, and then raised it to stroke his head.

"Imam," Sharif pressed, pushing open the kitchen door. "Use the back staircase or you will not get past the crowd."

Ahmad squeezed past the contingent of French police and firefighters who were charging up the service stairway. Several of the emergency responders yelled orders for him to clear out of the building. They began to converge on the kitchen, the flashing strobe lights of the fire alarms reflecting off their helmets and equipment.

Sharif stood in front of the oven. He felt complete calm as he prayed and pushed the auto clean button, and set the timer to 7:14. Then, in the last act of his short life, he twisted the temperature dial to the number 471.

When Ahmad stopped running from the site of the explosion, he found himself inside a dark and narrow alleyway in an unfamiliar Paris neighborhood. It was late in the evening and there was no one about to catch sight of the anxious stranger sprinting through the streets. Dim lights shone from the windows of homes where families were finishing their supper, carefully sipping the last of the wine with a few bites of cheese and fruit.

As Ahmad flew by the open windows, he caught snippets of laughter and music, intermingled with the occasional shouting he knew was part of a nightly ritual that included the obligatory arguments revolving around the ever-deepening, dismal prospects for the world's future generations.

Ahmad could still hear the sound of sirens flying by on the main thoroughfares. He changed direction each time one approached, ducking into the maze of small streets and alleyways that zigzagged through Paris, traveling always opposite of the speeding police cars and ambulances. The smoke from the conference site soon disappeared behind him.

Ahmad had been running at a mighty clip since slipping out of the Hotel de Ville in the ensuing chaos. Now, his lungs and legs were on fire with the effort and Ahmad stopped in an alleyway to gather his thoughts along with his strength. Leaning against the cool stone of the wall lining the alley, he bent over, hands resting on his knees, instinctively easing the effort of bringing great volumes of air into his burning lungs. He began to mull over his options.

Ahmad guessed he must be two or three kilometers from the conference site. He should have stopped running long ago to avoid attracting attention, but the adrenalin coursing, full speed, through his bloodstream would not allow him to rest. He had not run this kind of distance since leaving the training camps in the mountains bordering Afghanistan on Pakistan's northwestern frontier. He was surprised at how much ground he covered in so short a time.

As his breathing slowed, Ahmad reached into the inside pocket of his trousers and pulled out a small key ring. The ring contained keys to a black Peugeot sedan waiting for him on a local street in the Latin Quarter, a few blocks outside the quarantine zone. It was the vehicle that had been meant to carry him, and his cell, out of Paris and back to the safety of the hilltop château outside of Saint-Gatien-sous-Bois. His dilemma, at present, was figuring out where the hell he was and getting to the car without being caught. Surely, someone at the scene had given the police his description by now, perhaps that nosey man at the bar. He figured it was a miracle the police had not apprehended him already.

Ahmad puzzled over how he would get back to the car and out of the wait uniform he had been wearing since that afternoon. The uniform was a dead giveaway and he had to discard it. It might be possible to break into a shop and steal some clothes but that would waste precious time, and possibly clue the police into his activity after the explosion. How ironic, thought Ahmad, to be caught stealing clothes after escaping the combined security forces of the French Police and Interior Ministry.

At first, he thought it might be best to go to Sholeh's parents' residence in Clichy to pick up his backpack and get out of France.

But his superiors expected him at the Château and they would protect him and have an escape arranged. He hoped they would agree the mission had been a success. The backup plan, though not as effective as the original, had worked, demonstrating to the world that the infidels were never safe from this holy war.

Straightening himself as his breathing returned to normal, Ahmad crept out of the alleyway and surveyed the surrounding neighborhood. The roads were practically deserted. Random cars were passing back and forth. Drivers, lost in their own concerns, ignored the lone man on the street. As he walked along, Ahmad slipped the key ring back into his pocket. Pulling out his cell phone, he scrolled through the contact list, selected a number, and after several rings, a male answered whose voice Ahmad recognized as his Paris contact, Firuz.

"Ahmad, is that you?" asked his anxious friend. "You are alive? Where are you? I have been watching the coverage of the explosion on television...there is nothing else. The place is still on fire. It sounded like you were all dead."

"No, my friend," said Ahmad, "I got out, the police even helped me. Sharif...may Allah shower him with every honor...detonated the bomb.."

"He was right to do it, Ahmad. Our sacrifices are not in vain. If the others had been captured and even one succumbed to the pressure of interrogation..."

"Yes," interrupted Ahmad. "Listen, Firuz. I need to get out of Paris right away. There is a car waiting for me but I think it is too dangerous to go back. I need help. Will you come?"

"Yes, of course, my brother. I will leave now. Where are you?"

Ahmad gave Firuz the cross streets and told him he would wait by the entrance to the alley opposite Le Plume Brasserie, less than half a block north of the intersection.

"Oh, and Firuz, bring me a change of clothes."

He turned off his phone and went back into the alley to wait. Within half an hour, Firuz pulled up in a dilapidated blue and white pickup marked, Ali's Carrosserie – 24 heures de remorquage. The truck's patina was gone so that now both blue and white melded into the same dreary shade of grey. A white Citroen DS4, not nearly as old as the truck, pulled up behind. A man Ahmad did not know stepped out of the Citroen. He got into the passenger seat of the pickup without saying a word or glancing at the stranger who had emerged from the thick darkness of the alley.

Firuz greeted Ahmad with a hug and a kiss on both cheeks and handed him a small canvas bag.

"Allah'u'Akbar. Here are your clothes, my brother. Take the car. It is yours."

"Ma'a Salaama," replied Ahmad, throwing the bag onto the back seat, and jumping into the auto.

"Bettawfeeq," called Firuz as Ahmad pulled out from the curb and sped away.

Safely behind the wheel of the Citroen, Ahmed left the Paris city center and sped down the motorway en route to the province of Normandy. Ahmad's thoughts raced through his mind as swiftly as the countryside raced past his vision. While struggling to keep the speeding car from drifting off the road, he frantically pulled off the jacket, tie, and stiff white shirt of the wait uniform.

Reaching over the seat, Ahmad grabbed the canvas bag with his change of clothes. Gripping the wheel with one hand, he held the bag in the other, unzipping it with his clenched teeth. He dumped its contents onto the passenger seat, his eyes darting between the road and the clothes that spilled out of the bag. Firuz had stuffed a clean yellow and brown flannel shirt, and a pair of faded blue jeans, into the sack and Ahmad slipped on the wrinkled shirt, leaving the jeans for later. When he finished, he rolled the discarded clothing into a ball and jammed them under the front seat, intending to dispose of the bundle, along with the trousers he was wearing, as soon as it was safe enough to stop.

As the kilometers rolled by, the adrenalin that fueled Ahmad's escape finally began to wane, and the vehicle slowed. He was alone on the road, traveling along the rolling hills of Normandy's halcyon farmlands.

When he was nearly halfway to the château, the grief that had been overtaking his thoughts, in sync with his decelerating speedometer, became unbearable and Ahmad began to unravel. Blinded by exhaustion, looking for a safe place to stop, he pulled off the motorway and he turned onto the road leading to Gravigny. Driving slowly past a cider apple orchard, Ahmad noticed a small gate that had been left open for tractors and other farming equipment.

Taking his car as far into the trees as he could, he turned off the ignition and sat weeping, both hands clutching the steering wheel as he rocked back and forth with his head butting against its worn leather handgrip.

"Hovallah! Hovallah!" Ahmad cried out, over and over, his incantation a plea for solace and forgiveness. "God, forgive me! Sharif, my dear friend, forgive me. I beg of you, my brother. I have let you down. I have failed you. I have failed my teachers, and I have failed God. I am a hopeless sinner…my life is worth nothing. Please, God, forgive me."

Dripping with sweat, Ahmad flung open the car door and fell over onto the ground. Crying still, he buried his head in his hands and continued supplicating for forgiveness from Sharif, and the Divine, for his great sin.

"How could I have let this happen?" he moaned. "Why, Allah, has this happened? Why did You allow Your divine mission to fail? Why did Sharif have to die…so young…he was so young."

As Ahmad's anxiety began to grow, he stood up and started pacing back and forth in front of the car's headlights, still railing at his fate and the fate of his fallen friends.

"Is this really Your divine will? What is the purpose of this test? I cannot bear it! I am being punished for not honoring Sholeh's wishes! I should have listened to her parents. Why didn't I listen?"

At this last thought, Ahmad pounded his fists into the hood of the car then sank down once again to the ground. He was leaning against the well of the front wheel, knees pulled up and his head resting on his arms, when he heard a small cry above the din of his vociferous grief.

Slowing the violent hitching of his chest, but not daring to look up, he listened more closely, leaning left into the direction of the sound. Suddenly, the feeling that something was crawling on his leg startled him. Screaming, Ahmad shot up, the branch of an apple tree sweeping the top of his head, knocking him off balance and causing his arms to flail about.

Falling to the ground, cursing, Ahmad began pounding at the monster gripping his trousers, the flesh of his thigh searing as his attacker's claws dug ever deeper into his flesh. Finally, Ahmad's blows hit their mark. The creature howled and jumped off, making a lightning sprint for the hedgerow.

Catching a glimpse of the animal in the beam of the headlights, Ahmad realized his attacker was merely a small feral cat. He chuckled to himself in relief.

"You scared me, my little friend! I guess I got my own back though, didn't I?"

He paused a moment, watching the hunched cat stare back through the brush.

"Poor little cat," said Ahmad, relenting. "I have terrified you. You were climbing into my lap for a little warmth and friendship, weren't you? I'm sorry, I frightened you away."

Ahmad remembered a small paper bag on the front seat that had fallen out of Firuz's pouch along with the clothes. On a hunch, he went back to the open door of the car, slid into the driver's seat, grabbed the bag and began rummaging around in it. He found what he was looking for; an apple, a croissant, a can of foie gras and a few slices of fine white cheddar. Ahmad, eyes raised, silently thanking his brother Firuz, kissed the bag, broke off a slice of the cheese and climbed back out of the car.

"Come, little cat," said Ahmad in a whisper, hoping to soothe the frightened animal.

"Share my cheese. We will be friends. You will know how sorry I am for all the trouble I have caused."

Ahmad waited, patiently hunched on his heels, and watched the reflection of the headlights in the terrified cat's enormous yellow eyes as the animal unfurled its gray and white tail. Ahmad persisted for several minutes, holding out the cheese and cajoling the cat to abandon its hiding place. Just as Ahmad was about to pop the cheese into his own mouth, the cat crept out of the bush and slowly closed the gap between itself and Ahmad's gift.

"Aha!" Ahmad chuckled, letting the cat creep toward him ever closer. It snatched the cheese from his fingers, ran back into the hedgerow and sat, on its guard, devouring the pungent morsel.

"You're crafty, aren't you, little one?" Ahmad laughed, amused by the ravenous cat. "You weren't going to lose a chance at a free meal, now were you? Truly, you are a cat after my own heart." Ahmed, amused, let out a laugh, startling the cat again before it returned to the banquet.

As the hungry feline hunched over the best meal it had eaten in some time, Ahmad continued breaking off small pieces of the cheese, throwing them to the cat. When the cheese was nearly finished, he rose from the ground, spread his arms, looked skyward and began to chant.

"Hovallah! Hovallah! Assist your loved ones, oh Allah, to bear our tests with fortitude, and to remain firm in the Divine Will." As his chanting became more and more intense, a sense of urgency began to take shape in Ahmad's weary mind. He must get to the château and contact his superiors. They needed to know he was alive and that he intended to continue on, as planned, to the next phase of his mission.

If he wasn't captured tonight, he could leave France without fear of being identified by the authorities at the ports. By now, the computer program Roshed bin Hamid loaded into the security system's database would have destroyed his identity. An hour, maybe two, and he would reach the château and freedom would be his. But before then, Ahmad looked forward to spending a few days in hiding at the château; a few days to stop running, to stop planning, to stop thinking, to catch his breath.

Ahmad opened the can of goose liver and left it, along with the rest of the cheese, next to the starving cat, believing this act of kindness to be a kind of atonement. Then he got back into the car and, leaning out the window, he wished the cat a long and happy life, full of savory cheeses and warm laps in which to curl up. Slowly, he backed the car out of its hiding place in the orchard. If he kept a steady pace, he calculated, he would be at the château in little more than an hour.

As he drove along, the confidence he was feeling about a painless escape began to fade. Ahmad had forgotten about the man at the bar. But now his thoughts were preoccupied with the memory of the stranger's face. He looked so familiar, Ahmad thought, and he insisted we met sometime in the past. What was it, he said, about a fountain in Tehran? What if he recognizes me...recalls how he knows me? What if he remembers my real name? Maybe he was killed in the blast...can't take a chance on that...I'll have to leave France right away, no time to rest.

The smell of salt air blowing in from the English Channel signaled that Ahmad was close to his destination. The château was just outside a small village beside the coast. The commune was tiny with only a few quaint buildings and he passed through the town center quickly and unchallenged. Soon now, he thought, another kilometer, maybe less.

When he rounded the bend, just passed Deauville Saint Gatien airfield, he caught sight of the château. There it was, standing majestically like a lighted monument of stone and glass, rising from the ground as though it grew up naturally from divine seeds. Ahmed smiled.

An Unusual Kind
of Fire

Château de Lumiere was once the centuries-old summer residence of a flamboyant French monarch. The granite and limestone castle stood on a rise in the verdant Normandy countryside, overseeing, like its former owner, the apple orchards and dairy pastures, the people, the town and the land, all of which, in times past, belonged to the king.

The roads leading up to the château were unlit and Ahmad was forced to slow his car to a crawl, winding along the rural roads, as he searched for the mansion's main gate. Finally, spotting the unmarked entrance, Ahmad turned the car onto a narrow cobblestone driveway lined with tall pines standing at attention like sentinels. Moving ever so cautiously along the serpentine drive, he paused at the entrance of a small stone bridge, one of several, crossing the streams that flowed idly through the estate.

He studied the house as he approached, looking for signs of movement. There were mature beech trees on each side of the château. Sculpted shrubs of various varieties lined the facade. The darkened windows suggested the house was unoccupied but, when Ahmad traced a line along the steeply pitched slate roof to one of the chimneys, he noticed smoke. The caretaker must be here, he thought. He cautiously drove toward the mansion, stopping in front of its grand entryway.

Locking the Citroen, he found and followed a gravel path that wound around toward the rear of the building. Ahmad's footsteps crunched on the gravel, sounding thunderous against the quiet night. When he reached the side of the building, the path split. Curious, he took the right fork leading away from the house, in spite of the noise the gravel made as he walked. The path was lined with ornamental topiary and, after a short walk; it ended at a knot garden. The box-wood hedges of the parterre, accented with rosemary and lavender, were cut into symmetrical patterns. In the pale light of a three-quarter moon, he could see a shape, barely discernable, sculpted from the shrubs and sitting prominently in the garden's center. It was a symbol he had known since childhood; a symbol of reassurance that he was safe at home.

Ahmad returned to the fork and followed the left path around a pond until he came to the service entrance. He tapped lightly on the windowpane's beveled glass diamonds, waiting in the dark, until the rear lights came on. Five minutes went by. Ahmad stood in a cone of bright light, wondering where the caretaker could be, until finally, he heard the sound of the door being unlatched. A frail looking man, wearing what appeared to be workman's clothes, stood there; his face and head clean shaven, his eyes the same gunmetal color as the weapon hidden under Ahmad's shirt.

The man looked at the stranger, and said, "Bonsoir, je peux vous aider?"

Ahmad introduced himself.

"Come in, monsieur, we are expecting you. Where are the others?"

Lowering his eyes, Ahmad said, "Killed…I am the only one left. May I ask your name?"

"Excusez-moi. My name is Gaspard. I am the groundskeeper and caretaker. I am here alone, until morning, so you will not be disturbed. Your auto...where did you leave it?"

"At the front entrance."

"It must be moved, before it is seen. Come, monsieur, we will hide your car."

Ahmad allowed Gaspard to guide him through a labyrinth of passageways until they reached the grand hall of the front entryway. The entrance was more spacious than the rail terminals in most small cities. The room had a twenty-foot high ceiling and immense stained glass cathedral windows, set into the front wall. On each side of the room, two massive marble staircases swept upward to the second floor. Between the staircases, twelve medieval suits of armor stood gleaming under spotlights, each armored suit holding a shield with a sword or battle axe. On each shield there was painted a coat of arms belonging to one of the original Teutonic Knights; men who had gathered, long ago, in the Castle Marienberg.

Gaspard unlocked the massive front door. To Ahmad's surprise, it swung open, effortlessly, on invisible hinges. Once in the car, the caretaker directed Ahmad back along the cobblestone drive, to a turn-off leading through the perfectly tended apple orchard. They drove between rows of apple trees with the windows down, enjoying the pleasant night air and the pungent aroma from hectare upon hectare of apple blossoms. The car stopped in a dimly lit clearing, occupied by brick and stone buildings and an assortment of farm equipment.

"What is this place?" Ahmad asked.

"This is where Calvados Brandy is made," Gaspard replied. "They have been growing and fermenting apples here since Charlemagne's empire." Pointing to several outbuildings, he said, "Over there are the sorting and pressing sheds; just beyond are the fermentation and distillery buildings; to the right is an old cider house for the workers, and this is the equipment shed. We will leave your car here, out of sight, until it is needed."

"Where are all the workers?" Ahmad asked.

"At this time of year we have only a maintenance crew. Château de Lumiere does not entertain visitors. Come, we have a long walk back."

The two men shared little conversation on the hike back to the château. Both had been trained to be circumspect with strangers, even those in their own inner circle and, as such, surmised it safer not to talk rather than inadvertently disclose privileged information. The walk was a strain for Ahmad who was, by now, past exhausted. Loath to show any sign of weakness, the Iranian concealed his fatigue.

After Ahmad finished a reheated meal, prepared by Gaspard earlier in the evening, they ascended the servant's staircase to the bedroom level. The caretaker handed Ahmad a sealed envelope. Moving to the end of the long corridor, he unlocked the door to a bedroom suite. Murmuring a brusque good night, he brushed past his guest and disappeared, turning off the lights behind him in the hallway.

Ahmad stood alone, shaking his head, wondering why this man would leave him in the dark. He entered the room, sat on the edge of the bed, and opened the letter. Inside were his escape instructions and the combination for the ignition to an airplane waiting for him at the small airfield, nearby. He committed the information to memory, then threw the letter into a large fireplace crafted from hand-carved stone, lit it on fire and watched until it was reduced to carbon. Returning to the bed, he turned off the lamp and fell asleep.

By the faint light of a single low wattage incandescent lamp, Gaspard carefully negotiated the winding and creaky hickory steps leading to the château's wine cellar. He slipped between huge oak casks, then past rows of wine racks, until he located an old style black telephone, without a dial or keypad, which sat on an antique wooden stand. The groundskeeper lifted the receiver to his ear, and waited until he heard a click. There was never a voice or a greeting, just that damn click. He cleared his throat and said, "One arrival…name, Ahmad…others, dead." Then he dropped the receiver back onto the cradle and waited for instructions.

The golden symbol of the Brotherhood lay in the center of the table. Its brilliance stretched between the past and future like a bridge of light over which generations of its members traveled. Around the table, twelve members of the Grand Council readied themselves for a difficult discussion, for things were getting out of hand. The sealed council chamber had soundproofed walls, windows, and an arrangement of inner and outer doors, to trap any conversation, no matter its volume.

"Gentlemen," said the Grandmaster, interrupting the low buzz of conversation in the room. "Shall we bring the meeting to order?"

As the members quieted, he continued. "I would like to thank everyone for traveling...some from far away...to be here, in person. As you know, by now, the operation in Paris did not fully meet our objectives. We are still evaluating the degree of success and will know more once the casualty list is released. Details of the exact outcome are expected soon from one of our brothers...a high ranking member of the French Ministry."

Another member, sitting opposite the Grandmaster, stood to address the Council. He had deeply sunken eyes and the pin spotlight hanging above his head shone down, casting shadows of light and dark, creating the macabre illusion that his face was an empty skull. He formed a steeple with his fingers and spoke in a baritone voice that filled the room with a sound akin to a rumbling locomotive heard off in the distance. He had failed in his interrogation of Brian Saunders and the failure put his ascension to deputy Grandmaster in question. His urgent task was to restore the confidence of those sitting around the table.

"Brothers, several months ago, we caught up with Haji Shaykh Mahmud Azzizi. After some...*convincing*...he admitted to removing the original founding charter from our vault."

"How could that be?" questioned a man with fine snow white hair and a matching white beard. "Are not all these things inaccessible?"

"We do not know for certain how he acquired the document," continued the baritone. "Azzizi was well trusted by our predecessors and, when he vanished, they may have thought he simply disappeared into retirement. There is a complication, however...for reasons, not known to us, the old fool befriended a young newsman in Iran and gave the scroll to him."

"Any potential to expose the foundations of our organization jeopardizes the future," bellowed another member, dressed in a traditional caftan that was made from fine kutnu fabric. "This ineptitude is unacceptable!"

Unfair as they were, his vituperations were clearly aimed at the baritone.

"To allow a single rogue member to place us in this position is an outrage," observed a man wearing aviator style glasses, jabbing his index finger into the table.

His comment agitated the men, provoking a chorus of protests to break out in the room. The baritone, who had remained on his feet, called for order.

"Gentlemen, please! I took action the minute this information was disclosed. I contacted three U.S. based members. Together, we discovered the identity of the newsman and dispatched a...representative...to retrieve our property and keep the incident quiet."

"Please then, tell us of your success," the man with white hair demanded.

The Grandmaster rose and motioned for the baritone to be seated. He looked around at the table, pausing to fix his gaze on each individual before proceeding.

"My brothers, it is not a trivial matter that compelled me to request your personal attendance here today. What has happened, has happened, nothing can reverse that. The facts are these: David Anderson of Global News is the newsman who received our document from Haji Shaykh Mahmud Azzizi but, so far, there is no evidence of any disclosure. Remember, this is written in an ancient language and, we believe, this man may think of it as an antique the Shaykh gave him as a gift. A second issue involves the loss of a Holy Qur'an, and a set of coded cards, by Ahmad Hasan as he was departing from the activities in San Francisco. A young woman who accidentally stumbled across these items, apparently, recovered them."

"I do not understand...can you explain how these events relate?" a member asked.

"Yes, of course," replied the Grandmaster. He picked up a sheaf of papers from the table, shuffling through them until he found the proper page.

"A man named, eh...Brian Saunders, was sent to contend with this Anderson business. His first attempt failed and he was brought in to answer for his failure. During questioning, he disclosed he had discovered the identity of the woman who found Hasan's lost items.

Apparently, she contacted, and met, with Anderson in the belief she had discovered something newsworthy related to the attack. Anderson turned her down and she retained possession of the items. Saunders was then dispatched, along with another man, to reacquire our belongings. According to Saunders' account, they tried to gain entrance to her apartment through a bedroom window. The woman had a pistol and exchanged gunfire with Saunders' escort and both were killed. Saunders claims, he began to search for the items but the police arrived and he narrowly escaped."

"His story strains the bounds of credulity," the white haired gentleman commented. "The man is either the unluckiest human in the world, incompetent, or a liar!"

"Agreed...I find it unconvincing...in fact, this whole thing is unbelievable," declared the man wearing the caftan.

"As do we all," the baritone assured them. "The police report is inconclusive so we can't disprove Saunders' account. However, I do not trust him."

"Neither do I," echoed the Grandmaster. "Obviously, he has not earned our trust, or his pay, but Mister Saunders is currently keeping track of Anderson's whereabouts...so we know where he is. We have not heard yet whether his presence in Paris affected the outcome of events there."

"And what if it did?" asked a council member.

"There is no sense speculating," insisted the Grandmaster. "We'll know soon enough. For now, we must focus on hard facts and take action. I suggest we first contend with Ahmad Hasan. His identity may be compromised and we cannot allow the authorities to question him. He is resting comfortably at Château de Lumiere so dealing with this will be relatively simple.

"Secondly, let Saunders complete the final activities in Turkey...once accomplished, the prayer book and accompanying cards are of no value. Since he is not trustworthy, and represents a liability to the organization, arrangements must be put in place so he will never leave that country. Lastly, we will isolate Anderson in New York, retrieve our founding scroll, and convince him that silence is golden. After that, we can resume our normal course of conduct."

"I am not comfortable with these tactics," the man with the white hair insisted. "They're unseemly and counter to our principles."

The man wearing the caftan nodded in agreement as did most of the council members.

"Brothers," said the baritone, "we all deplore these tactics! They are but a short term means to an end in these troubled times. If we don't act, and act now, who will? I beg you all to consider that during your deliberations."

A chime interrupted the proceedings and the Grandmaster unlocked the entrance to the soundproof room. Several waiters entered, carrying trays of food. They set out a banquet that included twelve entrees, each specially prepared at each member's request.

While dining, the Brotherhood continued the discussions, pouring over different strategies, referring to charts, matrices and decision trees, designed for members to game all known possible outcomes then trace back their logic. By the time the members finished eating, they had unanimously determined to follow the Grandmaster's recommendations.

At the end of the meal, after all the food was cleared away, each member recited a favorite passage from one of the ancient epistles. Each recitation was in the member's native language. Lastly, the Grandmaster rose and recited their founding precept:

"Our moral purpose is to keep ourselves, and our members, unspotted in a decadent and corrupt society; our intellectual purpose is to bring together all that is known; our spiritual purpose is to discover universal truth, and to work in harmony as part of the connected whole."

With a single fluid motion, David Anderson pulled open the double French doors of his suite and stepped out onto its tiny balcony. He leaned against the wall, one foot resting on a low, bronze railing, its patina now green with age and looked across the square. To the right of a huge white obelisk, standing in the center of the plaza, smoke from the still smoldering fires at the Hotel de Ville rose above the buildings and filled the skyline. He tucked both hands into the small of his back, tormented by the horror of all the lives lost in the recent attacks. The world is under siege, he worried, and there must be something more that can be done to stop it.

The breeze that had refreshed him only yesterday now whipped the smoke into surreal shapes, shifting, at will, from sublime to terrifying. As he watched, David wondered if the outcomes, for all the different possibilities of life, were like the shapes he saw in the smoke – a product of his own conscious choice.

He reentered the suite, reclined on the couch, and glanced at his wristwatch. It was nearly four in the afternoon, the scheduled time of the official news conference with French authorities. David was positive someone at the reception would recount his involvement with the evacuation. Indeed, by that morning, rumors and speculation appeared all over the Internet. The press wanted to know why David yelled 'fire,' and how he knew to rush the guests down the Grand Staircase, when security did not.

David did not want to become part of the story, and even more importantly, he wasn't completely sure what it was he saw. So he asked Mike Lussardi to fill in for him at the news conference. With that settled, David reached for the remote and began surfing through the television channels.

He watched as dozens of international news teams, anxiously reporting on the day's events, converged at the Elysee Palace. Each had experts lined up to speculate on the reason the conference had been attacked; each was prepared to press the authorities for information and their official statements. They had come here to cover what was meant to be a historic meeting of world leaders, but instead, they found themselves covering another international tragedy. All anyone knew, so far, was that there had been a deadly explosion causing a fire that left the city's sky filled with thick black smoke and eerie blue flames randomly licking at the night.

The French President's press secretary was the first to address the media, providing only sketchy information. He also reported that the president and several staff members were uninjured but, keeping with protocol, they were, currently, undergoing a standard medical evaluation. He promised the president would, in short order, deliver a brief statement from his office that he would address to the world.

Next, Inspector General Francois Michelet appeared, accompanied by Andre Noiret and a contingent of police and other officials from the Interior Ministry. He stood facing dozens of cameras and began fielding questions from the anxious press, explaining what was known so far.

"At present, all we know is an explosion has occurred in the kitchen, near the Salle des Fetes, during the opening ceremonies of the conference. Fire and emergency personnel responded to the scene within minutes of the explosion and have now succeeded in controlling the ensuing blaze."

"Inspector, has there been any loss of life?" asked a reporter from France Televisions.

"My understanding is that initial loss of life was confined to the kitchen staff where the explosion occurred, but others in the dining room, who were unable to get out, died of smoke inhalation." replied Michelet.

"How many have died, sir, and who?" asked a reporter from the BBC.

"We do not have names, or those figures, at this time, madame," answered the Inspector.

Calling out over the other reporters, Mike Lussardi asked. "What caused the explosion…was this an accident or a terror attack?"

"It would be premature to comment on that, monsieur," replied Inspector Michelet. "All we can say is that an explosion has occurred and, we believe, many of the guests at the reception were safely evacuated through the excellent planning and swift action of the security staff."

A journalist from Israel shouted, "What about the rumors?"

"I do not comment on rumors, monsieur," Michelet insisted.

The reply ignited the news media and they began firing a salvo of questions toward the officials.

"What about the story circulating that David Anderson discovered a bomb and alerted people to leave?"

"How about the reports from several families of the delegates claiming their relatives were injured or killed?"

"I interviewed several policemen about the problems with the traffic signals, who claim all the security systems are disabled. Any comments?"

"Has the Ministry identified possible suspects, or groups, that might be responsible?"

"What type of an explosive was used? Have you recovered any traces or evidence?"

Andre Noiret positioned himself next to the Inspector and raised his hand to silence the press corps. Standing hands on hips, he shouted down the crowd, "Please, please…for all we know, this was nothing more than a gas leak! All the storytellers out there… you must stop making things up!"

Startled and dismayed, disbelief spreading over his face, Inspector General Michelet pushed Noiret a step back. The Inspector couldn't fathom why his subordinate would say such incredible things to the press, let alone, break the etiquette of rank by stepping forward without being asked.

"Commissaire Noiret," he began, attempting to contain the damage, "is simply trying to illustrate there are many possibilities and we will pursue every avenue of this investigation until an answer is uncovered. Now, we must get back to work. Thank you all for your patience. We will have more announcements as the situation unfolds."

The Inspector abruptly left the room, his retinue following close behind. Andre Noiret was the last to exit.

Incredulous, David looked on as Noiret disappeared. Like the Inspector General, he couldn't imagine why anyone would make such a misleading statement. He watched awhile as the disappointed correspondents mulled around, strategizing their next move, before turning off the broadcast. He picked up the phone and waited several rings for the hotel operator to answer.

"Bon après-midi," came the cheerful voice.

"Please connect me to Ron Eyota's room."

"Certes monsieur, vous avez une bonne journee."

"Hello," Ron answered.

"Hey Ron, it's me. I spoke to John and he has a plane standing by to fly us home tonight. I thought you'd want to know so you can pack."

"Eh…Okay, I'll be ready to go within a half hour, or sooner, if need be. Are we all leaving?"

"You bet. Global will continue the coverage from our Paris news bureau. And don't hurry, Suzanne and Mike won't be back for at least an hour."

"What's up with the rush to get out of Dodge, anyway?"

"I've been thinking, Ron. By tomorrow, the latest, the police will have interviewed some of the conference delegates and piece together the story of what really happened at the reception. Add to that, the information you gave to Noiret, and it makes us the focal point of the investigation. They will, likely, confiscate everything you showed them for evidence and detain us until they get whatever it is they want to know. I don't relish ending up in some Byzantine police process and out of circulation."

"They can, of course, send someone stateside to interview us, you know…right?"

"Sure, but without preferring charges, we can't be detained, or forced into separate interviews and no one can touch Merilee's items or your laptop. A court room is the last place these guys want to be."

Ron could tell, from the concern in David's voice, there must be something else on his friend's mind, so he asked, "Tell me David, what really set off that famous Anderson alarm bell?"

David chuckled. "You know me too well." After a moment to think, he explained, "Something's a little off here and it's making me suspicious. First, the tirade from Noiret yesterday…just out of the blue…and then, a few minutes ago, he steps in front of his boss to make an inane statement about a gas leak? He knows it wasn't an accident!"

"Are you suggesting a cover up?" asked Ron.

"I'm suggesting that, once our evidence is in Noiret's possession, it's a simple matter to blame the whole thing on a broken gas pipe or point the finger at any terrorist group. It'll be, 'he said, she said', and the truth, as usual, becomes so convoluted it winds up lost in the background noise. I'm also suggesting that we…at least, I… need time to wrap our heads around this and find competent authorities who can help us."

"Makes sense," Ron assured his friend. "One thing though, David...don't you think the police may try to stop us if we leave for the airport?"

"It's possible...Suzanne was thinking the same thing. She's coming back with a camera crew and we'll put our luggage in the empty equipment cases...so when you stop by, bring your bags. They'll take it to the plane while we go to dinner and then the studio...business as usual. After dark, we'll head for the airport in a news van. At that time of night, private aviation gets very little scrutiny."

"Sounds kind of like a spy parody...queue the theme music," Ron quipped, muffling a chuckle. "Very well, then...see you in an hour."

David kept the receiver to his ear for several minutes after Ron hung up listening for a click, or any sound that might alert him to the fact their conversation was monitored. Satisfied, he returned to the balcony and resumed the business of waiting for Mike and Suzanne. The newsman started laughing when he thought about Ron's comment. *He's right. I'm acting like a cliché from a Pink Panther movie.* When he looked again at the horizon and saw the smoke, it occurred to David that this wasn't really that funny, after all.

Returning late that evening, Mike, Suzanne, and two crewmembers, found David and Ron in the anchorman's suite, discussing events over a bottle of Saint-Emilion.

"Don't you guys look comfortable," Suzanne quipped, stacking the equipment cases. "David, I did a little more research and guess what I found?"

"It will have to wait," David insisted. "You can tell me in the car. Right now, I need you and Mike to gather up all your stuff so the crew can make sure everything fits...I'm anxious to leave."

Suzanne and Mike hurried off, and David followed Ron out onto the balcony to toast the Parisian skyline one last time. The friends stood together in silence, looking across the pointed rooftops into a glittering sea of lights, until David raised his glass, "Here's to Paris...may its lights never dim."

"Well, that's out of character." Ron said to his friend.

"What is?"

"The fatalistic tone of voice. You giving up?"

"Maybe," the newsman said, with a shrug. "This won't be easy to unravel."

"Turn him to any cause of policy, the Gordian Knot of it he will unloose."

"Henry the Fifth, right?" said David, acknowledging Ron's encouragement. "Let's see what Suzanne's come up with, and go from there."

The news van dropped them off at a quaint bistro a block away from Global's Paris studios. Overhead, a gibbous moon, dimmed occasionally by a wayward cloud, glowed brightly in the eastern sky. Since the explosion, the streets were quiet and the restaurant was empty, except for a single couple, so enamored, their passion far exceeded the past day's vicissitudes.

The restaurant's owner, overjoyed at having other customers, offered them any table in the house and a complementary glass of wine.

Once they were seated, Suzanne cooed, "Isn't that nice."

"Isn't what nice?" David asked.

"Romance," she answered, admiring the couple's unfettered display of affection. "Isn't romance nice?"

David shot a quick glance at Ron, "So, what is it you're so eager to tell me, Suzanne?"

Rolling her eyes, Suzanne explained, "Remember yesterday, at the reception...I mentioned the EU bank's president...he told me they were going along with the IMF reserve currency?"

"Vaguely," David said, rubbing his temples. "I was, kind of occupied with something else at the time. So tell me now."

"Okay, let me just grab at my notes." As she retrieved a small notebook, David, Mike and Ron leaned in to give Suzanne their full attention. "Let's see...Kurt said, a few years ago, the International Monetary Fund published a paper..."

"Kurt?" David inquired, a mocking smile in his eyes.

Ignoring David's innuendo, she continued without missing a beat. "...for transitioning to a super-sovereign reserve currency from the dollar. It cited looming currency wars, devaluating dollar value and the sovereign debt crises as justification."

"Not converting to dollars for global trade would be a big boost for them," Mike added. "It might solve some of their internal problems...at least temporarily."

"Didn't the Treasury Secretary from a past administration say they were open to an IMF global reserve currency?" David asked. "If memory serves, when the wild swing began in the currency markets, they recanted the statement. I'm not sure it's politically tenable."

"Well, it's becoming more tenable," insisted Suzanne.

"The Pound Sterling lost ninety percent of its value when it ceased being the reserve," David argued. "A similar loss of liquidity in the dollar would have catastrophic consequences for the US economy."

"True, but the IMF is now an integral part of the global financial community," Mike observed. "They've arm twisted more than a few governments with draconian bailout terms."

"That's what Borchert was telling me," Suzanne pointed out. "Many European politicians are secretly scared to death that the global financiers are becoming more powerful than their national governments. We should do a story on this."

"I agree, Suzanne," David said. "Right now, though, I need you to dive into the picture archive and find a photo I took when I was in Iran. It will be of a boy, in his teens, next to a fountain. I am sure he's the guy behind the bar. Run the facial recognition software and get a name."

"And then what?" she asked.

"Then we're back in New York with access to Global's archive system. We'll let it sort the clues so the attacks are in context and we have a coherent narrative. After that, we'll look into your currency story."

"Works for me," Mike agreed.

"Me, too," Ron said. "But finals are coming up and I have to get back to the University. I'll return as soon as I can."

Incomplete, and far from perfect, they now had a purpose and a plan. Mike had faith in the extensive research locked up at Global. Ron had faith in the hand of Divine guidance. Suzanne had faith in

David, and David; he had a glimmer of hope, and that was at least something. For now, they were happy to forget their immediate problems and focus solely on the anticipation of a fine meal and returning home.

It was just after nightfall when Ahmad returned from Deauville St. Gatien airfield and quietly entered the château by the service entrance. That morning he slept until noon, and when he finally woke, found a tray with an assortment of tartines and croissants, jams and butter, a pot of café au lait and a tall glass of fresh orange juice, but no Gaspard, or anyone else for that matter. The night's rest had completely rejuvenated him and he walked the four, or so, kilometers to the airfield and back, and found, as stated in his instructions, an airplane, parked and ready to fly. By the time he returned, it was evening. He had not eaten since breakfast and was now starved.

"Gaspard," Ahmad shouted. "Is dinner ready? I am hungry."

Hearing no reply, he tried to search the château but many of the rooms were locked, including the entrance to the cellar. After searching in vain, Ahmad decided to prepare his own meal, but found the kitchen pantry and the refrigerators also locked. There was a small cupboard containing dried biscuits and another with several cases of bottled water. On one side of the center island, wire baskets of assorted fruits were hanging from the ceiling. He made a snack tray from the foods he found, and went off to his suite.

Ahmad was relaxing on the sofa, munching on an apple slice, and reading the aeronautical charts he took from the plane. He sat, calculating the airspeed, fuel and distance needed to escape when, from the corner of his eye, he spotted movement by the arched windows in the grand bedroom. The draperies were shifting, back and forth, in a staccato cadence as if someone were jabbing at them from behind.

Ahmad shot up, carefully scanning the room, adrenalin pumping. Setting aside the charts, he stole towards the bedroom chamber, hesitating for a second, looking back at his jacket thrown over a nearby chair, realizing he left the gun in its pocket.

Standing beside the king bed, Ahmad pushed back the curtains. Relieved, he closed the open window, and securely latched the sash, brushing off the incident, when a voice whispered his name. Spinning around, toward the sound, he spotted a metal box with a proximity sensor, protruding out from under the bed frame. It took a second for him to identify the threat and only a split-second more for him to respond.

Ahmad raced back toward the lounge, hurtling himself over the coffee table that stood in front of the sofa, blocking his path to the exit. Twisting to grab the door, a bomb exploded, throwing him into the air. His body crashed against the wall with such force it left a huge, gaping hole in the plaster. Framed pictures and furniture shattered, glass and wood lay scattered on the bedroom floor. Unconscious and barely breathing, his nearly lifeless body was lying slouched, against the wall.

Gaspard, back working in the kitchen and well away from the blast, heard the enormous explosion from where he stood, peeling potatoes and popping them into the pot on the stove that would thicken the fresh fish soup he was preparing for dinner.

"Au revoir, Monsieur Ahmad," said the man, out loud, "I sincerely hope you did not know what happened to you."

Gaspard was aware the fire and smoke from the explosion would be seen from the airport and the town. Putting the paring knife down on the marble countertop, he crossed the room, picked up an elegant white portable phone hanging on the wall, and immediately dialed emergency services. Before he finished speaking with the eager young woman taking down his information, fire trucks, sirens wailing, arrived at the elaborately ornamented gates of the château. Two police cars and an ambulance accompanied the fire fighters.

The caretaker had been well rehearsed by his superiors and, as the first police gendarmes arrived on the scene, Gaspard appeared at the steps of the mansion, directing the emergency vehicles to the rear of the château, confident that his story would be entirely plausible to the men who would soon be interviewing him.

"There is a man," yelled the caretaker to the emergency workers, "He was in the south wing of the house, where the explosion occurred. Please find him, poor man. He must be desperately injured."

The caretaker's words were not lost on the gendarme who walked up the drive toward him.

"Hello, monsieur," said the gendarme, extending a hand holding his identification, "My name is Inspector Jean Bissette. I am assigned to..."

His words trailed off as the medicopter, sent from Saint Joan's emergency department, flew over and hovered above the château, gauging a place to safely land.

"Pardon, Inspector," replied Gaspard, as the chopper found a spot and touched down, "I missed that last part."

"I am here to investigate the accident," said Inspector Bissette. "Can you tell me what happened?"

"Certainly," said Gaspard, "I was in the kitchen, preparing our supper, when I heard the explosion. It was horrendous! I knew it came from the direction of the suite occupied by a guest, so I dashed there as fast as I could. Because of the smoke and flames, I could not enter the room. I immediately dialed one-twelve. Thank God, you made it here so quickly. Perhaps he has a chance..."

"He was your guest?" interrupted Bissette.

"Yes," answered the caretaker. "He had been staying with us for the past several weeks."

"What was...is his name, monsieur," asked the Inspector.

"His name is Ahmad Hasanzadeh," replied Gaspard.

"He was foreign born?" asked Bissette.

"He has an Iranian passport with a French student's visa," said the caretaker.

"You asked him for no other identification or credentials, monsieur?"

"No, Inspector. He is a guest of my employer."

"Yes, of course," the detective said, nodding in agreement. "You said he was Iranian. Did he speak French?"

"Oui, Inspector," said Gaspard, "He spoke French quite well. Not like you and me, of course, but well enough to sound as though he's lived in France for quite a few years. He said he's been studying at the university."

"Interesting, monsieur. It is not often you would find a university student vacationing in a place as opulent as this château. Did he tell you why he was visiting here?"

"Yes, of course. Ahmad represents his father, a wealthy Persian investor. He was exploring financial investments with the owner," replied Gaspard.

Just then the Capitaine working on the case with Inspector Bissette, Louis Lamare, stepped out of the front door of the mansion and came down the steps.

"How is our victim, Louis?" asked Bissette, "Have you talked to him?"

"Not a chance, Jean," replied Louis, "Comatose...he is barely alive...I doubt he will last the night."

"Well, I will come right away then," said Bissette, "Don't want our chief witness dying on us before we get a chance to talk to him."

Turning back to the caretaker, Bissette asked, "Who owns the château, monsieur?"

"His name is Ambros von Lightchild," replied Gaspard. "He is an international investor and financier. He has, of late, taken up property development. He is quite renowned for buying antiquated and abandoned properties all over Europe, refurbishing them, and then selling them as resorts to hotel chains. They make fine palaces for the nouveau rich. The property market has been drying up for quite some time now, with the worldwide economic problems...a shame, really, since he had been restoring historical places all over Europe."

"Please call him, immediately, and tell him we want to speak with him," instructed Bissette, "We will be back here tomorrow, at the very latest."

"Oui," said the caretaker, "I will do my best."

"You must do better than your best, monsieur," Bissette insisted.

"What will happen to Monsieur Ahmad?" asked Gaspard as the gendarme walked away.

"You'll have to ask them," replied the Inspector, pointing upward as the noise of the medicopter rose, once again, from behind the mansion.

Gaspard began another query but the noise of the chopper continued to grow, drowning out his voice as the members of the gendarmerie disappeared into the mansion. The fire brigades were finishing up and he would have to deal with them next.

Entering the house, the caretaker laughed aloud thinking, unfortunately for you, Inspector, you will never know the true reason Ahmad was staying at the château or who owns this entire compound. You won't ever find out that this is a preplanned escape route and your gravely wounded captive serves a purpose known only to the Brotherhood. So spin your wheels, Inspector, because, even the most meticulous intelligence will not discover the investment story is a front.

Gaspard's work, to help install Brotherhood members into the highest financial circles in Europe, was just about complete and, after assuming a new identity, he would soon relocate to Quebec. Gaspard knew Inspector Bissette would never speak to von Lightchild, for he was not a citizen of France or even of his native country; he was a citizen of the world and a very powerful one at that. As for Bissette's other queries: they would soon come to an end along with Ahmad Hasan.

Ahmad spent his first hours, after the explosion, at Caen's regional medical hub, with the emergency room staff of Hospitalier du Saint Joan de Arc.

The hospital was the closest facility to the château equipped with a state-of-the-art trauma unit, capable of adequately caring for patients with extensive injuries. The staff at Saint Joan's was frantically working to save the Islamic warrior. Despite this good fortune, Ahmad was barely clinging to the razor's edge of life.

Detective Jean Bissette accompanied the patient. He was the commandant and divisional inspector assigned to investigate the case.

"The victim was identified as a man by the name of Ahmad Hasanzadeh," Bissette reported to the attending physician. "We have not confirmed this as his real identity."

"His documents...a passport or driver's license...they were not found on him or in the château?" queried Dr. Paul Juneau, the emergency room physician. As he spoke, he wrote down the name given him by the detective on the patient's chart.

"No. If they are discovered, it will not be in the château. What was not blown up in the suite was destroyed, or badly damaged, in the ensuing fire. My assistant tried to question him but he could only stare into space."

"His state of shock appears profound," an adamant Dr. Juneau insisted, trying to impress, upon the detective, the critical state of his patient. "Dare I say, he will not be able to respond to your questions for some days, if he awakens at all. I suggest you forego your questioning until we have a chance to help him survive."

"If he dies before I have a chance to question him, we may never find out what happened in that château," replied the insistent detective.

"Yes, that may be so, but I must insist we not delay his treatment for another second. It is the duty of the health professionals in this hospital to put the patient's well being first, before any other consideration. I ask you to respect that. Thank you, Inspector Bissette."

The physician turned away and sauntered off to treatment room three, where Ahmad's gurney had been wheeled, closing the door securely behind him.

"Doctors…" Bissette mumbled as he left to find his partner.

Capitaine Louis Lamare was waiting for him in a patrol car outside the hospital lobby. The two colleagues nodded their greetings to each other as the Inspector opened the passenger side door and slipped onto the front seat. Clicking his seatbelt into the lock, he said, "Let's run back over to the château and see what's happening at the scene. Perhaps they have found his papers."

"Did you get any information?" asked his colleague.

"A waste of time," replied Bissette. "The doctor in charge wouldn't let me anywhere near the man. I can come back tonight and perhaps they will let me get in a few questions…should our victim survive and wake up. Even if I am not able to speak with him, I will push for them to allow fingerprints to be taken. At least then, we can send the prints off to Interpol and see whether he has any criminal history."

"Sounds like a good plan."

"Well, it may be the best we can do at the moment but I have a bad feeling about this situation. I tell you, Louis, that man has 'terrorist' written all over his face. Merd!"

"What gives you that idea?" asked Louis. "He could just be an unlucky tourist."

"Oui, perhaps you are right," said Bissette. "But young Middle Eastern men don't usually get blown up while on vacation. Besides, the site has the distinct look of a deliberate and planned explosion. Something is going on and I want to know what it is. I will insist that, at least, we take his prints tonight. In the meantime, I want to know who owns that château, where he is, and what he knows about our suspect. When we get to the château, I want you to find the caretaker, so he can be questioned in detail. I don't like him either."

Mirroring the urgency in his superior's voice, Louis snapped on the vehicle's siren and sped off to the scene of the explosion. As the patrol car turned onto the motorway, heading back toward Château de Lumiere, the last thing on the Inspector's mind was how difficult a time he would have identifying this suspect. Fingerprints would prove fruitless. Ahmad had no criminal record, either in Europe or abroad. For now, Ahmad would remain as he came to France: simply another foreign student taking advantage of the opportunity for a western education.

The emergency room staff worked for hours repairing Ahmad's injuries. First, they meticulously monitored and corrected his fluids and electrolytes, acutely aware that the slightest abnormality in such a sick patient could precipitate a cardiac arrest. Next, he was wheeled up to the Operating Room, where the surgeons mended his wounds.

Recovery room nurses monitored Ahmad's vital signs every fifteen minutes. Emilia, Ahmad's charge nurse, sure her patient was sufficiently stable to be transferred, called Renee in the surgical intensive care unit to find out whether they had a bed available.

"Yes," she told Emilia, "the patient in 'three' is scheduled for transfer to a regular floor today but the room won't be ready for another two hours."

Emilia informed her nursing assistant, Henri, he must begin to ready Ahmad to 'travel' – the arduous task of transporting the patient with all the portable equipment and hookups needed to sustain his life.

Henri was a diligent aide and, following Emilia's instructions, immediately set about gathering the instruments and equipment needed for Ahmad's trek to the intensive care unit. The high tech equipment Ahmad relied upon to keep him alive would be disconnected and replaced by portable versions of his breathing and monitoring equipment, his intravenous fluids and medications re-hung on a movable pole and, finally, a portable defibrillator attached, just in case he suffered a cardiac arrest en route.

"Call me when you are finished," instructed Emilia, "and I will recheck it with you. We do not want to be caught, unprepared, if anything goes wrong."

The charge nurse always kept close in her memory an incident during her training when, trapped in a stalled elevator, her patient's portable ventilator failed. They had forgotten an ambu bag – a hand-held device pumped by hand. She, and the nurse in charge, began to perform continuous chest compressions and artificial mouth-to-mouth resuscitation, praying the elevator would move but it stayed where it was. They grew tired, nearly unable to continue, and the patient almost died. Luckily, they were rescued in time but the incident made an indelible imprint on Emilia's consciousness.

After a final inspection, Henri was on his way. He maneuvered the bed around, smacked his hand against the metal wall plate that swung open the wide double-doors of the recovery room, and wheeled the comatose patient down the hall to intensive care.

The familiar sound of bleating heart monitors greeted them, as the gurney carrying Ahmad's nearly lifeless body was wheeled into the room directly opposite the nurses' station.

Ahmad's medical team met to develop a rigorous plan of care to sustain him through the first critical days of his recovery. Ahmad would require support for hemodynamic stability so his organs would continue to maintain adequate blood supply and function. To protect him from a blood infection that could overwhelm his already overtaxed immune system, he would receive prophylactic intravenous antibiotics. His airway needed to remain unobstructed to prevent respiratory compromise and his ventilator would require frequent adjustments as his condition changed.

Among the first priorities of his medical team was to reinitiate feeding their patient to support his immune system and ability to heal. Ahmad was being held in an induced coma, so he would not fight the artificial ventilator that regulated his breathing and, consequently, it was not possible for him to eat. The hospital's dietitian devised an intravenous formula, based on Ahmad's weight and medical condition, setting his calorie requirements at twice his usual needs. He would continue to receive this feeding until his bowel function improved.

The sounds and sights of the SICU, the soft ka-plunk-whoosh of the ventilator, the blinking lights on the instruments, the beeping of the monitors, the conversations among the doctors, nurses and medical technicians, filled the recovery room in which Ahmad lay. But his mind was unaware of his physical surroundings and, instead, descended into a darkness blacker than the deepest cavern burrowed, over eons, into the earth's crust.

Ahmad stood in the center of a black disk, not more than four feet across. Its metallic surface was smooth and matte-like. Around its edge there was a faint glow, like the embers of a dying fire. Ahmad couldn't see past his hand but he knew, beyond that glow, there was a bottomless abyss. Screams rose from its depths and, in the surrounding darkness, he heard the taunts of his victims, the cries of Sharif, and the pleas of Sholeh. An angry voice whispered in his ear, urging him to take a few steps forward and end his pain. This was not the halcyon paradise he'd come to expect and he cried out in a loud voice for an angel of deliverance.

BROKEN WITH A
CRUSHED SPIRIT

The surgical intensive care unit is not unlike a war zone. Except for the absence of gunfire and exploding shells, the heightened state of urgency, tragedy, and triumph can be every bit the same. The missiles in the SICU are the alarms that scream a patient is dying, organs failing. The machines become an extension of the unconscious mind, as they flash and bleep their constant stream of data, blaring red warnings when a patient's vital signs slip out of normal range.

Staff in intensive care become as addicted to the adrenaline rush as those in combat. Much like a career soldier, they may spend many years in this environment, despite the physical and emotional punishment.

Some choose not to stay. Those who remain learn to manage extreme stress, some coping with drugs or alcohol, others finding that detachment, balance, and focus on the positive aspects of their work, will save them from self-medicating. In any event, those who make it past the stress, who embrace the stress, discover something much more than just an adrenaline rush to keep them coming back, day after day.

Patients in the unit are some of the sickest in the world, and many will not survive, despite the heroic efforts of the medical and surgical teams. In spite of this fact, there is often an ineffable state of transcendence; something about the very sick and dying that brings most everyone who cares for them into a state of grace and reverence. The medical teams find, as years pass, that death, for the dying, is not repulsive but, often, more an experience of joy than grief.

In a real sense, this is a gift: to be present during a journey that we all must face someday; to have the privilege of witnessing a special grace, perhaps glimpsing the sublime beauty that lies in store; watching the great dread many carry all their lives, transform into a transcendent sense of serenity and to be the recipient of many last words of remembrance and wisdom that come from a life well-lived.

On early morning medical rounds the following day, Ahmad's medical team discussed whether it was time to wean him from the mechanical ventilator. The doctors tried reducing Ahmad's sedation to see whether he would spontaneously awaken. The trial was a success. Ahmad could open his eyes and blink when the attending physician spoke to him. The settings on his ventilator were then decreased to allow him to partially breathe on his own.

Ahmed tolerated the change quite well and the team, encouraged by his progress, continued cranking down the settings, allowing him to progressively assist the vent, until he was breathing entirely by himself. Doctor Breton, the physician in charge of Ahmad's case, remarked that it was a good sign, indicating the respiratory center of Ahmad's brain was functioning.

"The question remains, however," the physician speculated, "will Monsieur Hasanzadeh be able to remember, speak, and move once the breathing tube is removed."

Not only did the Global News building rise prominently above the skyline in midtown Manhattan, it was anchored deep into its bedrock. Here, far below street level, the builders constructed a vault that would house a unique information gathering and analysis engine. Its ability to capture, aggregate, retrieve, index, sort, interpret and present a broad spectrum of information, in real time, from every electronic source imaginable, was the envy of industry and governments around the world.

The engine's holographic information was stored in photons, parked deep inside a crystal memory bank and enclosed in a specially designed and insulated container. It was no bigger than the small refrigerator one might find on a boat or in a college dormitory, but its temperature, hovering around two degrees Kelvin, was cold enough to instantly kill anyone who might open it. The staff at Global News referred to it as the tabernacle, and the space above it, the sanctuary.

The indicator display on the only public access elevator permitted to descend below street level, read B6. It lit up as Suzanne and Ron stepped into the security anteroom of the sanctuary. This was the only entrance to the GN archive control room and very few employees had security clearance to enter. Although Suzanne was part of that elite group, she was required to obtain approval for Ron to accompany her from both John Stavos and Lance Rodgers. The area had dark grey concrete walls with wavy lines masoned into its surface and the indirect LED lighting emitted an unnatural orange glow.

Suzanne approached a stainless steel door and stopped at the kiosk to insert her identification card. She placed the fingers of her right hand on a biometric reader and looked up at the camera, brushing the hair away from her face. The door slid open into the wall and they entered the security verification room. The guards rechecked Suzanne's credentials and the computer authorization for Ron. They were handed access badges that opened a second ponderous door.

"Follow me," Suzanne said, motioning to Ron.

They approached a hub of workstations in the center of a cavernous, darkly lit space and, picking one at random, sat down. Ron turned to Suzanne. "I'm surprised there isn't access to this archive from your office. It seems a bit of a time waster to come all the way down here."

"Oh, there is." She paused to logon. "Every GN office, and employee around the world has access but it is segmented…

compartmentalized...we each have certain permissions and can only see a small portion of the data stored here. There are only two places where the entire archive is accessible - this control room and Lance Rodgers' office. David's archive can only be viewed at his desk and he hasn't arrived yet, so..."

"Why don't you just call him for his password?"

"I've tried that, more than once, and...well, you can guess the rest."

A Machiavellian thought flashed across Ron's mind. "I'll bet there are a lot of secrets one could learn, about very powerful people, if you spent a few hours noodling around this database."

Suzanne winked her nose at Ron, bowing her head in a conspiratorial nod. "Look above us. That camera records everything we do. Every keystroke I type is recorded and analyzed, and if it does not match the search parameters approved before we came down, the system locks, and then...we're screwed."

"How?"

"They come and arrest us."

"No, really?"

"Relax...just kidding."

"I'll tell you what, though. The CIA wishes it had security like this."

She whispered, "This probably is the CIA."

The look on Ron's face caused her to laugh out loud.

She entered a simple string of search terms, exactly as David described in Paris, pressed 'enter', and waited for the result set.

It took just seconds for the picture of a boy to appear on the screen. He was standing in front of a stone fountain, wearing a brown robe and holding a book. He appeared restless, in a hurry to get somewhere, or maybe, he just didn't want to be photographed.

Suzanne framed his face with an expandable box and selected the 'aging' software from the menu. She responded to several prompts for criteria and she and Ron watched as the face of the boy was transformed into that of a young man.

"I can hardly believe this," she exclaimed, looking sideways at Ron. "It's the guy from the bar!"

"Well, it's certainly a close match," Ron said. "Before we jump to any firm conclusions, let's get David's confirmation."

Suzanne navigated to a second screen and asked the computer if there were any identification details for the pictures. The system responded, instantly, with a short list of details common for both; a name, school records, and some travel details, but nothing to indicate this man was wanted or had anything suspicious in his background.

"There's not a whole lot here," Ron said. "Primarily educated in Iran, attended the university in France. It might explain why he was working the bar there."

Suzanne was thinking of logging out when the system asked, 'Do You Want More?' She raised one eyebrow, pausing a second, and pressed 'yes'. The monitor displayed the heading, 'All Instances of Picture Two'. Below the heading was a list of cities sorted by traffic and security cameras. She selected a few of the entries on the list and pictures appeared of public spaces, some crowded, but all with a highlight indicating where in the picture the target subject was matched.

Whoa, this guy really gets around!" Suzanne said.

"More than just a student, I think." Ron replied. Suddenly, his mouth dropped open.

"Soooo…what's up?" she asked. "You look freaked out!"

"Many of the locations on this list are the same as those on Merilee Brunswick's cards…or they are routes you might travel to go from one card location to another. I think it may be time to call the police."

"We ought to call David and see what he thinks."

The phone on the desk rang. The lines had only internal access and Suzanne knew it was from someone upstairs. "Hello," she answered. "Hi Lynn…he is…okay, I'll be right up."

"No need to call David…that was his admin. He's sitting at his desk."

"Say Suzanne, can you print all this out?"

"I can do better than that! I'll save this session and we can view it in David's office."

By the time Suzanne and Ron got up to his office, David was gone. He spent the morning arranging a service for his father and he was down in the lobby, handing the funeral director a check. Ron and Suzanne waited, Lynn telling them David had made the decision when to hold the funeral after consulting family by phone.

The professor sat forward, his fingers steepled, listening intently, while Suzanne, slumped in a chair, was holding back tears.

Lynn left, but not before she asked the two to sign the office sympathy card the admin had tucked into a plain folder. Suzanne straightened when she noticed Ron regarding her. "Something wrong?" she asked.

"Nothing at all," he replied, still staring, "I was just wondering why, when you heard about David arranging his father's funeral, your mood changed."

She responded with a shake of her head.

"Are you all right?"

Suzanne swallowed hard, and found her voice. "With all the activities of the past few days, Ron, I haven't thought about the tragedy of what happened, but now...I guess it's catching up to me...David's father...Merilee...all the others. I never met Eric Anderson, but I feel terrible he's gone. I should've given David a condolence card...or done something...but I kept thinking it wasn't the right time. I feel really stupid!"

Ron planted his hand on Suzanne's shoulder. "You, like the rest of us, were waiting for David to acknowledge his father's passing. Talk to him now, or send a card."

"I wouldn't know what to write."

"Keep it hopeful and personal...something like, I fly across time, born as flesh, reborn as spirit, guiding those I love."

"That's perfect," Suzanne said, "Did you make that up?"

"Yes, and feel free to use it."

Suzanne was thanking Ron, when David returned to the office and sat down behind his desk. Eyeing the two, he asked, "What's going on?"

"We were just saying how sorry we feel about your dad, David," his producer replied, her voice still husky with tears. Clearing her throat, Suzanne changed the subject. "Sign in and take a look at the last 'saved' session."

Suzanne shot a grateful look at Ron and walked around the desk to stand behind David. Placing a gentle hand on the newsman's shoulder, she leaned across him, pointing out the items they found.

"What do you think?"

"Well, no question, that's the boy I met in Iran," David said, turning away from the screen to look up at Suzanne. Returning to the screen, he said, "Hmmm...Ahmad Hasan. Funny...over the years, I sometimes thought about him and wondered about his name... now, I know."

A hint of melancholy fell across the newsman's eyes and he sat there, transported back in time to a faraway place.

Ron interrupted his reverie. "Do you see the locations where our friend has been?"

"Yes," said the pensive newsman. "I can't help but conclude he was involved with the attacks. I could never have imagined when I was talking to that kid...he even promised me..."

"Promised what?" Ron asked.

"Look," Suzanne interrupted. She was pointing to a prompt, flashing in the lower right corner of David's screen. "Click on that and see what it is."

Ron joined them, standing behind his friend, as together they watched several images of passports appear. Each had a different name and issuing country, all had Ahmad's picture. Ron moved to the front of David's desk. He looked grim and serious. "David, we ought to inform the authorities. Right now!"

"Oh, no, we won't!" Suzanne shot back. "Global News is going to break this on tonight's broadcast. Right, David?"

"I have to agree with Suzanne, Ron. Investigative reporting is what we do. Listen, if we wanted the authorities to have this first, we could've stayed in Paris. Anyway, I don't think a few hours will make a difference...I'm pretty sure Mister Ahmad Hasan died in the explosion at the Hotel de Ville. I'd better get downstairs and start putting this together. Suzanne, why don't you see about the graphics and meet me there?"

"On it!" She responded, picking up the phone. "I'll fill John in, too." Suzanne loved it when David was in this mode.

David got up, went over to Ron, and sat down. Leaning into his friend he whispered, "Just between you and me?"

"Yes, of course."

"After I spoke to Rodgers, I phoned an old contact at the Agency, and told him why I pulled the alarm. I asked him to check out our friend and keep it quiet."

"Smart idea, bro," Ron was relieved.

"What are your plans, now?" David asked his friend, rising from his chair to leave.

"I have a flight out this afternoon. I'll grade final papers and finish up the semester. I expect to return in a few days. Have you picked a date for Eric's funeral?"

"It's not firm, yet, but I hope it will be next week. I'm just waiting for several family members to make arrangements and finalize their travel plans. I'll let you know. See you, Friday?"

"You bet!"

David gave his friend a hug before hurrying down the hall.

When Suzanne hung up the telephone, she looked towards David's empty chair. Getting up from where she was sitting, she went over to Ron and gave him a kiss on the cheek. "Thanks for the haiku...among other things."

This was one of the few times in his life Ron Eyota found himself completely surprised, and he stammered, "I...err...that is, I'm not sure I did anything."

"Have a safe trip, professor." Then, she too, disappeared into the maze of Global News.

Antoinette Soubirous perused Ahmad's medical records from the time the patient was admitted to the emergency room, right through the last twenty-four hours, including the notes left by the night-duty nurse and the on-call medical resident.

Crisp white sheets and a thin blue cotton blanket covered Ahmad all the way up to his armpits. Bandages laced with manuka honey from New Zealand, having special properties to protect wounds from morbid infection and sugars to promote rapid healing, covered the wounds on his arms, neck, face, thighs, and scalp. In spite of a severe, worldwide shortage of medicines, intravenous lines, exiting every visible vein, were hooked up to a pharmacy of medications, fluids, and blood products.

Ahmad's wounds were profoundly grave but Antoinette had seen too much to be unnerved by them. She surveyed the monitors above Ahmad's head, making sure that his heart was beating adequately to provide sufficient perfusion to his vital organs.

Humming softly, Antoinette began changing Ahmad's wound dressings. "Who might you be then, Mr. Hasanzeedee!" The nurse practically sang out the words.

"No," she grinned, amused by her own ineptitude pronouncing the foreign name, "that can't be right!"

Antoinette glanced up at the plaque, above Ahmad's head, that bore his name.

"I still cannot make heads or tails of it." She shook her head.

"Oh, heck! Let's just call you Monsieur Ahmad, shall we, my honey? I hope you will take no offense. I mean less disrespect by calling you by your Christian name...excuse me, your given name...than in the fracture of your surname. I'm sure I will hear, exactly, how you will want me to address you, soon enough...that is, if we can even understand each other."

As Antoinette continued to sing and talk to Ahmad, the subtle changes on the patient's face seemed to indicate he was conscious and aware of her presence.

"I can't help but wonder how, on earth, you managed to get into this mess," she said to the recumbent man. "The police inspector followed you here and has come calling for you on a regular basis. Get ready for some very pointed questioning when you awaken."

A patch of sunlight was moving slowly across Ahmad's face. The nurse pulled a heavy white linen curtain, hanging from a chrome track on the ceiling, to shade the patient.

"We cannot have you overheating, can we, my honey? Don't worry, you'll be awake and off this awful ventilator, in just a few hours. Then you can tell me what you need. I am sure you would approve of that!"

During the course of the day, sedation was fully withdrawn and Ahmad's mental status kept improving. By late afternoon, Ahmad opened his eyes. Sweat formed on his brow, as he struggled to orient himself to the strange surroundings. When asked by the nurse, he could squeeze her fingers and move his limbs.

Antoinette was removing Ahmad's wrist restraints when he began, with a raspy croak, to speak. "Where am I?"

"Aha, you are speaking French," was Antoinette's cheery reply. "We can understand one another."

"Where am I?" repeated Ahmad.

"My name is Antoinette…"

"Why will you not tell me where I am?" Ahmad persisted, trying hard to bellow but his voice was thin and hoarse, his face red with effort and annoyance.

Antoinette did not reply.

"Why can't the infernal Europeans ever answer a question?" Ahmad hissed.

"You are in hospital," she said, foregoing personal offence, recognizing her patient's fear and frustration. "You were very badly hurt…almost killed…in an explosion that occurred in the château up on the hill outside of town…of which, dare I say, the police believe you were the target."

Ahmad's eyes widened. Antoinette could see he was anxious for the whole story but she wasn't positive he was ready to hear it.

"I do not remember…" Ahmad's voiced trailed away.

"I think you have had enough stress for one day. Your color is not the best and you can barely speak."

"My throat feels like it is on fire," complained Ahmad.

"You had a large tube placed in your throat to help you breathe while in surgery. I will give you something for the pain, so you can sleep. We will finish our chat when you are stronger. If you awaken and feel any discomfort, ring this bell," she instructed, as she guided Ahmad's fingers to the buzzer hanging on the bedrail.

Ahmad, enervated and preoccupied with the pain in his throat, did not pursue all the questions swirling in his head. Instead, he surrendered to his fate; his eyes following the nurse, as she hung an intravenous medication bag onto a pole. The bag dripped into a tube, the end of which, covered with white gauze, appeared buried in the skin of his upper chest. Before she was finished adjusting the equipment that kept Ahmad's medications draining into his veins, he fell back asleep.

The staff, at Saint Joan's, were not the only ones interested in Ahmad's well being. Once David Anderson broadcast Ahmad's story on the Global News Network, embarrassed law enforcement from various nations, practically stood in line to interview him. Extradition requests poured in to the French Government from intelligence agencies hoping to interrogate and persuade Ahmad to identify his accomplices.

The inspector in charge, authorized by his superiors, agreed to offer the wounded man a bargain: a confession and relevant information, for their promise not to proceed with rendition to a country where he could face torture and the death penalty.

Interpol agents and the local police authorities checked on Ahmad's progress every day. Bissette assigned policemen to remain as close to Ahmad's room as the head nurse would permit. They would man their posts round-the-clock, not only ensuring Ahmad did not escape, but guarding him from the person or organization that, apparently, wanted him dead.

In spite of the turf wars among the intelligence community, they ardently agreed on one thing: Ahmad's case could be a potential breakthrough in the recent rash of terrorist attacks. If there was a story, they were determined to be present when Ahmad was well enough to tell it. His fragile health, they cared about not a whit, so long as he was able to provide the information they needed to kill or capture the masterminds of his organization.

The Boeing 737 looped past World Trade Center, Number One, on its descent towards LaGuardia's Runway Four. Ron was admiring how the sun's rays reflected from the Freedom Tower when he spotted his destination mixed into the skyline of New York. Pleased the school term had gone so well, with final papers graded, he was returning a day earlier than planned.

Just as David had forecast, the news about Ahmad spawned a flood of investigations from governments and news outlets worldwide. The Internet was abuzz with conspiracy theories that pointed to people, alive and dead, and organizations currently active or, long ago, consigned to history. He noticed, with interest, that one group was missing from the speculation. David wanted that name to be the subject of his next story, but first, they had to figure out exactly what that story was.

With this goal in mind, they nicknamed themselves the 'Paris Posse' and planned to meet in John Stavos' private conference room directly after the evening's news broadcast. It was small, accommodating only six to eight people. Here, the group wouldn't attract attention from the news staff, curious to know what David Anderson was planning now that the word on Ahmad was out.

"How was the trip, Ron?" David asked.

"Good to see you again, professor," Suzanne said, her bright smile acknowledging their new bond.

"Welcome," Mike Lussardi added, "recover from our last adventure yet?"

After a short but congenial conversation, David finally settled everyone down and logged into the GN archive. "So guys, any ideas how we advance this story?"

"Can someone fill me in on any new developments?" asked Ron.

"We received an official list of casualties from the French Government," Suzanne replied. "We've begun looking into their backgrounds, talking to colleagues, checking sources, reviewing past interviews, searching records…the usual stuff. So far…nothing of interest."

"On the plus side, we have our first pattern analysis, thanks to CARIS," David said, pointing to the display screen on the wall. "Near as I can tell, all the officials, killed or injured, were opposed to the IMF's new reserve currency…the supporters all seemed overcome by some mystery illness and left the conference…that, in itself, if interesting, doesn't make a compelling story…yet."

Ron looked puzzled. "CARIS?"

"Capture, aggregate, retrieve, index, sort," Suzanne explained. "It's the techie name for the information engine down in the tabernacle."

"I see," Ron said.

David went back to the keyboard, called up several pattern analysis templates, and the information about Ahmad uncovered by Suzanne and Ron. "Anything else?" he asked.

"Pop in 'the Alliance for Global Advancement'," Lussardi suggested.

"Good idea," Suzanne said. "Put Noiret's name in there too. After scaring the hell out of me, he deserves it!"

"I'd recommend including the Brotherhood and their symbol," Ron added.

"Alright...done...now let's see what we get," David said.

They waited while the tabernacle crunched the data, and a matrix of results appeared on the screen. David selected an entry concerning the organization named the Alliance for Global Advancement. The system showed a list of officials from countries the group claimed stood in the way of essential change. Several names matched the list of casualties provided by the French.

He clicked a related entry and found the group's current funding came via an anonymous trust fund whose only trustee was a man with vast international financial holdings, named Ambros von Lightchild. An associated entry indicated one of his many real estate companies owned a block of apartment buildings in a small suburb of Paris, named Clichy-sous-Bois; one of the apartments matched the address on the student visa issued to Ahmad Hasan.

Exploring further, David discovered the name of an ambitious young man, beginning his government service career, who had been promoted to director of the French Visa Services. He was the man who approved the issuance of Ahmad's student visa. His name was Andre Noiret.

David paused for a moment to look around the room. The import of what they had found, sinking in, produced a silence, so profound, it was deafening. Suzanne, despite years in the news business, was pacing the room as though she was looking for an escape route. Ron, unmoving, sat detached, as ever, like a scientist studying a specimen under a microscope, and Mike wore a cynical smile, shaking his head, as though to say, I should have known this all along.

Most alarming of all, was finding that more than half the results were labeled BLOCKED. David skipped down and randomly picked one of the entries. The screen displayed a message that read:

PROHIBITED
YOUR PRIVILEGES DO NOT ALLOW YOU TO VIEW THIS DATA
IF YOU BELIEVE THIS MESSAGE IS IN ERROR
CONTACT YOUR SYSTEMS ADMINISTRATOR

David tried several other restricted entries and, each time, the same message appeared on the screen. He looked perplexed. "Strange...never seen that message before."

"Here," Suzanne urged, handing him the phone, "call the sys admin."

"I doubt it will do any good."

"Why not?" she asked.

"Because they're obviously restricting any query that has anything to do with the Brotherhood," Ron said, stealing David's line. "I guess the joke's on me. There are inviolate secrets down there."

"How do we get the information then?" Suzanne asked.

"We don't," David assured her. "Only Lance Rodgers is authorized to see it and we can't, very well, get him involved...not yet...noooooo...this is going to take a bit of artful investigation."

"Wait a second," Suzanne insisted. "If we make Hasan the locus of the next story, show him arriving in Mexico and slipping across the border just before the San Francisco attack; arriving in Paris just before that incident, then tie in Noiret...maybe it's a cover up, maybe not. At the very least, shouldn't the French police have known there were two passports with the same picture...and, how about the apartment buildings, in Clichy-sous-Bois, owned by von Lightchild? Well?"

"Hmm...let me think a second," David said. "We can't imply any cover up because we don't have hard facts to support such an accusation. If we lose our credibility, the story is blown. We might put Noiret in the hot seat with his boss, but that's about it."

"What about the video of your argument with him?" Suzanne pressed.

"Or that lame performance at the press conference after the attack," Mike added.

"Meaningless," David assured them. "So what if Noiret's a useful idiot? It's not a crime. Neither is owning a building. This von Lightchild apparently owns lots of real estate and contributes to all sorts of organizations."

"And the list of officials?" Suzanne asked pleading for a story line they could pursue.

"Viewers might see it as a fluke and the lists don't tie directly to Hasan so there's no continuity to that narrative. We're going to need a little more evidence."

"So what should we do?"

"Keep investigating," David suggested. "Something will turn up...it always does."

"We have to find a way to get that information," Suzanne insisted. She spoke with that steely determination David liked but knew could spell trouble.

"Suzanne, please don't do anything until we have a chance to talk...promise?"

"Alright!" she said, exasperated with David's caution. "What about Brian Saunders? We haven't put him into the mix."

"Let's see what we get," David replied, adding him to the logic matrix.

CARIS returned more than one million occurrences for the stand-alone search but zero results when crossed with the Brotherhood or any of the other search parameters in the logic framework.

"It's too common a name," David said. "Even if he's in there, we can't chase down a million leads."

"Try adding 'police detective' as a qualifier," Suzanne recommended.

"No result, at all, here," David reported, within seconds. "I imagine, if the FBI couldn't trace him, then..."

"If we only had his picture," Suzanne said, speculating that an image would pinpoint Saunders in the search results. "Why don't we try..."

They were interrupted when John Stavos entered the room.

"Well gang, find anything?"

"Some interesting items popped up," David offered, "but I think they are too premature to air at this point, though I'm sure Suzanne would disagree." David grinned at his producer.

"David's afraid we're going to lose our news cred," Suzanne complained. "Let's show John the data and let him decide."

John stepped back and raised both hands. "Hold on! David's the executive editor. If he thinks the story isn't ready, then we wait. Anyway, we have some legal issues brewing you ought to know about."

Glancing up from following David's electronic meanderings, Suzanne asked "What kind of legal issues?"

"The kind requiring us to marshal the legal department," answered John.

That grabbed their attention and they all turned towards John at once.

"This morning we received a request from Justice for the FBI to interview David. They want to know, among other things, just how he discovered Hasan's identity. They're threatening to subpoena him if we don't comply. On top of that, the State Department has a request from the French to send representatives here for a conversation regarding the incident at the Hotel de Ville. I'm trying to convince legal not to cave. First Amendment Shield Laws…that sort of thing."

"I was expecting this," said the newsman. "Not that I have anything to hide. I simply recognized him…"

"It's the principle, David. I have to protect Global's sources and methods. Which brings us to your new assignment."

"Which would be?" prodded David.

"There's an evolving story in Turkey," John began. "Sounds damned interesting, if you ask me. Besides, it's an opportunity to sequester you away from the gathering pack of wolves."

"Turkey? What's going on there…another attack?"

"No, but come to think of it, an attack could certainly be reason for concern."

"Well, what about it, boss? Why am I going to Turkey?"

"Whoa, buddy! I'm gettin' there," laughed John. "You'll be going to a small town on the Aegean coast called Ephesus. You leave next week...after we return from your father's funeral. That gives you plenty of time to get everything organized with our local news operation."

"You're really trying to bury me, eh?"

"Not at all," replied John. "Actually, this could turn into a good story, although it is not getting a lot of media play at the moment, which doesn't surprise me. At any rate, it should get the authorities off your back until I sort this out. Doubt anyone will chase you to Ephesus."

"So, why the interest?" Suzanne asked.

"There's a group of religious leaders gathering there," John explained. "It seems the idea started to take shape over a decade ago through the interfaith movement, here in New York, as a reaction to the terrorist attacks at the World Trade Center."

"I know about their group," said Suzanne. "They collaborate on community development projects to promote unity and tolerance."

"That's right," John continued, "and the group has invited their counterparts from around the world to consult at Ephesus."

"So why is this news?" David asked.

"According to the press release," said John, "they're concerned that the world's governments have lost their moral authority and replaced it with an ever-increasing police presence. Some believe the heightened tensions between Christians, Muslims, Jews, and other religious groups during the past several years, have been intentionally inflamed to distract people from the real problems caused by economic stress and other social ills. The summit materials outline goals for reestablishing a moral base for civil society and a plan to ensure the different faith communities remain united. They've invited every relevant dignitary, both religious and secular, that you can imagine...it will be interesting to see who actually shows up! Since you covered that part of the world for years, David, I'm sending you back."

"I don't know, John," said David, his usual confident comportment yielding to reluctance. "Religion is not my strong suit. What if Suzanne comes along?"

Suzanne, excited by the prospect of a new adventure, jumped in. "Actually, I would love to go!"

"Sorry, folks. My executive producer has been out of pocket long enough. I really need her here. Besides, she may have to cover for me, should push come to shove, and I have to deal with the authorities. Oh, and Mike...I need you back at the White House. A few staff members are heading down, later this evening...if you hurry; you can fly out with them."

"Well, guys, it's been fun...duty calls...ciao." Mike, grabbed his belongings, slipped on his jacket and hurried off.

Suzanne and David looked at each other, sharing a sigh. They didn't protest. John was right; she was needed at Global's headquarters. Suzanne had already been allowed a very generous sabbatical and was not about to challenge her boss on this one.

"You'll do fine, David," she assured him, a smile grazing her mouth, "I think you have more feeling for the spiritual than you know."

Appreciating her ability to recognize his gifts, David smiled back at her.

"Ephesus sounds like an awfully long way to go for a powwow," David commented.

"I can't say why they chose Ephesus, David. I suggest you enlist our extensive research staff to help you find the answer before you leave."

"Perhaps, I can save him a bit of time," Ron chimed in. "I might know why they chose Ephesus."

"Go for it," David perked up. His natural curiosity was brimming over into the room, like a pot of coffee left too long to percolate.

"Well," Ron began, "to make a long story even longer, in the fourteenth century, a German mystic, named Anna Katharina Emmerick, had visions of the Virgin Mary traveling to a secluded spot, just outside of Ephesus, with the Apostle John...you know...the one Jesus loved. Some authorities maintain Mary, eventually, returned to Jerusalem, and passed on into the next world there, but local Turkish tradition says Mary lived the remainder of her life in the vicinity of Ephesus in a small stone cottage, built by John for her, surrounded by shelter trees."

"Have they ever found any evidence for the existence of such a place?" asked David.

"As a matter of fact," Ron continued, "a Lazarist priest convinced two friends to venture with him up into the mountains overlooking the ruins of Ephesus. In July of 1891, after an exhaustive search, they finally found the remains of a stone house alongside a spring. It was protected by tall trees with smooth bark, just as Anna described, and in better condition than a far more modern chapel in the area. Since no other grotto houses from that same period survived, it seemed, to the men, to be exactly as portrayed in the mystic's visions and they came to believe the vision was true. When they returned to town, their story spread and, eventually, the site became a place of pilgrimage for people of many faiths."

"That's odd," said Suzanne, "I attended Catholic elementary school and never heard that story. I wonder, why?"

"I'm surprised," Ron said to her. "In 1957, Pope Pius XII wrote to the archbishop of Smyrna, praising him for the zeal his congregation had shown toward the Virgin Mother and acknowledging the sacredness of the place. Meryem Ana Evi, he called her. He blessed the Shrine, and its surrounds, as a Centre of Marian culture where Christians and Muslims both venerate the Mother of Jesus."

Suzanne looked dubious. "Christians and Muslims worshiping together?"

"Exactly right," asserted Ron. "Little do most Western cultures realize, but the Virgin Mary is highly venerated by a variety of Islamic sects. She's mentioned in the Qur'an no less than thirty times and an entire chapter is dedicated to her. At the shrine, Christians and Muslims still pray in separate rooms but it is the only place on earth that is a shared place of worship for both. They even celebrate her anniversaries together."

"Well," David said, "I can see why they chose that venue."

"Precisely," answered Ron. "What better place to call for the world's religious leaders to shepherd their flock through the rising challenges of the emerging world culture? What better way to begin collaborating on solutions? What better place, than the Shrine of Mary at Ephesus?"

"Bravo, Ron," said John. "That was thoroughly engrossing and I liked the dramatic touch at the end. You just saved David's staff a heck of a lot of hunting and pecking."

"No problem, Mr. Stavos. It was my pleasure."

"Listen," said John, looking intently at the professor, "how would you feel about going on the ride with David. You'd be a great resource on this assignment. We'll sign you on as a Global News contributor, get you on the air, all expenses paid, and you'll be on company time. As a personal favor to me…what do you say?"

Ron's excitement stretched his smile into a wide grin, "Game on! I'd love to go along. If you think it will be worthwhile."

"It already is," said David with a wink.

"It's a deal, then," said Ron, shaking John's outstretched hand. "Oh man! I'll have to fly home and pack."

John was obviously pleased. "First, Ron. I need to introduce you to Bronwyn, down in Human Resources, and get your paperwork done. Carry on, guys."

They left the veteran anchor and his executive producer behind to plan out the production schedule that would take David and Ron to the ancient city of Ephesus and far, far away from New York, from Global News, from the Paris Posse, and from pursuing the hidden information about the Brotherhood.

WILFUL BLINDNESS

The sun was streaming through the windows on the morning following Ahmad's first meeting with Antoinette. Fully conscious for the first time since the explosion, the wounded man noticed his throat did not hurt as much as it did the day before. It left him with the realization that the rest of his body hurt like hell.

Ahmad groped for the control console wrapped around the bedrail. He pressed the buzzer with his thumb. Presently, he heard a female voice wafting from an intercom somewhere above his head. "Yes, monsieur, how may I help you?"

"I need the nurse," was Ahmad's curt reply.

"She is in morning report, monsieur. She will be in just as soon as she is finished." Ahmad heard a click and the voice was gone.

"Brainless French woman," he mumbled in annoyance.

Moments later, Antoinette, pushing open the glass door, greeted Ahmad, "My, my, you look considerably better this morning. How are you feeling?"

"I need more medicine for pain," Ahmad grumbled, "and I want to know what happened...why I'm here."

"Yes, well, it is no wonder you are in pain," said Antoinette.

"Pain, yes," Ahmad repeated, "I want to know how I got here and when I am leaving."

The nurse picked up Ahmad's bedside chart and began perusing the vital signs, recorded during the night, before repeating the doctor's evaluation.

"Well, my honey, you suffered some burns and terrible wounds when a bomb exploded in your suite at the château. The police describe it as a deliberate attempt to kill you. When the medics arrived on the scene, you were in severe shock from a great loss of blood. Your heart stopped a number of times, and you had to be resuscitated. The medical team stabilized you as best they could and then brought you to Saint Joan's hospital...it's not far from the château. This is where you are now. Luckily, this hospital has a trauma unit and a topnotch trauma team. You needed surgery...and even more blood. We barely managed to save your life."

Antoinette paused, searching the chart to see if there was anything she left out, "Oh, yes...you lost your right kidney...you should do fine with only one...if the remaining one heals. We are not sure...we are hoping."

"They should not have interfered," moaned Ahmad.

"Interfered with what, monsieur?" queried Antoinette, creases of concern knitting her brow.

"Saving my life!"

"Well, that point is moot," said Antoinette with a sigh. "The medical team is not the only ones determined to save you. Government officials and police are just outside the unit, waiting. It seems, somehow, the press got hold of information that you may be linked to terrorist activity. It also seems that they know you were working under an assumed name. You are fortunate that the police have decided not to let the press know of your whereabouts, for the time being, or even that you where not killed with the others in Paris."

Antoinette reached over and placed her hand on the collar of Ahmad's hospital gown. Ahmad reacted instantly, pushing it away. "What do you think you are doing?"

"I am your nurse, monsieur. I wish to check the sites, just here, under your collarbone, where your intravenous lines are located. I want to ensure they remain properly connected and covered, with no signs of infection. Will you please allow me to do this for you?"

Ahmad did not answer but allowed the caretaker to proceed. As Antoinette quietly went to work, redressing the bandage covering Ahmad's central line, she began to note that her patient was looking more and more agitated. Finally, she said, "Monsieur, is there something you need...something you wish to know?"

"I am a legal resident of France," the annoyed patient yelled. "They have no right to harass me."

"Yes, well, at the moment the authorities intend to protect you from the hordes of press anxious to uncover the facts of this story and, lest we forget, the angry mobs of Frenchmen, quite sick of losing life and property at the hands of foreigners. But I doubt the authorities will protect you for long. They are here, every day, waiting for you to awaken to talk to you about what happened at that château. They want to know who you really are and what you are doing in France."

"When will that be?" Ahmad asked, sounding anxious and exhausted. He let his head sink into the pillow.

"Soon...very soon, I suspect," replied Antoinette. "I think you have had enough talk for today. You look tired and should rest."

"I must leave here," insisted the injured man.

"You aren't going anywhere," said Antoinette. "You need to heal. You wouldn't make it halfway across the room, I daresay. Leaving, before your body has a chance to recover from the horrible wounds you have suffered, is unthinkable."

Antoinette grabbed Ahmad's bedside chart and began to write down the data on the monitors.

"I will not rest until I have completed my mission," Ahmad said.

"Completed?" asked Antoinette, surprised, not expecting him to be so candid. "Complete what? Blowing yourself up? Were you making explosives in the château to blow up another building...the rest of the city...more world leaders...the rest of France, perhaps? The police say they have evidence that you had something to do with the attack at the conference in Paris. Interpol and the American FBI will be with them."

"Did they all die?"

"All of your friends? Yes."

"God forgive me," Ahmad whispered.

"Forgiveness for what," asked Antoinette, "that your friends died or that everyone else did not?"

"This does not concern you, Madame," Ahmad insisted. "Western Civilization will soon come under the banner of the Prophet, His Holiness, Muhammad, peace be upon Him."

"You are talking about hirabah...yes?" asked Antoinette.

"This is jihad," retorted the patient. "We are waging Holy War...our mission is no sin!"

"Wars are never 'holy,' Monsieur Ahmed," replied Antoinette. "When Muhammad spoke to the people of The Book, he told them, 'Our God and your God is one and to Him are we self-surrendered.'"

"Christians and Jews, your so-called 'people of the book,' do not accept the Prophet of Islam. This cannot be tolerated," Ahmad said.

"Then you would take God's place as judge?"

"The West has imposed its secular culture on every other land that it has invaded and you do not complain. But no matter, once everyone is under the banner of Islam, all men will be my brothers."

"How could a loving, all-merciful God want His children to fight and die over religion?"

"This is blasphemy!" Ahmad shouted.

Ahmad only stared past Antoinette and out the window. He looked as though he was a million miles away, or perhaps, just transported to another place from his past, a simpler time, where everything was set in stone; there was no dispute, only one belief and complete submission.

"You know," the nurse, continued, "did it ever occur to you that we are all God's favored?"

"I do not think it is possible, Madame Antoinette. I have lived among you. Your only interest is in winning and accumulating wealth and power. You are too different from us. How can one have any meaningful dialogue with people who need several drinks before they can even say 'hello'? It disgusts me."

His nurse hung the chart back on the hook at the foot of his bed and readjusted the bedding, pulling out the ragged corners of the linens, gently smoothing out the folds and wrinkles, expertly tucking in the edges, while Ahmad watched her without uttering a word in protest.

Preparing to depart, she said, "Yes, well…you are certainly stronger and more alert than anyone could hope for…still, I have taxed you, greatly, I'm afraid. Good day, monsieur. Rest well, my honey."

Antoinette crossed the room and, Ahmad's scowl not lost on her; she left for the day.

It's an extraordinary feeling, trying to understand the likes of a terrorist. Antoinette saw the path Ahmad's life had taken; a path inevitably leading to this place; a place where only holy war and a martyr's death were viable and honorable life choices. Ahmad's choices had been hijacked by men without courage; who stole his youth and destiny, setting him, and all his victims, on a path to destruction.

In her eyes, theirs was not a forgivable offence, but she was keenly aware only God would decide their fates in the worlds beyond.

Ahmad, blessed like all people with free will and a soul, was not without guilt. Antoinette hoped that somewhere in his deepest recesses, this man still had a remnant of the universal voice that whispers to all of us when our actions are wrong. This she counted on as she began her day caring for Ahmad; not so concerned with the body as the spirit.

"Bonjour, my honey!" she said, sweeping into his room, her robust energy overpowering her patient's protests at the easy familiarity with which the woman seemed quite comfortable. She was holding a sparkling clean white terry washcloth, soap, and had a huge bath towel slung over her shoulder. The nurse began filling a basin and humming a French country song, elevating her spirit, hoping it would do the same for her patient.

"What is all this?" asked Ahmad, his voice rising.

"It is about time you had a bath, monsieur. Come, I have a busy schedule today." She snapped closed the curtain with a resolute tug.

"Bath? You will not touch me. You are an infidel and a woman. You will stop what you are doing and leave me alone...now!"

"Monsieur Ahmad," she said, with one perfectly raised eyebrow. "I understand how you feel. I am truly sorry that I cannot accommodate your request but there are no male nurses on this ward trained to care for patients with the extent of your injuries. The point is moot, at any rate, since I have been caring for you since you arrived, changing your bedclothes, your linens, and, if you will pardon me, monsieur, checking your urinary catheter. Besides...we are all infidels here."

Antoinette set her mouth, the fierceness that shot out of her steely eyes a testament to her resolve. "So, Monsieur Ahmad, you may allow me to bathe you and redress your wounds or you will have to take your chances and do it yourself. You will then be responsible for whatever infections you acquire and, probably, your own death. Is this what you want?"

Exhausted, in pain, every limb on fire, Ahmad hesitated, but knew the nurse was right. He ceded to her argument with a deep sigh and let his eyes close, blocking out the indignity; telling himself he could accept any humiliation for the sake of the sacred mission with which he had been entrusted. He silently swore to fight this battle to the very last, and that none, save the Hand of God, would end his life. He prayed to be sent to his reward as a martyr.

He lay there, silent and pensive, while Antoinette quietly finished her work, caring for him with all the tenderness and respect that she could give. With the last dressing applied, Antoinette opened the curtains surrounding his bed and, adjusting the linens, she went off for morning rounds.

After the noontime meal, Antoinette returned with another woman at her side. "Monsieur, this is Mademoiselle Michelle Yusef. Her parents fled to France during the Iranian Revolution. You should have much in common with her."

"Bonjour, Monsieur Hasanzadeh. Please call me Michelle," said the pretty young woman. "I am your physical therapist. I am here to help your body heal."

"I am too tired today," Ahmad complained squeezing shut his eyes. "Come back tomorrow."

"No, monsieur," Antoinette replied, her voice firm, "You are making remarkable progress and these exercises, which are very gentle, will ensure you heal even more quickly."

"What's going to happen to me?" asked Ahmad, positive that he would not dissuade Antoinette.

"Michelle is going to help you walk again," said Antoinette.

"I only need a little of your time," said Michelle.

"I do not need anyone to help me walk," balked Ahmad, waving her away with his hand. "I am not getting out of bed!"

"Suit yourself, monsieur," said Antoinette, pretending to give up. "The doctor cannot allow you to leave intensive care until you walk on your own without assistance. Michelle, I am afraid…"

"Yes, okay, fine," snapped Ahmad, annoyed that Antoinette had won again but not ready to fully concede. "I will give you five minutes."

"Give me ten minutes today," Michelle bargained. "We can do some stretching, and maybe, bring you to the side of the bed to sit upright without support. The exercises, I teach you, will strengthen your back and abdominal muscles. Your muscles have been atrophying during the time you have been immobile."

"Excellent!" beamed Antoinette. "I'll just leave you to it then."

"Shall we get started?" asked Michelle.

Ahmad nodded an anxious consent.

"I see you have an Iranian name," said Michelle, as she pressed the button that raised the back of Ahmad's bed. "I'll adjust your position as much as possible. You have been hurt badly, so expect to feel some pain."

"Ow! You are hurting me, woman," he growled, now sitting, legs dangling over the bed's edge.

"My parents are from Iran, too," said Michelle, bending one of Ahmad's legs, ignoring his protests and the grimace on his face. "My parents had to leave Iran when the Shah was overthrown. The people who arranged the escape wanted a great deal of money. My parents did not have it, but their friends paid the men, knowing there was no alternative. Once they made it over the mountains into Turkey, it took over a year to get a French Visa."

"If they had to escape, they must have been part of the Shah's criminal regime," retorted Ahmad through gritted teeth. He recalled the tales his male relatives recounted about the 1979 Revolution when the despised Pahlavi regime was overthrown.

That event marked the end of the twenty-five-hundred-year old reign by the Shahs – the Iranian monarchs. The last remnants of the glorious Persian Empire, founded by Cyrus the Great, had been relegated forever to the history books, as the revolutionary forces swiftly transformed the newly installed government into the first Islamic Republic in the Middle East. The return from exile of the Ayatollah Khomeini brought a joyous celebration that swept, like wildfire, over the country and, along with it, an era of power by the holy Imams. Khomeini's return was a triumph for the conservative element of Ahmad's countrymen, who believed that the Shah had become a puppet of the United States, committed to imposing secularization on their society. What Ahmad would not acknowledge was that many of Khomeini's staunchest supporters enforced his regime by brutality and oppression.

"Actually," said Michelle, completing her story. "My parents were members of a religion condemned by the Ayatollah Khomeini. If they had stayed in Iran they might have been imprisoned or even condemned to die."

"This is a lie!" roared Ahmad. "Get out! Get out, you filthy liar!"

Michelle backed away from the shouting man. A moment later, Antoinette rushed into the room.

"What on earth is going on in here? I could hear you down the hall," said the nurse.

"I was telling Monsieur Hasanzadeh the story of my parents," said the contrite physiotherapist. Turning back to Ahmad, she said, "We have a common bond and I thought it would distract you from the discomfort of the therapy. I am truly sorry. I did not mean to upset you, monsieur."

"Let's get his legs back onto the bed," suggested Antoinette, glaring at the patient. "He is probably in pain. Perhaps that explains this outburst."

Michelle offered her apologies once again, adding, "I will come back tomorrow, if you like. Perhaps you will be ready to stand." Then she bade them, goodbye. Ahmad did not say a word but only glowered at the physical therapist as she went.

Antoinette strode over to his bedside.

"Monsieur Ahmad, that young woman was trying to help you. I am certain you will be more cooperative tomorrow."

"She was making a false attack against the holy rulers of my country."

"Attack?"

"She claimed her parents were threatened by the mullahs. It is a lie!" Still gritting his teeth, Ahmad wriggled himself further into the folds of the bed coverings. "They could have pledged their allegiance to Islam and lived in peace."

"I was taught the path to heaven is between the individual and God alone," observed Antoinette. "Not even the angels know."

"How can you pretend to know the thoughts of angels? You talk too much for a woman."

"You are very angry, my honey, no?" she asked.

Ahmad's head jerked back in surprise. He feared and resented the feelings he had whenever the nurse was in his presence. Eyes narrowing, he snapped, "You should not call me honey. I do not know you!"

Antoinette stood silent as she heard his voice rising. The rage that had been seething in Ahmad all his life, finally burst forth like a locomotive from a long, dark tunnel. Ahmad's face flushed with anger.

"Even now our lands are infiltrated from the West. They try to change the way we live, the way we think, the way we dress, even the way we worship! This change will not happen. I swear this by my life!"

"Monsieur Ahmad," pleaded Antoinette. "Listen to your own holy book when it tells you that 'in order to enter heaven, your faith must be completed and, in order to complete your faith, you must love completely.'"

"You are not of my faith," replied Ahmed. "You cannot pretend to know what the holy Qur'an tells me. There is only one true faith"

"You are certainly right, Ahmad," agreed Antoinette. "There is only one...ours!"

"Islam is not just a religion," Ahmad insisted. "It is a theocratic government and sovereign nation. Our religious leaders and scholars are there to interpret the law and to administer justice. Our holiest Imams are divinely guided."

"Your own people kill each other, instigated by clergymen who claim to be divinely guided. How could this possibly represent divine guidance?"

"You are talking rubbish," said Ahmad. "You are against me."

"No, Ahmad," was Antoinette's reply, "I am just for everyone else as well."

"You talk too much for a woman," said Ahmad, wrinkling his nose at the nurse, "You tire me."

"Well, Ahmad, you are making progress," Antoinette said with a gentle smile. "I pray that what we have shared will not be without gain. I know that you speak from, what you believe to be, the truth."

Ahmad's rage flared again. "Why do you come here, madame? Why are you trying to take my faith from me? I will go to hell for listening to you!"

Silently, Antoinette continued to work, waiting for the relentless wheels of Ahmad's outrage to finish their grinding. In a while, Ahmad took a deep breath, trying to shed the tension cramping his muscles but it only added to his pain.

Finally, in a voice as soft as the patter of steady rain, she said, "Oui, monsieur, perhaps you are right. I must stop talking. For who can ever change? We all seem to be relentlessly who we are. Maybe we don't change because fear overwhelms us. I'll leave you to rest now."

She slid closed the glass door but stood outside and continued watching him, while at the same time fighting back the doubts welling up inside.

Inspector Bissette leaned in over the laminated countertop at the nurse's station waiting for one of the staff to turn around, not realizing they knew full well he was there, and why. Growing impatient, the inspector wrapped lightly on the countertop, holding open his wallet to display the identification inside.

"Hello, I am Inspector Bissette. I am assigned to guard Monsieur Ahmad Hasanzadeh, or whatever is his real name. I need a minute with him today."

"Pardon, Inspector," replied Marion Marchant, the unit's supervising nurse, "generally, no one, except immediate family, is allowed on the unit without express permission from the hospital administrator. Would you kindly have a seat in the waiting room and, as soon as I reach her, I will come and speak with you."

"If I must, madame," said Bissette, "I will wait as long as needed."

The inspector sat in the waiting area of the Surgical Intensive Care Unit for a little more than three hours and, by then, he had read every magazine on hand. He had pleasant conversations with a variety of people waiting to see relatives or receive some word on their condition. They had all come and gone.

During his wait, Bissette contacted the precinct office several times to check the progress of other open cases. Louis called him on his cell phone, twice in the last hour, to report his latest findings and ask for marching orders. His business completed, he continued to wait.

After waiting another hour, Bissette was becoming quite irritated. He began glancing at his watch every five minutes. This can't be happening, he thought, fuming. The infernal nurse had more than enough time to contact the damn hospital administrator. Finally, reaching the outer limit of his patience, Bissette got up and pushed past the doors that led into intensive care. He proceeded to the nurses' station with the demeanor of an erupting volcano, this time rapping loudly on the countertop.

"Pardon, I have been waiting a very long time to see the patient in bed four and the nurse…"

The inspector did not have a chance to finish his sentence when the clerk replied, "I am so sorry, Inspector, but I am afraid you will not be seeing that patient any time soon. Another of our patients has taken a turn for the worse and is in very grave condition. The staff has been busy working on this man and must have forgotten you were waiting. Unfortunately, the hospital administrator would have gone home at least an hour ago now. Please accept our apologies but I am afraid you will not be able to see Mr. Hasanzadeh until you can speak to her. I suggest you check back tomorrow."

"What does that mean?" Bissette demanded.

"I am sorry Inspector, but you know the law. I am not permitted to discuss the patient's status with anyone except immediate family."

Angry and frustrated, Bissette stepped back, his eyes incandescent. "I will return tomorrow, madame...with a warrant. I will not stand by and allow this man to die before I have had a chance to interview him. Sparing him from the stress of a police interrogation is not as important as sparing the lives of countless others who might still be saved with the information this man may provide. If you compel me to use force...I will use force!"

"Yes, I understand," the clerk responded meekly. "I will let them know at once."

The next morning Antoinette returned to Ahmad's bedside. Her patient was resting and the nurse occupied her time reviewing his medical charts. Always, in the back of her mind, there were misgivings and reservations over her ability to reach this man. Keenly aware she still had much to accomplish before her time with Ahmad was over, she could only pray for guidance.

When Ahmad opened his eyes, he did not move and would not speak. The nurse sat beside him, telling stories of many lives and the part she had played in them.

She talked to him about long, luxurious treks up into the green, rolling hills overlooking a village she so loved. She told him tales of afternoons spent among garden roses, teacups, and visiting friends. She shared childhood recollections of siblings playing in the olive grove where the gnarled old trees possessed a magic of their own. The gentle breezes, blowing in from the English Channel, turned over their leaves, creating a mysterious and enchanting silvery luminescence. She told him of many lives, their sorrows and joys, crises and victories, and how, although she helped them, sometimes she yearned to be a part of them.

"There is magic and mystery everywhere, Monsieur Ahmad," she whispered. "The things we cannot see are sometimes beyond the imagination, but they are ours if we wish."

The smallest of smiles began to creep over Ahmad's mouth as he listened with greater and greater attention. The spell was broken when a grey haired man entered the room with a group of students.

Ahmad looked past Antoinette, a cloud of apprehension sweeping over his face and pooling in his large almond-shaped eyes like the long shadows that gather at dusk. He did not answer the nurse but, instead, stared intensely at the physician approaching his bed. The doctor was wearing a white lab coat and a grim expression.

"Good morning, I am Dr. Landau. We are very happy to see that you are better today, monsieur...you have been through a rough time. We were not sure that you would survive it."

The physician then proceeded to ask Ahmad a series of short questions: whether he knew where he was, who he was, and what day it was; all were meant to test if Ahmad's mentation was satisfactory. The patient just glowered at the doctor.

"Monsieur Ahmad," said Antoinette. "Can you understand? Please answer the good doctor, if you are able."

"I hear you," Ahmad finally replied. "Are you going to turn me over to the police now?"

"It's nothing like that," insisted Antoinette. "Dr. Landau would like to review your progress."

"Do you feel well enough for me to review your case, monsieur?" asked the doctor.

"I am well enough, yes," replied Ahmad, suppressing a groan born of apprehension.

With the calm, professional demeanor of a seasoned physician, Dr. Landau explained, "Well, monsieur, I am sorry I must bring you this news but we must perform a procedure today to debride your burn wounds. It might hurt a bit."

"You cannot touch me. I will not allow it!" Ahmad began to rise from the bed and pull at the wires and tubes connected to him.

Antoinette took a firm hold of her patient's shoulders, imploring him to stop thrashing about. "Please calm down, Monsieur Hasanzadeh, you will pull out your lines. We will pray together. God will hear our prayers, monsieur. He hears all sincere prayers."

Ahmad fell back upon his pillows and snapped shut his eyes. Together, they prayed as the medical team began to unwrap the bandages covering Ahmad's burns. As the physician began to lift the bandages, Ahmad began to scream; great wails slicing through the usual peacefulness of the unit. Antoinette scooped up Ahmad's hand and squeezed it tightly in her own.

Ahmad's face turned the same color that remains at the bottom of a fireplace the morning following a roaring fire. Twisted in pain, he began to cry out as Dr. Landau slowly removed a piece of dead skin from Ahmad's right thigh. The physician described, over the patient's vociferous protestations, the procedure to the medical residents. The surgeon had performed the procedure many times, and the patient's screams did not seem to affect, in the slightest, the enthusiasm with which he instructed his students.

"The dead skin is removed," the surgeon explained, "so that the new, healthy tissue underneath can grow unfettered and free of infection. See the beautiful, pink tissue forming beneath the eschar?"

Ahmad caught a glimpse of Antoinette, his eyes pleading, make them stop!

"Hold on, Monsieur Ahmad, my honey," Antoinette said, squeezing his hand tighter. "They are just about finished. I know how painful this must be, but the procedure will help prevent infection and you will heal more quickly."

"I need more medication," he begged.

"You are exceeding the recommended dosage already. If we give you any more, it will depress your ability to breathe. You could end up back on the vent." Bending over him, Antoinette whispered in his ear. "You don't want to miss anything, do you?"

Ahmad quieted. He did not want to be re-intubated, just the thought of it made him feel as though he was trapped by his captors in a cruel experiment.

With the procedure completed, the medical team redressed the wound and went on to the next patient. Ahmad's thigh was still throbbing but the searing pain was gone.

"When will my leg be healed?" he asked, seeming to read Antoinette's thoughts.

"Soon, I should think. You are young and healing very quickly. God has given you quite an efficient metabolism and He has answered your prayers."

Ahmad made a subtle gesture acknowledging her kindness.

"Don't thank me," she smiled. "Thank the One who gave you this grace."

"In Iran, we have a saying, 'Trust in God, but tether your camel.' You are my tether. I thank Allah for sending you to me."

Antoinette looked at him in a way that was both surprised and tender. She nodded and said, "Well, my honey, all this excitement has made me late for rounds."

She turned off the bright light hanging over Ahmad's bed and, fully intending to see him the next morning, bid him a good day.

For patients in intensive care, it is impossible to measure time. There are no timepieces or calendars, no sunsets or moon phases, no tides, or seasons, or stars. In fact, there aren't any of the devices people use to synchronize themselves with nature's clockworks. Much like a womb, artificial umbilical cords sustain and monitor their lives. Movement is restricted. The only sounds, providing some connection to reality, are the rhythmic bleeping of the monitors.

Ahmad, confined to intensive care for some unknown number of days, was not able to answer even the simplest question of 'how long'. The curtains were drawn so he could not tell night from day and the twenty-four hour darkness nearly drove him into what is known as 'ICU psychosis'. The medical staff would come by at random intervals to prod and poke. They maintained an air of strict professionalism, aloof from the humanity of their patient, going about the business of medicine without much in the way of casual conversation or expressions of concern. Ahmad longed for Antoinette to return.

Under these conditions, it took great effort for Ahmad to maintain his sanity and the perpetual scowl that had become his trademark remained a firm feature on the landscape of his face.

One morning, on early morning rounds, the surgeon told him the abdominal stitches would be removed, his intravenous medications and nutrition could be discontinued and the lines in his chest detached. It took great effort for him to suppress his relief and joy when the medical resident announced that he was to be transferred to a normal room in the trauma ward and the hospital dietitian would visit him to help progress his diet from liquid to solid food.

Ahmad could no longer hide his delight when a case manager mentioned that for the remainder of his stay in hospital, he would occupy a bright and sunny room, facing southeast. His physician told Ahmad that he had gained a notoriety all his own and, at the insistence of the authorities, he would be placed in a private accommodation, usually reserved for patients who were rich or famous.

All in all, Ahmad was very pleased and thanked Allah for his remarkable healing; never expecting to feel as well as he did at that very moment, ever again.

Later that morning, two nurses and a medical resident wheeled Ahmad into his new room. It had been cleaned, just before he arrived, by a very thorough and diligent janitorial staff, and the faint smell of antiseptic cleaning agents still hung in the air.

By early afternoon, Antoinette returned with Ahmad's lunch, keeping her promise of visiting him.

"Well, if it isn't my favorite patient," said Antoinette, as she walked into Ahmad's room and set down the tray. "How have you been, my honey?"

"I am surprised to see you," answered Ahmad. He tried to hide how glad he was that this extraordinary woman, unlike any woman he had ever encountered before, had kept her word.

Antoinette smiled, "I have great news for you this morning."

"How can that possibly be, madame," interrupted Ahmad, in his usual dour manner. "We are in France, after all."

"You cannot bait me…I am too happy. Your physical therapists are very proud and the physicians are astounded by your progress!

You may be leaving the hospital sooner than any of us could have imagined!"

Ahmad, his gaze far away, did not reply. Instead, he fell back against his pillows, staring out the window. Antoinette could detect a quiet unease in his manner.

"What is it, monsieur?" she asked, "You seem apprehensive, almost alarmed."

Ahmad, looking past the bucolic French countryside that lay beyond, said, "Who will protect me from the police once I leave here? They will come for me soon...I must leave...I cannot let them question me."

"Listen," Antoinette reassured him. "You have not been discharged and, until you are, the police will have to wait!"

She crossed the room and stood in front of a set of French doors that opened onto a small veranda. Pushing aside the curtains, the nurse swung open both doors. Ahmad groaned at the perfusion of bright light that flooded the room. His eyes hurt after so long in the dark of intensive care. Antoinette fixed her gaze on him for a moment, "You are a silly man! Don't you agree you need fresh air and sunshine to help speed your recovery? Time to enjoy the outdoors, wouldn't you agree?"

"No, I would not agree," Ahmad growled, "I think, I need to be left alone by European infidel women who believe they know what's best for me."

Ahmad, still grumbling under his breath, swung his feet off the bed, slipping them into the flimsy disposable hospital slippers lying on the red tiled floor, all the while, expecting the nurse's next admonition. She helped Ahmad to the terrace where he would be able to partake of the sweet, fresh breeze and warm sunshine for the first time since the day of the explosion.

"Will you take your lunch on the balcony, monsieur?" Antoinette said with a light heart. "There is a lovely salade d' epinards, followed by poulet au porto on the menu."

"Can't a man get a decent shirazi and kebab morgh around here?" Ahmad said with a scowl.

Antoinette laughed.

Her patient, encouraged by the nurse's good humor, began a new rant. "What kind of civilization do you call this? This is why your culture must eventually yield to the religion of the Prophet, may my life be a sacrifice for his loved ones. If you do not do this, your world will be consumed in the fire of Satan and you will be forced to eat this horrible food forever in hell."

"I am not sure what you mean," Antoinette chuckled. "We need to change our culture to yours because you don't like French cuisine? That seems a little extreme, don't you think?"

The glint in Ahmad's eyes vanished; his face grew grim and serious.

"The West has rejected God and His Holy Laws," Ahmad said with fervent passion, repeating the doctrine he learned as a child. "They embrace a decadence which is most unseemly and unclean. Many in your, so called, civilization have denounced the living God and, those who have not, allow the unbelievers to rule over them and their children. We cannot allow this filth to infiltrate our culture and steal our youth from us."

"That is quite a condemnation, monsieur. I have tried to tell you, not everyone in the west is like this. There are sincere, hard-working, and devout souls who also cherish the value of God's words."

"Devout?" Ahmad shot back, the contempt in his voice unmistakable. "There are more practicing Muslims in France than practicing Christians and we are a small percentage of your population! Your government forbids us from praying in public because they claim France is a secular nation...but we are a social religion, our prayers and beliefs embedded in our everyday lives...so we defy you...and soon the nation of Islam will rise up and prevail over your country and all of Europe."

"Prevail? Why not try just living with the 'infidels' in peace?" asked Antoinette.

Ahmad, shaking his head in disdain, replied, "People of 'The Book'...I scorn you. Your pride is no more in your righteous and heavenly acts, as it was in the days of the Christian martyrs, but in your relentless pursuit of material luxuries and animal appetites! A lazy and complacent culture you've become, demanding to be entertained and cradled in the womb of a corrupt government.

Your children are repulsed by words of the spirit, rebellious against their parents, glorifying idols of their own imaginings. Their only talk of God is the sound of their swearing and contempt in denying His existence! When are they encouraged to speak of Him with reverence and praise or perform good works in His name?"

Ahmad stopped and looked at Antoinette. His eyes were fierce and hot. Antoinette returned his look and nodded, but she did not reply. After a long silence, Ahmad continued. "You have had two thousand years to follow in Christ's footsteps and you have failed. The change will come shortly, madame, and sooner than you think." The intensity in his voice remained unchanged; the fire in his eyes undiminished. "Why leave any remnant of so evil and hideous a culture? It must be swept aside along with anyone who defends it."

Antoinette spoke plainly. "Is what you propose justice…to kill those who are different than you? Can you justify killing innocents and still hold onto the belief that you are righteous?"

"Don't speak of justice to me when your soldiers invade our lands!" Ahmad demanded. "We will fight for our lands with stones and clubs, if need be. Our holy warriors will outlast your armies and bankrupt your nations. This mission is a sacred trust. We will not fail because Allah protects and guides us. All the peoples of the earth will submit or fall under His sword."

"If you are telling me you fight for land, power, control…then say it, outright," Antoinette insisted. Her eyes were now like his, aflame. "Yes, this is your free choice, but do not hide behind the Almighty and use His holy name as an excuse to kill."

This time, Antoinette's outburst did not shock Ahmad. He thought about her strength, her resolve, her insight, the kindness and tender mercy she showed him. He thought about her smile, as though she knew just what he was thinking; it made Ahmad turn his eyes away from the woman who had nurtured him back to health.

When Ahmad finally spoke, his voice almost soft and his face drained of color, it was with a contriteness Antoinette had not heard before and did not expect. "We only mean to defend that which is ours and given to us by Allah…to live by the words in the Qur'an and the teachings of the Prophet, peace be upon Him. For this, you fear and hate us…so how can the search for peace and justice be anything but fruitless…there is no answer."

"Yes," the nurse admitted, "but it's not too late. There is still time to discover our true selves."

Then, much to Ahmad's astonishment, the nurse gently took his hand, the spark of compassion shining brightly in her eyes.

"You have spoken to me from your heart and I, in turn, have revealed my heart to you. Maybe, someday, people will be united through understanding, respect, and steady, unwavering love. Then you will have your justice and the world will have its peace."

Ahmad looked dumbfounded, for indeed, she knew his heart, and he had willingly shown it to her. He rubbed his temples, trying to think. Antoinette retreated to the foot of the bed where they stood watching each other, sharing the silence of their thoughts.

Glancing at the sturdy watch on her wrist, its flexible silver band gleaming in a shaft of sunlight, Antoinette smiled while stepping backward towards the exit.

"It is time for you to eat and for me to continue on…my work here is nearly complete."

"What work? Continue where?" Ahmad demanded, trying to stop her, his frantic wave insisting that the nurse should stay.

"The work of healing…and not just your body," she said, pulling the door closed before he had a chance to protest; his words dying on the doorstep of his open mouth.

Suzanne, eyes fixed on the floor indicator, nervous energy rocking her from foot to foot, waited as the executive elevator shot to the top of Global's headquarters on its way past the news rooms, studios and staff offices. Her heart was racing, the thumb-thump of its pumping pounding in her ears. So far, so good, she concluded.

Avoiding being discovered by the pesky night cleaning crews roaming the floors was smart, she thought. Yep, early morning was a lot better; no one would arrive for, at least, two hours and Rodgers, along with most of the executives on this floor, were on their way to New Town to attend the funeral for David's father.

It was a dangerous gambit sneaking into Rodgers' office, sitting behind the CEO's desk, turning on his computer, trying to guess the password, but how else in the world would she ever get a glimpse at the Brotherhood's restricted information and know, for sure, what was hidden deep inside the tabernacle?

She stepped from the elevator holding her breath, knowing well the consequences of her actions. If she was caught, and lucky enough to escape prosecution, at the very least she would face dismissal, ejection from the building, shame, the end of her career in journalism, and the loss of friends and colleagues. More than anything else, she worried about what David would think of her. Still, she brushed all this aside, continuing towards Rodger's office, eyes watchful and her body tensing at every perceived sound. At last, she arrived at the double doors that bore the name, Lance Rodgers. There were no security cameras and she had plenty of time; these were her only allies.

Suzanne passed through the outer suite where Lance's assistants sat each day following his commands with the precision of NASA engineers. She slipped into the CEO's huge office that occupied an entire two corners of the building's floor. Nice view, she mused, taking a seat behind his desk. She pulled a headshot of her employer out of the valise that sat on her lap and propped it up for the visual recognition system to scan, grinning as the computer screen flashed to life. With all due care, she selected a screen icon, the symbolic link that led to the tabernacle and, at that point, ran into a roadblock as the system's access control asked for authentication.

"Damn it," she muttered as she began searching through his desk, hoping that, like most people, he had written his passwords down somewhere. She opened the first draw, carefully inspecting the contents, taking pains to return each item exactly as it was found, moving to the next, and the next, expecting one would give up the password list. When the effort proved futile, Suzanne turned to the only other item on the desk besides the computer. It was Rodger's journal.

Slowly turning the pages, she was surprised that Lance had meticulously recorded his personal reflections, day after day, and she stopped herself from becoming lost in the diary's notations, merely glancing for any signs of anything that might be a password. One name caught her attention, however, and she could not help reading the entry, which said, von Lightchild phoned and expressed his concerns. I've heard that name before, she thought, trying to remember where. Suddenly, she heard a muffled voice in the outer office.

Glancing at a rare, antique, gold and black enamel clock on a far shelf, Suzanne realized almost an hour had passed and the executive staff would soon begin to arrive. Time was now the enemy.

Her pulse quickened as she frantically shut down the computer, placed the diary on the exact spot where she found it, and hid the picture, stuffing it back into her valise. She moved to the door to listen, alarmed there was no other exit. Alma, Rodgers personal assistant, was talking on the phone, "Yes, Mr. Rodgers, I'll see he gets it right away…I'm just running down to the cafeteria for tea. Will you be back in the office this afternoon? Yes sir, I will wait. Please convey my sympathy to Mr. Anderson. Goodbye."

When she heard the receiver drop and the outer door close, Suzanne knew she had only seconds to save her career and her reputation. Moving like a cat chasing its prey, she bounded down the corridor toward the elevators, treading softly on the pads of her feet, eyes and ears on high alert, hoping and praying the offices she passed were empty, thanking fate and Divine Providence that they were.

Clenching her teeth, Suzanne pressed the elevator call button. A rapid burst of energy pouring down her arm made her finger hit the button, over and over. Her weight shifted side to side, and Suzanne prayed no one would be in the car when it arrived, again thanking the powers on high. She stepped into the elevator holding her breath until, at her floor, the doors slid open. The tension in her muscles began to unwind as she saw she was still alone.

Back in her office, Suzanne fell hard into her office chair, disgusted by her failure to break into Rodgers' computer, already exhausted at eight in the morning. The smartphone in her pocket began to chime a reminder that she was booked on a nine o'clock Amtrak train. She had just enough time to meet up with John and the news staff attending Eric's funeral. Suzanne started gathering a few items to take on the trip when she recalled just how she knew the name, von Lightchild.

Her eyebrows shot up. Nah, can't be, she thought. When Ron's admonition to David, 'it's only a coincidence until all the facts are known,' came into her mind, a tumbler clicked into place. Slowly, like the fade to black in a movie, a smile crossed her face, for perhaps, she had discovered something about the Brotherhood after all.

Suzanne imagined the triumph of presenting these new facts to David and Ron, when another troubling thought popped up: how do I explain it? As she absent-mindedly placed Rodgers's crumpled publicity headshot into the shredder under her desk, Suzanne decided to wait until after they returned from their Ephesus assignment. This would give her plenty of time to figure out what was going on and construct a plausible and newsworthy story.

Suddenly, Suzanne shot to her feet, hands frantically searching each pocket and then her valise, repeating her search for a second, and then a third time. "Damn it, damn it, damn it" she yelled, realizing that she dropped her identification card somewhere behind.

Her mind began to race in a hundred different directions. She knew there could be no explanation if it was found in Rodger's office and, holding back tears, she cursed herself for being so impetuous. Suzanne froze as two men, wearing Global News security uniforms, knocked on her office door.

"Ms. Biasotto? Are you Suzanne Biasotto?"

"Yes," she answered; her voice so breathy the guards could hardly hear her.

"Your ID card was turned into the security office. It was found in an elevator. You need to be more careful, miss."

Trying to keep her hand from shaking, she took the card from the guard. "Thank you, I will. Oh, who found it? I'd like to offer a reward."

"That won't be necessary," one said as they walked away.

Her smartphone reminder chimed again. Suzanne jumped, startled by the sharp ring. Grabbing her handbag, she ran off, on shaky legs, to catch the train.

The wall clock in the nursing station chimed the midnight hour, its echo fading, as Ahmad, aroused by a surreal dream, opened his eyes and looked about the darkened room. As his eyes adjusted, Ahmad saw Antoinette standing at his bedside. She switched on a wall lamp, folded her arms and stood in silence, watching him as he became aware of his surroundings.

Finally, Antoinette spoke, even, flat, businesslike, "The police are waiting for you. They believe you are a terrorist and mean to put you in jail for the rest of your life...the room is guarded and locked. But this is not your destiny. I am here to give you a chance at redemption."

Sitting up, confused, he asked, "You are going to give me a chance at redemption?"

Ahmad fell back onto the pillow, the crisp linen, like fine rice paper, made a crinkling sound as his head sunk deeper. Lying there, unable to understand, he said "How can you save me from the police?"

"Redemption does not come from earthly authorities...it comes from deep within your spirit and is evidenced by your deeds. So, I ask you, monsieur...will you allow God's love to take the sword from your hand?"

"Then...you will do nothing to help me escape?" Ahmad repeated.

"I am helping you escape. I am freeing you from the limits of rigid doctrines that are your true prison. Will you allow me to do this?"

Ahmad indicated his concurrence with a subtle nod of his head, encouraging the nurse, but in his eyes she read apprehension, reluctance, maybe even fear.

"Look carefully through the mist, Ahmad, see that small boy sitting there, alone...can you feel this child's distress...his fear...his loneliness?"

"I put these things out of my mind long ago," retorted the boy, now grown. "They made me weak." Pulling the pillow around his head, he cried, "Stop this, please!"

But Antoinette pressed on. "We all need love, Ahmad. Tell me...did Sholeh's love make you weak...or did you find great strength in her love?"

"I will not listen to this," raged Ahmad. "She was murdered by your countryman!"

"Passing the blame to the police is not going to heal you," Antoinette said.

Despite the pillow wrapped around Ahmad's head, the man could hear every word; he thought it was almost as if the nurse's voice came from somewhere inside him. "Sholeh pleaded with you not to go that night but you ignored her. She tried to warn you and was killed in the riots. Can't you accept some responsibility for her death and, for that matter, Sharif's death? Can't you see where violence leads?"

Ahmad flung the pillow at her but it seemed to pass through the nurse and struck the wall. "That's enough, woman...do not speak to me this way!"

"It's a terrible feeling, isn't it, Ahmad, to feel loss...to feel fear...to feel pain. You have known what it is like to grieve for your friends and now you know what it is like to suffer at the hands of those who wish you harm. Surely, you can grieve for the great pain and loss you have brought upon your victims."

He grew quiet. Antoinette knew things no one should know and he could not explain it. She knew all the secrets of his broken heart.

Antoinette moved into the middle of the room. Her garments began radiating a blinding white light. Then Ahmad saw her standing in a wide green field, lush, verdant, looking changed, as if she was no longer the physical being he had come to know so well. She remained recognizable to him as his nurse and friend, only now, she appeared much younger and, somehow, more perfect in a manner he could not quite describe. An inexpressible glow lit her face and Ahmad couldn't help but think he was in the presence of an angel, or how he imagined an angel might appear.

The field behind her seemed enveloped by a filmy substance, somewhat like looking through the rising morning mist, or layers of fine mosquito netting. A whisper of music sounded at the edge of his awareness. There were people scurrying about, working together, eating together, playing, laughing; a diverse group, all dressed in their own special garments, typifying them as of a particular place. Antoinette looked at him and began to speak, her mouth not moving but, every word, clear and distinct.

"Welcome, my honey. Mankind has never seen the likes of this field, although it has been waiting since before the beginning of time…the day of harvest approaches and a new garden has begun to bloom."

"Is that paradise?" asked Ahmad, astonished and afraid.

"Heaven cannot be seen by mortal eyes. It must remain a mystery until the hour of death."

"Why must that be?"

"If its glory were known to men…none would consent, for a moment, to remain on earth. Before your death, Ahmad, you must finish the work of your own redemption."

"But how can I do this? I can barely walk."

"The heart of God is healing. You will be well before long and you will leave this place. You will know the right path."

At that, the vision abruptly dissolved into a haze, as Ahmad's eyes darted about the room, trying to separate delusion from reality, present from past. Calculating an uncertain future, he lay back on the bed, his head too heavy to lift. "How…how?" he called out.

As if in reply, Ahmad heard a voice echo through his entire being. Whether it was Antoinette's voice, or his own, he could not tell. "Put down your sword…let the gun fall…let your hate and rage fall with it."

Ahmad squeezed shut his eyes and wept, the tears streaming down the sides of his face, soaking the bed sheets, his chest heaving up and down in short staccato movements. After a long while, when all his deepest feelings had been spent, he opened his eyes. His nurse was gone and Ahmad was alone.

THE HEART WILL
UNDERSTAND

Ahmad awoke slowly to the memory of his last
encounter with Antoinette. He could hear her
answering his bitter assertion, that a heart could
not be changed, with her own passionate assertion. Yes, she insisted,
of course, it could be changed, just as a mountain could be changed
by the act of gentle and, seeming, inconsequential droplets of water
falling steadfastly, one by one, year after year, eon after eon.
Eventually the mountain tumbles into the sea and the jagged crusty
rock is molded into smooth clean stone that finally crumbles into
sand. Each mountain, each rock, each stone shift their form in
deference to a finer purpose, a grander purpose; as the tiny grains
that remain, commingling in a single sparkling bed, nurture every
creature, large and small, that comes to live within the shores of its
strong and fertile protection.

He was eager to tell Antoinette that, the night before, he dreamt
she was an angel. He began to worry she might decide befriending

a terrorist was a bad idea. He certainly could not blame her for feeling that way. The truth was Ahmad felt the same about befriending an infidel. Still he had to admit, in spite of himself, he missed her and, in all honesty, their friendship had become important to him.

When his mind finally cleared, he realized several things at once: he was in a room that was not the same room in which he fell asleep; he was connected to a wall of machines with digital displays and blinking lights; his arms were restrained so he could not pull out his lines. Ahmad began to yell out, "Where is my nurse...why am I tied...get Antoinette Soubirous...please, get Antoinette Soubirous! Is someone there?"

A slender young woman he had never seen before, with red hair and round green eyes covered by a pair of narrow black-rimmed eyeglasses, entered the room, her movements brisk and efficient. She was wearing white cotton slacks and a lavender checkered pinafore with wide pockets on both sides. A stethoscope was draped around her neck and she dragged a small medication cart behind her, letting it come to rest at the foot of Ahmad's bed.

"Bonjour, monsieur," she said, "It is good to see you awake and alert."

"Why am I tied," demanded Ahmad darkly. "I am anxious to leave."

"Leave?" laughed the woman. "Why, this is impossible, monsieur. We just woke you. I must say though, you look extremely well for a man who spent a week in a coma!"

"A week in a coma?" said Ahmad, alarmed. "What are you saying? Who woke me?"

"Your physicians, monsieur," replied the nurse. "Yesterday, you began breathing on your own and the doctors removed your ventilator. Dr. Breton, our chief intensive care physician, decided it was time to wake you up. You were in a horrible acciden...."

"Don't be ridiculous!" snapped Ahmad. "I know I was in an explosion! I know Doctor Landau removed my kidney and that I nearly died...more than once. I awoke over two weeks ago. I left intensive care last week. I have been having physical therapy every day...yesterday, I walked without help!"

The woman looked at Ahmad with dismay. "No, monsieur, I am afraid that you did not leave intensive care until yesterday when they took you off the respirator. Your kidneys are fine. You suffered burns on your thighs and some head trauma. There is no doctor on staff named Landau." Then, to reassure him, she added, "You are healing remarkably well. I am certain with the progress you have been making, you will be sent home very soon."

Ahmad was on the brink of panic.

"Are you insane?" he asked the woman, whose face now turned ashen. "Please, leave my room. I want you out! Get my nurse. I want to see my nurse!"

"Monsieur," she replied, her voice trained to sound calmer than she felt, "I am your nurse. My name is Noel. I have been your nurse since you were admitted here."

"Get me Antoinette," commanded Ahmad. "Get me my nurse, now!"

"Antoinette?" asked the nurse. "Who is Antoinette?"

"I have said she is my nurse, you ignorant woman," Ahmad yelled, losing control. "I insist on seeing her, immediately."

"Pardon, monsieur," replied Noel, an irritated tremor stealing away the calm of her voice. "I have been your nurse since you were brought to intensive care a week ago from the surgical recovery room. I was assigned to continue your care when they transferred you to the ward yesterday. There is no nurse, in this hospital, whose name is Antoinette, I assure you."

Ahmad, now white as a sheet, could not speak.

"Listen," she said, trying hard to regain her composure and soothe the distraught man. "It is very common for people in a coma to think they have been awake."

"What in Allah's name are you saying," raved Ahmad. "I must speak to Antoinette now!"

"Monsieur," pleaded the young nurse, "I am so sorry…there is no such…"

"Liar!" Ahmad exploded. "Are you telling me that I did not feel the pain when one of your so-called doctors scraped the dead skin off my thigh, and that Antoinette did not come to my bedside in answer to my cries?"

The young nurse's mouth fell open as Ahmad related this event.

"Are you telling me that I would not have died if Antoinette had not changed my dressings every day; if she did not argue with the physicians to adjust my medications to speed my recovery; if she had not forced me to work with Michelle, the physical therapist, and if she had not reminded me of all the things in my life I have left unfinished, encouraging me, every day, to recover?"

His nurse, staring at him with a bewilderment bordering on shock, finally stopped him and told Ahmad, "You are describing some things that I have done and may have said, even things about your care I may have discussed with your physicians, but my name is Noel. I have never spoken with you, monsieur, because you were not awake. This is our very first conversation, except for the little things I whispered to you as you slept. Yes, your physical therapist is a woman named Michele...how you know this I have no idea. She comes every day to move your arms and legs so they do not atrophy and...you have never spoken to her."

"Why are you lying to me," moaned Ahmad. "What is the purpose?"

"You could not have possibly remembered these things...you were in a medically-induced coma until the swelling in your brain subsided. We tapered your sedation, just yesterday. Perhaps you were dreaming."

"I was not dreaming," insisted Ahmad. "Don't you think I can tell the difference between a dream and my life? Now, please...I beg you, let me see Antoinette."

"I know of no one named Antoinette," Noel repeated.

Ahmad pinched shut his eyes upon hearing Noel again deny that Antoinette was his nurse; or that she worked there; or that she even existed. His anger was growing inside him like expanding magma pushing against the earth's crust.

"Leave! Leave me alone," Ahmad bellowed, the inevitable eruption just moments away. "We cannot continue this chimera. I will not see anyone until Antoinette returns."

Noel became concerned by her patient's rage, and thought it best to do as he asked, hoping to mitigate the possibility that Ahmad's anger might become destructive. Perhaps, she thought, the brain injury Ahmad sustained caused him to hallucinate as he was awakening. She had rotated in intensive care for over a year now, and though she was not yet a veteran, she certainly had seen enough mental status changes in patients with head injuries to know that this was a possibility.

"Listen," said Noel, "I will talk to the nursing supervisor. Perhaps there is a nurse on another shift named Antoinette that I have not met. She will surely know. I will send her in to speak with you as soon as possible. How would that be?"

Ahmad just shrugged and waved the young woman away.

Noel hurried to the nurses' station in search of Marion Marchant, supervisor for both the medical and surgical intensive care units. She asked the unit clerk whether Marion was available. "It is important that I speak with her as soon as possible. The patient in Room 147 is quite agitated."

The clerk, a pale and vacuous woman, refusing to look up, informed her, "Nursing administration is conducting their monthly meeting in the second floor conference room...might last another half hour...might run longer."

Noel nodded, despite the fact the woman was not looking at her, and asked the unit clerk to relate her message the moment the supervisor returned. She headed back to the medication cart to finish her rounds. Progressing from room to room, chatting with those patients who were alert, she deliberately gave Room 147 a wide berth, rationalizing that, if he needed pain medication, Ahmad would call. Her decision to hold his antibiotics and fluids was more personal than medical. She was hoping against hope that if Marion, with the apparent authority of a supervisor, was standing beside her, Ahmad could be persuaded to calm down, listen to reason, and cooperate with his medication schedule.

Marion returned long before the dour clerk predicted, and before entering her small office, she read a note pinned to the bulletin board hanging on the door. Moments later, the supervisor was searching for the young nurse.

"Noel, what's this about Monsieur Hasanzadeh?" Marion asked. "Sounds serious."

Noel, quite relieved to see her mentor, confided to her the events of the morning. The details were sketchy, her mind still clouded from the shock of the patient's wild claims. Marion listened attentively, forming several possible explanations in her mind about why the patient in Room 147 believed he had been awake for several weeks.

"If this is true," she told Noel, "it is an extremely rare event... most patients have little or no memory of the time they spend under sedation. They're far better off unconscious of the pain."

Marion paused to consider the problem. Trying not to alarm Noel, she carefully selected words to express the conclusions she was still forming in her mind.

"If this patient does remember anything about this past week, perhaps it is similar to the phenomenon of what happens when someone, who is clinically dead is brought back to life. They can describe everything in the room, including conversations and events. Who knows what's possible?"

"Yes," said Noel, agreeing with her superior, "I should have thought of that."

"Perhaps the patient simply mistook you for someone named Antoinette. This interests me a great deal. I have never heard of a patient seeing and hearing everything going on while sedated or comatose...and then developing a personal relationship with his caretaker at the same time. Lord, he has even given her a name... pretty impressive."

"It is, isn't it," said Noel.

"Well, enough with the conjecture about this mysterious and ephemeral caretaker," smiled Marion. "This is probably all drug induced, so let's go and talk to the man and see if we can calm him down."

Tentative and cautious, Noel entered Ahmad's room and greeted her patient. "Good afternoon, may I introduce Madame Marchant. She is the nursing supervisor for this unit and hopes to be of help and comfort. I am certain she can answer some of your very pressing questions better than I have been able to do."

"Yes, I fervently hope so," replied Ahmad. "Please have a seat, madame."

Marion, keenly aware the police suspected the man of terrorist activity, took the seat closest to the door. Noel, frightened even though he was restrained, pardoned herself and left them alone.

"Well, Monsieur," said Marion, "you are a rather famous fellow here at Saint Joan's. You have recovered faster than any patient we have ever seen with your type of injuries. No doubt you are well pleased with your progress."

"I am," said Ahmad. "But right now, what I am most concerned with is my nurse."

"You are not pleased with Noel's care?" asked Marion, feigning ignorance of the patient's early morning outburst, hoping to hear, in his own words, the complete story.

"I am quite sure Mademoiselle Noel is competent, Madame," said Ahmad. "I really cannot say, we have only just met."

"Yes, of course, you have only just awakened. May I assure you, Noel is an excellent…"

"No, Madame Marchant," interrupted Ahmad, the pitch of his voice rising again. "May I assure you that I have been awake for several weeks now…and I am not insane! I do not understand why you continue to insist that I have only just awakened."

The two looked at each other in silence, not knowing where to go from here, until finally Ahmad, trying to appear and sound rational, inquired again, this time in almost a whisper, as though he was afraid to hear Marion's reply. "My nurse…her name is Antoinette. Tell me why she does not come any longer."

Marion sadly shook her head, and with a sigh, the only visible sign of the regret she felt at having to convey such unwelcome news to a patient that fought so hard to live, slowly replied, "I am so sorry for your distress. It is obvious that you truly believe this experience was real. I understand you have grown attached to the woman you have imagined, but that woman is Noel, I promise you. I am so sorry."

"I cannot imagine that I could make up someone like Madame Antoinette," insisted Ahmad. "She was much too different from me. Why would I imagine a middle-aged, petite, white woman with blue-green eyes? She is the first European with whom I have ever had a genuine conversation. We, of course, did not agree but she was my friend."

"Monsieur, the entire staff has worked diligently to help you survive. We would never hurt you by lying...for the last time, no such nurse works here by that name. I acknowledge that your experience is very remarkable; everything about your recovery has been very remarkable. I would even call it miraculous. I believe your injuries, and subsequent treatment, have produced this...effect, and it is not entirely explainable."

"Then you refuse to help me," said Ahmad turning away from the nurse. "I will miss having an infidel call me 'my honey'."

Marion was startled. "What is that you say, Monsieur Hasanzadeh? What did she call you?"

Ahmad, upon hearing the change in the nurse's tone, turned back to face her. "Why do you look so surprised?"

"She called you 'my honey'?" asked the nurse, searching.

"Annoyingly, yes, and all the time," said Ahmad. "I cannot believe I wish to hear her say it now."

Marion looked at the newly awakened trauma patient with an incredulity that she had never felt before in her life; feeling at that moment, like she had been whisked into a strange world, a dream world, where nothing was real or certain any longer.

"Monsieur Ahmad," said the nurse, her voice wavering, "When I started here as a young nurse...very much like Noel...new, naïve, maybe somewhat too innocent...a man, that is, a patient, was admitted to my ward. He was a notorious villain running from the police. He wrecked his car and his injuries were much like yours. When he awoke from a coma and saw me, the reaction was quite similar. He told me a fantastic story...much like you are telling me now...almost word for word. Your story prompted my memory of it because, he too, claimed to have seen a nurse who called him by a pet name, but I do not remember what it was – it was so long ago. But how could you know this while you were comatose?"

"This man, what became of him?" Ahmad asked.

"He recovered and confessed everything to the police, telling us his punishment would be just! It must have been a remarkable dream."

"I was not dreaming. I swear this on my honor. She was most certainly here...this must be a trick of the police!"

"No, Monsieur," argued the head nurse, "it is impossible! You could not have met anyone because you have not been conscious until we woke you this morning. This must be some extraordinary coincidence! I promise you on my honor...this is not a trick."

"I am not insane," Ahmad exploded. "She healed me when I was dying. A man does not forget a woman who is willing to do such things for a stranger...an enemy!"

Marion's mouth dropped open again, as she heard Ahmad go on to describe the events leading up to the moment he awoke that morning.

"Monsieur," said Marion, now exhausted, "the burns you sustained, not only to your legs but to your airways, made it necessary to intubate you. We considered removing your life supports to allow you to pass away peacefully in your sleep but...but that night your condition improved. It was miraculous according to the doctors, but then, there are many things in medicine that are true even though they are not logical. I do not pretend to explain how you recovered."

"I am telling you, Madame," Ahmad persisted, "Antoinette was here with me and there is nothing anyone can say that will convince me it was only a dream."

"I am sorry, Monsieur Ahmad," said the forlorn nurse.

"Oui, Madame...as am I."

"Yes...well," said Marion, smoothing the wrinkles on her pinafore. "I regret having to insist on the matter, monsieur, but sometimes we have to constantly reorient patients who have been in a coma. Please, do not be too concerned, your reaction is not uncommon and I am certain you will recover fully."

Ahmad was past arguing, but the nurse would not go away.

"I have yet more unfortunate news," she said. "The police have been waiting all week to interview you about the attack in Paris. It was our duty to inform them of our intention to awaken you. They are sending someone to speak with you this afternoon. Do you think you are up to it?"

"It is inevitable," said Ahmad with finality.

"Then, monsieur," replied the nurse getting up from the chair. "I will let you know when they arrive."

Like an animal caught in a trap, Ahmad raged, pulling again and again against the restraints, his head whipping from side to side. The futility of his struggle was bigger than his endurance and he let his arms fall. He felt despondent and desperate, like any unwilling captive. He quieted when the supervising nurse returned to his room.

"Monsieur Hasanzadeh, may I interrupt you?" said Marion Marchant. Her frown, and the rueful smile on the face of the man behind her, told Ahmad he was not going to like what she was about to say. "Since you are alert and recovering so well, the police inspector is here and would like to speak with you."

Silence.

Directly behind the nurse, exactly one step behind, stood a tall distinguished gentleman with broad shoulders and a mustache, wearing an inexpensive blue suit and matching tie. "May I introduce Chief Inspector Bissette?"

The silence grew.

"He has asked for a few minutes of your time."

Ahmad's stony silence became deafening.

The policeman, a thin smile on his face, glared at Ahmad with piercing eyes, a look of determination firmly setting his mouth, and nodded his greetings.

"Monsieur does not wish to speak?"

"An animal does not speak to its captors," Ahmad said with a menacing growl.

"I understand," said the policeman tilting his head in the direction of the restraints, indicating the nurse should remove them. The sound of plastic ripping filled the room, as the Velcro straps were pulled apart.

"There," remarked Bissette, "you are human again. Now we can talk as men…no?"

"You are not really asking," said Ahmad, rubbing his wrists and flexing his arms, careful not to dislodge the intravenous tubes.

"I suppose, I am not," replied Bissette, a wave of his hand prodding the nurse to leave. The nurse willingly obliged.

Ahmad, his arms folded defensively, as though they could shield him from what was about to come, asked, "What is it you want?"

"I see it won't be too long before you are fully recovered from the injuries you sustained in the explosion," began Bissette. "Our forensics team tells me that your suite had a bomb planted next to the bed. It must have been on a delayed proximity fuse, triggered by your appearance at the window. The delay...small as it was...saved your life."

Ahmad only grunted, refusing to comment, his expression not, in the least, altered, a fact that did not escape the veteran inspector.

"You do not seem concerned...or even surprised. Why would someone want to kill you, Monsieur Hasanzadeh?"

"Why would someone want to kill me?" echoed Ahmad. "Frankly, Inspector, I do not believe I was the intended victim."

"And whom do you think was the intended victim?"

"Isn't that something you should tell me?" Ahmad said, mocking his inquisitor.

It was now clear the interview wasn't going to yield a quick and easy result. The chief inspector decided to change tack, hoping he would get Ahmad to open up and tell him what he really knew.

"Well, monsieur," said Bissette, his weak smile fading, replaced by the stone-like expression of a gargoyle on a Parisian cathedral. "It appears this is going to take a bit more time than expected. I have your name listed as Ahmad Hasanzadeh. Is that your real name?" Bissette moved the chair close to Ahmad's bed and, pulling out a notepad and pen, sat down.

"No, it is not," replied Ahmad.

The inspector's eyebrows shot up in surprise. "May I ask your real name?"

"Yes, of course," said Ahmad. "It is Ahmad Hasan."

"We found no identification on you, monsieur," said Bissette, surprised by the candid response, though he was trained not to show it.

"It must have been incinerated along with the rest of my things," replied Ahmad.

"What is your business in France?"

"I live here on a student visa and study engineering at the university in Paris."

"You live at the university?" asked Bissette, pressing on.

"No, I share an apartment in Clichy-sous-Bois…you must know of it from the demonstrations…perhaps you should visit and see the suffering of our people."

"All people suffer, monsieur, and I have been there on many occasions during the street riots…or as you call them…demonstrations. Why were you staying alone at the château?"

"My parents" Ahmad explained, "want to own a business in France. I was looking over the property for my father. The owner allows potential buyers to survey the estate before they decide…it is a huge investment…one should be certain."

"Yes, I am sure," replied Bissette leaning forward. "What are you…eh, your parents, intending to do with the château?"

"My father might convert it into a hotel and spa," answered Ahmad. "That is, if the accountants tell him there is profit to be made."

"You are staying there under an assumed name…why?" Bissette asked, pushing forward, trying to connect the dots and complete the sketch in his head.

"My father did not want the owner to contact him if they decide against buying," replied Ahmad without hesitating, "They do not like being harassed by anxious sellers."

"We discovered a car…with a forged registration. Where did you get the car, Monsieur Hasan?"

"I know of no car. I arrived in a limousine arranged by my father."

"Then I won't ask for the receipt," the inspector said with a sneer. "One last question I must ask you…for now…can you account for the three days before you came to the hospital?"

"I was at the château," replied Ahmad. "I spent the time looking over the buildings…the fields…the machinery…trying to get acquainted with the place. My parents must have returned to Iran or they would be here at my side. They must be very worried!"

The Chief Inspector felt, knew, and smelled something was not quite right with the man lying before him or with the man's answers. He stopped to think for a moment. He considered how he might shake up his suspect; something, perhaps, that might cause him to let something slip. He took a deep breath. Here goes, he said to himself.

"Tell me, what is your connection to the terrorist activity at the Hotel De Ville? Who was the intended target?"

Inside, Ahmad froze. Had he been identified? He felt trapped. His thoughts raced. He began tracing and retracing each step of that day, an avalanche of 'what ifs' striking against his consciousness.

"I'm sorry, but I am not sure what you mean...what terrorist activity at the Hotel De Ville? Why do you accuse me? Is it because I am Muslim?"

At this last remark, Detective Bissette rose briskly from the chair and angrily pulled it away from the bed. Leaning over the patient, almost eye to eye, he spoke his next words as though it was a formal indictment. "Are you asking me to believe you have no knowledge of the attack in Paris...events known to the entire world?"

"Inspector, I am a student trying to be a good son...abiding by my father's request...there was no time for televisions, or internet, or newspapers at the château...I had only a simple cell phone and did not know of this event."

Bissette straightened, pocketing the pen and note pad. Glaring at Ahmad, he said, "I don't believe a word of this. I will check every fact, beginning with your father...there is someone, something that will trap you...a cell phone picture, a witness...it will turn up, monsieur, count on that! I will be back...count on that too! Oh, and one other thing...I am leaving policemen outside to guard your door."

"I am a prisoner?" asked Ahmad, his obvious dismay apparent to the detective.

"You have not convinced me you are telling the truth, monsieur," replied the inspector, "But if you would like, think of the policemen as here for your protection...we wouldn't want your mystery assassin to reappear...now would we?"

Moments later, Chief Inspector Bissette was back in the car conversing with his partner, Louis, and hoping the 'two heads are better than one' theory wasn't just a mindless bromide.

"Well," said Bissette to the junior man, "I don't believe him, something isn't right."

"I tried telephoning the caretaker while you were interviewing Hasan," Louis offered, "but he appears to be traveling. No forwarding address, according to the repairmen working on the mansion."

"Troubling, Louis," said Bissette. "I would be willing to bet we will not see this caretaker again. I have that bad feeling. The hackles on the back of my neck are up and buzzing like I have just touched a live wire at the top of a cattle fence. It's the hackles, Louis...you develop them over years and years working at this job. Ignore them at your peril. My instincts tell me Hasan has something to do with Paris...his answers are perfect, too perfect, too quick, too sure... life is not so perfect, Louis...life is messy. I think he's as phony as a Nigerian lottery ticket."

"We'll keep going then!" Louis insisted, his admiration for the veteran policeman driving his agreement. He knew Bissette's reputation and the man was never wrong.

"I want you to get me all the information on him that exists in our system and through Interpol," Bissette instructed his partner, tearing a page from the notebook. "Find his father, check his apartment, get his computer, talk to his friends, telephone the university. Most of all...get a copy of that Global News story and check on the passports. I want to know everything there is to know about Ahmad Hasan and where he has been."

"Oui, Inspector," replied Louis.

"First, let's get some dinner, mon ami," suggested Bissette as they drove away. "I'm starving. Oh, and Louis...find that damn caretaker!"

It took the insistence of a trusted physician, who once treated his wife, to convince Inspector Bissette to relocate the police guard standing outside Ahmad's room.

"Inspector," explained the doctor pointing out a stark reality, "the patient is stable and no longer requires monitoring or intravenous medication so we are removing his lines. He can walk the halls of the ward, regain his strength and, possibly, he can be released in a few days. On the other hand, the physical therapist can spend two weeks rebuilding his atrophied muscles, your choice."

Bissette acquiesced, but not before placing two armed men just outside the hospital ward's double entrance doors and sitting two others in front of the fire exit. When the inspector was satisfied with the security arrangements and finally left, he swore to return within forty-eight hours, assuring the physician he expected to take the prisoner into his custody.

The ward was pedestrian and functional; not at all like the place Ahmad remembered from his dreams. The rooms were painted a dull taupe in place of the bright periwinkle blue of his memory. There weren't any French doors leading out onto a veranda where a patient could sit and enjoy the provincial countryside; only a plain metal sash window that did not open, looking out at parking lots and rooftops. Gone, were the full-length chintz drapes with the large yellow cabbage rose print that framed the veranda doors; replaced instead with sterile white blinds that remained half open, regardless of the time, day or night.

As the hours ticked away, Ahmad worked on his journey back to wholeness, walking up and down the length of the hospital ward's hallways, at first needing a walker but soon managing with only a cane. Determined and driven, in preparation for his escape, he continued this monotonous routine for hours on end but, in reality, he walked as an antidote to missing Antoinette.

As he walked, Ahmad became keenly aware that he was lonely. Antoinette put him in touch with his need for human relationships and he realized this feeling of loneliness was quite familiar to him; a burden he carried since childhood, as far back as he could remember. While walking the halls his aloneness became more acute, an omnipresent and disturbing phenomenon, calling out, with every step, the isolation that was his life.

There was the loneliness he felt as he walked past the policemen assigned to guard him; alike in every way Ahmad could think; talking together, neither glancing up or acknowledging him as he went by, arguing the way friends do. Ahmad remembered how Shahin would call across the stone wall for him and how, because of his studies, he would refuse to play with his only friend.

There was loneliness as he walked past the nurses' station and watched the excited young women chatter about the new engagement ring one had received; Ahmad wondering whether Sholeh's mother still kept the ring he had given her daughter on the night before she died.

There was loneliness as he passed each patient's room, the talk and laughter of their visitors floating out into the hall; Antoinette's reproaches and encouragements, no longer swirling in with the low din, creating a cavernous ache in Ahmad's chest.

There was loneliness in the photographs of frolicking children, taken and donated by staff members, lining the walls on either side of the corridor; calling forth the memory of children playing in the yard outside the madrasah without him, never him. He had not been included, nor had he wanted to be. Now he could see the pride he took in his aloneness had been a buffer against the pain.

There was loneliness with every step he took: in the patients sitting in wheelchairs looking down at their withered and fragile hands, perking up only when a passing staff member asked how they were feeling, then patting a shoulder in a gesture of kindness and comfort; in the maintenance man who swabbed the hallway floor without ever glancing up at passersby; at the camaraderie of ardent physicians intent on their medical revelations, huddling together as they moved with lightning efficiency from room to room and patient to patient; at the people and cars he could see through the open window at the end of the corridor, hurrying along the road, engrossed in their fevered affairs.

He observed the plight of a struggling honeybee trapped in the web of an enterprising spider. Its steadfast partner striving, at grave risk to its own life, to liberate its friend from the spider's snare; it left Ahmad to wonder whether there was a living soul on earth who would have done the same for him.

A loud thud interrupted Ahmad's reflections when an orderly, pushing a hospital bed upon which lay a jumbled mass, slammed open the swinging doors at the end of the hallway. Ordinarily, Ahmad would not have given a second thought to this sight but today there was something remarkable about the bed being wheeled and maneuvered through the ward's corridor to a room just opposite his own. The bed appeared huge in comparison to its occupant; a tiny wisp of a very old woman, with silver hair and huge eyes the color of the deep Persian sea. She was lost amongst its jumble of sheets, pillows, and blankets.

As she was wheeled into her room, Ahmad overheard the orderly giving a brief report to the nurse, emphasizing that the full report, laboratory results, and patient history were all in the medical chart that sat on the mattress at the end of the bed. The patient was so tiny that her feet missed the chart by at least ten inches.

The orderly, now out of Ahmad's range of hearing, maneuvered the bed against the right wall opposite a small wardrobe with misshapen wire clothes hangers, banging against each other as the bed rolled past, tinkling out the secrets of the sick and dying who had hung clothes, robes, and old memories on them, year after year.

The orderly continued his report by telling the nurse that the patient had been sent to the hospital from the nursing home for treatment of pneumonia. The little lady had spiked a temperature overnight and the staff could detect rales in her lungs on auscultation. The patient's name was Betty Rosner, a ninety-six year old woman with Chronic Lymphocytic Leukemia and senile dementia.

"Merci, Marcel," said the nurse, thanking the orderly. "We are quite familiar with our Betty."

"I suppose you would be," replied Marcel. "She has lived in the nursing home for some time now."

"Yes," said Noel, "and her condition has been fairly stable, yet she does come to us for periodic flare-ups of leukemia. This is her first bout with pneumonia though. I hope she has the strength to recover from it."

"Sorry for having to leave her," said Marcel. "I know how challenging she can be, especially on the ward where there are so many ill patients who have to tolerate her incessant ravings. All I can say is bonne chance."

"Except for her crying, she is one of our favorite patients," said Noel. "All the nurses and aides are quite fond of her."

"There is something special about her," agreed Marcel, nodding to the nurse as he headed back to the dispatch office in admissions for his next transfer.

An hour later, Ahmad, returning for noon prayers, caught sight of Noel leaving the new patient's room. As he approached, he heard a frantic voice pleading, "Help me. Somebody help me, I'm dying! I'm dying!"

Ahmad briefly peeked into the woman's room and seeing her in grave distress, turned and hurried back to the nurses' station. He said to the ward clerk behind the counter, "The woman in the room opposite mine is crying out…she seems to be having trouble."

"Just try to ignore her, monsieur," said the clerk.

Glancing up and seeing Ahmad's astonished face, she added, "Everyone is used to this so no one pays attention. She cries out like that whenever she's awake. She will fall asleep soon…I hope."

The clerk went back to her work but when she glanced up again, Ahmad, unsatisfied, was still standing there.

"The aides make fun of her to ease the frustration of listening to her all day," said the clerk, trying to break the embarrassed silence.

Hoping Ahmad would take the hint, she added, "She quiets immediately though when someone enters the room and resumes her cries as soon as she is alone again…there is really nothing we can do. She'll be quiet soon."

This time, realizing that she was not satisfying Ahmad's concerns in the least, the clerk got up and went back into the nurses' lounge, no longer willing to abide his accusing glare.

Ahmad returned to his room and, in disgust, slammed closed the door, causing the guards to jump at the startling sound. Hanging his cane in the wardrobe, he went into the lavatory to perform his ablutions and followed these by laying down a clean white cotton bath mat. It was a poor substitute for his Persian prayer rug, carried with great care from Iran.

The rug had been a treasured gift, woven by his grandmother prior to his departure for the madrasah in Tehran. Elegant and sturdy, its red, gold, and blue threads were interwoven into an elaborate array of exotic birds and animals roaming amidst intricate patterns of swirls and flowers. The rug kept watch over the boy when he prayed. It was Ahmad's sole connection, throughout his trips to distant and inhospitable lands, to the beloved Iran of his memories and dreams. Each night, when he knelt upon it in prayer, it would fly him home, as if Persian magic were woven into the fine silk threads by his grandmother. Destroyed in the fire at the Château, he would grieve its loss forever.

Kneeling on the hospital bath mat, hands clasped together and pressed tightly to his forehead, Ahmad tried to pray. The cries across the hall were so piercing and persistent he finally rose and sat on the bed's edge, thinking what to do.

"I will not endure this torture one moment longer," he said to the empty space. "I cannot pray with this noise. I will demand a new room at the other end of the hall."

With every intention of marching down to the nurses' station, Ahmad found himself stopped outside the little woman's room. He decided to speak with her and insist she cease her foolishness. Followed by the suspicious eyes of the police officers, he stepped inside and found Betty lying in bed, very frail, and wondered how she had lived so long.

Noel, Betty's nurse, was connecting a bag of antibiotics into the intravenous line that was placed into a fragile vein in her forearm. She was singing a quiet tune that seemed to calm the agitated woman.

"She's demented," Noel told Ahmad, when she finished the song. "She cannot help calling out the same things over and over. Her tired brain has finally given up and all she can remember is this one little mantra. It is her way of surviving, of protecting herself, so to speak. You don't need to keep running in here, monsieur. It is very kind of you to try and comfort her but I'm afraid she cannot appreciate your efforts."

Ahmad remained quiet, thinking the nurse had no need to know the real reason he had entered Betty's room.

"Of course," continued the nurse, "if you should happen to want a break from walking the halls and decide to come in and sit with her, we would all be ever so grateful for a break from her constant crying."

"Yes" replied Ahmad, not knowing what else he could possibly say.

"You would like that too," said Noel, gently brushing the old woman's hair back away from her face, "yes, Betty?"

Betty just watched unmoved, her eyes following Noel as the nurse circumambulated the bed, smoothing the linens.

"Well," said Ahmad, "I should be going now."

"Jumping ship so soon?" laughed Noel. "You'll be back, I am sure."

And he was. Ahmad made his way across the hall and entered Betty's room the very next hour, having been able to tolerate her noisome crying for just a little over forty minutes. He stood at the foot of her bed considering the old woman, thinking, I must get her to stop this insufferable screeching. At the sight of the man, Betty quieted and Ahmad asked the woman to explain her lamentations. Betty just stared with an intenseness that belied her dementia but she did not answer him and since Ahmad didn't know what else to say, he departed.

In a matter of minutes, Betty was at it again but Ahmad, worn out, walked slowly back toward his room, passing the police officers on the way. They snickered at him, mocking him with biting sarcasm, but Ahmad ignored their taunts, closing his door without a word.

After a short discussion, the police officers made a decision. Speculating their suspect was planning an escape; they tried to prevent Ahmad from further visiting the old woman. But the nurses objected. "He's willing to keep her company so she doesn't disturb the other patients. What harm is there in this?" The officers relented and agreed to let him continue, quite willing to shirk their responsibility for a chance at some peace and quiet.

Later that night, seeking a way to escape the monotony of hospital life but telling himself it was to stop Betty's crying, Ahmad went across the hall again. As long as he kept talking, the woman remained wide-eyed and silent, which suited him just fine. At first, he asked after her health and told her about the happenings on the floor. Betty just stared off into space, without the slightest hint of comprehension and Ahmad realized she could not understand. He ended the visit by reciting the Qur'an, which seemed to please the old woman. He kept at it till she fell asleep.

Early the next morning, Ahmad was startled awake by his neighbor's particularly ardent cries of "Help me! Help me, nurse, come quick. I'm dying! I'm dying!"

Still half asleep, Ahmad climbed out of bed, put on a robe and slippers then went off to wash. Taking a particularly long time, he hoped that when his shower was ended, Betty would have quieted again. To his dismay, when he finally dared to leave the lavatory, he could hear the old woman's cries across the hall.

"Help me, help me, please!" she insisted, "I'm dying! I'm dying!"

Ahmad couldn't help himself; he dressed and went, immediately, to the distressed woman's room with the suspicious policemen following close behind.

"You're not dying, Madame Rosner," he assured her.

"I'm dying!" Betty insisted. "Get my nurse."

"I've never seen anyone dying as long, or as loud, as you, madame," Ahmad replied, scolding her.

Standing at the doorway, the two policemen laughed and taunted their charge; one of them remarking, "Jew's do not discriminate...see...she even quiets when a terrorist enters her room."

Ahmad, frustrated as much by the officers as by Betty, confronted the men. He reminded them they were supposed to be guarding the exits, not harassing him. The police returned to their assigned posts. It wasn't their prisoner's admonishments, but the woman's screaming that forced their hand. Once they were gone, Ahmad decided to begin his own rant as retribution for Betty's vociferous and repeated complaints. He concluded it was safe, after all, Betty was demented and would not understand a word of it and the policemen were out of earshot. He started to speak, spilling out his uttermost secrets. Betty just listened, so captivated it would have made any stage actor jealous.

Ahmad began his rant with a diatribe about why the Jews must be annihilated. "Soon, we will drive Israel into the sea. You will see."

Somehow though, Ahmad's fulminations lacked their usual fervor and, as time passed, his words took on the characteristic of one friend chiding another, such as the way it would be if the two were watching a sporting event, each rooting for the opposite team.

When Ahmad's invective ran itself out, he left the room willing to deal with the inevitable resumption of Betty's cries, but returned shortly when Betty changed her hourly mantra. It would bring Ahmad running and it, in itself, changed her relationship with Ahmad forever.

"Somebody, come quick," she screamed, "Take me to the morgue. I'm dead. I'm dead!"

As Ahmad entered, Betty's screams got louder and more urgent. Ahmad told the little woman, "You are not dead, Madame Rosner, you are screaming."

"I am dead! I'm dead. Take me to the morgue," she cried again, this time with greater insistence.

"You cannot possibly be dead, madame," he replied with sincere ardor. "You are yelling so loud a nuclear bomb could have been detonated and who would know?"

She stopped screaming. Her eyes followed him back and forth as he paced the room. Though she remained silent, Ahmad noticed her eyes had narrowed to slits and had taken on a peculiar focus and sharpness to them. One of her brows was raised, her long slender nose, with just the slightest curve to it, made her look almost shrewd, not like a demented person at all. All in all, he thought, she is rather like a hawk searching for prey. The idea unnerved him.

Finally, he said, "I am going now. I hope you will not begin to cry out when I leave. Stop whining. Why are the Jews always whining?"

As Ahmad walked away a tiny voice from the supine figure spoke with stinging mockery, "Oh, like the Arabs never whine…the biggest moaners on the planet."

"What did you say? Did you speak to me?" asked Ahmad in astonishment.

"What a yutz," replied the old woman. "You can't hear, or something? I said, oh, like Arabs never whine? We call it sarcasm, boychick."

Standing there, gaping, Ahmad's next words froze on his tongue. Finally, he said, "You, woman, sound about as demented as a logician."

"What would an Arab know about a Jew, anyway?"

"I am not Arab, I am Persian," Ahmad proudly informed her.

"Big difference," quipped Betty.

"Persians are not the same."

"Who gives a shit?"

"I do."

"Yes, but you shouldn't. Why is it so important to be better than someone else? Why does your culture have to be better than mine? Who cares about fighting over which prophet is the 'true and only one'? Moses, Jesus; Jesus, Mohammed; it's exhausting already! Maybe Jesus was the Messiah. What does it hurt to say so after five thousand years of waiting for one to show up? As for the Muslims and Jews, it's pathetic that brothers can't get along!"

"Muslims and Jews," he continued, ignoring her comments, "will never tolerate each other."

"Ah, tolerance…it's drek…garbage," squeaked Betty. "It means you really think you are better. I'll put up with you to appear magnanimous and open-minded. This way everyone can feel okay about their own bullshit."

Ahmad considered the woman with a measured silence, wondering if he could believe his ears while she completed her thought.

"We need to share some love, maybe some food…celebrate our differences instead of all this mishegoss."

"People will not let their own culture get entirely lost," he retorted.

"The flowers live together in one garden and each adds its own special beauty to the rest. What shnook says they can't grow together because they're not the same? Even weeds are just plants…but the noxious weeds? The noxious weeds…these we should pluck out."

Ahmad was tempted to ask Betty if she knew of Antoinette but held back. He was afraid that, in addition to being a terrorist, she would now think he was insane.

Betty squinted. "There is something on your mind that you are afraid to say…say it out…don't be a coward."

"The nurse who took care of me and saved me from dying after the explosion that brought me to this hospital…she gave me the will to live. Only now the nurses say I was only hallucinating…that she never existed. They say I could not possibly have seen her because I was in a coma."

"What the hell do they know?" Betty snorted. "Trust yourself; be a mensch! Doesn't it say in the Qur'an that the next world is closer to you than your neck vein! Don't you believe your own book over the cynicism of a silly nurse? Anyway, bubele, she is around you."

"What are you saying?"

"She is here...around you," replied the old woman, "I can sense these things...it's something new...dying people see things...you can talk to her anytime you like."

"What do you mean...see things?" asked Ahmad, anxious to know if perhaps this tiny Jewish woman had seen Antoinette.

Betty looked away, into a future that was now closer with each passing moment. "Sometimes I see my husband and my parents...all long gone from this toomel place...standing at the end of my bed. They are waiting for me now. I talk to them. They say I will be with them soon."

"How do you know they are real?" asked Ahmad.

"I'm mishuggah...just a demented old dying lady. What do I know?" She said it with a smirk while patting Ahmad's hand with her slender gnarled fingers; the delicate skin of her hand like tissue paper. Her hands seemed to Ahmad to be like two wizened old trees with a hundred years of history to tell - history and a woman that Ahmad was coming to see as astonishingly beautiful.

"You think Antoinette is still with me?" asked the anxious man.

"Always, bubele, always...as long as you want her to be."

Her expression hardened and she looked at him with the same intense sharpness as before, "You and me, young man, we are the same. My people and your people, along with eons of many peoples with many names...we all have the right to resent the injustices heaped upon us, and yet, why is it that two wrongs never seem to make it right? Pray for what you want but don't insist, my young Iranian friend. Your insistence on justice has turned you into a killer. That is not what you want to be."

Aghast at even the thought of reconciliation with the Jews and exasperated by Betty's comments, Ahmad blurt out, "What can two people do?"

"Two people can do more than one and one can do much, but we have to have koyach." Ahmad looked puzzled so Betty, pointing to her chest, added, "you know...inner strength."

"And do what?" Ahmad demanded.

"Heal this never ending woe between Muslims and Jews. We could show the world it is possible to replace hate with compassion. If only our people could begin it. Such an astonishing sight that would be, no? God willing, the blessing would spread to all nations and all peoples."

Ahmad looked at Betty as though he had never seen her before. Betty noticed this and said, "What? You look like you have just seen a ghost."

"I have...you!"

"I'm not a ghost now" laughed Betty. "But during the Holocaust... *then* I was a ghost."

"The Holocaust? You...in the holocaust? I don't believe it."

Betty pushed up the left sleeve of her dressing gown revealing what appeared to be faded numbers imbedded in the fragile skin of her inner forearm.

Ahmad just stared.

"This is my number from Treblinka," she said. "I rarely show a soul nowadays...don't want to be bothered going through the story...I've told it so often but now I am too old and too tired."

"You are not really going to try and push that tale on me, are you?"

"Listen," said Betty, her eyes cold as ice, narrowing to slits. "I don't give a bupkes whether you believe me or not. If you think an old woman had her arm tattooed in the event she would someday meet a Muslim terrorist then you are not only irreparably brainwashed, you are hopelessly delusional, as well."

"Why are you showing me this, madame?" asked Ahmad, his discomfort growing and discernable in the changed pitch of his voice.

"Because you need to understand that everyone is given a chance at redemption...everyone. Some of us get many chances; some get only one. I certainly did. After the war I was a ghost. My entire family was killed in the camps. I couldn't eat or sleep. I had night terrors. All I could manage to do all day was to wait for death to come so I would not have to face the night. It is a wonder that I survived the war at all but something kept me going. I was given a choice...live or die. I chose life...left Poland...went to the United States where a kind American soldier helped me. I was very young when I arrived in the States and utterly alone. But ten years later I found that soldier... we were married and lived in Williamsburg, that's in Brooklyn. While serving in Europe, my husband became enchanted by some of the things he saw. We returned and he began an importing business. We traveled to Europe often and eventually he transferred most of his operations to France and we came here, started a family and stayed. It was a wonderful life but the memory of those camps kept an iron grip on my heart. Sometimes to keep going felt almost impossible. Sometimes I thought about killing myself. Do you understand?"

Even though Ahmad nodded, Betty did not believe he understood. "I would look at my children," she said. "I decided that they would not have to live with the same nightmare. I did not want death to be their legacy. God gave me children...they were my chance at redemption. I did not have to accept redemption. I could have chosen otherwise. Only love has the power to redeem us. I chose love for my children. In the end, love saved me! You have been given a chance at redemption. This is how I see it...it is up to you...now choose!"

Ahmad objected one final time. "Why will anyone listen?"

"I need a good sleep now," Betty said, her voice thick, eyes heavy.

"Yes, of course." Reluctant to leave the room, he watched her drift off to sleep and whispered, "Rest well, Madame Betty."

Ahmad, leaning against the bedrail, stood over the sleeping old waif. He watched her even and peaceful breath; her eyelids moving in an ever so gentle flutter as she dreamed. A lone wisp of her shimmering silver hair was lying across her face.

Contemplating the mystery of their relationship, Ahmad found himself wondering if it would be safe to touch her; just lightly on the cheek, to somehow acknowledge their remarkable relationship but also for reassurance that she was real. He had come to have genuine affection for this little Jewish woman, almost as though she was his own grandmother. The feeling Betty gave him through the gift of her time and great wisdom, reminded Ahmad of a similar feeling he had experienced once, long ago, when a stranger sat beside him at a fountain in the square. Until that day, Ahmad had felt utterly alone and isolated from real human contact, his only companions the ubiquitous flies that swept past his face.

Now, many years later and a world away, here was Betty: a woman he had been taught to shun as one of God's rejects, for hers was the most unclean race and his greatest enemy. Nevertheless, the only emotion he could summon was this damnable feeling of pure affection. Perplexed, yet sure of his feelings perhaps for the first time since Sholeh died, bending past the bedrail and over the sleeping woman, heart beating palpably, he placed, ever so briefly, the tenderest of kisses on her lined and hollow cheek and brushed the wisp of hair away from her face.

Marveling at himself, Ahmad thought perhaps this was Antoinette's message all along: that love is the only true reality, its limitless power, alone, able to unravel the mysteries latent in the universe…and in the human heart. Then whispering her name once more, Ahmad wished her "bien dormir," and slipped out of her room.

Once back across the hallway, hidden from the curious eyes of the police and medical staff, Ahmad became overwhelmed with emotion and found it difficult to draw a deep breath. He could barely believe he touched a Jew, let alone, kissed her as if she were his own grandmother. At that moment, Ahmad decided that he must leave France now, before it was too late, before his will was broken or the police could take him in for interrogation.

Unable to sleep, he devised an escape plan for slipping out the next night during the quietest time, when the patients all slept and the guards drifted off. This left enough time in the morning to see Betty and give her his blessings and farewells. The Islamic warrior started to drowse and fell off to sleep rationalizing the myriad meanings from the remarkable events of the past days, determined these things would not change the course of his life.

Ahmad arose early for morning prayers refreshed and energetic. The morning was breaking toward a beautiful day and the anticipation over his pending liberation brought about in him a renewed state of sunrise vigor.

"Bonjour, monsieur," sang a nursing assistant, named Monique, as she entered. "And how is the most esteemed patient of Ward Two this morning?"

Monique stood there beaming. A grin, wider than the Persian Gulf, spread across her face. Ahmad was curious, but unable to think of an appropriate response for such an effusive greeting, simply folded his arms and waited.

Ignoring Ahmad's look of impatience, the nursing assistant chattered on, "Perhaps you have not heard? You are the new hero of Saint Joan's."

Ahmad's expression was now morphing into restiveness and he replied, "I am afraid you have the wrong patient."

"Oh, no, monsieur, you are much too modest," said Monique, waving away Ahmad's dry declaration. "I only meant to thank you for transforming Madame Rosner. She is in her room, happily eating breakfast without a peep or a whimper for the very first time. We are all very grateful for the respite. The night shift reported there was not one complaint! You are a miracle worker! Well, I must finish my rounds. I am terribly sorry to have disturbed you."

After the nurse departed, Ahmad listened carefully and could hear nothing from across the hallway. The revelation caused Ahmad to burst into peals of laughter, leaving the guards outside the door to conjecture, with their ever-abiding disdain, whether their usually somber charge had finally gone off the rails.

Donning the drab blue hospital robe and paper-thin slippers, Ahmad prepared to execute the first step of his escape plan. Using the cane as a prop, he exited the room with an exaggerated limp to begin the daily constitutional up and down the hallway the police had come to expect. Two things were immediately apparent: Betty's door was closed and one guard was engrossed in flirting with the nurses. Still another was choosing pastry from the morning breakfast cart. Stupid and weak were the two adjectives that popped into his head.

He continued walking up and down the corridor without even the slightest scrutiny on the part of the guards. He moved down the corridor, stopping at the door of a room where a man lay comatose. Ahmad entered and quickly rummaged through the chiffonier, found a collared shirt and lightweight zipper jacket and wrapped both around his waist, carefully concealing them under the robe he was wearing. Stepping back, checking himself in the mirror, happy with the result, he returned to his room to hide the stolen clothing.

Earlier, he took note of a second man, whose height and weight were close matches with his own. When the patient was taken off the ward for medical tests, Ahmad stole his pants and shoes, concealing them in the same manner and hiding them in the same place. He was almost done now.

Later that morning, Ahmad slipped into the empty medical staff lounge directly after hearing a 'code blue' announcement. He stole small amounts of cash from several purses before returning to his room. The captive was now fully prepared for departure. First, he must say goodbye to Betty.

Just after finishing lunch, Ahmad was visited by the ward physician. He was closely followed by a team of medical residents awaiting their mentor's expert pronouncements, each anxious over the rigorous interrogations of their mentor in his pursuit to test their apprehension of the case. There was one other unexpected person mixed in with the group: Chief Inspector Bissette.

Pleased with the examination results, the doctor said, "Well, monsieur, I anticipate that you can leave the hospital within the next few days. However, we expect you to require physical therapy for a while yet and are sending you to a rehabilitation unit for two weeks. Then we will refer you to a facility near your residence for outpatient therapy to assist you in what, we believe, will be a full recovery."

"No, doctor," interrupted Bissette, contradicting the physician. "I will be taking the prisoner today. There is an armored van coming to transport him…and Doctor, any interference will be dealt with in the harshest possible terms!"

"Oh, I see," fumed the irate physician. "I am not aware that you have such authority. If this patient does not recover fully I will hold the Ministry of Justice responsible!"

"I assure you, doctor, I do have the authority. In fact, I could have removed this man at any time and had him placed in the prison infirmary." The inspector spoke with a calm and even voice cultivated over many years. Bissette had been patient enough with the hospital staff and was not about to be dismissed any longer. Glancing at Ahmad, he concluded, "Your patient looks quite well. The rest is an act."

Stunned by Bissette's display of disdain and the smug look of victory on his face, the physician scowled at him and pushed past his medical team. As he was leaving the room in utter disgust, he said, "I will return at the end of my rounds, Monsieur Inspector, and I certainly will not discharge a patient who has not sufficiently recovered."

Ahmad and Inspector Bissette watched the cadre of medical personnel file out of the room behind the doctor, all mirroring their mentor and retreating in a manner that by no means suggested surrender, the hauteur that accompanied their medical training ever-abiding in their collective gait.

Hiding the rising alarm he felt, Ahmad asked, "Where do you expect to take me, Inspector?"

"You, my terrorist friend, are going on a ride through the countryside...although, sadly, the delightful scenery will be obstructed by the steel mesh across the window. You will become a guest of the French Government...the accommodations at La Santé Prison may not be as nice as these...in fact, I guarantee it...but the conversation will be ever more interesting and lively."

"Explain to me, Inspector, what possible information you could obtain from interrogation that I have not already given you? I will not allow you to interfere with my recovery!"

"I am afraid you will be spending a great deal of time with us," the inspector asserted with a menacing voice, "a very long time! We have been investigating your past. I have many hands tracking your history and what we have gathered, so far, is quite alarming. We have not been asleep, I assure you."

"Utterly ridiculous!" Ahmad shouted. "This is harassment. If you would please leave me..."

"Weren't you a student in Tehran at a radical madrasah?" The inspector shot back with an accusing roar. "Tell me, why were you in every location over the past year where a major terrorist attack occurred? Why are there passports in your name from different countries? If you are such a diligent student, tell me why your attendance records at the University are so spotty? You are under arrest. You will be in our custody and will undergo prosecution for the murder of those who died at the Hotel De Ville and, as an enemy of the state of France. Believe me, monsieur, this is not over and your cooperation at this point would serve you well."

"I am merely a student," cried Ahmad, growing weary of the argument.

"Yes, a student raised in a radical madrasah," Inspector Bissette replied.

"That proves nothing," Ahmad bellowed. "You cannot hold me, I will not allow it!"

"Oh, but we can and we will," Inspector Bissette yelled back, his voice booming. "We have ample circumstantial evidence to hold you for quite some time for further questioning. Whether you are discharged by your physician or not, you will be escorted from this hospital to La Santé where you will remain in our custody."

"Have you forgotten, Inspector, that I am the victim?"

"Yes…the victim of your own actions. We believe whoever tried to kill you hoped your death would eliminate any trail leading to the Paris attacks, leaving us in the dark. It is the only explanation that fits. We can find no evidence that you were engaged in any legitimate business whatsoever."

"If you call the caretaker he…"

"The caretaker has vanished, monsieur, and the owner appears above suspicion. We have left a change of clothes for you with the nursing staff. They will bring it to your room this evening. By then, your transportation should be here."

Ahmad held his tongue. In his blazing eyes there was defiance so steely it almost unnerved the seasoned officer.

"There is no point evading the issue," said the inspector. Turning to go, he added, "The police are quite good at extracting whatever information they need…of this I can assure you."

Then, as an afterthought, pausing in the doorway Bissette said, "Your photograph, your fingerprints, and your biography, such as we know it, have been transmitted to every intelligence agency around the world, Monsieur Hasan. Should you try to escape, it would be most unfortunate. You will not last long on the streets, I assure you…Good day, monsieur." The inspector lumbered away while the smoke from both men's wrath hung heavily in the air.

Ahmad went into the lavatory to wash his hands and face. The water rinsed away his agitation, his mind calming as each splash of the cold clear liquid shivered his cheeks and soothed his eyes, his thoughts returning, like a surgical laser, sharply into focus.

It was obvious now that he would not be allowed to leave this institution a free man and, inevitably, the police would learn about his connection to the recent attacks in San Francisco and Paris. Ahmad was headed for incarceration in a French prison or maybe even worse: rendition to a country where torture was not only practiced, it was a perfected art form.

I will have to leave sooner than planned, Ahmad thought. They'll be coming for me tonight. This is my last chance. He sat for a long time revising his original plans. After careful consideration, he decided the five o'clock dinner service would afford the best cover.

Later that afternoon, just before dinner, a nurse brought a plain brown paper package and set it on his bed. "The Inspector sent this over for you."

Ahmad just stared so the nurse opened the parcel and pulled out a blue chambray shirt labeled with the name of the prison, denim jeans, white cotton undergarments, a pair of black nylon socks and athletic shoes, also dark blue.

The nurse took each item of clothing from the package and placed it in the closet opposite Ahmad's bed. "The Inspector wanted you to wear these so you do not have to travel in your hospital robe. I am so sorry you will not be going to our rehab center." She waited for Ahmad's reply. Ahmad had nothing to say and, within a few minutes, the nurse was off to see other patients.

Ahmad waited motionless for his dinner, posed like a big cat ready to spring. The minute the tray was delivered he asked for privacy to pray and closed the door. Then he shaved and dressed in the stolen street clothes, stuffing the pilfered cash into his right front pocket. Now he was ready, or as ready as could be. Set to see Betty one last time, he slipped on his usual blue hospital robe, hoping the guards would not notice, that underneath, he was dressed in street attire and not the prison garb brought to him by the nurse.

Ahmad, never glancing at the guards, crossed the hall and entered Betty's room. They looked at each other for what seemed like a long time, the old woman's face radiant, alight with a slight fever.

"Are you well, Madame Betty?" asked Ahmad, concerned.

"Who knows what well is?" Betty said. Although she did not look well, she was smiling. "Have you come to say goodbye to a mishuggah old woman? No need...our separation is only temporary...but you must go or you will miss your chance and that would be a real shondah. You think you got tsooris now? You don't know what's coming. The road ahead will be hard and painful but, remember, unless you put ore into the fire you will never get gold. Don't fear the fire...it is where the clay of self is molded. Now go...before I get all verklempt."

At that moment the door to Betty's hospital room swung open and in popped Ahmad's nurse, Noel. "I thought you might be in here, monsieur. I, um..." Seeing Ahmad shaved and in street clothes confused the nurse and she stuttered. "I...err, came in to ask you to get dressed...but I see you are ready. You look very different, monsieur...umm...strange. Never mind, the inspector persuaded your doctors to discharge you. Perhaps you can finish your visit with Madame Rosner now so that I can go over the physicians final instructions before you leave. The transport will be here within the next hour."

Ahmad did not move or speak.

Again Noel asked. "Would you like to say goodbye to Madame Rosner? I would prefer we speak privately, in your room."

Neither Ahmad nor Betty uttered a word.

"Shall we return to your room then, monsieur?" The nurse offered once more, holding wide the door.

Ahmad remained frozen, until, in frustration, Noel went to speak with the guards who were enjoying the company of the nurses.

"Monsieur Ahmad will not leave the old woman's side," she said to one of the policemen. "Perhaps you can convince him it's time to go."

When the guard entered Betty's room, Ahmad knew he must escape right then or he would not escape at all. With his heart pounding in his chest, his hands growing ice cold, sweat breaking out on his palms, and panic mounting, Ahmad instinctively, swung the bed table around and pushed it toward the guard, driving him backward and to the floor.

He instantly rushed to the window, tugging at its heavy frame, Betty's hospital bed now the only obstacle between him and the fallen policeman. The snap of a holster resounded in the room as the guard drew his weapon, shouting for the escaping man to stop. Ahmad, desperate and wild eyed, cursed the fates that brought him here.

"Turn around now, monsieur, or I will be forced to shoot," yelled the guard.

Ahmad ignored him, trying with all his might to pry open the frozen window. The window would not budge, not even a few centimeters. Beyond the glass he could see freedom and the sight tormented him.

The guard rushed to the side of the bed, raised his gun and shouted, "I order you to halt, monsieur."

Betty, fueled with adrenalin from the memories of the holocaust, shouted "No, no, no." Raising her hand, more quickly than the guard could anticipate, she grabbed hold of the policeman's arm, pleading with him to stop. The frantic guard, ignoring the tiny woman, continued to shout. "Stop! This is your last warning."

When she saw the guard pull back the hammer, cocking the gun in preparation to fire at the escaping suspect, Betty reached up and grabbed the policeman's hand and pulled on the gun. Her weight caused the policeman's arm to drop as he fired at Ahmad. The deflection was just enough to send the bullet through the right side of the old woman's frail and ailing body and blood from the exit wound spattered across the bed.

When he heard the shot, Ahmad instinctively spun around and saw the guard aghast, unmoving, a vacant stare glazing his eyes. In a single blur of motion, Ahmad leaped over the bed grabbing Betty's walker as he flew and with one powerful swing slammed it into the guard. The man fell unconscious to the floor, his body, a crumpled ball, slumped against the door.

Betty lay dying and looked up at Ahmad's grief-stricken face.

"I will not leave you here to die alone, Madame Betty," cried Ahmad.

There was shouting in the hallway. The door, blocked by the unconscious policeman's body, was slowly being forced open.

"Turn your face to the light," counseled the old woman, her voice barely audible. "I will be praying you follow it and that your shadow will always remain behind you."

He kissed her on the top of her head one last time. "Shapakeh, mama jan, Allah'u'akbar." Betty Rosner lay motionless on the bed, the tension gone, a serene smile gracing her aged face.

Ahmad looked up as the shouting guards pounded on the door. He launched his body over the bed with the agility of a cougar pouncing on its unsuspecting prey. In midair, he grabbed a bedside chair and, coming down, slammed it into the window, smashing the pane outward. Shards of glass spewed into the setting sun, sparkling like a shower of falling stars as they fell to the ground.

The police, still shouting, crashed through the door. Jumping onto the window ledge, Ahmad heard a gunshot meant to bring him down but the enraged policeman's bullet missed its mark. Hoping his weakened legs would propel him far enough out into space to reach the branches of the old oak tree, which had kept careful watch over the hospital grounds for a century or more, Ahmad sprang up and out into the void, arms open wide to the universe, agreeing to whatever fate would bring, trusting fully, the noble oak would catch him and secure his freedom.

His weary hands found purchase on an outermost branch. The tree, reaching out, hoping to save the desperate, frightened man from what would certainly be a fatal fall, extended a branch that yielded with swift kindness, bending toward the earth until Ahmad hovered just ten feet above the ground. In that instant, the escaped prisoner decided to go for the free fall. With only thoughts of liberation filling his mind, Ahmad refused to consider what fate held in store for his still fragile legs when they would meet the green earth below. Holding his breath, releasing his hands, he plummeted towards the ground while silently thanking the tree for its great bounty.

THE HUMAN STORM

Ahmad's body hit the ground at the same time he heard the tortured screech of car tires. He looked around for an escape route opposite the direction of the car he believed contained his captors. Still disoriented from the fall, Ahmad rolled onto his back. While gathering his strength and wits, he heard a woman's frantic voice.

"Monsieur, are you alright?" She flung open her car door, jumped out, and came running to help the fallen man. "What in God's name happened? You fell from the sky and nearly scared me to death! I almost hit you!"

Just behind her, Ahmad could see the open door of a small yellow Volkswagen hybrid, absent its driver, idling on the road that ran past the hospital and into the commune. The woman stayed at Ahmad's side as he rose on shaking legs and tried to regain his balance. She put her hand out to steady the faltering stranger, but Ahmad pushed her aside and stumbled toward the open car door.

The woman, watching Ahmad limping toward her unoccupied auto, began screaming but her cries were drowned out by the wail of sirens in the distance as police cars made their way to Saint Joan's.

With only moments to spare, Ahmad dove through the open driver's side door and pulled it shut. He gunned the engine and, slamming the gears into reverse, backed up, turned the car around and drove away from the sound of the sirens, nearly colliding with another passenger car coming toward him from the opposite direction.

Racing along the road, speeding by the homes and businesses of Saint-Gatien-des-Bois, Ahmad whispered farewell to Saint Joan's Hospital, imploring Antoinette and Betty to guide and protect him on his way.

Ahmad had planned his escape with great care, sneaking one night behind the receptionist's desk at the nursing station to grab the local phone book. The directory had a street map that included the area surrounding Caen and extending as far as Saint-Gatien-des-Bois.

He navigated the car's route by comparing the hospital address with his memory of the map. He knew it would take him to the airfield by way of Route D74 and he thanked Allah for having been given a means of escape. Now he could only hope that his luck would hold out and there would be no police cars along the route. He could still hear the sirens screaming behind him and he pressed down on the accelerator. Tears stung his eyes as the memory of Betty, dying in his arms, on his behalf, flooded his senses. Saying a silent prayer for Allah to take her into his care, Ahmad wiped away the tears and set about completing his mission.

As the car sped down the road, Ahmad calculated his next move. He needed to contact Farzam, Sholeh's brother, and ask him to bring the satchel Ahmad left in Habib's care. In it were the documents he now urgently needed, a change of clothing, and the small sum of money originally stowed in preparation for his escape after the Paris attack.

Grabbing the green leather handbag left on the passenger seat when the owner fled her car, Ahmad pulled open the flap and turned it over, dumping its contents on the seat beside him. Picking out the woman's cell phone, Ahmad flipped it open and began to fiddle with the buttons. The phone was a quick study and Ahmad was presently pressing the keys connecting him directly with Sholeh's brother.

"Salam."

"Ahmad, where are you? We have all been so worried."

"I am well, Farzam-joon, but I need a favor."

"Anything, Ahmad. You know I would do anything for you."

"Praised be to God for sending me such a brother."

"What is it, Ahmad? What can I do for you?"

"Do you remember the backpack I left with your father?"

"Yes, of course."

"Do you know where he is keeping it?"

"I am not sure but I will ask."

"No, Farzam. I do not want to worry your father now. It is best that he does not know. In due time, I will contact him and explain everything."

"I have never deceived my father, Ahmad."

"I am asking in good faith that you do this, not only for me, but for the glory of Allah and as a protection to both your parents."

"I will do what you ask, Ahmad, my brother. You know I have always trusted you. I am certain I will find your belongings...the apartment is small and there are only a few places my father could have hidden it. I will help you in any way I can."

"I am in your deep debt, Farzam. There is a small private airfield just before you reach the town of Saint-Gatien-des Bois. Do you know of this town?

"Saint-Gatien. Yes, of course, I know. It is in Normandy."

"Yes. You will need directions. Do you have a pen and paper?"

"Of course. Just a moment."

Ahmad waited only a few seconds before Farzam's voice told him he was ready. Ahmad dictated directions to the Saint Gatien Airport.

"You will follow the directions, exactly. If all goes well, and you find the backpack, you should arrive just after sunset. As you approach the airfield, you will see small aircraft lined up along the perimeter of a parking field just off the runway. Beside it, is a farm with fields of corgettes. When you come to the field, slow down and dim your lights. There is a small, whitewashed cottage with a high-peaked, thatched roof along the road. It is an abandoned farmhouse bordered by a white split-rail fence running in front of the hedgerow. Turn off your headlights and pull into the drive and come around to the rear entrance. The windows are boarded up and you will not see any lights. I will be waiting for you at the back of the house among the trees. Do you understand, my brother?"

"Yes…yes, of course. I have it all."

"If there is a light in the window, or any evidence the house is occupied, drive past. If you see any police patrols on the road do not stop. Drive into the town, turn around, and wait a while. When you come back, if you sense it is too dangerous, drop the bag in the weeds on the opposite side of the road from the airport sign and go home. I will retrieve it. If you are not here by ten o'clock, I will know you could not find the bag. I will leave without it. Can you do this for me?"

"Of course I can…and I will. It is a privilege for me to be able to help, Ahmad-joon. Where are you going…can I ask?"

"I must leave the country, right away. It is best that I not discuss my plans right now."

"I want to go with you, Ahmad!"

"Ah, my loyal friend and brother, you are my salvation and my blessing, but I cannot allow you to follow me at present. Right now, it is too dangerous, Farzam-joon. Perhaps in due time…we shall see."

"Why? Where are you going? Are you putting yourself in danger? Will we ever see you again?"

"I must leave France. That is all I can say right now, my brother. Please do not ask me to explain. In due time, you will know exactly where I am and why…when it is safe. Do you understand?"

"Yes, you will contact me and let me know you are safe?"

"Yes, Farzam, yes, somehow I will do that for you, my brother. Allah'u'Akbar."

Once Ahmad finished the conversation, he pressed the power key, turning off the phone, so that his whereabouts could not be detected and, placed it deliberately into his jacket pocket.

Ahmad arrived at Saint Gatien Airport and began to look for a place to ditch the yellow Volkswagen. He decided to pull into a deep stand of trees on one of the secondary roads that ran alongside a wood bordering the airfield. He would walk from there to the outermost perimeter of the wood and remain in the safety of the trees, watching for any possible police activity in the area. Soon, he was able to steal across the road and force his way into the abandoned farmhouse.

By ten o'clock that night Ahmad was ready to leave France. Farzam arrived at the little cottage only forty-five minutes past the time Ahmad calculated. He had been especially careful to avoid the extra police patrols in the area but now, sure to his word, Farzam had brought Ahmad's belongings. Farzam greeted his friend with a warm hug and then pulled the backpack from the car's back seat and handed it to Ahmad.

With an anxious laugh and a slap on Farzam's back, Ahmad knelt down and opened the bag. A great sigh escaped his lips as a quick survey of the bag's contents revealed all the original items were there and untouched.

"Praise be to Allah and may Habib be blessed with all His bountiful favors," Ahmad prayed.

The joyful reunion lasted only a moment, replaced with regret and sorrow as Ahmad, giving Farzam a final insistent directive to get in his car and head back to Paris, watched his friend's vibrant body change from intense excitement to a dejected boy as he rolled the car away with sad reluctance.

Ahmad watched the car disappear down the drive, then walked back into the deserted house and spilled the contents of the bag onto the floor. An hour later, he had deciphered the sixth card and knew his destination was to be Selcuk, Turkey.

Selcuk, hmmm, Ahmad pondered. Why does that place strike a familiar cord?

Several moments went by as Ahmad, carefully returning everything to the bag, puzzled over the question. Slipping on the backpack, Ahmad headed out to the airfield, preoccupied with thoughts of the flight ahead.

"Where have I heard this name before?" He rolled it around, again and again, the question dogging him.

Ahmad put the idea out of his mind and continued through the field of nearly ripe corgettes. He pulled two of the largest from their vines and stuffed one in each pocket of his jacket. As he crossed the field, Ahmad scanned the area for signs of life but there did not seem a soul about. He remembered Gaspard mentioning that the airfield was saving a small fortune by suspending night security.

Noticing the bright orange windsock hanging from an aluminum pole fluttering with lazy ease in the gentle night air, Ahmad calculated the wind's speed and direction for takeoff; the sock reminding him of a kite he, and his only childhood friend, flew in the fields behind his boyhood home.

"My God! That's it!" muttered Ahmad. "Shahin! My mother wrote me that he moved to Selcuk. I wonder how he is faring. What did she say he was doing? What was it?"

As he reached the edge of the field he thought, I know, she said he bought a fruit and vegetable stall in the souk. Allah's blessings be upon you, Shahin. Shouldn't be too hard to find you...I will make a point of it.

Ahmad crossed onto the tarmac where a row of five small aircraft slept for the night bathed in the dim glow of the yellow and red lamps lining either side of the runway. Ahmad headed for the plane at the end of the row that seemed to be waiting in anxious anticipation of a pilot. The plane was a little silver beauty with gold and purple feathered detailing and, on the tail, an emblem: the same golden symbol proudly displayed at the chateau and, indeed, the very same symbol on the outside of the madrasah he attended as a boy.

Ahmad caught his breath in awe and reverence at the magical sight of the Pilatus PC-12. The thought that he was about to steal, and probably destroy, this state-of-the-art, fully-outfitted, multi-million dollar aircraft filled him with a perverse sense of satisfaction, tempered with a twinge of sadness. He praised Allah for this gift, the means of his escape, and hoped that the plane's gas tank was full and that one tank would manage the distance to Selcuk.

Shaking off any worries, Ahmad ducked under the plane's nose and pulled away the wheel chocks that kept the plane from rolling, tossing them onto the grass. He then disconnected the tie down cables, throwing them sufficiently off to the side to ensure they would not tangle in the wheels as he left the aircraft's parking spot.

When that was done, Ahmad circled once around the plane, and then circled once again, inspecting the wings, windshield, and wheels, looking out for any signs the plane had been tampered with and might not be worthy to fly. Satisfied the aircraft was intact, Ahmad opened the cockpit door and hopped inside, stowing his backpack behind the seat. Groping through the semi-darkness, he found a small interior light and, flicking the switch, caught sight of the aeronautical charts stowed in the narrow compartment anchored to the floor beside his seat.

Looking more closely at the interior, Ahmad could see that nothing had been touched since his last visit. He fastened the harness tightly over his chest and hips, feeling fortuitous that the plane, meant for the cell's escape after the Paris attacks, had been sitting idle, waiting for his return.

Ahmad quickly checked to ensure his trim, flaps, and all other control surfaces were working correctly. Once satisfied, he punched the code given to him by Gaspard into the keypad, unlocking the aircraft's ignition and flight systems. Turning the battery switch to the 'on' position, he proceeded to check his radio, the calibration of the instruments, and fuel gage. He was happy to find the tank was full.

Next, Ahmad needed to set the course he would take to Selcuk; a matter made infinitely easy by the use of the plane's Honeywell Primus Integrated flight and navigation system. It contained the entire package of equipment needed to fly the plane, from basic instrumentation to advanced GPS based navigation. It even had weather radar which would tell Ahmad what could be expected as he flew through variable weather conditions over Europe.

The package also contained a Traffic Collision Avoidance System that would keep his plane from colliding with any other aircraft in his vicinity. The system would receive a signal from approaching flights yet they would not see Ahmad once he turned off the plane's transponder. The sky was a big place and primary radar would have a difficult task tracking his small, composite aircraft as it flew out to sea in the dead of night without navigation lights. It made him virtually invisible.

Ahmad fired up the GPS and typed 'Selcuk, Turkey' into the keypad on the touchscreen, waiting for the instant search function to complete its work of listing the possible airports into which he could fly. Although Ahmad would ditch the plane without ever touching down on the tarmac, he selected Selcuk Efes Airport, and set his system for the airport's non-directional beacon: a navigational aid located within the airport that would prompt his GPS to plot the most direct route. In seconds, all the information required to fly to Selcuk appeared on the screen.

Ahmad started the engine and began to roll. He turned the plane onto the taxiway and, moments later, arrived at the intersection that would take him onto the runway. Upon entering the runway, the spotlights from the control tower came on in a blaze and his radio crackled to life.

"This is, Jean, in the control tower," said the disembodied voice. "I have no flight plan filed for you. Please identify yourself."

Ahmad continued to accelerate, as the ground controller's voice grew louder and increasingly emphatic. "You must stop your plane! You are not authorized to leave this airport. I will track you…"

Ahmad turned off the radio and began to gently pull back on the yoke. As his plane gathered speed he heard, over the roar of the engine, sirens from the control tower begin to sound. In the next instant, the plane was in the air, climbing at five hundred meters per minute, heading north by northwest. He glanced down to see a line of police lights whirling through the streets below, headed toward the airport. Commanding the aircraft to make a one hundred ten degree turn, east by southeast, he headed out over the English Channel.

The GPS informed Ahmad there were fifteen hundred and sixty-four flying miles to Selcuk. At his preset cruising speed, he'd arrive in approximately five hours. He would abandon the plane an hour before daybreak, with approximately one hundred eight miles of fuel to spare - more than enough to send his very expensive toy out into the turquoise of the Aegean Sea, on autopilot, while its human pilot parachuted to safety.

Ahmad cruised along over France at an altitude of twenty-five thousand feet. With the plane fast approaching the border, he left behind, for the final time, a journey that began with so much promise. Mulling over the events of the past few years, the young Iranian national wondered what might have been if Sholeh had not been killed and he had followed her into a different future. He thought of how their future once looked so bright and how there had really been no choice, once she was gone, but to follow the course given to him by the mullahs of his childhood. To him, it seemed, God had chosen his destiny.

Ahmad, shaking off the sadness, turned his thoughts to Paris, imagining countless ways in which he could have thought quicker, planned smarter, and acted more efficiently. As he analyzed the events at the Hotel De Ville, he remembered the stranger at the bar, the familiar stranger who seemed to recognize him.

While he scanned the instruments and the sky for other aircraft, Ahmad was also scanning his subconscious for clues to the identity of the man at the bar. Did I see the man pull the fire alarm? How did he know of the attack? Who was he? Where have I seen that face?

The hours zipped by and soon the instruments alerted Ahmad he had arrived in Turkish airspace. The computer guided the airplane's descent to three thousand feet. He had programmed the route so the plane would fly in from the west over the Aegean Sea, make a tight turn at the airport, and head east, back out over open water. He would jump about one mile in from the shoreline and aim for Wild Pamucek Beach – ground zero for a soft, unobstructed landing.

The range display indicated there was about fifty-five miles of fuel: enough to send the plane back over the Aegean where it would fall out of the sky into the Ikaria Trough, sinking to a depth of thirty-seven hundred feet and guaranteeing that recovery would be virtually impossible. Since the owners of the plane would never be identified, the plane's disappearance would remain, forever, a mystery.

The aircraft turned over the airport and headed back out to sea. Ahmad could imagine the air traffic controllers having a heart attack as they heard the sound of the unidentifiable aircraft. He slipped off his harness and into the parachute. The rectangular chute, a ram-air model used by BASE jumpers, was designed to inflate in such a way as to lessen the jolt of the parachute's deployment. It afforded Ahmad excellent control over his speed and direction as he fell.

At three thousand feet, a height reserved for experienced jumpers, Ahmad pushed open the plane's door against the wind, slid over the wing, glancing one last time at the fine aircraft, and jumped out into the darkened sky. Almost immediately, his chute opened with a whoosh and dragged him abruptly upward, the pressure making him lightheaded. As he ascended, an image flashed across his vision: it was a vision of himself as a boy, sitting at the fountain outside the madrasah with a young man beside him. In that instant, Ahmad connected the identity of the man at the bar with the man at the fountain. Gliding down through the cool night air, expertly steering the chute toward the tranquil beach that lay below, illumined by the sparkle of the setting moon on the gently lapping waves, Ahmad strained his memory. What was his name? Ah, yes, David Effendi, is what I called him. I made a pact that day, a sworn oath.

When he landed on the beach, Ahmad rolled up the parachute and found a break between two rocks and jammed it inside. He pulled up some of the grasses and other foliage growing on the dunes and stuffed them on top of the chute, hoping it would be many days before anyone might notice the site and catch a glimpse of the red and yellow canopy.

Climbing up the bank through the brush, he found himself on a shore road that traveled north and south. Walking north, about a quarter mile, Ahmad came upon a luxury resort, its many buildings surrounded by a stone wall about five feet in height.

Midway down the length of the wall, Ahmad spotted a gate. He peered through the bars into the darkness within and saw an open door, its illuminated interior revealing what appeared to be an entryway into the resort's kitchen. Leaning against the outside wall was a bicycle with a large delivery basket attached to the front handlebars.

Ahmad glanced around and found no sign of anyone in the yard. He pushed against the gate and it swung open. He stole down the walkway and, in the next few seconds, was riding down Dr. Sabri Yayla Boulevard with the deliveryman's bicycle, enjoying the crisp predawn air, his backpack neatly resting in the basket. Happy that the four mile trip into Selcuk would be short and sweet, he peddled faster.

Upon the first signs of habitation, Ahmad left the bike just outside the city, standing against a tall and twisted olive tree; ancient, glistening in the early rays of dawn, its leaves changing color from deep green to silver at the whim of the sea breezes blowing in from the Aegean. Although he could not remember why, the tree reminded him of Antoinette.

Walking the rest of the way into the town center, he asked directions to the souk and wound his way through the city streets toward the bazaar. The marketplace was teeming with life as its vendors, intent upon the business of the day, shouted at each other over their stalls, while setting out displays of fresh fish, meats, and produce; coffee, teas, dried peas and beans; fresh-baked breads and cakes; jewelry, clothing and all manner of household wares.

Ahmad's mouth watered as the delicious aromas of the souk filled his nostrils, reminding him it had been many hours since his last meal. Hunger trumped his search for Shahin. Rummaging through his pockets, the ravenous man pulled out several bills from the top pocket of his shirt and bought breakfast at a stall whose merchant would accept the European notes he offered. He sat down at a small round café table, watching the rising sun, when a stranger came over and asked if he could share the table. Ahmad nodded and the pair ate in silence until the newly arrived fugitive struck up a conversation.

"Pardon me, effendi." Ahmad said in broken Turkish. "I am looking for a Persian gentleman who operates a produce stall in the souk."

"Ah, of course," replied the man, instantly, "You must mean Shahin."

"Why, yes," Ahmad said, surprised.

"You will find him selling his fruits and vegetables in a stall with some Capucian nuns at the end of the lane. The nuns care for St. Mary's Shrine and Shahin sells the vegetables they grow...kind man...I am sure I would not sacrifice part of my own income for a bunch of nuns. He takes the Quranic injunction, exhorting us to be kind to Christians, a little too seriously for my taste." The man let out a thunderous laugh and downed the rest of his coffee. "The nuns use the money to pay for their humble living expenses. I guess he will go to heaven for that."

"Yes, I suppose he will," said Ahmad in a perfunctory manner.

The stranger rose, thanked Ahmad for the hospitality, and hurried on his way.

Ahmad finished his breakfast of yogurt and dill, scooped up in a still warm pita, savoring every delectable bite, wiping his mouth on his sleeve when he was done. He sat a while, sipping coffee, enjoying the atmosphere of the souk. With his belly satisfied and his mind refreshed, Ahmad set off down the lane in search of Shahin.

I wonder if I will recognize him, Ahmad thought, as he strolled along, surveying the multifarious wares of the merchants along the route. I wonder if he will recognize me!

Ahmad found Shahin exactly where the stranger said and, to his delight, recognized his old friend straight away. Still, he felt a bit shy about approaching the busy man, his stall already jammed with early-bird shoppers, bargaining over prices, vying with their neighbors for the best and freshest produce. Shahin learned to come extra early to the market for the customers who insisted on being there even before its official opening. He was often sold out of some items before he finished unloading the first crates from his truck. Ahmad hung back in the crowd, observing his friend, a small but discernable smile on his face. His friend looked happy and prosperous and that made Ahmad glad.

The sun was at its midday zenith when the crowds finally began to thin. Shahin glanced up and noticed a man standing off to the side. He bent down to fetch another crate and began to restock his tables when, suddenly, he stopped and peered back at the stranger. A grin burst upon his mouth, lighting up his face like a flame, and he began to laugh, pointing at his friend.

"Ahmad?" he shouted, "Could it really be you?"

Shahin dropped the melons he was holding and practically jumped over the stall's tables. He sprinted over to Ahmad, threw his arms around his old friend, and lifted him in the air.

"Thanks be to Allah! I never thought I would see you again! What in heaven's name are you doing here?"

"Shahin, my friend! You remembered!"

"Of course!" Shahin said. "Of course, of course, I remember my boyhood friend...but what happened to the skinny kid that went off to Tehran?"

Signaling for Ahmad to wait, Shahin turned around and walked back to the stall, whispered a few words to one of the nuns, who was haggling with a customer, then pulled off his apron and threw it into the back of his truck.

"Come, my friend. I will take you to visit my home."

"I did not mean to interrupt your business. I can come back later, after you have closed for the day."

"Nonsense, my friend, the nuns can handle the stall for a few hours. Allah knows I have done it many times for them."

"Are you sure?"

"Yes, yes. Come. You must meet my wife. She is very beautiful... a Turkish lady...but what can you do? At least, she makes fine love and can cook food for the gods."

"I had not heard you married."

"Married, why, yes...yes! And children...praise be Allah, we have two healthy, strong boys and another on the way. My wife is hoping for a little girl to dress up like a doll. Typical woman! What brings you to our part of the world, Ahmad?"

Ahmad muttered something about a business deal. Shahin regarded Ahmad's comment with one eyebrow raised but deferred to his friend and dropped the matter.

Shahin asked about Ahmad and his family, whether he had married and, when Ahmad replied that he had not, Shahin slapped his friend on the back and quipped, "Not to worry, my wife will find you a fine Turkish princess in no time."

Ahmad just smiled, wondering what Sholeh would think about that.

Shahin's wife, Bahar, whose name meant 'spring of life', was every bit as beautiful as she had been described, with warm, amber almond-shaped eyes sparkling under lush, black lashes. She was every bit as gracious, as well, and the food she set out for her husband and his guest was what certainly could have been described as a Turkish delight beyond measure.

Bahar never spoke a word beyond her greeting, but she listened intently to the two men as they laughed and ate, reminiscing about boyhood adventures in the time before Ahmad was sent away to the madrasah.

Shahin wanted to know every detail of his friend's life since they had played together in the countryside surrounding Shiraz but Ahmad was an insular man, of necessity, adept at turning the attention back to Shahin with every query. He did tell him about his time in Paris with Sholeh and her family, and the tragic events that led to her death.

"Yes, I was following the riots in the news, as was everyone," said Shahin. "I am most very sorry to hear of your loss." Bahar, still silent and attentive, nodded her head in agreement, her expression conveying, with subtle eloquence, the compassion she felt for her husband's closest boyhood friend. Her husband had spoken of Ahmad many times over the years and Bahar felt as though she knew him too. Ahmad, seeing the kindness in her eyes, thought Shahin had chosen well. Bahar was as beautiful inside as out.

There was a long silence as the men finished their coffee. Bahar, up and clearing the table, laid out plates of sweets, the centerpiece of which was a hand-painted ceramic platter with many shades of blue, containing diamond-shaped pieces of baklava dripping with thick, rich honey.

The samovar on the table gently bubbled a fragrant jasmine tea and Bahar poured both men a glass held in cup holders with delicate filigree patterns cut into the silver. They piled their desert plates high. Shahin invited Ahmad to sit in the lounge while his wife repaired to the kitchen to clean up after the meal.

Ahmad asked his friend many questions about life in Turkey, partly as a way to avoid discussing his own clandestine past, but mostly because he was sincerely fascinated by the colorful details of his host's stories. Shahin especially enjoyed telling Ahmad about Turkish culture and history, something Ahmad missed in a school focused on Islamic studies.

Shahin described the importance of the Selcuk area and the House of the Virgin Mary, the Meryem Ana Evi, on the Hill of the Nightingale.

"I must take you to visit there, Ahmad. It is just seven kilometers from here...such a peaceful place of prayer for both Christians and Muslims. You can meet my nuns!"

"Are these the nuns...the ones at the market with you...who live there?" asked Ahmad, his attention slowly morphing into alarm as the adrenaline started to pump. The stilted change in his voice was not lost on Shahin.

"That's right," replied Shahin, "I have been helping them for the last several years. It is my offering for all the good they do at the Shrine. It is not much but it is something to repay their charity."

Shahin went on. "There is a path behind Mary's House that climbs up to the top of the mountain and ends at a rocky peak from where you can see all of Ephesus and the sea studded with islands. The house, itself, is surrounded by fertile hills and grottos that once served as homes – now, all but Mary's are gone. The trees have smooth trunks and the pyramidal shapes they cast on the ground make them seem like sentries protecting the mountain. I will take you there. Bahar will prepare a lunch for us."

The thought of this made Ahmad twist in his chair, his body now turned slightly away from his friend. Shahin noticed the small gesture of discomfort but thought it best, for the moment, to hold back any comment.

"It is becoming quite famous, you know, Ephesus. They are holding a conference of religions here this week. That is why there were so many more tourists than usual in the market this morning. We will go together, you and me. It is a most auspicious occasion...a great honor for us...they have even sent David Anderson from America to cover the event worldwide on Global News."

"David Anderson," repeated Ahmad, practically in a whisper, echoing his swirling thoughts.

"Why, of course," said Shahin, "Surely, you must know of him...the entire world is watching his reports since the poor fellow lost his own father in the San Francisco attacks. I don't know how he goes on reporting, night after night...he was almost killed in Paris at the Hotel de Ville…surely you have heard…he must have the courage of a lion."

Ahmad finally connected all the dots: the man at the bar in Paris with the press badge on his lapel; the man whose face he saw as the parachute opened; the man at the fountain in Tehran - they were the same man and now, bursting forth from the deepest well of his memory, he heard a boy on the cusp of manhood say, I swear to never harm you or any of your family.

Noticing Ahmad's skin turning the color of dusty sandals, Shahin could not ignore the dour look on his friend's face, or the truth, any longer. "You are in trouble, my friend…I have seen your picture on the news reports…except now you look very much different. The police believe you were involved in the Paris terror attack. The world is looking for you, Ahmad. Are they lying?"

Ahmad rose from the chair, legs shaking, his voice trembling, "I beg you, my brother, to hold your tongue. There is something I must do and, if I survive, I promise to tell you everything. Will you do this for me?"

Shahin did not hesitate for a second. "I have a small bungalow behind the house for our guests. You may stay there as long as you like. The police would not think to look around here."

"There is nothing I can ever do to repay your kindness. May Allah bless you, and your family, for all time."

Shahin went over to a heavy ornate desk sitting in the far corner of the lounge. He opened the top draw and pulled out a key. Handing it to Ahmad, he said, "Enough for this afternoon, my friend. You look exhausted."

"I have not slept in two days," Ahmad responded.

"Go. Have a warm bath and a good sleep. Bahar will leave a light supper in front of your door in case you awaken and feel hungry. I will see you in the morning, my brother."

Ahmad thanked his friend and left the house. He found the bungalow small but comfortable, and he took a long, hot bath. When he felt thoroughly cleansed of the last several days, he climbed into the bed and fell fast asleep. Dreaming dark dreams, he awoke in darkness, the sun well below the horizon. With the stars and moon rising overhead, it was time to go and meet his cell.

Its silver discolored or missing in spots, its glass cracked, hanging from a frayed wire, the mirror reflected more than the image of the man standing before it. Indeed, it was an abstraction of the shabby room where it hung, capturing the seedy surroundings while, at the same time, part of them. The man standing in front of the mirror was completing touchups on his face; a dab here, a brushstroke there. When he was done, he stepped back to admire the delicate and meticulous handiwork before closing the lid of the theatrical cosmetics kit and on his former identity.

A darker complexion, a wider nose, full salt and pepper short-cropped beard, brown tinted contact lenses; all made the transformation remarkable and, more, impossible to detect. Brian Saunders was positive he could easily sell his newly acquired Middle Eastern persona.

After rechecking his weapon, for the third time, and stuffing a small Qur'an into an empty pocket, Saunders was ready: ready to assume the role of leader, captain, imam, mentor, ready to assume Ahmad's authority, ready for anything, but mostly, for redemption in the eyes of the Brotherhood. Checking the alarm clock next to the bed, noticing it was almost eleven, he departed, rushing to meet the cell members who would carry out his orders and the Brotherhood's plan.

Saunders slid into a black Škoda Fabia, a super mini compact whose engineers, he thought, must have designed it for children. Squeezing into the front seat, the steering wheel pressed against his chest, he drove to the outskirts of Selcuk, stopping in front of a cheerless whitewashed building constructed from concrete block.

Saunders pushed open the door and scanned his surroundings, making sure it was safe to enter the building. He found four men in the middle of a large, open space, lounging on aging wooden chairs, drinking Turkish coffee, and playing Tawula.

A wave of satisfaction swept over him as Saunders noticed, with pride, how his own appearance matched, so closely, that of the men in the room. When he stepped inside, their activity came to a sudden stop. The man closest to Saunders drew a pistol. A second stepped forward.

"What is your business here?"

Saunders didn't respond. It was a risky move but he enjoyed the adrenaline high of danger. Reaching into his coat, his slow and deliberate movements meant to quell the fears of the man pointing a gun at him, he produced the Qur'an. Opening to a bookmarked page, he read out loud a highlighted passage, slammed shut the prayer book, and glared at the men with aggressive authority.

The men backed off and acknowledged their leader, just as Saunders knew they would. Each produced a card; one side printed with an embossed gold mark, the other side, with short incantations in Arabic. The cards were handed, without a word, over to Saunders. He went to the table, pushed aside the Tawula board and authenticated their identities.

Pleased with the results, and a newly discovered feeling of power, Saunders called the men over and instructed them to sit and listen up.

"From now on, you call me Hadi. I know I speak different from you...but I was sent to America when I was a kid and raised there...so I could move around undetected, get it? Now they send me here. If ya don't mind, we speak English. Any questions?"

The man with the gun, an intemperate Albanian named Lorenc, glanced at the faces of the other men, and asked, "Why would they send someone from America?"

"All I know is the guy that was supposed to be here disappeared and they sent me in his place. I don't ask questions and you shouldn't either!"

The answer was less than satisfying and tension was growing in the room. Saunders suggested praying for success and to the glory of the 'Almighty,' as he called it. He lowered his head and, with feigned humility, asked the men to select an imam. It was his usual routine and much like the act he pulled standing outside Merilee Brunswick's door.

There was little doubt about the matter, and the men chose a prayer leader; a gaunt man, short of stature, with drawn eyes. The man, turning toward the Qiblih, began to lead the men in prayer.

Saunders followed him closely, duplicating every motion as the men prayed, trying to look like this all came naturally to him, hoping the others would not notice his hesitant and awkward movements.

"Where are the weapons?" asked Saunders, moving swiftly to the next order of business when the prayer ended, feeling confident his authority would go unchallenged.

"There, in those crates." replied the prayer leader. "RPG 32s...smuggled by al-Qaeda during the Libyan uprising. We should thank the American government for deposing Gaddafi."

"Yes...thank you," said the man with the gun, staring at Saunders.

"I told ya, I ain't American." Saunders snapped. "I was sent there...that's all there is to it...okay?"

"Yes...yes..." the gunman said, relenting for the moment.

"How many we got?" Saunders asked.

"Four launchers...eight antipersonnel grenades and four antitank grenades," replied the prayer leader.

"Those are freakin' big crates for a few launchers."

"There are six Kalashnikovs with ammo as well."

"Good...good." Saunders was pleased. "That should be enough ordnance to level a small town and hold off the security forces. And the other stuff?"

The man who first confronted Saunders, a bald man with tired eyes, brought over and opened a medium sized trunk. "The costumes are in here."

Saunders, looking inside, noted various religious garments: bisht, thowb, kufis; black and grey clerical shirts with white collars, cassocks, habits in several colors, tricivara, rabbinical robes. More than enough to cover all the religions coming to the conference, he figured. Reaching into the bottom of the box and fishing around, Saunders pulled out a package marked: Attn: Hadi. So far everything was going well - right to plan.

He gathered the men into a tight semicircle and spilling the contents of the package onto the table, said, "Ahh, excellent. Here's the credentials we'll need to walk around the conference grounds. The security requirements are not so strict for religious leaders as for your secular government types, so I don't think anyone will bother checking too closely…it ain't like the Pope will be there."

Displaying a map, included in the package, he continued, "Look here. This half circle that looks like a football stadium cut in half, is the Odeon Great Theater. We'll use it as our point of reference. In front of it, you'll see a group of flat roof buildings…the toilets, first aid station, and police are there. Now, you see this road in front of the theater? It's called Harbor Street…between that road and the buildings…right in front of the theater…they set up tents for the conference. The closest one is the media tent; this one in the back is for the food service and these two are for delegate meetings."

Pausing, and looking around the room, Saunders asked, "Everyone savvy…I mean, do you get it?"

"We understand," replied Lorenc, gesturing for Saunders to continue.

"Good…good…we're on the same page." Pointing with renewed enthusiasm at the map, Saunders kept going. "So…as you can see the Great Theater is built into a steep hill with some trees and good brush cover. Okay…tomorrow…say about four in the morning, we'll go to the top of that hill from the other side. Directly behind the theater, right here, along the tree line, we stash the RPGs here and the AKs one hundred feet away on each side…here and here. Then we'll come back and change into the clerical outfits, get the IDs and go to the opening event. The conference schedule says invocations and opening remarks are to be held starting at daybreak, about five miles away at a house at the top of Bulbuldagi mountain…here…called Mary's Shrine. We will attend, all dressed up in our pretty little costumes, and walk back in the procession to the theater."

"Why must we walk," asked one of the men.

"Good question. It's a long walk, about two hours. During it, you try to strike up a conversation with people in your religious group. Your job is to plant seeds of fear, conspiracy-type stuff that makes them think other groups are plotting an assassination. Whip 'em up…get them at each other's throats, express outrage at insults to the Prophet Mohammad…whatever it takes. If we are lucky, it will even start a few riots. Mostly, make sure the reporters hear it…that's the key. The scripts, here on the table, have some ideas."

Flipping through one of the scripts, the prayer leader asked, "What purpose is it to make them believe there are groups from the other religions insulting their holy messengers or plotting to kill them?"

"I don't know and I don't question orders! Our orders are to bust up this meeting and that is just what we are going to do. By the time we are done, they'll hate each other forever. When the procession gets to the Great Theater, they'll start making speeches. We slip back up the hill...you two, take up the flanking positions and you and me will handle the RPGs. When the speeches are over and they go into the tents, we'll fire as many grenades as we can, then hightail it out, back down the way we came up. A car will be waiting. If anyone comes up the hill, you guys fire at them with the AKs. Oh...I almost forgot...do you know how to use these weapons?"

"We know!" The prayer leader insisted.

"I know the weapons; I don't know you." Lorenc said with a menacing roughness, his hand inching slowly toward the gun.

Brian Saunders quickly produced his pistol and glared at the man. "Don't do it, partner...I may not like you, you may not like me, but I was assigned to lead this mission and I'm gonna lead it. Now, if you want to...what the hell was that?"

"A noise...outside...I heard it." said the man with tired eyes. He went over to the cache of weapons, removed two AK 107 assault rifles and handed one to the transient prayer leader.

Saunders raised his weapon, motioning for the men to be quiet. He stood perfectly still, prepared to fire on anyone entering the building. Several seconds passed as they waited, turned off the nearest lights and waited some more. While holding their breath, in the semi darkness, they kept waiting. A tap-tap-tap came from the door, then a man's voice reciting several lines from the Qur'an. The men looked at each other, puzzled, anxious.

"Identify yourself," Saunders yelled.

"Ahmad Hasan," came the reply. "I am coming in."

Every light in the room was switched on as Ahmad approached, both assault rifles trained on the stranger with the pensive grey-black eyes. Lorenc, intending to frisk Ahmad, moved cautiously toward him but he stopped in mid-stride, a grin stretching the corners of his mouth, "Ahmad Effendi...welcome...welcome, my brother." Turning to the others, he said in Arabic, "Put those guns down, this is Ahmad Hasan. We trained together in the camps...you must recognize him from the news...this is the imam from Paris...a great man...a great servant of Allah...an instrument of punishment for the Great Satan."

In English, he told Saunders that Ahmad was their leader.

God damn it, was the first thought in Brian Saunders head, things aren't going so well any longer. It was no surprise, considering his line of business. Saunders didn't expect Ahmad to show up but the orders were to kill him if he did. Now things were complicated. The other men embraced Ahmad and it was obvious who they would choose as their leader. He fumed inside, these camel-jockeys all stick together, they hate me 'cause I'm not in their goddamn club. I can't whack Hasan now; they'll kill me for sure...I'll get the bastard later, when this is all over.

Cunning was Brian Saunders' greatest talent. With the guile of a sideshow huckster, he joined the group, pushing aside the prayer leader, grabbing hold of Ahmad's shoulders, shaking him like a favorite nephew or an old high school chum. With a sigh of relief, he said, "Thank God, you're all right. We thought you must have been killed or captured in Paris. Whew! It's a good thing you showed. You're in charge now."

Ahmad, still troubled by the attempt on his life at the château, did not trust Saunders. He broke free from his grasp and said to the men, "In the great wisdom of Allah, my faith is being tested, but through the strength of the Most Holy One, I am here to finish my work. Praise be upon Allah and His holy prophet."

"Praise be to Allah," echoed the men.

"Yeah, praise be, praise be," Saunders mumbled. Returning to the table to get the map, he explained to Ahmad the plan's details. "I think I covered all the bases...you got any other ideas?"

"You have done well for a foreigner, but I will handle the other RPG. These men will flank us and provide cover against the security forces. We will each target a tent and, if there is time...a second shot into the crowd."

"My brother," said the man who led the prayers, "have you a place to hide? I fear the authorities may recognize and arrest you. You must keep off the streets."

"I am blessed with the hospitality of an old friend, may gifts from Allah shower upon him. I will stay there until we meet at the appointed time."

"But if someone along the procession route should recognize you, my brother, what..."

"Don't ya worry about that," Saunders announced, "I got make-up stuff...when I'm finished, you won't recognize him. I'll bring it with me."

"When?" Ahmad asked.

"After we hide the weapons; when we come back for the costumes...it'll only take a few minutes. Okay?"

"Yes, that will be good."

The gaunt man, the one who earlier led the prayers, said, "Imam, I am troubled...will we not also kill our own brothers in Islam?"

"They are apostates," Ahmad replied. "They gather with infidels at a conference to spread lies about the Prophet and sow seeds of doubt about our holy mission. Satan has them now and the law is clear, the enemies of Islam must be killed."

The men understood Ahmad's answer and all agreed: Shari'ah, the holy Islamic law, was divine and the only law to which they were subject, the only law needed on earth. There was little else to discuss. The participants understood the plan and its divine design, for which each of these men was ready to sacrifice his life. The hour was late and after a short prayer, Ahmad dismissed them.

Riding back on the bicycle he had taken when he left Shahin's house, beneath a tarpaulin of brilliant stars, the rhythmic clinking of the bicycle chain breaking the nighttime stillness, Ahmad's attention wandered aimlessly from one distraction to another but he could not still the voice within him. Ahmad Hasan heard a woman's voice telling him this was wrong, that it was not the will of Allah but the will of men. The voice was soft, its message fragile, and Ahmad, preoccupied with a plan for killing infidels, and the puzzle of who tried to kill him, refused to listen, having not yet learned the timeless warning: it is with great peril we ignore the inner voices that guide us.

Exhausted and troubled, Ahmad, picking up the basket of food left by Bahar, let himself into the little bungalow. He stood for a while in the darkened house, accompanied by shadows cast from the moonlight streaming in through a small window. Exhaling a deep sigh, he settled into a sofa stacked with pillows and watched the fragile lace curtains dance to the soft rhythm of a gentle breeze. While running over the meeting in his weary mind, Ahmad fell into a fitful sleep that was full of fragments of impenetrable dreams.

Waking in the predawn hours, sweating and cold, Ahmad ran his fingers through his hair, turned on the floor lamp beside the sofa, then went into the bathroom and splashed cold water on his face. He returned to the couch with the basket of food and devoured the meal, washing it all down with a lukewarm bottle of fresh grape juice.

He sat quietly, reprising Saunders' plan, looking for faults, when a lingering reluctance – a feeling things weren't quite right – came upon him, sparking an internal battle between all his tightly-held beliefs and his newly acquired awareness that, perhaps, compassion and love was a more effective remedy than war.

Ahmad argued with his own thoughts, telling himself that the infidels knew nothing of compassion and that, although he was sorry, love could not abide without justice. Besides, he reasoned, why am I allowing the coma-induced voice of a ghost and the rantings of a demented Jew to affect my sacred duty?

When this would not suffice to quell his disquiet, Ahmad dove into the mundane task of preparing for the morning's attack, distracting himself enough to put the feelings out of mind. Ahmad carefully checked his weapon then retrieved the backpack stuffed under the bed and sorted through its contents. He pulled the cards out and, in preparation for his next mission, decoded the name of his next contact.

The final item pulled from the backpack was a video camera; the one he used on the roof to film the attack in San Francisco. With all the strange events of the past several weeks, at times prompting him to question his sanity, he wondered whether San Francisco was just another hallucination or if it had actually occurred. The camera contained the proof, he thought, and offered an anchor to help ground him in the steely determination needed to complete his assignment.

Ahmad retrieved a video cable from the backpack, connected the camera to a small portable television sitting on top of a low dresser opposite the bed, turned on the television, pressed play on the camera, and sat down on the bed waiting.

An image appeared on the screen, fuzzy, then sharp, then fuzzy again, as the auto focus ran through algorithms trying to find the right focal length. Finally, he saw the bridge, its center span missing, dark objects teetering, others falling into the water below. In the background, the distant wail of sirens sounded – some wobbling, some screaming; fire truck horns with their low guttural voices demanding the traffic move aside. The picture was telescoping, in and out, trying to find a point of interest on the bridge, as its cables swayed in groaning spasms, finally resting on one focal point. Ahmad realized, as he watched, just how poor a cameraman he was.

In the background, Ahmad heard his own voice saying, almost time now. The camera panned the San Francisco skyline and, searching, it found the Omni's top levels standing in proud splendor above the other buildings. The serenity of the scene was cut by a few puffs of smoke and dust. The building shuddered, taking a deep breath, a final dying breath. A bright flash of light blew out the windows and, suddenly, the building was ablaze. He heard the sound of his own gasp and the sirens, screaming through the streets, as gleaming shards of glass fell like condemned angels cast from heaven.

The camera panned the gruesome scene, morphing into a streak of pixels trying to capture all the panic, all the terror. Then the picture sharpened as the telephoto lens zoomed to its maximum, capturing a flock of white birds hovering around the building.

Mesmerized by the scene, confusion began to creep onto Ahmad's face. Astonished, he wondered aloud, "Why don't they fly away?"

Ahmad snatched the camera from the top of the table, and pressing slow motion, he sat engrossed in perusing the video, trying to make sense of what he was seeing.

There was a man standing on a ledge of the burning skyscraper. He bore an undeniable resemblance to David. Ahmad knew, instantly, who the man was. It looked as though David's father was being attacked by birds – no wait, he thought, they are moving away – with the man still in their grasp. Carrion birds? Perhaps they want him as food; they can carry large fish and small animals in their talons – but a man? How can this be?

There were seven birds on each side. Then Ahmad saw something else – a woman? A woman in a glistening gown hovered just in front of the flock carrying the man. Ahmad could see her lips moving – as though she was directing the movement of the birds. They obeyed at once, disappearing into the clouds above. Just as the woman was ascending, her face came into view.

Ahmad hit the pause button and stared in disbelief. He cried out in anguish, fell to his knees, his tears freely flowing, sobs wracking his body, never suspecting, until this moment, that there was this much emotion lying hidden within him.

"Madame Antoinette! It is you. It is you," Ahmad cried covering his eyes. "I'm so ashamed! You told me the truth and I turned away! You brought to me healing grace and I spurned you! Please, please tell me now, what I should do?"

Ahmad, praying for guidance and forgiveness, lay motionless on the floor before the vision and wept for a long, long time. When he lifted his head the first rays of confirmation were coming in from the eastern horizon. It was clear to Ahmad what was to be.

The weary, Islamic soldier rose, pulled the digital flash card out of the camera, grabbed his Qur'an and, with a penknife, meticulously cut a slot in the prayer book's back cover. He inserted the video flash card and taped the slot closed. Leaving behind all his worldly possessions, Ahmad placed the Qur'an with the six cards into his backpack and fled. First, he would meet with the cell, as planned, for the procession from Mary's Shrine. Then Ahmad would find David Anderson.

THE CHILDREN OF MEN

R
on Eyota never imaged he'd be standing in front of a camera telecasting to a global audience but, just as John Stavos promised, here he was shooting background video on location in Ephesus. With a spectacular landscape as a backdrop, Ron was guiding the viewers on a tour of the ancient city ruins, describing both its historical and sacred nature. So novel and exciting was this that for a moment the professor thought of trading his classroom for a newsroom.

Ron was standing on the first of nine steps leading to the Library of Celsus. Its two-story marble façade, beautifully appointed with Corinthian columns, was glistening softly, like newly fallen snow, in the morning sunshine. He was describing the feminine statues of the library, embodying the qualities of wisdom, knowledge, thought, and virtue when the producer signaled for him to wrap up the segment and introduce David.

"…in antiquity, this library, originally constructed as a tomb, contained over twelve thousand scrolls…the accumulated knowledge of the preceding five hundred years. It was as important as the Library of Alexandria and it suffered a similar fate when the Goths attacked, setting the scrolls to flame. The knowledge…that allowed the Ephesians to call into being an advanced new world was destroyed by the dark side of human nature…returning it to a tomb, once again. This is Doctor Ron Eyota, for Global News…now over to David Anderson."

Flanked on each side by white stone columns of differing heights, many predating Jesus, David Anderson walked along the Marble Road, a glimpse of the Odeon over his left shoulder, explaining the conference events and the imminent arrival of dignitaries from the world's religions. In front of him a camera dolly, pulled by two grips, made steady progress toward the area where the 'Unity Procession' was to enter the Great Theater.

As the procession drew near, Turkish security forces, flying two UH-60 Blackhawk helicopters on loan from NATO, hovered low overhead, drowning out the audio. In his earpiece, David could hear the sound engineer complaining that the noise and interference from the unexpected airborne patrol was proving difficult to screen out. The anchor stopped, until the choppers flew past and the noise subsided, then continued the coverage as the initial delegates arrived. They were trickling in, one or two at a time, until hundreds of clerics and officials of the various faith communities filled the area.

Reporters from Europe, Asia, the Middle East, and the Americas, microphones in hand, lined the road firing questions at the clergymen. None answered. Instead, they formed a stately procession and headed toward the Odeon, smiling and nodding their official greetings to the reverent and enthusiastic throngs of participants and spectators, with news crews following close on their heels.

David planned to catch the crowd of dignitaries as they entered the Odeon. He and the cameraman began to set up the site, just beyond the arched entrance, when Ron appeared, crew in tow.

"David," he called, "where do you want us?"

"The first two rows of the orchestra are reserved for the press, grab the spot in front of the podium...I'll meet you after some interviews."

The interviews didn't go as planned. The conference attendees deferred David's in-depth questions, preferring to provide only brief descriptions about the upcoming conference. Instead, they referred the newsman to preprinted material, maintaining he would find all the answers to his queries in upcoming speeches. After asking the same questions, over and over, as the participants passed by, David grew frustrated. Without the sound bite he was looking for to capture the essence of the conference, David joined Ron in the press area. They watched, in amazement, as the ancient Odeon filled with people much as it had thousands of years ago.

In time, correspondents from other news organizations joined them in the press area. David spent some time in casual conversation with many of his colleagues, always mindful to introduce Ron as Global's subject expert. Ron noticed that when David described the professor's illustrious background, it raised a few eyebrows and Ron received more than a few slaps on the back. The reporters and crewmembers, in boisterous camaraderie, seemed like a cadre of best mates at a college reunion.

David was sharing an anecdote with a reporter from Moscow's major news outlet, when he caught sight of a familiar figure on stage. "Hey Ron, isn't that your friend, Oriastro?"

"The Cardinal is a friend to us both...wouldn't you say?"

"I would. Let's go say hi."

They removed their audio equipment, and leaving the camera crew behind, went to greet the Cardinal, who was standing beside a man dressed in traditional Islamic garments.

"Professor, we were just speaking of you...I'm delighted to see you both. May I present my counterpart, his eminence Shaykh Abdullah ibn Hakim al Salah, Grand Mufti of Saudi Arabia?"

"An honor to meet you," Ron said.

"The honor is mine, Professor. I do hope that I may someday visit your university. The Cardinal has told me much about it. And this young man?"

Written on the face of the Grand Mufti, David saw the same openness that was once a gift from another shaykh, in Iran, when he was a neophyte journalist exploring the power of the mass media. Hoping not to offend, but unable to resist seizing the opportunity, the newsman decided to take a chance. "I'm David Anderson from Global News, Your Eminence. Could I perhaps impose on you, and the Cardinal, to answer a few questions?"

Amused by Ron's pained expression, Cardinal Oriastro quickly replied, "I think we could entertain a query or two…alright, Abdullah?"

"I would be pleased to speak with this young man, if his questions arise from an earnest heart."

"Thank you," David said, producing a small note pad. "I've listened to several Islamic scholars, today, who condemn restrictions on religious freedom…yet when I look at Islamic countries, the reality seems to be quite the opposite…Muslims converting to Christianity are treated as heretics, churches are burned during holy days, calls for the extermination of the Jews persist. Can you explain this dichotomy?"

"I have hope for a world where all faithful will practice their own beliefs and traditions without fear…hope that the widespread use of modern communication methods will facilitate understanding so we can move toward a brotherhood of mankind. Of course, if a Muslim converts to another religion and acts against Islam…that is not permissible among some of my co-religionists."

"And the punishment is…what…torture, death? After a thousand years of violence, conditions do not seem to be improving for the citizens of these regions. Several years ago, the world was encouraged by the spread of the 'Arab Spring' movement as dictators fell. We hoped this might bring peace to the region but, instead of democracy and tolerance, extremism and intolerance only escalated."

"Yes, perpetrated by unenlightened men, hungry only for power, who would kill the human spirit rather than rule with equanimity and true justice. No, my young friend…this must be a time of healing the human spirit, not killing it. I confess there are those of my faith who do not understand these things, let alone embrace them.

This is the reason we are gathered here: to build not cast away; to love not hate; to speak out not remain silent."

"That's a beautiful sentiment...but what does it mean in practice...how does it change the lives of those who live under the continued threat of violence and oppression?" David pressed.

"The world is in crisis." The Islamic scholar answered. "Businesses run without ethics; wealth is obtained without producing value; unprincipled politicians seek only power. In short, my young friend, there is no longer a moral absolute. In a world of relative thinking, how do you define morality, compassion, and responsibility? How stable and durable is our global society if people cannot define and judge their own behavior? Look at the chaos in the world. The only way to end the chaos is to build a common set of values where justice is the cornerstone of all our dealings. We are here to begin this greatest of tasks."

Scribbling, so fast, he thought his fingers would fly off his hand, David looked up, and asked, "Can I quote you?" When Shaykh Abdullah indicated his accession, the anchorman, addressing both clerics, asked, "Isn't this all part of the human condition...with the outcome preordained? As Rougemont said, 'If my neighbor is stronger, I fear him; weaker, I hate him; equal, I trick him.' How do you factor in the natural tendencies of people into the solution?"

"May I, Abdullah?' Cardinal Oriastro proposed with sanguine confidence. "I have a simple answer for you, David...compassionate empathy and recognition of how we are all the same."

"Compassionate empathy? That's the simple solution to the world's problems?"

Ron's face was, by now, quite contorted, underscoring his disquiet with the aggressive manner in which David was pursuing his line of questions. When his pained expression caught Oriastro's attention once again, the prelate turned to Ron, and said, "My friend, don't let these questions make you uncomfortable. We welcome the rare opportunity to discuss these vital matters in an open and frank way. Your friend is a skilled and honest interviewer."

"In other words, Ron," said David. "Chill. It's my job."

"David," the Cardinal said, turning back to the journalist and his questions, "only the strongest among us can admit their weakness, only the richest among us realize their poverty in virtue and justice, only the most learned perceive how great is their ignorance in comparison to the All-knowing God. There are many mysteries of the universe that cannot be measured or explained, and only the most humble can see the greatness and sanctity of every living soul. Therefore, if I, knowing my poor and imperfect self, can ask for God's love and be assured of His forgiveness, why can't I love and forgive all those around me in that same way?"

"So, you're saying, 'if God loves me, he must love everyone, and so must we'," David said.

"Exactly, David," replied the Cardinal. "The paradigm for the future must be our essential oneness and God's loving embrace of every living soul."

"With all due respect, Your Excellency, there are few of us with such profound insight into our own behavior, whether, or not, we are believers," posed David.

"Then our job is to enlighten them, Mr. Anderson," replied Oriastro.

"Well, then," David said without the slightest hesitation, "Your job must also be to tear down the wall in Mary's chapel that separates Christian and Muslim worshipers, correct?"

"Ahh, you are a deep thinker, David," replied Oriastro, "Yes, someday, this too will come, God willing. Just like love and forgiveness, we cannot force such a profound idea. Such a thing must be embraced out of free will and wisdom."

David, impressed with what he heard, could not help but wonder. Since his mother's death he had, steadfastly, doubted the existence of God. In this place, holy to so many believers of different religions, he was facing men who should have an answer. "May I pose one last question?"

"Yes, of course," said Oriastro.

"Why do you think, in this day and age, it's becoming so common to proclaim that God is dead?"

"Ah yes…a quote attributed to Nietzsche that over the years has become part of our cultural zeitgeist." Oriasto smiled. "People often repeat it without realizing Nietzsche said this in reaction to the horror of human atrocities during World War II. I recall he said something along the lines of, 'God is dead and we have killed him. How shall we, murderers of all murderers, console ourselves?' Nietzsche was asking: how do we console ourselves when there is so much evil in the world and we have willfully created it? Now we search for consolation in the material world, looking to our own experiences for the meaning of life. But the truth is, no government, no object, no experience, no amount of money, wealth, or fame can ever be a substitute for a true sense of meaning, joy, and higher purpose."

David closed the note pad, the Cardinal's answer touching a personal struggle he had undergone since his mother's passing. Minutes went by before he looked up.

"That is a very profound and hopeful message," offered the newsman. "Look, I'm just thinking out loud but I wonder if you would grant me an interview on camera. All of Global's outlets will carry it; you have my word on that. You can bring this message to a worldwide audience."

"What do you think, Abdullah?" Oriastro asked.

"I think this young man is sincere. I like the idea."

"All right, David. Meet us in the media tent at four. I'll arrange to have representatives in attendance from all the religions here at the conference."

"Great," David exclaimed, extending his hand, intending to 'shake on it' and seal the deal. Instead, he took the Cardinal's hand and kissed his ring.

"Thank you, your Eminence," David said. Turning to Shaykh Abdullah ibn Hakim al Salah, he said, "Many thanks, your Eminence. I have to fly if I want to pull this together."

"Before you leave, may I ask your help with something?" Oriastro said.

Glancing towards Ron, David said, "Sure, I'd be happy to help...if I can."

"There have been some unsettling rumors circulating that are becoming quite disturbing. They suggest that one religious group here may be planning to attack another," began the Cardinal. "I wish I could be more definitive. The 'who and what' of the plan, I don't know."

"What is it you want from me?"

"We would not want the journalists reporting on disunity among the faith groups that doesn't exist. It would defeat the whole purpose of our gathering and greatly hamper our consultation. As a favor, I am asking if you would use your considerable investigative talents and get to the bottom of this. Oh, and please, use your influence with the other journalists. Ask them to hold back reporting this matter until we find out more about what's reailly going on."

"I will certainly help out in any way I can, Your Eminence. I'll see you this afternoon."

David left the Odeon through the stone archway and sprinted through the crowd, Ron Eyota not far behind. David stopped when he reached the media tent and began to search for Tahir Korkmaz. He was the executive producer at Global's station in Izmir, which was a large metropolis in western Turkey. Tahir was acting as their field producer, guide, and general all-around 'Mister Fixit'.

"David," a winded Ron asked, "what's going on?"

"I have to find Tahir. Can you spot him?"

"He's right over there," Ron said.

David ran up to the producer. "Do you have the satellite phone?"

"Right here, why?"

"I need to call New York."

"Whom do you wish to call…wait…it's three in the morning there!"

"Never mind that! Get Suzanne Biasotto on the line."

Tahir searched the contacts list on the satellite phone until he found Suzanne's home number in Manhattan. He pressed 'select' then 'send.' The signal, along with his dream of someday working at Global's headquarters in New York City, flew across the Atlantic.

Suzanne awoke to the sound of her cell, lying close by on her bedside table. After a few seconds of staring into the blackness of the bedroom, she was able to clear the grogginess in her head and lift the receiver to her ear. "Hello," she said, slurring the word.

"Hi Suzanne, it's me, David."

"Hey, David…I was just…dreaming about…" Then, in a snap, she was alert, sitting up and yelling into the handset, "David, are you okay? What's all that noise on the line?"

"I'm fine, Ron's fine, everything is fine. We're calling from Turkey on a satellite phone. Can you conference John in?"

"Are you kidding? It's three in the morning, he'll kill me!"

"Please, Suzanne, and hurry up."

"All right, okay, hold on for a second."

When John picked up, his voice was thick and heavy, "Hello."

"Hi John, it's Suzanne. Please, don't get mad. I have David and Ron on the line."

"What the hell...do you know it's three in the morning?"

"I know, I told them. David and Ron are on the line, do you want to..."

"Yes...put them through, and this better be good!"

"Okay, hold a sec...David, we're on, go ahead."

"Sorry to wake you, John, but look, I scheduled an exclusive interview with a panel of high-level delegates representing all the religions in attendance at the conference. Their message is impressive and I think our viewers would like to see it. I need you to arrange to have all, and I mean all, of our channels telecast it. Preempt other programming, if you have to. And, by the way, there are rumors of a conspiracy that we are investigating."

"Number one, David, I am half asleep, and two, that's a tall order."

"I know, but you have to trust me. This is an important story and I gave my word."

"And just how do you plan to broadcast this live? The uplink you guys have has limited resolution and bandwidth."

"We plan to tape it. Tahir will shoot up to Izmir and transmit it to New York from the studio there. It's about a forty-five mile drive...shouldn't take more than an hour. You'll have it before noon your time."

"And what about this plot thing," John asked.

"We'll start nosing around right after we finish the interview prep. Anything I find, I'll do live over the uplink. Agreed?"

"That's fine, but if you uncover anything about a plot, you find me, no matter where I am. Got it?"

"Yes, John, I've got it. Suzanne, can you whip up a fast promo?"

"I guess so...John, can I?"

"Okay, go ahead. David, we'll talk soon. Suzanne, now that I'm wide awake, please stay on the line for a moment. Oh, and David, my wife has a few choice words she would like to share with you when you return."

"Tell her, I'm very sorry and I owe you guys a dinner…Ron is sorry too. Hey, John thanks…you too, Suzanne. I'll call back, right after we finish taping."

When the call ended, David and Ron rushed off to make preparations for that afternoon. The crew, meanwhile, staked out a spot in the media tent and set up for an interview that promised to be one of David Anderson's most compelling ever.

By noon, David and Ron were sitting in the commissary composing the questions for the interview, enjoying a lunch of stuffed eggplant, chicken skewers and a fresh green salad. Ron helped by explaining the more esoteric theological concepts and the interrelationships among the religious doctrines. They spent an hour in preparation, partly because John would come through and arrange a huge audience - one that would be expecting the highest level of depth and integrity from a David Anderson telecast - but mostly, to pay respect to the intelligence and spirit of the men and women that would be seated on the dais.

Once David was satisfied, his notes organized and ready, he and Ron began mixing in with the crush of delegates engaging in casual conversation and, where they could, both men tried to uncover any leads about the Cardinal's suspected terror plot.

Lorenc, working alone behind the meetinghouse in Selcuk, was in a foul mood. Saunders had ordered him to break up, and dispose of, the empty gun crates. It was menial work, below his status, but he obeyed. He had gathered up the last of the evidence and was burning it in a steel drum, when he noticed the shadow of a man lying across the ground. Cursing under his breath for having left his gun on the table inside, he spun around expecting to be shot.

The man standing there was well groomed with refined features, definitely European. The image of the flames from the steel drum reflecting in his eyes made the man look sinister and frightening. He was holding the Albanian's gun by its barrel.

"You are Gaspard?" asked Lorenc, beginning the recognition sequence.

"Oui," replied the stranger.

"Where will you be going?" Lorenc continued.

"To Canada."

"With whom?"

"In a lonely world, I travel alone," replied Gaspard, completing the recognition code and handing over the weapon. "It is dangerous to leave your pistol so far from you, monsieur, no?"

Tucking the gun into his waistband, the Albanian said," I was expecting you. What are my instructions?"

Reaching into the inner pocket of his jacket, Gaspard hesitated. "It's okay?"

"Yes, I trust it is you."

"Good," replied Gaspard, pulling out a sealed envelope and handing it to Lorenc. "Here are your instructions. You are to kill Ahmad Hasan during the attack."

"Why? Why must this be?" asked the Albanian, in shock.

"We cannot risk his capture. That is all you need to know!"

"Anything else?" Lorenc asked.

Pausing for a second to 'size up' the sour looking man standing before him, Gaspard continued. "Oui, there is something…after the job is complete…during your escape…you are to kill Hadi also. Understand?"

"I understand. It will be my pleasure to kill him!"

Lifting a shopping bag from a department store in Paris called Galeries Lafayette, Gaspard continued, "There is a belt inside with high explosives…in case, monsieur, you are captured. The police must not take any of you alive."

"I will take many of the infidels with me."

"Très bien," Gaspard said. He did not offer a trace of sympathy for this man who just agreed to take his own life and Lorenc did not expect any. "Well then, monsieur, I must be going. The tour bus will be leaving shortly. Bonne chance!"

Lorenc followed Gaspard down the alley and watched him get into a waiting car. When the car door closed behind Gaspard, Lorenc removed the explosive belt from the shopping bag and stood there, alone, for a long time, holding it and contemplating a martyr's death.

At four o'clock that afternoon, Ahmad Hasan stood in the long shadows of the media tent, furtively looking around for David Anderson. He was carrying his backpack and wearing an Islamic cleric's white cotton slacks, a white thowb, or tunic, covered by a lightweight grey gauze shirt called a bisht. On his head, sitting high upon his brow, Ahmad had a beautiful kufi of black hopsack, the rim of which was decorated in fine white silk embroidery. He looked and felt like a true Muslim brother, and it felt right, like he was finally walking around in his own skin, in his own homeland, once more.

The participant's badge Ahmad wore around his neck hung from a red lanyard. It was printed on both sides with the Conference logo and identified Ahmad as Siyyid Haji Ali Mustafa, an official of the Aqa Jamal Mosque in Tehran. He stopped at the entrance of the tent while his badge was inspected, passing through the checkpoint with nothing more from the Turkish guard than a glance from Ahmad's face to the picture on the badge and back again. A cursory inspection of the backpack, showing nothing but a Qur'an inside, was followed by a bow of respect from the Turkish security guard as he waved Ahmad into the tent.

David Anderson was unaware that the man who killed his father had entered the media tent and was silently watching from a short distance away, waiting as David conferred with his production staff. The swarm of activity surrounding the anchor intrigued Ahmad. The news crew was making final preparations for the interview with the conference delegates.

David, oblivious to all the activity, stood with Ron and Tahir, intent upon one last review of the interview questions. Lighting, audio, and camera technicians, busy with last minute checks of the equipment, ensured the production quality would be perfect, or as perfect as they could manage from this remote location.

The persistent chop of the helicopter blades was gone, thanks to a request by the U.S. State Department to reposition the Black Hawks for the taping; a request initiated by Global News in New York.

Hair and makeup artists, with their own unique brand of doggedness, buzzed around David's head like mosquitoes on a sweaty hiker laboring along a trail in deep woods, stopping only when the producer called for a camera check.

David, picking up the microphone, began. "Leading delegates of the world's religions, participating in a three day conference in Ephesus, Turkey, have arrived from all over the world to consult with each other on world matters affecting their respective congregations. Today, they will present their views to the world."

"How's that?" David asked, handing the microphone to a production assistant.

"There's a technical problem, David. Try again," responded Tahir.

Ahmad stood a long time watching David. He waited for an opportunity to approach the man he had first laid eyes on as a boy; the man to whom he had broken a sacred pledge. He was thinking about that day, feeling for the first time much like the boy at the fountain. The newsman glanced up and saw him standing beside a tent pole. Their eyes met for only a second before David returned to his work.

A few moments passed and David looked up again. He stared at Ahmad with intensity and intent, the unmistakable light of recognition on his face. Ahmad felt alarm and, thinking David might alert security, prepared to flee into the crowd but willed himself to stay where he was.

Handing the producer his notes, David whispered, "Wait. Wait, just a second. Wait right here." Pushing past his colleagues, he approached Ahmad.

"You're here," he said, peering at Ahmad with quiet rage. "What do you want?"

"I broke my vow…a sacred oath I made a long time ago," Ahmad said. His voice low and trembling. The fervent and sorrowful sound held back David's seething wrath.

"Yes." It was all David could say.

"I cannot take it back, even though it is what I wish to do. I cannot ask your forgiveness. There are things we can never make right." Ahmad was almost pleading now, thinking the words not merely inadequate, but hollow. "I must try..."

"Try what?"

Ahmad held out the backpack. "Please take this. I want you to have it."

"What is it...a bomb?"

David's contempt was not lost on Ahmad. He had little time left, so he thrust the bag into David's reluctant arms.

"Please, here are the answers you seek. I promise you, it will help you heal."

Ahmad had no time left for words. He turned abruptly, and walking briskly toward the exit, glanced back at the newsman to see if he was being followed.

"Hey!" David yelled at the retreating figure. "Just where the hell do you think you're going?"

Ahmad did not answer, disappearing into the crowd. The anchorman stood there, his mouth open, his assistant now tugging, furiously, at his arm.

"David, come on. We need you on set! The Conference organizers are here waiting for the interview!"

Without a word, David thrust the backpack into the bewildered production assistant's hands and ran after Ahmad.

The stunned assistant shouted, "Come back...where are you going? David, we'll miss the story! Are you crazy?"

One of the cameramen, having witnessed this preposterous scene, called after David. "Hey! You're kidding, right? The world is waiting to see this..."

David did not hear this last entreaty. He was out of the tent, pushing past the people invited to watch the interview. His eyes were glued to the man in the black kufi sprinting up Harbor Road.

Pursuing Ahmad, David melded into the crowd. He pulled out a cell phone, and called the segment producer.

"Tahir...it's David."

"David! Oh, thank God! Where did you go?"

"Listen! Tell security I think there is going to be an attack. I am trailing a terrorist. He is heading up Harbor Road in the direction of the Odeon."

"No, David, goddamn it! We're missing the interview. We'll all be fired, for God's sake. You're reputation with these people could be ruined!"

"Call security. Do it now!" David clicked off. Ahmad was still in his sights.

Ahmad pushed his way through the crowds. Some of the delegates were leaving the amphitheater for a much needed rest; some were milling around the ancient site getting to know their fellow pilgrims with stories of home; others discussed their hopes and dreams for the future of mankind and this nascent branch of the interfaith movement. In total, there were close to three thousand souls who had gone to great lengths to come to this conference. They prayed and debated the spiritual issues of the day; they sat through addresses by the many religious leaders that inspired and galvanized them. Although the day was long, the good will was palpable – even to Ahmad who had led a most insular life where good will, with few exceptions, had been in short supply.

Ahmad entered the Odeon, glancing back over his shoulder, every so often, to check whether he had been spotted. He missed David, who positioned himself behind a small, motorized food cart selling Turkish deserts and coffee. When he was sure no one was following him, Ahmad began to sprint to the top of the Great Theater. Reaching the uppermost row of seats, he climbed over the low wall, hopping into the stand of trees and brush growing in luxuriant array behind the Odeon and rising to the mountaintop. During the early morning hours, beyond the break of a grove covered by thick growth, the cell had hidden the cache of weapons that would be used in the assault. This is where Ahmad headed.

David waited at the stone entrance of the Odeon, still unnoticed by the Iranian ascending the mountain, wondering what Ahmad would do next. David was watching the terrorist disappear into the woodland, when a cameraman stepped up beside him. He was out of breath and the camera felt like the weight of the world on his shoulders.

"What the hell are you doing here?" demanded the newsman.

"Mr. Anderson, for a guy who sits behind a desk, you sure are fit!"

"Get back to the media tent!"

"But sir, with all due respect, this is breaking news…I have my duty and…"

"Stop! Enough already." By now, Ahmad had disappeared from sight, irritating David further. "Look, you want this story…fine. But I'm not waiting for you to drag that camera along and get us both killed…is that clear? You wait here until I signal you! Understood?"

The cameraman, burdened by the heavy video equipment, nodded his reluctant assertion and David took off in pursuit of Ahmad. He ran past the stage, sprinting up the aisle two steps at a time. Heart pumping, blood pounding in his ears, thighs burning, he forced his body by the sheer power of will to keep ascending, the singular thought of a boy at a fountain driving him upward. In response to Tahir's alert, Turkish security forces searching for David were already entering to the Great Theater.

On the hillside, Ahmad looked around the woods. Finding his bearings, the Iranian hurried toward the area where Brian Saunders was supposed to be assembling the RPG's. As he approached the clearing where the launching site was set up, Ahmad spotted Saunders loading the weapons.

"Ahmad!" yelled Saunders. "We were afraid something happened to you. Our boys are at their posts ready to rock and roll. We're just about there, brother!"

Saunders picked up a rocket launcher and held it out to Ahmad. "Grab this baby and find a comfortable position. It's a beauty. Allah be praised for the leftovers from our Libyan friends and their little foray into freedom!"

Saunders put his head back and laughed; it was a vicious laugh, jagged and jeering, the kind heard from the mouths of assassins in gleeful anticipation of a deadly strike.

Ahmad just stood where he was, staring at the terrorist, recognizing, for maybe the first time, the sight of pure evil.

"Put the missile launcher down," Ahmad said. His voice was dark and menacing. "There will be no attack."

"Whaddaya, mean? You go nuts or somethin'?" Saunders, in shock, could not hold on to the small semblance of Middle Eastern decorum he had been struggling to maintain. Pulling out his Glock semi-automatic, he pointed it at Ahmad.

"I am the leader," Ahmad insisted. "Put the weapons down and step back."

Saunders dropped the RPG he had been holding out to Ahmad. It hit the ground with a dull thud. "You're chickening out, you rat bastard!" Saunders snarled.

"Put the gun down, it's over." Ahmad held his position but Saunders was sure he heard defeat.

"The death of a martyr is too good for you," Saunders jeered, pulling back the Glock's hammer. "So long, you miserable coward!"

David heard the gun click as he entered the clearing where Saunders and Ahmad faced each other. He was no more than one hundred feet away.

It took only a moment for David to comprehend the unfolding scene. He shouted, "Drop the gun …the police are on their way. It's over."

The assassin was caught off-guard by coming, face to face, with David Anderson - the man he had been unable to kill; the man who almost cost him his life; the man who always bested him.

"Go to hell, Anderson," he screamed.

Saunders raised his weapon and, enraged, fired several times.

David folded, throwing himself behind a wild bramble, the random shots whizzing close by his head. The leggy bush, with its sparse leaves, was hardly an adequate defense against a hollow point bullet. David knew he would not be so lucky a second time. He prayed Tahir had done what he asked and called the authorities.

Saunders, seething, readied his stance. Aligning his hips perpendicular to the target, legs apart, clutching the pistol with both hands and looking carefully down the sight, he cocked the Glock's hammer again. He told himself that this time, there was no way he would miss his mark.

Ahmad reacted with lightening reflexes the moment Saunders took his eyes off him. Reaching inside his tunic, Ahmed drew the

9mm Beretta he was carrying from a hidden shoulder holster. Screaming, his eyes wide and wild, he got off a round.

The bullet pierced Saunders' wrist, causing his hand to spring open, the gun flying into the woodland brush behind him. The sting forced Saunders to shriek in pain. Before the howl fully escaped his throat, he was hit with a second bullet from Ahmad's gun. It struck Saunders on the left side of the head; half his skull exploding outward, leaving blood and brain matter splattered on the shrubs and surrounding trees, and a viscous red liquid, along with bits of human tissue, dripping from the leaves.

Ahmad's gun slipped from his hand. Focused on nothing else in the world, he sprinted toward the place where David lay.

The other members of the terror cell, hearing the gunfire, began running toward the staging area, ignoring the din from the distant security helicopters as the sound began to build.

Lorenc and his partner arrived at the clearing only to discover Saunders' lifeless body lying twisted in the tall grass. Turning the prone man onto his back, the Albanian said to his accomplice, "This one is gone."

Just then, the prayer leader and his partner appeared. "Who has killed Hadi? Where is the Imam?"

"There," Lorenc replied, pointing to Ahmad's retreating figure.

In the next instant, Turkish Armed Forces swooped into the area and the terrorists began to scatter. A booming command from a bullhorn ordered, "This is the TAF...you are surrounded...stand down and drop your weapons!"

Lorenc, could see shadows in the woods moving towards them. He began spraying the forest with the AK107. The security forces answered, returning fire, and began to fan out.

In the distance, Blackhawk Helicopters, flown by Turkish pilots, waited for their guidance systems to compute the target. Each machine was equipped with eighteen acoustical sensors able to detect the supersonic shock wave of a bullet in flight. Its onboard computer was so precise it could guide them to the exact spot where any gun, even with a silencer, had been discharged. The pilots were hovering at thirty five hundred feet over open fields three miles northeast of the Odeon. When the alarm sounded, they set off at maximum speed, in the direction indicated on their navigational display.

As they flew in, the pilots could easily spot the muzzle flashes of the gun battle from their cockpits. One chopper stopped to take up a defensive position, hovering five hundred feet above the tents, while the other came roaring in for the confrontation.

The prayer leader, catching sight of the loaded RPG, took hold of the weapon, kneeling and aiming at the approaching army. Just before he could fire the rocket, the Black Hawk swooped in, the deafening sound of its blades drowning out the gunshots. It fired a burst from the onboard Gatling gun. The fifty-caliber rounds practically cut the terrorist in two. The chopper veered away, flying out of range and over the mountain, its pilot executing a tight circle so he could prepare for a second assault.

Lorenc saw the futility of the fight and ordered the other men to surrender. Reluctant, but obedient, they followed his commands, and with hands in the air, gave up. The inexperienced lieutenant in charge ordered a halt to the shooting. He gave several dozen security men a command to, 'approach the assailants with caution and apprehend them.'

The ground security forces surrounded the terrorists, the men closest, confiscating the AK's and RPGs while others pushed in to restrain the captives. With a dozen security personnel around him, Lorenc cried, "Allah'u'Akbar," and detonated the explosive belt.

The gun battle and explosion behind Ahmad propelled him forward even faster, as he urgently ran toward David. The anchorman stood up as the first Black Hawk completed its circle, moving in their direction. David charged in front of Ahmad, ripped the press credentials from the lanyard around his neck, and held them in the air waving his arms, signaling to the chopper's pilot to stand down.

The pilot pulled hard on the cyclic and the helicopter veered off, roaring up and away, leaving the two men unhurt. The Black Hawk crew hovering above the tent area, seeing the explosion, came buzzing in fast behind the first chopper and did not see David's signal. They sprayed a short burst of fire from their Gatling gun. Ahmad, diving toward the journalist, pushed David to the ground but it was too late. A bullet tore through David's trousers, grazing his leg.

David heard Ahmad scream and turned in time to see the man fall and grab his bleeding thigh, attempting to stem the gush of blood spurting from his femoral artery.

Pulling himself up, the newsman limped to Ahmad. He saw the massive wound below his groin, the blood spreading out, staining the white trousers. He ripped at the fallen man's pant leg, tearing a strip of cloth from it. Scrambling for a stick, he tried tying a tourniquet, but seeing the color drain from the Iranian's face, David knew the effort was futile. Ahmad Hasan was dying from massive blood loss.

"Hold on there, buddy." David said, trying to disguise his shock. "The security people will be here in a second. If they don't shoot us, they'll take us to the hospital."

A moment passed between the two men as David and Ahmad looked into each other's eyes for what seemed a long time.

"I should have taken you with me," whispered David.

"I beg your forgiveness, David Effendi. I forgot you were my friend. I have put down my sword. I have let the gun fall."

Then Ahmad looked past David. Staring through the ether of the empty blue sky, he said, "They've come to take me, David Effendi, but know this…they are always with you, my brother."

Before David could reply, the security team converged around them. The helicopters pulled away, hovering just above, waiting for ground security to signal that all was clear. David flashed his press badge, motioning for security to step back. They did as he asked.

David lifted Ahmad's head with careful tenderness. The boy at the fountain was gone, on his face, a look of repose the newsman never expected to see there. He laid the man's head gently back down on the ground. Medics arrived. Some tended to Ahmad, pronouncing him dead at the scene; others turned to David, bandaging his wound and guiding him to a stretcher.

The medics carefully carried the cot through the underbrush, down the steep steps of the Odeon, past the stone entrance and onto Harbor Road where the cameraman joined him.

"Thank God you're all right, Mr. Anderson," said the cameraman. "I caught some great footage from here. It was incredible."

David nodded and reclined on the stretcher. As he lay back, David heard a remarkable sound. It was a cacophony of song, yet he could not make out a specific melody.

David, propped himself up on his elbows, looked around in amazement and called to the cameraman, who was following close behind.

"Hand me a mic, quick!" he said.

The cameraman rushed forward and gave David a microphone.

"First," David instructed, "pan the crowd then put me on camera."

The cameraman did as he was asked and David began to speak.

"This morning, malicious whispers invaded this gathering; rumors of an impending terror attack by one group of delegates against another; rumors intended to spread fear and division. Indeed, there was an attack, but not by these delegates. As I look around, there is not the chaos one would expect in the wake of a terror attack intended to bring this gathering to a horrible and irreconcilable end. On the faces of these delegates, I see courage and resolve; I see them praying together; I see joy and I hear, not one discernable voice, but a symphony of spiritual sounds at once, blended and beautiful; glorious and grand. I am reminded of angels, who once proclaimed, 'Peace on earth to all those of good will.' Reporting from Ephesus, Turkey, this is David Anderson."

A GLIMPSE OF THE
ETERNAL NOW

T he stone used to build Château de Lumiere came from an indigenous carboniferous deposit of granite and it was upon this the foundation of the château was constructed. The site was chosen centuries ago; partly, because of its elevation above the surrounding countryside and, partly, because building materials were abundant and the groundwork solid but, mostly, because its owner discovered unique magnetic properties within the rock.

Ambros von Lightchild was now descending the narrow stairs leading to the château's wine cellar. Ducking under low wooden beams, he pointed a flashlight toward a stained and worn floor mat lying in the farthest corner of the room. Lifting the mat, he signaled to the nearest of the two men with him to unlock a small concealed square hatch cut into the floor.

"One moment, Grandmaster, I have it here somewhere," a man said in a deep, reverberating baritone. After checking his pockets and producing a four-sided key, the baritone inserted it into a slot, using extra care to avoid triggering the canisters of deadly gas protecting the entrance from intruders. The hatch began to slowly lift open.

Kneeling at the rim of a black hole in the floor, Ambros von Lightchild shone a light beam against the far wall, until he located a reflective photo sensor. Leaning against the hatch to steady his aim, he entered a pass code using the flashlight's on/off switch.

.. ⁻.⁻ .... .——— .⁻ ⁻. .⁻ .⁻.. ⁻.... ⁻ ... .⁻ ..⁻. .⁻

Immediately, the room below illuminated. An aluminum ladder extended down to the floor, and a chime sounded, signaling the second-stage intruder defense was deactivated. "Shall we, gentlemen?" the Grandmaster said.

They descended to an empty chamber hewn from rough stone. Marks from the cutting blades used to carve out the room created unusual patterns and shadows. The granite's face was damp with condensation and the space appeared to be nothing more than unused storage.

Holding an irregular granite fragment, aligning it with the rock's pattern, Ambros von Lightchild fit it into a void on the wall. The rock face slid open, revealing a heavy metallic door. The third man with them, a man wearing tinted glasses in aviator frames, entered a series of numbers into a keypad beside the door. When the door opened, they entered a tubular capsule. Von Lightchild stated his name, ignoring the buttons on the panel, any of which, once pressed, would bring them down to one of several decoy rooms designed to confuse and trap intruders. The capsule, riding on three solid metallic rails, dropped through a seven-foot diameter shaft, bored through four hundred feet of granite, to a vault deep in the rock.

'The Vault' was the Brotherhood's holiest space. Cut into the granite walls were forty two glass cases, each temperature controlled, and filled with an inert gas. Above each, a set of instruments displayed the health of the case's internal environment.

Each case held one of the original epistles written by the Brotherhood of Purity. Two other cases, mounted atop solid stone bases, stood prominently in the middle of the room. One case was empty. The other contained the Brotherhood's most revered and sacred document: the order's greatest treasure; its forty-third epistle. It was called 'The Light of Revelation', and although every member knew of it, only those in the highest echelon were given the opportunity to read and discuss it.

Ambros von Lightchild was staring into the empty case, when the man with aviator glasses walked over. "I feel as though a piece of my own heart is missing," he said.

"We all feel the emptiness," replied von Lightchild, "but this will soon be a memory."

"Why not just offer Anderson a reward to return the scroll?" asked Aviator, hoping to avoid any further bloodshed.

"We considered that," said the baritone joining them, "but how much is enough? Too small an amount might not induce him; too large, and he might question what it is that's so valuable. In any event, given the man's proclivity for investigation, any contact might pique his curiosity. We do not need him investigating our organization. The risk of directly contacting him seems unduly high...wouldn't you agree?"

"I imagine so," came the reluctant reply.

"There is no need to rehash this topic," von Lightchild insisted. "The Council has already decided!"

"And our plans going forward...what's next?"

"We will evaluate the effects of our recent actions, both good and bad, and plan our next stage from there."

Staring into the case with a rueful look, reflecting on the scroll before him, the man wearing the glasses intoned, "Here lies the journey towards renewal and the promise of quiet light. When...when does the moment come, the point, in that time you speak of, so solemnly, that we may proclaim this to the world?"

"Why would you ask such a question?" the baritone demanded.

"Many knights of the council believe the time has come. We have deferred our own wishes in deference to you, grandmaster, and your direct lineage to the founding knight, Andre Saint-Omer."

"When the world is ready," the grandmaster answered. "When people are truly prepared and their hearts are open to accept the word, only then can we share this glorious message. I humbly ask for your trust until that day. Come, brothers, let's finish today's tasks so we can resume our other work."

Many hours later, after a grilled lunch enjoyed on the château's rear patio, overlooking a large lily pond, they prepared to depart for Saint Gatien Airport where a private jet was waiting to fly them to Marienberg, Poland. While packing the car, von Lightchild commented, "Next time we visit, our new domestic and grounds keeping staff will be here."

"That's a relief," replied the baritone. "I doubt we could tolerate my cooking much longer."

They laughed and with the car loaded and his colleagues set, Ambros von Lightchild locked the front entrance of Château de Lumiere, thinking that tomorrow a new group of people would arrive; some would tend the grounds, some would care for the castle and its guests, but not one would ever know they worked above a vault carved from solid granite.

It was the end of another busy day in the newsroom when Suzanne stepped out from the subway at Seventy Seventh Street. Strolling along with the grace of a dancer, she headed east toward Central Park. The sun was just beginning to set behind her, the temperature was perfect, the streets were still teeming with people, the city alive. Since David's return from Ephesus, the 'buzz' was back.

Using the key David gave her, Suzanne entered the newsman's apartment to find Professor Eyota in the living room, working on his laptop. Beside him, on the sofa, were Ahmad Hasan's empty backpack and the sixth card. On the coffee table, opened to the same marked page, lay the two Qur'ans with a set of cards, ten in all, matched together in five pairs. Ron was typing furiously, comparing, decoding and chewing on a pen cap. He appeared excited.

"What's up...where's David?' Suzanne asked brightly, casually throwing her jacket over the back of a nearby chair.

"You are not going to believe it," Ron exclaimed, "You guys are going to love this! I knew it all along...the sixth card was the key!"

"What are you raving about? What key?"

"I'll explain when David is here."

"Really? Okay, fine. Where is David?"

"He took a nap after the doctor left...should be up any time now," Ron answered, without looking away from the screen.

Watching Ron work fascinated Suzanne. He sat bolt upright staring at the screen, playing the computer's keys like a pianist, mouth pinched, eyebrows locked in a furrow on his forehead. Suzanne marveled as Ron's lips stretched into a wide grin and he threw back his head, in amazement and delight, as the secrets of the Brotherhood's cards revealed themselves.

Suzanne could not wait a moment longer. "Look," she said. "I'll tell you a secret if you tell me what's so interesting."

"All right," Ron agreed, looking up, "You first!"

"Okay...check this out. Last week I snuck into Lance Rodgers' office and tried to log into the Tabernacle to get the restricted data on the Brotherhood."

"And..."

"And nothing...I couldn't find his password but I did discover some interesting information about our CEO."

"I heard that," David yelled from the bedroom. He limped into the living room and plopped into an overstuffed chair. Setting aside the cane, he scolded her. "You know, not only could you be fired for a stunt like that, you could be arrested! I need you here, not in jail!"

"Hi, David," she said with a demure smile. "Feeling better? By the way, the Global web site almost crashed again today. So many people are viewing the Ephesus video...I bet your audience triples. We should give that cameraman a bonus."

"S u z a n n e, don't change the subject."

"Fine, okay," came her exasperated answer. With a petulant toss of her hair, she sat down opposite the newsman. "But how are we ever going to investigate these Brotherhood of Purity guys?"

"May I interject?" Ron volunteered. "These five cards, along with the Qur'an from Hasan's backpack, are identical to the ones Merilee Brunswick gave us."

"So what do they say about the Brotherhood?" Suzanne asked.

"Nothing explicit," replied Ron

"Noiret?" she pressed.

"I'm afraid not."

"Von Lightchild…anyone…anything?"

"Nope…sorry."

"Then what…I don't get it!" Shaking her head, Suzanne sighed, "Two steps forward, one step back."

"Hold on," Ron insisted. "The cards originally produced information about the past two attacks. With the sixth card, everything opens up…it's the key. Now we have details on backup targets, cell contacts, safe house addresses, methods, tactics, weapon sources…all kinds of stuff. Best of all…ready? You're not going to believe this…a date to meet the next group in Quebec…a week prior to the Global Climate meeting."

"That's next month," observed Suzanne.

"Good," David said. "That gives us some time to investigate without putting anyone in harm's way. Even if there are no hard facts tying the Brotherhood to all this, something might turn up." Teasing Ron, David added, "Of course, this could all be one big coincidence."

"Not funny."

"You okay with that, Suzanne?"

"Sure."

"I would suggest that you turn this information over to the authorities ASAP," Ron prodded. "They'll need time to organize a capture team, start surveillance, and set a trap."

"There's something else to consider, Ron," the newsman assured him.

"Which is?" Ron asked.

"Why doesn't our Government already know all this? I don't understand how come our intelligence assets and the French authorities seem so blind. I suspect Noiret is involved somehow and maybe other officials as well. No matter who's in charge, a free and honest press challenges the power structure…it's what we do."

"David's right. Global should break this story then press the leadership for answers."

"Okay, but then you tip off the conspirators and they get away," Ron assured them.

"That's our dilemma," replied David, "one of balance and timing. I think we need to bring John in and get his opinion. The other puzzle is, who the hell is…eh…was Brian Saunders and what was he doing in Ephesus?"

Suzanne, looking pensive, said, "Before we do anything else, I have to tell you guys about the entry in Lance Rodgers' journal."

"Please don't tell me you read his journal," David pleaded. "Please, I'm begging!"

"He wrote something about this von Lightchild being upset."

"Upset about what," asked the newsman.

"He didn't elaborate but don't you think it's interesting that Rodgers knows him?"

"It could be anything," David responded. "The guy is a big time financer and Lance comes from that world…they might have investments together."

Suzanne looked down, thinking for a moment, before suggesting, "Why don't we go through Ron's findings and pull together a narrative for John."

"All right," David agreed, "But I'm feeling a bit peckish. How about a bite to eat, first?"

"Where would you like to go?" Suzanne asked. "How about that new place on the corner? The menu looks great."

"I'm not sure I want to go limping through the streets just yet. Let's get something delivered."

"Ahh, New York," she rhapsodized, "the takeout capital of the world. I would rather take a little walk and pick it up, myself. Any preference?"

"Just surprise me."

"Okay…but no complaints."

"I'll go to help carry the food." Ron volunteered.

"You see, David," Suzanne chided, "there are still a few gentlemen left."

Slipping on her jacket as Ron opened the door, she turned to David, "You need to catch up on your voice and e-mail messages. They're really piling up."

Through the apartment's door David could hear Suzanne chatting away, explaining to Ron the meaning of the Cardinal's sheep story, her muffled voice fading as they walked through the hallway toward the elevators.

Even the constant hum of the traffic below seemed to fade as Ron and Suzanne disappeared down the hallway. David sank back in his chair enjoying the quiet solitude. The apartment darkened as the orange glow of the setting sun vanished behind the skyscrapers, melting first into twilight, and then into dusk. Thinking back on the personal losses of the past month, he felt, somehow, blessed by the good fortune to still be alive.

Mindful of the pain in his leg, he rose slowly using the cane, just as the physical therapist instructed. He began to limp around the room straightening up the bits and pieces Ron had left strewn about.

At the sofa, David sat down and settled into the spot where Ron was working. Picking up the Qur'an Merilee Brunswick gave him, he thought about his promise and how she trusted him. He remembered the innocent smile, her naiveté, the way her brown eyes darted nervously around the restaurant when they first met. Still haunted by his promise to her, David resolved, right then and there, to investigate her death when he flew to San Francisco to settle Eric's estate.

In a few moments, it would be dark in the apartment, yet David had no need for artificial light. He sat in the darkening room as the sun's rays sank beneath the horizon, still gazing out the window over the city below, marveling at the strange and new sense of illumination he felt. It seemed to impart a light from within.

Just as one sees a reflection in a mirror, David could see, in his mind's eye, a reflection of his recent journeys. They seemed to have brought miraculous revelations into his life. Despite the sorrows, or perhaps because of them, he felt a sense of peace that had eluded him since he was a boy.

David decided, at that moment, to stop and listen first the next time he was tempted to judge another human being. He remembered his father admonishing him not to judge a man until he walked a mile in his shoes. He had not realized, at the time, what vital advice that had been. Amused, David recalled his father's joke that then, if you judge the man, you will be a mile away and still have his shoes.

He decided to roll along with the idea of giving religion a break, like the cardinal suggested, and seeing how that would unfold.

He thought, as well, about his relationship with God, knowing that, although he wished it to be otherwise, this was the hardest challenge of all. His father was gone and the mistrust he felt about his vision, persisted. He decided he would have to settle, for now, with learning to live with this impasse, wondering if he might have to struggle with it the rest of his life. Still, truth be told, he was grateful for it all and it lightened his spirit.

Leaning over, David switched on a lamp. He picked up the prayer book given to him by Ahmad, and slowly turned the pages, thinking Ron was right: both Qur'ans looked the same. Wishing he could read the text, admiring the beauty of the craftsmanship that went in to making it, he slowly scrutinized the book, hoping for some insight into Ahmad's world. The newsman was about to return it to the coffee table when he noticed something odd. The back cover of Ahmad's Qur'an had a small lump near its center. It was almost unnoticeable; it could barely be felt and David wondered how Ron had missed this. Perhaps, David thought, he was distracted with decoding the sixth card.

Taking great care, David pulled open the back cover, stretching the binding, half expecting something might go 'boom', and saw, cut into the book's cloth, a tiny slit covered with clear tape. He opened the draw of the accent table beside the sofa, searching for something sharp, and found a decorative brass letter opener - a souvenir from the Oriental Hotel in Bangkok.

He gingerly poked at the tiny slit, trying not to damage the prayer book's beauty or the contents inside, until it finally opened enough to give up its secret treasure. A small video flash card fell to the floor. David retrieved the card and held it up to the light, pondering what might be recorded on the miniature device. There were thousands of possibilities. He speculated on what prompted Ahmad Hasan to hide the video in the first place and, why in the world, he would ever hand it over to an infidel.

A sudden notion occurred to David: the video must contain the missing piece of the puzzle; the connection between the attacks and the Brotherhood of Purity. This had to be what Ahmad meant when he told him the answers he sought were inside.

Stopping to picture Suzanne's excitement, Ron's astonishment, the anticipation of John's enthusiastic approval, and the reaction of his audience, he wondered if this moment might prove to be the pinnacle of his storied career. Still, he struggled with an internal debate. Should he wait for Suzanne and Ron to return, or watch the video now, and show it to them later?

He decided to come down on the side of decorum and wait for his companions. He set off to find something to drink in the refrigerator but, halfway to the kitchen, David's inquisitive nature overwhelmed his better judgment.

Fired up, a slight quiver running up his backbone, his eyelids fluttering just for a second, he returned to the living room and brought the flash card over to the entertainment center. He inserted it into the proper slot on the side of the flat panel television and stood there looking at the black screen, for a long while, before turning it on. An exotic dance of photons, left over from the moment of creation, bathed the room in white static.

The newsman headed to the kitchen to retrieve a cold beverage. Limping back to the sofa, he found a comfortable position and popped open the can, pouring its contents into a glass. Nervous about what Ahmad might have placed on the card, David laughed out loud, took a deep breath, and a sip of his drink.

Then, leaning forward, heart thumping, adrenaline flooding every cell, his senses razor sharp, David Anderson lifted the remote from the coffee table, pointed it at the television screen, and pressed 'play'.

The End

Acknowledgements:

The authors are grateful to the following folks for sharing their insights, consultations and stories: Dov Levy, Sholeh O'Connell, Marlena Vega, Raed Hamdan, David Swatloski, Sam Gralnick, Tello Miniero, Turker Ayar, Michael Simon and Mostafa Hanif. Thank you for helping us enrich our story.

Thanks to the Naval History and Heritage Command for help with the Navajo language.

And a special thank you to Professor Brooks Landon from the University of Iowa for insights into great sentences.

Last but not least; we wish to express our deepest appreciation to all our friends and family who have been so patient and encouraging during the years. We particularly want to acknowledge our mom, who, throughout her life, was a constant source of love and inspiration by her keen intellect, her deep sense of justice, and her unconditional love, and encouragement. You are our special angel. Thank you dad for believing in us and keeping us laughing. Connie wishes to express her deepest love and appreciation for her darling husband, who supported her through this entire process, sacrificing his own comfort so that his wife could have the luxury to write. Tom thanks his loving wife and children for their unwavering support while writing this novel; this would not have been possible without you guys.

Contact Information:
We love to hear from our readers:
E-mail: Tom at: tdc@thebrotherhoodofpurity.com
E-mail Connie at: cda@thebrotherhoodofpurity.com
-or-
Visit us on the web: www.Thebrotherhoodofpurity.com
Discover background information, links to social media and the author's blog.